YEAR'S BEST
BODY HORROR

2017 ANTHOLOGY

Edited by C.P. Dunphey

Gehenna & Hinnom Books

ACKNOWLEDGMENTS

Thank you to all the fantastic authors who submitted to us, believing in our mission and trusting in us. We only opened our doors in April of 2017, and this anthology you are reading is our first major publication (aside from the bi-annual *Hinnom Magazine*). We received so many fantastic stories and it truly moved us to see the amount of passion from these writers. We hope to release this anthology annually, as the experience of this volume alone was filled with exciting and breathlessly inspired works.

Special thanks to all the authors included in this volume, and to the many members of the professional horror community for their unwavering support.

Finally, thank you to everyone who decided to Embrace the Unknown.

INTRODUCTION
By Shane Ramirez

Deconstructing Body Horror

(Originally published on both soundonsight.org and popoptiq.com)

Your muscles contort. Your skin bubbles and stretches. Your loins throb and your limbs writhe. You thrash in the throes of excruciating pain and agonizing pleasure. Before you even realize your body has betrayed you, like a snake shedding its skin, you are born anew. Perhaps the most visceral of the horror genres, body horror represents the most intimate of all fears. It's the inescapable sensation that the shell housing every synchronized component keeping you alive is under attack. Yet it is more than simple infection; it is metamorphosis, a mutation that does not always spell death. More so, it may even be the start of a beautiful new life.

The human body has long been the enemy of horror films. One only has to look as early as *The Invisible Man* or *The Wolfman* for manifestations of physical forms undergoing irrevocable change. But the body horror genre encompasses three distinct variations of organic terror: invasion via disease or decomposition, violation through mutilation or penetration, and transformation from a re-constitution of biology.

Whether psychosomatic or extraterrestrial, the dangers of invasive body horror range from the plausible to the fantastic. The 1956 version of *Invasion of the Body Snatchers* turned Cold War paranoia into physical terror with its tale of pod people replacing humans for the ultimate takeover of the planet. The fear of conformity has long driven the horror genre, but it was popularized during the '50s when things as mundane as suburbia and as threatening as espionage were seeping into the cultural zeitgeist. Twenty years later, the 1978 remake would adopt a more visceral approach to its alien replicants, as special effects were able to effectively depict the process in all its gooey glory.

Special effects technology has largely been a friend to body horror, which has escalated in extremity with each passing decade. John Carpenter's 1981 remake of *The Thing from Another World*, aptly renamed *The Thing*, envisions an alien organism not unlike its pod predecessors. The titular thing assumes the shape of other life forms in an attempt to imitate it, involving a gruesome synthesis of flesh, blood, and viscera. In both *The Thing* and *Body Snatchers*, the concept of the uncanny is used to ratchet up the tension; it is not just the fear of the other, it is the fear of the other in a familiar shape, in some instances, your own.

The Thing shares a kindred spirit with *Society*, Brian Yuzna's icky allegory about Beverly Hills' upper crust, an incestuous and mutated gaggle of snobs who literally feed off the poor. The quest for genetic purity drives both sets of movie monsters and permeates more relatable fare like 1995's *Safe*, Todd Hayne's "horror movie of the soul" about a milquetoast housewife (Julianne Moore) who develops an inexplicable aversion to her environment. There literally becomes no place to hide as everyday pollution, beauty products, and toxins seem to turn against her, and she seeks refuge in a New Age cult. The extreme lengths that characters resort to in finding a "cure" are as much a part of body horror as the illnesses themselves. William Friedkin's 2006 chiller, *Bug*, frames an ill-fated romance around a Gulf War vet's paranoia over the government using his body for experiments with insects. With each escalating suspicion, the measure to resolve or prove that suspicion escalates as well.

Victims of body horror are rarely willing participants in their transgression. The fear of one's own body is coupled by the fear of how that body can be abused or violated. Eastern and Western sexual repression has provided ample fodder for horror films wherein the body becomes a conduit for other entities to enter, explore, and often desecrate. What drives these films is an audience that is largely ambivalent about its bodies, perhaps even ignorant of them. Ridley Scott's *Alien* was one of the first psychosexual horror films to achieve canonical status within the genre. Its alien xenomorph reproduces through a parasitic "face hugger" that inserts a proboscis into the mouth of its host and releases an egg. That egg then gestates in the warm stomach of its carrier (in this case, poor John Hurt as Kane), thereby eventually bursting out to life. The phallic-shaped organism picks off its human prey by puncturing their skulls with its tongue, another proboscis with a maw of its own. In the genre, breeding and birthing are returned to their primordial state of life or death.

If *Alien* represents the male anxiety of penetration as a perceived non-masculine act of submission, then *Possession* represents the female anxiety of penetration as an act of subjugation. The oddball 1981 film stars Isabelle Adjani as a disturbed wife who falls out of love with her husband (Sam Neill) and into the bed of a tentacled creature, which she kills for to protect. However, the creature's wriggling state is merely a gestation period for its true nature—a doppelganger of her estranged husband.

Gender dynamics play a key role in body horror, where the differing orificial experiences of males and females are broken down to a singular sensual state. *Eraserhead's* slimy mutant baby pushes its reticent father to his psychological breaking point by all but damning the signature purpose of his biology. Clive Barker's demon tale *Hellraiser* repurposes gender discrimination through its equal opportunity sadists from Hell, who torture hapless victims by venting new holes in their bodies. A film like Stuart Gordon's *Re-Animator* redraws familiar gender lines for optimal discomfort, as in a scene where a deranged doctor tries to force oral sex on a woman via a disembodied head. And that one's a comedy.

Such varying levels of taste have given rise to the New French Extremity cinema, which has largely differentiated itself from the abhorrent torture porn genre by setting its aims on the psychological traumas of its characters. Of course, the defilement of the body is still front and center. *Inside* turns maternal anxiety into a horror scenario where a pregnant woman is in danger of having her baby literally ripped from her womb. *In My Skin* chronicles the descent of a woman who self-mutilates after a disfiguring accident. Cannibalism drives the narratives of arthouse director Claire Denis' *Trouble Every Day* and schlock director Xavier Gens' *Frontier(s)*. When the perpetrators of these atrocities aren't the main characters, they are usually villains devoid of humanity, who inflict pain that transcends humanity. Pascal Laugier's 2008 film *Martyrs* is the staple of the French renaissance of horror. In the film, a shadowy organization imprisons young women and subjects them to demoralizing torture. This savagery serves a higher purpose—to force the victim to experience pain so unimaginable, she reaches a state of transfiguration.

Viewer repulsion is a key component of body horror—leave the audience squirming in their seats, shielding their eyes, and holding back their lunch. No other horror element elicits this reaction better than the full-on mutation of the body and no other director better encapsulates the genre than Canadian filmmaker David Cronenberg. Cronenberg's filmography is replete with stories of bodies slowly decaying, melding with technology, or succumbing to peculiar afflictions. The characters, once frightened, become not just accepting of their new physical states but emboldened. Two of his earliest films, *Shivers* and *Rabid*, rely on more stereotypical features of the genre, using parasites and zombies as their basis. But *Video-drome*, made in 1983, throws its main character Max (James Woods) deep into the heart of a conspiracy to control the masses through a mysterious cable channel. The channel broadcasts a signal that induces brain tumors in its viewers, but for Max, creates a cavity in his stomach not unlike the slot of a VCR. "Long live the new flesh" is the conspiracy's slogan and would best serve as Cronenberg's motto. By locating the narrative impetus behind the simple infection allegory, he finds the necessary human element for convincing body horror. His 1986 remake of *The Fly* is the ultimate distillation of the genre, a grim disease parable about one man's scientific obsession. Jeff Goldblum stars as Seth Brundle, the brilliant scientist whose molecules form with that of a common housefly after a test with his teleportation pod goes awry. At first, the changes are thrilling: increased agility, strength, and sexual performance. But soon, his entire cellular structure changes, revealing more of the insect/human hybrid he will become. Special effects wizard Chris Walas' creature design grounds the gruesome metamorphosis in reality, but it is Cronenberg's adherence to his character's emotional response, equal parts elation and devastation, which sells the harrowing transformation.

Scientific pursuit is a common theme among transformative body horror. In Ken Russell's *Altered States*, William Hurt's Dr. Jessup undergoes a drug and sensory deprivation procedure in an attempt to achieve another state of being. In this case, his genetic makeup regresses from man to ape. Likewise, in the H.P. Lovecraft adaptation *From Beyond*, a group of scientists create a machine to expand the human perception of reality, but tear open an alternate dimension in the process. But science is not always a prerequisite for mutation, as in the Japanese cult classic, *Tetsuo: The Iron Man*, where a man is cursed with a disease that fuses his flesh with scrap metal.

Body horror sees the body as an open entity, a vessel willing to take in new parts, and sometimes, new partners. The process of reconstitution — physical, psychological, or emotional—is a violent one. The comfort of our flesh is used against us, as our rubbery encasements are revealed to be breakable, malleable, and most frighteningly, susceptible to changes beyond the capacity of human thought, pain, and imagination.

Body Horror Top Ten

The Fly
The Thing
Videodrome
Re-Animator
Tetsuo: The Iron Man
Alien
Altered States
Possession
Invasion of the Body Snatchers 1956/1978
Martyrs

Honorable Mentions

Akira
The Brood
Cabin Fever
Human Centipede
It's Alive
Leviathan
Slither
Teeth

Shane Ramirez has been a filmmaker and film writer for over ten years. His love for film in high school got him into video production, a passion which he took to college, where he studied English and Media Studies at Texas State University. His professional writing career began with online film criticism for examiner.com, soundonsight.org, and popoptiq.com, and has since expanded to script editing. His short films have screened at Texas State University and the 72 Hour Film Fest in San Marcos, TX and can be seen at the upcoming Lost River Film Fest. At present, he works as a videographer and documentary filmmaker in Texas while currently writing two feature length screenplays and a novel. Visit his work at www.shane-ramirez.com.

TABLE OF CONTENTS

SLOBBER
By Shaun Avery

T here.

That one.

See the way her body fits so perfectly within the sensible clothes she's changed into? Yeah. There's a woman that really owns her own skin. Skin still gleaming a little with moisture she worked up at the gym just across the road.

Perfect.

So I walk over to her, cutting across the crowded bar, but it's really more a swagger than a walk, a confident strut that I've worked hard on over the years. And I can feel a lot of eyes on me, but mine are only on the woman as I come to a stop beside her and say "hi."

She looks over, one eyebrow raised, appraising me.

"Hi, yourself," she says.

I can tell that she likes what she sees.

But then, why wouldn't she?

"What you drinking?" I ask. But I already know the answer, wouldn't be talking to her if I didn't.

Still, it's a stroke for my ego—now the biggest thing about me—when she says, "Cronenberg Water."

That's the most expensive water you can get, the most designer. It's endorsed by athletes. And the drink of choice of all the women I meet in bars.

"Me, too," I say. "Well, I was," I add, looking around the bar for an imaginary bottle of water, acting a little bumbling now, something I always do to make them think there's more to me than what they're at first seeing. "Only I appear to have drank it . . ."

"Going to get another?" she asks, and now her eyes meet mine. "Or just come back to my place and fuck me?"

Take a guess which one I pick.

Yep.

You guessed right.

She tries to kiss me a few times along the way. But I don't—can't—let her. Not yet. Instead, I content myself with holding her hand, telling her, "soon."

She looks at me, smirking, when I say that.

It's not a nice smirk.

"Not much for public displays of affection, huh?" she asks.

I nod. "Something like that."

Both temporarily satisfied, we carry on walking.

And soon we're there.

A sixth-floor apartment building.

She makes us jog up each flight of stairs, me hanging back to enjoy the sight of her tightly packed behind.

"Working up a sweat beforehand," she explains, looking back over her shoulder at me, brown hair swishing. "Makes the whole thing better."

Looking at those buttocks, I'm inclined to agree.

What a waste it will be, what I do to her. Such a waste.

But that all lies ahead.

For now, we reach her door, and I come up behind her as she begins to unlock it, letting my mouth find her, teeth nibbling at her neck.

"So much for not liking the public displays," she says, reaching back with one hand to touch my face.

"This is a bit more private," I reply. "Now open the door."

She does so.

I release her.

She walks backwards into the apartment, beckoning me to join her.

And I decide to have a little fun with myself.

The front door is still wide open behind me, I think, *and that could be dangerous.* I stifle the irony of this thought. *Anyone could walk in, do anything to us.* I watch her, now stepping back into her bedroom. *If she notices this danger—if her desire doesn't take over her brain—then I . . . then I won't go through with what I do. I'll just make my excuses and leave. And she'll be fine.*

I wait a second, wait for her.

She's stopped at the foot of her bed.

She's looking towards me.

The door—the *open* door—still visible behind me.

Will she notice?

Will she tell me to close it?

No.

Instead, she says, "come on. Now."

And just like that she seals her fate.

She's quick, too, this girl.

I look down at my feet, steadying myself, readying myself for what is to come ... and by the time I look back up she's completely naked.

She's sat up on the bed, pointing towards me.

"Come here," she says.

Foolishly still thinking she's in control.

I walk over to the bed, place my hands on her shoulders.

She starts sucking at the fingers of one hand. Looking up directly into my eyes as she does so. But never once seeing the true intention behind them.

"Honey," I say.

And pull her roughly off the bed, dropping her to her knees on the carpet.

I see the outrage in her eyes, the sudden fire. But I've played scenes like this many times before, and I know just what to say, telling her, "I thought we could work our way up to the bed."

It's the right thing to say, the words driving the fury from her gaze.

She reaches for me, kneads my pectoral muscles through my shirt, repaying the favour I did for her earlier.

"I like the sound of that," she says, and raises herself up to kiss me.

And finally, the moment is here.

She thinks, at first, that everything is fine. That I am just a passionate kisser. But then she realises what is happening, and her eyes go wide, and she tries to pull away.

But can't.

"Gmmph!" she cries. "Glmph!"

It's at this point that I could almost feel sorry for them.

But it's too late for that now.

The thing inside me forces its way up through my body, emerging from the place near my stomach where it lives. Following the long trail of its tongue which has already come out of my mouth and into hers.

And now it spews its full black discharge into her.

She falls back onto the floor, free now, no longer of any use to me.

"Oh my God," she says, placing her hands on her hips, already feeling them change from within, the skin stretching and widening. Eyes huge with panic, she looks up at me. "What have you *done* to me?"

I back off, wiping my mouth, feeling the thing inside retreat to its usual hiding place. For now.

"Afraid I lied to you earlier, honey," I tell her. "Real reason I didn't want to use the bed is I didn't want it to break . . ."

And she balloons in size, becoming a huge, doughy mess of flesh upon the floor.

"When *this* happened," I conclude.

I step over her, walk towards the door.

"Sorry, honey," I say over my shoulder.

But I'm not.

Not anymore.

See, I was her way once.

Well, not the way she was at the start of the night, when we first met. No, the way she looked when I left her . . . that used to be me.

I ate everything. More than I could afford. So, when money ran out and I was still hungry, that was when I started raiding bins.

That was where I found it.

The thing.

Looking up from beneath a pile of mouldy food and dirty nappies. Eyes small and beady, set back on a face that looked a little like a crow's beak. It saw me reaching in to grab a half-eaten hot dog and it said, "what in the hell do you think you're doing?"

Startled, I could only come up with the truth. "Um . . . looking for something to eat?"

It looked me over. Which took a while—back then, remember, there was a lot of me to see.

"Something *more* to eat, you mean," it said.

"Hey," I said back, prepared to get angry with it.

But then, all of a sudden, I started to cry.

I don't know why. I mean, I'd been doing this for months, and never once had I felt bad about it, accepting my bin-raking activities merely as the way things had to be. But somehow, looking into the thing's eyes, I saw myself as it saw me, as I guess the whole world saw me. And it hurt a hell of a lot.

"I'm sorry," the thing said, sounding sincere.

I looked at the half of a hotdog my hand.

Still full of disgust for what I had become. But also still hungry.

"What if I showed you a way you didn't have to eat that?" it said, eyeing the remains of the hotdog. "A way I could control your appetite and give you a normal body?" It paused, and I sensed a strange sort of smile upon its face. "Fuck no, a *great* body!"

I looked at the thing.

And honestly, I was doubtful.

This sounded like the kind of garbage they spouted non-stop on the Diet Channel. The sort of thing I have believed in before, and been disappointed every time.

But, you know, what did I really have to lose?

"Well," I said, and I think it sensed from the tone of my voice that I was already in, no matter what the thing asked. "I mean, what would I have to do?"

"Simple," it said. "Just eat me instead."

So I did.

Only "eat" is not quite the right word.

In fact, it leapt into my mouth and scurried down my throat and settled in my stomach.

I was so shocked that I dropped the hotdog.

Then I puked.

And puked.

And puked.

Next, I staggered back home, wobbling through the streets drunkenly. But I could already feel my body changing, and by the time I got home. . . .

"Holy shitting shit," I said, looking at myself in the mirror. "I'm thinner!"

Sure you are, the thing said, now speaking directly into my mind. *Tell you something else – you don't feel hungry anymore, do you?*

Truth to tell, I had not noticed that.

But it was true.

Don't get me wrong—I wasn't about to starve myself or anything. What the thing meant was that my appetite was now a *normal* one . . . that my days of having to rake through bins for extras were at an end.

That's right, it told me. *But I'm afraid there's a price to pay. . . .*

And there was.

I got even more thin, and then I started working out, got buff. But to keep myself that way, every couple of months I had to infect others with the way I once was.

Didn't have to be women I infected, of course. But since it took lip-to-lip contact, there was no way I was going to do that with a guy. That's why I had held myself back earlier tonight, when the girl tried to kiss me—didn't want her sprouting fat in the middle of the road, where everyone could see it.

But it's all taken care of for another few months.

No need to worry.

So homewards bound it is.

Except. . . .

The door hangs open when I get there.

That's not what sets my mental alarms off, though. I mean, for all I know, I left it open, myself, too caught up in the need of finding a new girl to infect to worry much about the security of my home. No, what disturbs me are the shadows I see moving in there—the shadows of people.

Big people.

I'm about to retreat when I feel something cold slide into my ribs.

I look down and see a gun.

One held by a pudgy hand.

Each fingernail painted a different colour.

I remember fingers like that. Though they'd been a lot thinner back then, as they'd slid down my abs to unzip my jeans.

"Move," says the owner of the fingernails and the gun. "Inside."

I do as I'm told.

Only now realising that I'm in real trouble.

It should have been the lights that tipped me off, you see.

I'd lost track of time—I often do, when I'm out on the hunt. I'd forgotten that it had been daytime when I'd set out. There should have been no lights on inside the house. But they are. And now that I enter, I see that they illuminate several nightmares.

Women from my past.

Their names still a mystery—either I never learnt them, like tonight's victim, or I've forgotten them over time. Still, though, I know their faces. Oh, yes. Their bodies, too. Bodies I've corrupted. Bodies I've made fat.

Two of them in the room before me.

"Ladies," I say, looking between them. "You haven't changed since we last saw each other."

"We can't," says one of them, a dark-skinned woman. Once possessing the lithe legs of a pole dancer, she now seems to have no legs at all beneath the blubber. "Whatever you've done to us, we're stuck with it."

Just like I used to be.

"How'd you find me?" I say.

"I knew you'd ask that," replies the dancing girl. "I knew you'd think you were smart, moving around the city, picking us all up at separate bars."

"Yeah," agrees the rainbow-nailed one. Frustratingly, she still stands behind me, giving me no chance to go for the gun. "But you can't hide the things you've done."

"Yes," says the third one, a well-spoken, bobbed-haired woman I'd picked up in a university bar, a real posh type who'd unleashed a barrage of gutter talk on the way back to the bedroom floor of her student accommodation. "We found each other online. Then we all staked out bars until we found you."

How the hell did I miss people this big?

"A few other people helped us out," the student says, as if sensing my thoughts. "So you wouldn't spot us too early."

"We found you in a bar a few weeks ago." Gun Girl again. "You mustn't have been successful that night. We followed you here when you left, found out where you lived."

"So why the wait?" I ask. Then, twisting the knife a little, point out, "I've done a girl tonight. You could have stopped that."

This seems to bother the student, who grimaces a little.

But not the former dancer, who says, "we had to get a couple of things ready for you."

"Right," I say. And I laugh harshly, hating them, hating all three reminders of the me I once was. "So, what you come here for? A cure? Ain't no cure, girls. There's just me." I pat my stomach. "And a little friend of mine."

"Good thing that's not what we're here for, then," the voice behind me says.

Then the gun cracks down across my head and I sink into black.

I wake up in. . . .

I don't know where.

Some building.

A sports building, I think.

There are rows of seating facing me, where an audience can sit. But my three captors can't use them. Things won't take their weight. Instead, they stand in front of the first row of seats, watching me.

I laugh.

"Do your worst, girls," I tell them. Then, looking around, realise I am in some sort of ring, a circle of hardened straw surrounding me.

They say nothing.

And somehow that angers me most of all.

"This a wrestling ring?" I say. "Ha! Go ahead! Send in a wrestler! I'll kiss "em! I don't like guys but I don't mind! I'll turn 'em all into tubs of guts—just like you!"

"Like you," says the student.

"We found all the old photos," the dancer adds.

"Shut up!" I say, screaming it, not wanting to hear them, wanting instead to blot the truth out with my anger. "Shut up, shut up, shut up!"

Then I hear footsteps.

Huge footsteps.

I think we might be in trouble here, the thing tells me. *Or at least you are. When there's nothing left of you, I'll just find another body to share. Like I did with all the people that came before you.*

"What?" I say, looking down at my stomach, at its hiding place.

But it speaks no more.

And when I look back up, I see that Rainbow Fingers is smirking.

"Remember I said a couple of people helped us find you?" she says. "Well, one of them is the guy that owns this place. He owed me a favour. And the guys that come here to train . . . well, when I told them what you did—what you *are*—they really wanted to meet you."

"Guys?" I say. "This place?"

"Ike's Sumo Ring," she says.

And I realise that even if it wanted to, the thing inside me would not be much help here.

As a dozen Sumo warriors come charging towards me.

ERUPTION
By Charlotte Baker

I run to the bathroom and throw up the remnants of my roast dinner; the carrot was not as digested as I'd have liked. I'd been sick into the basin and I peeled one of my hands free from the cold porcelain to wipe my mouth, covered in liquid sick. The food was contained: no overspill, which was one thing to be thankful for, I suppose. Then, I used my other hand to wipe the sweat from my face.

God, I hated being sick.

My body felt on fire and I was getting pain from the blood merely flowing through my veins. I must have been coming down with something, surely. I pulled myself closer to the bathroom mirror, noticing a bloodshot left eye. I pulled my eyelids open, peering into the mirror as a reflection I didn't recognise looked back.

That's when it happened.

The bloodshot moved. The red worm unravelled itself and moved. But when it moved, the one in my eye, so did the fifty or so in my face, rising to the surface like the first tremor of the start of a volcanic eruption.

I fell backwards, hitting my head on the red-hot towel rail. Falling to the floor, I noticed the hundreds of red worms wriggling under my skin over my entire body. My breathing was loud and raspy. Then, they disappeared as quickly as they came.

I threw myself to the basin once again and retched repeatedly, from shock. The same sick/sweat wiping ritual began and as I turned my head to the left, Mellissa stood there; her nightie covered in sick, her pupils beaming red and her eyeballs protruding from their sockets. Her skin was all veiny, but instead of the normal blue colours, it was bright red.

The veins moved. Then stopped, as if they were singing.

DEVIL'S TEARS
By Shadrick Beechem

It was ten minutes after midnight when Freddy saw the headlights of a car turning into the old lot. That was ten minutes too late, Al was never late. Hell, he was always early. This made Freddy uncomfortable. Something was off. But he shook off the weirdness as the El Camino pulled up next to him and both men got out of their vehicles immediately, both engines still running.

"Jesus man, why the fuck did we have to meet all the way out here? What's wrong with the back of J's restaurant like we always do it? And you're late. I don't think I've ever seen your ass be more than a cunt hair past the hour on getting somewhere," Freddy said.

Al instructed him over the phone that the scheduled meet up for this shipment was going to take place out past the old Mayfield airstrip, which was an hour drive on a rough desert road from Freddy's base of operations in Winona. Albert was in a hurry though, and spoke quickly as he pulled out the boxes from the back of his car.

"I know, I know, I'm sorry. I'll explain it to you later, man, but for right now I just need these fuckin things gone. They are hot right now, man, this is some top secret crazy shit right here. Military grade, literally. The shipment got hijacked from a facility in Phoenix just yesterday and this is CIA property, brother. They don't like having their toys taken from them, not one bit." As he said this, he pulled out two cases the size of cereal boxes and placed them on the hood of Freddy's pickup.

Freddy walked around the front to get a better look, and the headlights of the vehicles briefly illuminated the man's ruined body. Al caught site of the tightened lumpy scars and pink crevices of old healed burns that stretched across every exposed inch of Freddy's body, which included the left side of his face. Al knew about the meth lab explosion that was responsible for this disfigurement, and he also knew about the running joke going on between the small circle of associates he and Freddy had. They had given him the nickname Mr. Krueger, in honor of the infamous dream-invading blade-fingered villain from the eighties. Usually Freddy wore long sleeve T's, and baseball hats a lot of the time to hide what he could of his disfigurement, but he must've not given a shit about appearances tonight, because he was wearing an old white wife beater and letting his long greasy hair down. Al saw more than he wanted. Pretending not to be phased by the gross sight, he got down to business, time was of the essence here.

"Is that it?" Freddy asked, a hint of disapproval in his voice. He looked at the two small cases, not believing that this could be all he was getting after all this unnecessary precautionary bullshit Al had put him through. Al looked at him and smiled. Then he snapped open both cases. The inside of each case was lined with dense protective foam, and sitting on top of the foam was four vials of a dark purple fluid. There was a small glass dropper next to each vial, along with several orange CAUTION stickers, each bearing the BIOHAZARD logo.

Freddy picked up one vile and studied it closely with the light of his phone.

"*Carefulllll* with that. I know it doesn't look like much, but trust me, there are over five hundred doses in each vial. It doesn't take much. This stuff is absolutely insane, man."

Freddy looked at Al, then at the vial again, suspicious. "What is it? Does it have a name?"

"You're not gonna believe this, man, but this used to be a drug the CIA used as a truth serum in their interrogations. You know, fighting the war on terror and all that shit. They developed a couple different types of hallucinogens to try and get people to fess up about whatever information they were prying out of them when the waterboarding and car battery nipple games didn't do the trick. Well, this shit right here was discontinued after ten 'unsuccessful trials' or some shit like that. Everyone who dosed on it ended up going out of their minds. Almost all of them ended up cutting off a part of their body or doing some kind of fucked up shit to themselves. Six of the ten died from self-inflicted injuries, the other four ended up getting schizophrenia or some shit."

With this bit of news, Freddy quickly put the vial back in the case and rubbed his hand on his jeans, then looked at Al with disbelief. "What the fuck, Al? I need drugs that are gonna get people *high,* not make them go crazy and cut their damn peckers off. Why do you think no one ever buys that bath salts shit anymore? A couple of zombie episodes and suddenly everyone thinks its gonna make you go crazy. You think I want that kinda reputation, you dumbass?" He raised his voice, not caring who heard. They were out in the middle of the goddamn desert after all.

Al put his hands up placatingly. "Hey, hey, hey, dude, calm down, man. You didn't let me finish. I got this guy right? He's a dirty cop who runs shit for the mafia out in California and they swear by this stuff, man. The trick is you just have to take a very, very, *verrrrrrry* small amount. The potency is the problem, not the content. Sort of like old school black tar heads who blast up on fentanyl and overdose, cause that shit is a thousand times more potent than that garbage H they get off the street. The pharmaceutical industry, man, they know how to make their drugs, amigo, you know that yourself.

"That's why everyone's out buying Adderall and Vyvanse from college kids with scripts instead of that bullshit crystal you tried to swing. Long lasting, and cheap, that's what those kids want, and this shit right here?" Al gently tapped one of the vials. "Is right up that particular alley. One small drop of this shit is enough to blast someone off into a world of unending horniness and hallucinations so intense that you can't tell what's real and what's your imagination. It's not just a hallucinogen, it's a deliriant, and it can last for up to twelve hours, man."

Freddy looked at him, amazed and a little skeptical. "Bullshit, one CC is barely a fuckin squirt. You tellin me that a itty bitty blotter of that can blast you off?"

Al shook his head vehemently. "You betcha. It's only been on the street for about two months now so the specifics are a little sketchy, you know everyone's body is different and all that. But it's the real deal, amigo. And what's cool about it is that at smaller doses, if you can find a way to measure smaller than that, it's more like a high than a trip. A lot of upper big ball swinging businessmen like it, say it's like coke mixed with a really heavy hash high. But we're talking like amounts you'd need a damn microscope to see."

"Jesus, that is crazy," Freddy reflected. Convinced, he got down to business. "All right, how much for both cases?" he asked.

Al smiled nervously and asked, "How does twelve K sound?"

Freddy scowled his scarred face and shook his head.

Despite the clearly high balled price, he reached into his pocket and handed over two thick rolls of hundred-dollar bills.

"Now, how about this, you damn jew conman. Here's six neat up-front, cause I still aint entirely sure about this. If it starts selling like you say it will I should have the other half to you in two weeks. Deal?"

Al considered this for a moment, sighed and handed over the two cases, looking around nervously as he did so. "Yeah, yeah, whatever, as long as it's off my ass. There's only two guys in the whole world who are able to bring this stuff on the street and I know one of them directly and I'd be quite surprised if the government wasn't already looking into him. They keep this shit heavily guarded in some evidence lab. And Freddy, look, man, if you don't want a shit show on your hands, you need to listen to me carefully. Never, ever, ever, *ever*, *ever*, *EVER* give anyone a larger dose than four CCs. The tolerance for this shit builds up quick, which helps you in the long run, but man, even the most hardcore users short circuit after four CCs. There's been two overdoses on it confirmed out in San Francisco where this shit is real hip with the artists and musicians. Remember, no more than four. No matter what, you got me?"

Freddy shook his head. "Yeah sure, although it's gonna be hard trying to convince people that such a small amount will do the trick. They got a name for this stuff? Something that will ring a bell?"

Al was quickly putting up his little stash of boxes and looked up, smiling. "Yep. They call it Devil's Tears on the street, cause you gotta drop that shit in your eyes."

Albert Weaver was in relatively good spirits until about thirty minutes ago. After the deal with Freddy went down a couple weeks back, he had taken a little vacation with the fat wad of cash the deal brought in. This was gonna be his last big run, his retirement from the game. He sold almost all of the Devil's Tears, assuring plenty of easy living until he croaked or got killed, but he made sure to keep a small vial for himself. He had been hooked on the stuff for over a month now, and his tolerance was so high that he had been taking up to four CCs per trip in order to feel the most basic effects now, despite his own dire warnings he gave to Freddy about the nature of the drug. It just . . . felt so *good*.

His addiction was taking its toll on him although he didn't realize it. He had been masturbating excessively the past five days as he lay locked in his dingy trailer in a perpetual never-ending swirl of wonderful highs and crashing, disorienting lows. At least once every two hours he jerked off, and the bottom of his shaft where the urethra was located was bruised a dark yellow. The tip and meatus was a bright irritated red and was scabbed, bleeding along the corona as Al continued to throttle his member, helpless to stop the sexual urges that plagued him. Orgasms now hurt severely as his small wrinkled testicles, which resembled dried prunes, struggled to pump empty contractions into the man's worn penis. His bed was covered in several dry crusts of semen stains, and some of these crusty deposits were tinged red with blood.

Unable to slake his thirst with mere masturbation, he had been ordering hookers over the last two days. He had the money to blow on top shelf call girls, girls that were experienced and were willing to do just about anything you wanted if you could afford them. The last one that came by refused to do anything with Al, seeing his scabby, bleeding penis and thinking the man had a severe case of herpes or something.

And also, his eyes, But his eyes were probably the worst part. He had put over twenty doses of *L-Diamethaltriazamine* into both eyes during the course of a bender unseen to the likes of conventional junkies. His eyes were almost completely stained a muddy burgundy color, so dark that you could barely make out the shape of the man's extremely dilated pupils. To Albert Weaver, the whole world was one abstract purple nightmare, but that was all right. He had gotten used to the unending auditory and visual hallucinations, which went on even when he was coming off the drug. He bled from his eyes and ears, along with a gelatinous purple goo that now steadily leaked out of the corners of his eyes.

When Candice "Candy Cane" Lane knocked on the double wide trailer's door of Al's run-down sanctum, she stumbled back in horror as something barely resembling a man opened the door for her. To Candice, he looked like one of those comic book gray aliens with a horrible mascara day. The man's pale, almost translucent skin was waxy in the glow of the bare bulbs that adorned his living room. His thinning black hair hung in wild kinked curls above his scabbed head. "You must be . . . *Cannnnnnnndy* Cane, is that right, darlin?" he asked, and smiled a most terrible smile.

The teeth she saw were little more than rotted husks, a case of meth mouth which had been accelerated by the dry Arizona air. She recoiled. "I uh . . . No, I'm sorry I must have the wrong place. I'm sorry I need to be—" but Al grabbed the beautiful voluptuous blonde by the arm. He made sure not to grab hard, he didn't want to be threatening. He was just so desperate for human touch.

"Wait, please!" he said in a feeble voice. He was as much addicted to the sex as he was to the Tears, despite how both physically pained when he'd indulge. He shoved a handful of hundred-dollar bills in front of her, the crumpled pieces of money smeared some sort of violet fluid. "I'm not infected with anything I swear I just . . . I got something in here that'll change your life, honey. A drug you aint never seen before, a drug you can't find anywhere else except here, and I guess I been hittin it a little hard, got some side effects as you can see," he said, issuing a shrill barking sound that was supposed to be laughter. "I'm just . . . so lonely, and I need you, baby. I'll pay you whatever you want, and I'll give you some of the Tears. It'll be worth your while, sweet honey, just you see."

Candice stared down at the wad of bills for a long moment, thinking hard. She did need the money. She was trying to pay her way through an accounting degree and the tuition fees were kicking her ass. But god, this was so sketchy. She swallowed hard, and while gripping the bottle of mace she had stashed her in purse hard enough to turn her knuckles white, she reluctantly allowed herself to be led into this disgusting creature's house, despite every feeling in her stomach telling her to get the fuck out of dodge.

"Candy, honey, you gotta open the door, please. You got me worried out here, baby doll," Al said gently through the door. A series of thick, labored grunts was all he got in response. "God fucking dammit, dumb cunt barely even got a hit," Al muttered under his breath. Although this was not true. In his spun-out mental state, he had accidentally given Candice a four-CC dose of the devil's tears. His blurred purple-tinged vision unable to see the small measurement markings on the side of the syringe he used.

Finally losing his patience, he attempted to kick in the door. It was a flimsy particle board thing anyway, and he burst through easily enough. It wasn't like he was getting his damage deposit back on the goddamn trailer anyway after all the meth he cooked in it. He became aware of two things at once. The sharp tang of ammonia in the air, and Candice, stark naked and half-crouching in the corner of his bathtub.

He looked to his right and saw the bottle of ammonia he kept stashed under the sink, along with a bottle of bleach and Drano. They were all lying askew on the floor, some of the contents spilled. It took Al a long moment to register the dangerous effect of this combo.

"Oh Candice, you sweet dumb fucking bitch. What the fuck did you do? What the fuck did you—" His question was cut off with a loud moan, followed by a sizzling sound. A geyser of dark foam jetted from the back of Candice and she shivered.

"There was . . . there was something inside me, something bad. I realize that . . . now. Something in me that's been poisoning my body for years. And now . . . now I'm gonna kill it. Now I'm gonna poison it, the fucking parasite inside of me. Make it all end. It will all finally. . ." but then she yelled and a violent jet of foamy pink liquid rocketed out the back of her.

Her belly had swollen as well and in Al's distorted vision, it pulsated and continued to grow. She collapsed, forward, and Al saw her back.

"Holy. Fucking. Shit," he said in terrified awe as he realized the woman had given herself an enema using the contents he kept under the sink. As she lay twitching and yelling in the tub, pink jelly speckled with bits of dissolved intestine, fecal matter, and flesh erupted from her ruined orifice. Al tried to go over and help her but he stopped as he saw the ruined melted crater of her anus and vagina, dissolved together to form one bloody oozing maw of gore.

To Al's purple-tinged vision, his bathtub looked like the bottom of a jar of grape jelly. Smoke was rising from the wound, skin foaming up and dissolving around the edges of her ruined genitalia.

"Candice!" he cried, and then attempted to roll her over so she would at least stop shitting her insides out against his bathroom wall.

Despite the hellish scene of gore he was now entrenched in, what disturbed Al the most was the fact that when he managed to roll the woman over, he saw that her stomach had deflated but was somehow yet . . . moving? Was that what it was doing? Al couldn't tell. He looked longer, and sure enough, her skin was rumpling and dimpling as if something was moving around within.

"Oh my god," he whispered, staring at the woman's stomach with terror, ignoring the fact that she was likely on the edge of death, only slight spasms in her arms and legs as the acidic mixture dissolved into her nerves.

She was right, there was something in her, holy shit. What is happening? His fried brain struggled to understand what had just happened and what continued to progress. *You gotta kill it, man you can't have let her die in vain,* a stoic voice spoke in his mind. *Finish it, finish the job and then go bury her body out there at that special place in the desert where you put Jim and that cunt from Vegas.*

Resolute now, and also terrified of whatever fucked up creature was hiding in Candy Cane's sweet tummy, he shrank back from the bathroom, and went to retrieve his knife.

Before he did though, he stopped and grabbed the small vial of Devil's Tears and looked at the bottle. It had been full at one point, but now there was only a small puddle in the bottom. Perhaps five or six hits left.

"Fuck it," he said, pouring the remaining fluid into his right eye. It stung like acid and he was forced to sit on his bed while the wave of biting heat raced through his head. In that moment, he felt every single busted capillary and inflamed vein running through his optical nerve, becoming aware of his entire body. It was then that his mind broke after so many hits of the drug. He completely lost sense of who he was, *where* he was.

But he remembered his mission.

The girl.

Yes, he needed to kill the thing that was in Candy. He reached over to the head of the bed and pulled out his big Ka-bar, which he kept under his pillow at night. He pulled it out of its sheath, and studied it, mystified for a moment. To Al, it looked like some kind of glorious Excalibur, a noble blade forged from violet sapphire.

"I'll honor you, baby," he said in a brave voice, and proceeded towards the bathroom, the rusty dull-edged knife that he was so proud of thrust out in front of him in a mock fencer's stance.

He entered the bathroom again, and by now there was a gelatinous puddle of human matter sinking through a hole burned through the bathtub. Candice's midsection had caved in, dissolving the navel and revealing crisp white ribs and a few strands of muscle that were clinging from them, protruding from a dark green puddle of dissolved innards. A smell similar to burning plastic, barbeque, and rubbing alcohol filled the air.

Preparing to thrust his knife into the beige pink soup in his tub, he raised the blade, feeling like a glorious knight. He plunged the blade into the ruined body, and at first thought, the creature was attacking him. His hands deep in her fluid organs, he pulled up, revealing his skin was searing and burning.

He didn't really understand though, and continued plunging in. Eventually, acidic gore burned through the skin until the ropey metacarpal muscles and knuckles glinted through the filmy mess. With his muscles dissolving, he lost his grip on the knife and instead began running his boney exposed fingers through the muck, splashing his forearms and face with the terrible soup.

He was enraptured in the experience, the burning feeling like a cleansing as he spread the gore all over himself, coating himself in the gelatinous liquid as some sort of ritualistic rite, although at that point his thoughts were not coherent enough to assign any kind of philosophical meaning to his actions. He just wanted to be her, be in her, find a way in.

Then he heard three loud knocks on the door.

"POLICE, SEARCH WARRANT!" a voice boomed from outside, followed by a loud crash.

AN ANGEL AMONG US
By David Beers

"**N**ow I know," the preacher said, "that today's world don't believe in miracles. Modern society thinks the days of miracles—the days of Christ turnin' water to wine—them days are gone. I'm here to tell ya, to tell *all* of ya, that's just the Devil's talk."

A chorus of *amen*s erupted from the congregation. The church was hot, as it always was during summer Sundays. The two air conditioners attached to the windows couldn't keep the church-goers from sweating something awful.

The preacher, his name being Alfred P. Cunningham, knew this was his moment. Alfred came from a long line of preachers—indeed, his very Daddy had founded the church he now stood in. The elder Cunningham had retired ten years ago, giving control of the church—and congregation—to Alfred.

Both understood he was ready for it, and standing at the pulpit this morning, it was clear how much greater the Lord would work through Alfred than he had his father.

It wasn't that the elder Cunningham was bad at his job, far from it. Only, his son was *that* good.

Alfred walked to the edge of the pulpit and looked down at his flock of sheep.

"The Lord talks to us all, doesn't he?"

"Lawd, yes!" Ruphus shouted from the third row.

"Brother Ruphus knows. The rest of us do too, don't we?"

"Amen!" came the agreement.

"It's that tiny voice that speaks to us, the one deep inside our chest that tells us right from wrong. That's God talkin' right there." Alfred paused as any good preacher will do, letting his words sink into the people before him. After a few seconds, he continued. "The Lord's been talkin' to me, lately, and he's been tellin' me some important things." Alfred looked up from his feet. "Do you believe me?"

"Yes, Pastor," Aunt Jennie said from the first row. "We know he has."

"Yes he has. Yes he *is*. He's told me that he's tired of people not believin' in him. He's tired of the world denyin' his miracles, and he's tired of how people are ignorin' his word!"

"Amen!"

Alfred nodded, flames flicking in his eyes, revealing the intensity of his belief beneath them. Because the good Lord had been talking to Alfred a lot lately. He'd been detailing out a lot of things, and Alfred had kept it quiet for a while. Up until this week, actually. Six days ago, the Lord gave him permission to start talking, and so he had, first bringing in the Bilbox family. It was their son that God planned to work through.

Alfred was a messenger, nothing else, and he was happy with that. The Lord had many different needs and many different ways to serve Him. Alfred P. Cunningham was humble in both his ambition and ways. He was a messenger. The Bilbox family—and more specifically, Ryan Bilbox—was the person the good Lord wanted.

"Tell me, Aunt Jennie, do you believe in angels?"

"You know I do, Preacher. You know I do!"

Aunt Jennie was nearly in rapture, Alfred speaking to her personally almost too much to handle.

"I know you do," Alfred said. "I know we all do, ain't that right?"

"It is!"

"Yes, suh!"

He soaked it all in, feeling the moment nearly upon him. The temperature in the church was rising, if that was possible (but all things are possible through Jesus Christ, our Lord and Savior, amen).

"Ryan Bilbox, where are ya, son?" Alfred called into the congregation.

"Here he is, Preacher," Ryan's father, Terry Bilbox, said.

"Come on up here, son. Come on up and let's tell the world what the Lord's been tellin' you, okay?"

A boy rose from one of the wooden pews. He was twelve years old, though his size made him look ten. He was thin and pale, and he walked as if something large, black, and with massive claws might reach out at any moment and grab him.

He didn't shirk his duty, though, and Alfred was glad for that. The boy had a lot ahead of him. Important things that would change the entire world. This was the first step on that road, and him simply coming to the pulpit meant he *believed*.

Just as Alfred did. Just as his parents did.

Ryan reached the pulpit and Alfred took him by the hand, pulling him up. The boy came to just above Alfred's waist, and the preacher placed his hands on Ryan's shoulders, standing behind him.

"The days of miracles are to begin again, and I'm here to tell you that personally. Our Lord, my *personal* Savior, has told me so, and ain't nobody in the world gonna convince me otherwise. Ain't no book or no scientist goin' to tell me that the Lord is wrong. Are you with me?"

"AMEN!"

"I knew you would be because I know you all love Christ as I do." Alfred looked down at the top of Ryan's head. "The Lord is going to show the world miracles exist, and he's going to do it through this boy here. God has told me, told Ryan's parents, and Ryan himself, that he is to become an angel. This boy here, so meek, will rise up as God's own righteousness, and strike down the wicked of this world!"

2.

Alfred P. Cunningham was the pastor over a 60-person church, in a town of 64 people. The four people that didn't attend church were the Bernsteins—Jews that lived at the very edge of the town and had nothing to do with no one.

Good riddance, Alfred always thought. The chosen people that crucified Christ. They would get what was coming to them in due time.

To call Rineswald, Alabama a town was a stretch, and Alfred would be the first to admit that. The only jobs inside Rineswald were at the diner. If you wanted anything outside of a burger, you had to drive twenty miles east and there you had a Walmart, Stop-N-Go, and a Taco Bell. Even farther east and you started seeing more, but Alfred didn't concern himself with any of that. Most of the people in Rineswald didn't either, not outside of where they had to drive for work (most worked at the Walmart twenty miles east).

Alfred concerned himself with his flock that the Lord had entrusted him with.

And now God had bestowed a great gift upon Alfred and his congregation.

"It's not going to be easy," Alfred said, "though we can't expect something this great to be. We have to show our dedication, just like Abraham. Do you understand?"

Terry and Patricia nodded. Ryan was quiet, per his usual countenance. The four of them sat at Alfred P. Cunningham's dining room table. His wife, Ruth, was in the garage finishing up the final touches on what would be the first part of Ryan's *change*. She had been working on them for months, ever since the Lord started talking to Alfred.

"Before I keep goin', has the Lord started talkin' to any of you, yet? Tellin' you about how important this is?"

Both Terry and Patricia nodded again. "Oh, yes," Terry said. "We've both had dreams the past three days, each one better than the last."

"Good, good," Alfred said. He had known they would. The Lord told him as much, that once he started explaining the Lord's Will, He would make himself known to them, too. The entire town (except for those troublesome Jews out there on Route 41) would start dreaming soon. "The Lord has specifically told me how this is supposed to go, and I want to say I thank both of you for trustin' me with your son. I promise ain't no harm comin' to this boy, not as long as we keep doin' the Lord's Work. You understand?"

"Yes, Preacher. We definitely do," Terry said. Patricia nodded in agreement.

"Okay, then. The Lord has told me that this is to take three weeks, and at the end of three weeks, Ryan here is goin' to be possessed by an angel. Not just some regular angel either, but Gabriel himself. If we follow the Lord's plan just right, at the end of three weeks, Ryan will *be* an angel, and he'll bring all of God's strength with him." Alfred spoke louder at the open garage door. "Ruth, go ahead and bring 'em out. We're ready for 'em."

The door to the garage opened wider and something white emerged. It was hard to tell exactly what was being shoved into the kitchen, only that it was large, nearly stretching from floor to ceiling.

Ruth entered the kitchen next, a huge smile across her face. Just as the white thing she held almost stretched the height of the house, her smile nearly touched both ears.

She kept walking and another white monstrosity came in with her other hand.

Alfred looked at their glory. Tall and feathery. Indeed, those were real feathers. Ruth had plucked each one from the chickens out back over the past three weeks. They'd killed a hundred chickens from their small farm for this, the meat was packed in the freezer as proof.

"Wings. That's the first thing Ryan's got to have. The Lord said if the miracle is to happen, he has to play the part, and he showed me just what Gabriel's wings looked like. This is them right here."

Alfred P. Cunningham's wife held two large contraptions made out of aluminum wiring. They did indeed stretch from floor to ceiling, and they'd been wrapped in cloth. Ruth Cunningham hadn't known exactly how to make the feathers stick, but God told Alfred to simply lay some super glue down across the cloth and then attach the feathers that way.

The five people in the kitchen stared at these homemade wings, smiles growing larger and larger across each of their faces. Ryan was the only one not smiling. He stared at the huge apparatuses with nothing but terror.

3.

Ron Jerwin wasn't a doctor, but he was the closest thing Rineswald had to it. Terry Bilbox had talked to him *extensively* before allowing him to operate on Ryan, and he'd walked away convinced Ron could do a good enough job. That's all that was really needed anyway—a *good enough* job, because God would take care of everything else.

That's what the world outside didn't understand, and that's why Terry and Patricia had decided to pull Ryan from school for the next few weeks. Ryan went to school in Kentwood, and the people over there always turned their noses up at the people of Rineswald. They certainly wouldn't understand what was happening now.

Heathens, the lot of 'em.

Terry wouldn't hear nothing of it. He knew Ron well, known him since they were kids. Hell, he'd watched Ron patch up his younger brother at least nine or ten times over the years. The wings would be easy. It wasn't like it was *real* surgery. This was basically cosmetic work.

Pastor Alfred told Terry and Patricia that if God was going to put Gabriel inside their son, then they had to show Him they *believed*. They couldn't simply look up at heaven and ask for a miracle, ask for a *blessing*. No, the Lord needed dedication before He would bestow His grace upon them.

That's what the wings were for.

It didn't have nothing to do with Ryan flying away or any such nonsense. It was them showing God their faith.

Terry trusted Ron to do a good job, but he still sat in the room with his son. He'd kissed his cheek before they administered the laughing gas (Pastor Alfred had ordered some off the Internet, though Terry didn't ask too many questions about it. He trusted the Pastor.), and then stood over Ron as he started sewing the wings on.

The needle pricked his son's skin and blood immediately pooled. They were attaching the wings directly to his back, right in the middle on either side of his spinal cord.

"Pastor, how is he goin' to be able to hold these things up? I mean, they look pretty heavy, like they might just rip right out his back."

Pastor Alfred was in the dining room with Terry and Ron. It was *his* dining room after all, and Ryan was lying face down on the table.

A stream of blood rolled down the boy's rib cage and onto the newspaper they'd laid down before starting.

"He'll have to sit in a wheelchair," Alfred said, not looking away from Ron's work. His eyes were just as bright as they'd been at the pulpit days ago.

Ron slowly poked the needle into the boy's skin again, pulling it out the other side and stretching it away from the bone it rested on.

"Only for a few weeks though, Terry," the preacher continued. "As soon as God places Gabriel's spirit in the boy, he'll hop right out of that wheelchair as if somebody had placed a hot brand on his behind. Remember, this is just to show God we're serious. Nothing else. Three weeks in a wheelchair and then he'll be flyin' around this whole town."

Terry nodded, his own eyes wide with anticipation. He wouldn't tell this to the preacher—of course, not—but he was proud. It was *his* son the Lord had chosen, after all. His little boy that kids at school picked on. He was to be God's Avenger, amen.

He watched Ron work, the needle and thread moving in and out of his son's skin.

"Grab the wing now, I have to tighten it against his back."

Terry grabbed the metal wing, lifting it above his son. It wasn't heavy exactly, but Alfred was right: Ryan would need to sit in a wheelchair for a bit to make sure the wings didn't rip right out of his back and leave him with two huge holes staring out at the world.

That would be embarrassing and certainly wouldn't send the right message to the Lord.

Terry lowered the first wing onto his son, watching as Ron pulled the whole thing tight.

4.

"How do you feel?"

Tears sat in Ryan's eyes. He hurt. His whole back hurt worse than anything he'd ever known. Daddy said he had to sit in the wheelchair, that if he tried to stand up, the wings on his back would just fall right out. Ryan didn't want that at all. He *knew* that would hurt worse than what he currently felt, and he didn't think he could handle so much pain.

"Okay," he said, his voice as watery as his eyes.

The pastor squatted down in front of him; Ryan really didn't want to show how bad this hurt in front of *him.* Crying in front of his father and mother had been awful enough. Daddy had told him to 'man up' and while his mother's eyes were wet, she only said that this would all be over soon.

"Now, look, your dad told me that you've been crying a lot at home. Is that true?"

Ryan didn't move in the wheelchair. Not an inch either way. The only time he felt even a moment's relief from the pain in his back was when sitting completely still, and then the fire raging over his flesh died down to relative embers.

His dad stood behind the chair, but Ryan wouldn't have lied to Pastor Alfred anyway. He knew liars went to hell.

"It hurts," he said and felt ashamed as tears burst forward onto his cheeks.

"I know. I know it does," Pastor Alfred said. "That's why I brought you these."

The Preacher opened his palm and two little pills sat in his hand.

"You take these every few hours and you won't feel any more pain, okay? You'll feel right as rain."

Ryan looked up from the preacher's hand, tears still streaming down his face. He'd never felt so much gratitude. Not in his whole life.

"Yeh—Yes, sir. Thank you so much."

"It's my pleasure, son," the preacher said, smiling. He reached forward and placed his hand on Ryan's leg. Ryan was just glad he didn't try and hug him.

5.

Alfred lay in bed with his eyes open, wondering if Jesus was going to come. Alfred P. Cunningham had been expecting Jesus for some time, and in complete honesty, had started to grow a little bit worried. He'd told the Bilbox's that this would be done in three weeks (because *that's* what God told *him*), but the Lord hadn't given him all the information at once. Alfred only knew the wings were first.

Jesus needed to tell him what the second part was supposed to be.

And tomorrow was the weekly service. Alfred was going to wheel the drugged-up child onto the pulpit and show how God was already working through him. The congregation didn't have to know about the Oxycontin Alfred was feeding the boy. It was necessary. Local anesthetics wouldn't last as long, nor help as much. They only needed the pills for a few weeks.

But, without the next commandment from God, he'd simply be rolling out a boy wearing wings. There would be no *plan*, and Alfred needed to be sure of God's will in order to deliver a powerful sermon. If he was to get his flock riled up about this, then Alfred had to believe it himself.

As he lay in bed, he didn't feel much in terms of his faith. If anything, he felt scared that he might have made a horrible mistake. Perhaps he'd misunderstood what God wanted, and instead of demonstrating his dedication, he'd simply surgically implanted chicken feathers on a boy and then fed him illegal drugs to keep him from crying.

Alfred need not have worried, though.

That was the thing about God.

He always came when you least expected it, as if He was testing your faith.

Jesus came as he always did, through the bedroom window. A white light looked in on Alfred, starting small and then growing larger and larger until Alfred P. Cunningham could see nothing else.

6.

"Last week I told you all that God had chosen us, this place, to begin showing the world that miracles existed. Let me hear an amen if ya remember!"

"Amen!"

"And who here believes that I was telling you the truth?"

"I did!"

"I'm sorry," Alfred P. Cunningham said, "I didn't catch that. *Who* thought I was telling the truth?"

"I did!" more voices shouted, echoing off the walls.

There wasn't much to Alfred's church. It was humble, just like he was, and just like his father before him. It was a two-room church, with ten wooden pews right in front of the pulpit. The second room was a small office just behind the pulpit, with a single desk and chair in it. Alfred did the church's business back there, but he wasn't above a little showmanship every now and then, either.

Ryan Bilbox wasn't sitting out with the congregation today. No, sir. He was in the back and he was going to be rolled out just as soon as Alfred had these people in a roar to see him.

The Lord was speaking powerfully through Alfred today. He was using His servant well—Alfred walked all over the pulpit, making eye contact with the people in each row; his voice was in fighting form. The night before had been beautiful and Alfred was ashamed he ever doubted his God.

For his God was powerful, just, and above all, loving.

"Now the Lord came to me last night, brothers and sisters. He came and He spoke long, and He spoke well, and He told me what we're to do! You see, did God simply give Job everything he wanted?"

"No!"

"No, he didn't! Did he make Job show his faith? Show how much he loved God?"

"Yes!"

"Yes. Yes, he did," Alfred said, growing very, very serious. "And he won't give us something even greater without the same sacrifice, without the *exact same show of faith* . . . Will he?"

"No," the congregation whispered back.

"No, indeed." Alfred looked down at his feet for a few seconds, feeling the crowd's emotion. They were waiting on him, their leader, to show them the way—just as he had waited for God to show him last night. "I love each and every one of you," he said, still not looking up. "Love you like you were my own children. What I'm about to show you the rest of the world might scoff at. They might look at us and call us crazy." His voice rose as he spoke, each sentence slightly louder than the last. "They might say we need to be in the looney bin over there in Birmingham, but we don't believe that do we?"

"No."

He looked up, his face flush and those flames dancing again in his eyes.

"I said, do we believe that?"

"NO!"

"No we don't! Because we have the Lord our God telling us the truth, leading us! We don't need man, and we don't want man telling us what to do! Those people that might scoff, well when our angel arrives they're going to have a lot of explaining to do, aren't they?"

"YES!"

"That's right! Terry, bring your son on out here, the boy that's going to bring God's righteous wrath down on all those that doubt Him *and* us!"

Alfred stepped to the side and the door behind him opened. Terry, dressed in his absolute best Sunday attire, walked out of the back room pushing the wheelchair in front of him.

Ryan sat in the chair, and though no one could see it, Alfred knew the wounds in his back were bleeding. Before the service, they had done a good bit to try and stem the blood flow, but the wings were just too damned heavy—even with him sitting in the wheelchair all day.

They'd put an extra thick coat over him, as well as padded the back and seat of the chair with black towels. If any of the blood did leak out, it would be tough to see. Not that Alfred cared so much about the child bleeding; he knew the Lord would make the boy well as long as they held faith.

He just didn't think it would be a good idea for the congregation to see such things.

"Here he is! Our very own soon to be angel! Two more weeks, brothers and sisters! Just *two more weeks!*"

The preteen sat in front of the congregation, his eyes hazy and his lids heavy. The only tell that he saw anyone in front of him was the small grin he gave when the crowd erupted in applause. Alfred had his doubts the boy knew exactly what was happening, but he seemed happy enough, and that's what mattered.

The wings attached to Ryan's back were starting to look a bit dingy, but Alfred knew none of his congregation saw it. Alfred stood to the side, clapping vigorously, his eyes moving from the slightly yellow feathers to the crowd and back again.

He watched as one of the chicken feathers lifted gently from the super glue and fell lazily to the floor next to the wheelchair.

7.

"Are you sure, Pastor Alfred? I mean he's been using the restroom on himself the past few days. And his back . . . I just don't know. I mean, when we clean the wound, it's starting to *smell*."

Alfred looked at Patricia Bilbox with a mixture of concern and calm.

"I understand, Patricia, I do. He's using the restroom on himself because we're giving him those pills around the clock, and that's to keep him from hurtin'. You know this."

Alfred watched as Patricia looked to Terry. The mother was concerned more than the father, but that was the natural way of things. They were the weaker sex—the Good Lord had told everyone that two thousand years ago.

"We're worried," Terry said. "I mean the smell coming from the back of him, and now this . . . it just might be too much, Pastor."

Alfred nodded. He thought something like this might come up. The boy was zonked out on Oxycontin, drooling on himself right now. He was sitting half naked in the wheelchair, and the mother wasn't lying—Alfred could smell the stench from across the living room. He knew what he had to do, though.

Alfred stood and walked over to the boy sitting in his underwear. He leaned the chap forward so that he could get a look at the surgery.

The smell was awful, but the sight might have been worse.

Puss and blood oozed from the holes in his skin. The antibacterial salve they'd placed across his back didn't seem to be working at all. Blisters were forming, too, and Alfred didn't even know how that was possible. It's not like the boy had been *burned*.

"This is the Devil's work," he said. "There's no doubt about it. He wants to stop us, but we're not going to let him."

"This next part, though . . . Pastor, I'm just not sure." The woman's voice shook as she spoke, but Alfred couldn't let her faith waiver. They had come this far, and there was less than two weeks before Gabriel took over the boy's body.

Alfred looked up from the drooling kid to Patricia. "Now listen to me, both of you. We're not going to let the Devil beat us here, are we? The bleach is going to clean this wound right up, and sure as I'm standin' here, God is going to put some healing potion in it too, and we're going to be able to take your son off these pills, okay?"

He stared at the two of them, and finally, slowly, they both nodded in agreement.

"Now let's get him in the tub so we can start healin' him."

It took a few minutes, but Alfred watched as the two parents undressed the child and moved him to the bathroom. His mother fed him another pill, because everyone knew the pain he was about to endure would be awful.

"How long's he got to stay in it?" Patricia asked.

"I've been thinkin' 'bout that," Alfred said. "The Lord ain't told me how long exactly, but I'm thinking three to four hours might be enough. Three to four hours will show Him we're serious, and it'll show Satan we're serious too. That's what we want, both of them to know which side we're on."

"Three to four hours?" Terry asked.

"Yes, I think that'll do it. Now let's pray before we put him in."

And they did pray.

8.

Alfred watched the boy the entire time. It was his duty, and to be honest, he thought the parents might grow weak if he were to leave. Growing weak now would only show God they *weren't* serious, and that couldn't happen. Not after the amount of belief the whole congregation had in what they were doing.

The tub was 1/5th water and 4/5th's bleach. Alfred had paid for all the bleach, and even hauled it over himself.

The boy sat in the tub, the liquid up to his neck. His body kept trying to slide down underneath, but Alfred or one of his parents would pull him up. The feathers were getting ruined, no doubt about it, but that couldn't be avoided. The wings were bent and wrapped around his body; the feathers had loosened and floated in the tub next to him.

They had opened the bathroom window and put a large fan inside the room as well, blowing the bleach fumes out.

It was slow going for a while, but eventually—about an hour and a half in—Patricia spoke up.

"Is he okay, Pastor? Look at his skin."

Had Alfred been dozing off? Perhaps. Sure enough, though, the boy's skin was changing, and not like Alfred had wanted. The point of this had been to *whiten* the boy's skin, making him look more angelic. That's what Jesus said He wanted, and it would certainly show their dedication to God's vision.

Red welts were rising on his arms. One of them had a trail of blood floating up into the clear liquid, looking like a red root rising to the ground's surface.

"That doesn't look good, Pastor. His skin ain't turnin' white at all. It's turnin' *red*."

Alfred suddenly wanted to grab the woman by her scraggly hair and jam her face into the damned mirror behind him. He could *tell* it was turning red. Everyone that *looked* at the tub saw it.

What's his back look like? Alfred wondered, but then shoved the thought away, half afraid the mother might read it and then start looking.

Alfred turned to his watch. It wasn't time yet. Three hours minimum and the kid had only sat in the bleach solution for half that.

"We have to wait, Patricia. Remember, it may look painful to us, but the Lord is in charge here."

A sick looking abrasion sat across the boy's penis, with a deep red line cracking down the middle like some sort of STD.

Alfred looked away.

"Another hour and a half."

No one said anything. Patricia moved a bit closer to the tub. Then they sat and waited.

Finally, almost two hours later, Patricia turned her head away from her boy and looked at the pastor with tear-filled eyes. "Can we get him out, Pastor? Please?"

The tub was full of chicken feathers and blood. The blood tinged the entire tub red despite the bleach. The feathers both floated on top and sunk to the bottom, hiding parts of the boy's body. Alfred didn't need to see the whole thing to know that it didn't look good beneath the chicken parts. The parents didn't need to see this, not if they were to keep going along with God's plan.

"Let me clean him up, Terry and Patricia. Ya'll go ahead on and I'll dry him and get him dressed. Leave one of them pills on the counter there." He stood, not looking at the two of them, not even going to give them the chance to brook dissent.

The two parents slowly walked out of the bathroom, their heads down.

Alfred waited until they were gone before he moved. He took his shirt and pants off, stripping himself down to his underwear. He looked at the red liquid and said a silent prayer that God would keep him from any disease.

He reached in and pulled Ryan from the murky water. The boy groaned on the way up, clearly the pain beginning to rise above the drugs.

The kid was heavy, especially with the damned wings, and Alfred barely got him from the tub to his wheelchair without falling out himself.

He sat down on the edge of the tub, the bleached bloody water cold on his ass as it soaked through his underwear. Alfred stared at the boy, growing more worried with each passing second.

This wasn't good. He couldn't sit here and pray himself into thinking it was.

The boy's body had begun to swell up, looking fat and disgusting. Blood dripped from the welts that covered his flesh, the bleach having eaten through his skin like some kind of parasite. Alfred had told the parents that God would put some type of healing potion in the water, but that hadn't been the case.

Christ no, it hadn't.

Red, bleeding welts stretched from the kid's neck down to his feet.

"Oh, God, what have we done?" Alfred whispered. He couldn't hide it from the parents.

And yet . . . he couldn't be wrong about this. He just couldn't be. The Lord had come to him too many times telling him what must happen . . . and Ryan's parents saw God too. In their dreams.

No, this was the Devil's work again, trying to confound the faithful.

Alfred would do his part. He'd cover the boy and explain to the parents what was happening. The Lord worked in mysterious ways and they had to understand that.

Alfred vomited in the toilet twice while putting Ryan's clothes on.

9.

The sun was hot on the final day of Ryan's changing. It beat down on the church's back lawn as if they had somehow offended it. The congregation was there, every single one of them.

Alfred P. Cunningham had promised a lot and today he would deliver. The Lord had come to him last night, laying everything out perfectly.

They were to have service *outside* today, underneath God's sky and the cleansing power of the sun. Ryan Bilbox was already sitting in his chair. The wings he wore were mostly destroyed, the metal aluminum beneath bent and twisted, poking through the cloth. A few scattered chicken feathers still stuck to them, but the magnificence had worn off.

"I want to thank you all for coming. Sincerely. From the bottom of my heart."

Alfred stood in the middle of the congregation, their chairs circling around him four rows deep. His hands were on the back of Ryan's wheelchair, and as he spoke, he turned the boy so they all could see him. Ryan wasn't smiling anymore as he had been last week at church. They'd loaded him up on so many painkillers, Alfred didn't think he had a clue where he was even at. A steady stream of drool rolled down his cheek, though the turtleneck he wore mopped it all up before it hit his neck.

The patches beneath his clothing were scabbing over for the most part, but there were many places that looked as infected as his back. The boy gave off a stench that smelled of rotten meat and spoiled milk, things left in the sun too long. Alfred had doused him with cologne before rolling him out onto the field, but that stench couldn't be hidden for long—especially not in this heat.

"Brothers and sisters, today is the day." Alfred looked back to the fourth row of circles. "Brother Brian, how long have you been with this church?"

"Forty years."

"FOUR-TEE YEARS!" Alfred shouted. "And you've been waitin' for a miracle ain'tcha? Been waiting on God to send someone that would take us all back up to heaven, ain't that right?"

"Amen!"

"Amen!"

The praises came up from all around him and Alfred was glad to hear it. His voice was taking their attention from the boy, which was good—if they focused too much on him, their enthusiasm might waiver.

It didn't matter, though.

God was nearly upon them and He would lift this boy up into His loving arms and replace whatever ailed him with the righteous power of angels. No more fake wings. No more red and bleeding skin. This boy would be perfect in just a few more moments. The Lord had said it and so it would be.

"I want to especially thank Terry and Patricia. They've shown more faith than just about anyone I've ever seen and God is surely to reward them for it. Not in the next life either, but in this one. In just a few minutes, to be matter of fact. Because their son . . . I can barely even believe it. Ryan here is moments away from being an angel. If you have faith, let me hear an amen!"

"AMEN!"

"Now," Alfred continued, "we've kept much of what we've done in private, but the Lord spoke to me and told me the last part is to be done in front of all you. Because we must show our faith as a congregation, not as individuals. And your participation is as important as mine, as Ryan's parents, too. You must watch and believe that the good Lord is goin' to deliver us from evil. Do you understand, brothers and sisters?"

The brothers and sisters affirmed their understanding.

"Good, good, good."

"Now, we've made this boy's body resemble as close to an angel as we can here on Earth. Because that's what God wanted. He commanded Jesus to go without food and water for forty days, and he commanded us to do this. But if He can keep Jonah alive in the belly of a fish, then He can certainly raise this boy high into the air. No doubt about it."

"None."

"Not a one."

Alfred nodded, feeling the moment approaching.

"Ruth, bring that on out here now." He looked out into the crowd as his wife approached. "The last thing we're missing, brothers and sisters, is a halo. And that's what we're going to do together. We're going to give this little angel a halo, and when we finish, there won't be nothin' little 'bout him no more."

Ruth made her way through the circles of chairs.

Her left hand carried a gold-painted, circular tube. It wasn't nothing more than a piece of an electric bug zapper that Alfred had laying around the house. He'd taken it apart and gave it to his wife, who then painted it and attached the three metal rods to it. The bottom of the metal rods would fit on Ryan's head, allowing the halo to stand high above it.

Ruth's right hand carried a staple gun.

She handed the gun to Alfred and then stepped to the side.

"Terry, come on up here," the pastor said.

Terry stood from the front row and walked to his son.

"Patricia, you too."

She did as she was bid.

"Let's hold hands," Alfred said. "All of you surrounding us hold hands too. Bow your heads as we bow ours and let's ask God for His grace and power." Alfred took the two parents in either hand and waited as his congregation did the same. "Dear God, our Lord and Savior, we come to you ready for your love and blessings to rain down upon us like the cleanest water to ever touch this Earth. These two parents here have suffered in your name, truly doing your bidding. Indeed, we all have, as we did what you asked. Now, though, at the time of truth, we ask for your strength and your guidance to carry us through. Because on the other side of this act is a glory that ain't none of us ever thought we'd live to see. I pray all of this in Jesus's name. Amen."

The crowd around him concluded the same.

"Now, if you two'll take your seats, we'll bring an angel down upon us, okay?"

Both Terry and Patricia had tears in their eyes and were smiling wide.

Alfred P. Cunningham returned their smiles and gently hugged them both. They *had* suffered and he was ready to relieve them of it. God was too; Alfred *knew* it.

The parents sat and his wife took their place next to the boy. They had rehearsed this late into the previous night. She took the makeshift halo and held it above the boy's head, while Alfred lined up the metal rods with the boy's skull.

Lord, thank you for this opportunity, he prayed silently.

He took the staple gun and placed it against the rod, pressing down hard so that the business end of the gun touched Ryan's skin.

He pulled the trigger.

He didn't look at what he'd done, but moved to the next spot. He knew that God wouldn't finish the job until *he* finished the job.

Boom. The staple gun fired in his hand again.

And finally, he stepped around to the last third of the boy's skull. He lined the gun up perfectly and shot the staple into his head.

He stepped back. Alfred could feel the electricity almost rising behind him, the people ready for their miracle.

Blood dripped down Ryan Bilbox's face. It streamed from six different holes, two from each staple. One had been pushed into the middle of his forehead, and the two streams dripped down either side of his nose; the left bloodstream mixed with the drool stemming from his mouth.

Alfred took another step back, unsure exactly how God planned on doing this, but knowing if he was in the way, he could be injured.

Another thirty seconds passed.

Ryan's head fell forward, his chin resting on his chest.

Patricia let out a small cry from behind Alfred, breaking his concentration.

The halo now tilted heavily from the boy's head, gravity pulling it toward his lap. The staples in the back of his skull still held it firm, but the metal rods were bending.

Blood dripped from the boy's forehead, splattering on his black suit.

"Ryan?" Terry said.

"One second," Alfred called back. Sweat covered his own brow and he felt his chest tightening up. There it was. That was the Lord's sign, that He was coming now. Alfred's hands went to his left pectoral, though he didn't know it. He was caught up in the rapture of the Lord's arrival.

Sure, his chest hurt, and sure a boy looked like he was dying right in front of him, but God had spoken and God would not lie.

Alfred P. Cunningham collapsed to the ground.

The congregation around him stood up, many gasping.

Patricia Bilbox began to scream—her voice sounding like a meadow full of pleating lambs.

Alfred P. Cunningham stared up at the sky and blackness started swimming on the outsides of his vision. His chest hurt, but that's only because the Lord was so powerful.

Darkness came over him quickly, and then he was in God's arms.

The rest of his congregation that he had led so faithfully for the past ten years stared at their dead preacher and their mangled boy. Many were sobbing, others only looking on with blank faces, as if still waiting for God to shine His holy light and end the madness before him.

In the end, God never showed up.

Lights did come though. The police from the town twenty miles east.

HUMAN-KINGS
By Austin Biela

We have known that the universe would one day die. We learned that early in our history. We had the theories of the Big Bang and of entropic equilibrium, of a universal state where there would be nothing, things that pointed us to one, inevitable ending and we accepted that. We accepted it like a child accepts death; tragic when it happens to others but inconceivable for ourselves. It was too far in the future to consider by those who first discovered this. There was nothing to fear. It didn't concern them beyond an idea to discuss with their peers. We focused on the present and the future we had ahead of us.

As human-kind developed, this looming certainty was shelved in the back of our minds. Within a few hundred years, human-kind began to explore its cosmic surroundings. We took our ships to the planets in our immediate solar system and colonized whatever we could, living out dreams of space exploration. In another millennium, we developed even faster ships that could take us even farther into the universe without tearing down, travelling along the expressways of sunbeams, and the technology suitable to make living in such a ship almost enjoyable. We fulfilled an existence-long ambition to meet the interstellar community. They gave us technology and in turn we gave them some of our own. The men and women who made these transactions described it as bizarre, "to think that such advanced life would trail behind in places where we have dominated." Though it had to be reconfigured for their biology, our gifts of medical technology and pharmaceutical substances gave the first impression of human-kind to all of the interstellar community who heard. We were survivalists and survivors.

The next several thousand millennia proceeded at a brisk pace. Human-kind was brought into the fold of the universe's culture, like the youngest child being taught all the tricks and secrets by their older siblings. We learned how to partake in universal politics, the best ways to discuss universal trade and even the proper, expected actions taken when engaging in war. Where there was disorder in the universe, this culture had maintained control. Those first alien races that had established this culture had passed down their values to its current occupants, the primary tenet being to make the best of the time they had now. Of course, there were always detractors and problem-starters. Warmongers, corrupt tradesmen, rambunctious races that decided they didn't want to maintain control at all. This wasn't us. Human-kind was glad that we were considered a valued part of the culture, an older sibling that needed to help integrate the next race that managed interstellar travel and met the challenge.

Still, there were times when human-kind couldn't help but feel like it was being amused by our older siblings. They would watch in fascination as we would colonize worlds that would never be fit for hospitable existence. Instead of just building space stations, they would smirk as we talked about landing and building colonies on barren planetary bodies. They didn't see the point in it. We could never live there naturally as a species. We could never grow cities the size of which we had on Earth or on other, more suitable planets. The same level of examination and investigation could easily be done with machines. What benefit was there to be had in looking at the rocks in person? We took it with a smile and laughed at how we just preferred it like this, while mumbling under our breaths and scowling when they weren't looking. Why couldn't they understand?

Other times, we were the ones who couldn't understand. From time to time, we would have the sudden rise of doomsday cults. They would often start small and then die out. Other times, they'd grow and grow until nearly entire colonies were converted, proclaiming either the end of the planet, the solar system or of the universe itself. Human-kind tried to keep such groups quiet, especially when our older siblings were around to hear it, like a teenager with an embarrassing fascination. Instead, our older siblings only laughed and seemingly commended the doomsday groups for their acceptance. Our older siblings thought that, while it may have been silly to expect the end of days to come so quickly or to be soon, their embrace of the end was an example we could learn from. It didn't sit well with us. In the collective mind of human-kind, our backburners began to heat up.

Thousands of millennia continued to pass. Human-kind saw many of our older siblings pass away. Their records and shared technology were all that was left of them. They had all been wiped out for various reasons. Victims of interstellar war that were caught off-guard and soon eradicated, a disease that boiled their bodies from the inside out and was too fast to properly diagnose, a freak accident of a meteor taking out their hive-mind collective. They all began to fade, until human-kind were the oldest sibling. We did our best to teach to the new ones what our predecessors had taught us, but our words were hollow. We discovered something about ourselves that we did our best to hide from those races under our tutelage. We had never really believed in the tenet of making the best of the time we had now. We had accepted it as individuals, but never as a race. Human-kind did not want to make the best of the time we had now. We didn't want to give up our time. We had come too far, hadn't we?

Apparently, others thought so as well. Soon, many of our younger siblings began to pass away, all for the same reasons our predecessors had. Yet human-kind remained, old and wise and powerful, having amassed the collective technology of the universal culture, including the technology that was no longer around. There was unrest in the culture. There were those races that called for human-kind to share the amassed power we had and to step back from universal politics. They began to call us, as best as we could translate, "human-kings." This was theoretical of course. Human-kind had no one political power or advantage over any other race. We may have made our mistakes, but as a whole, we did not control or strong-arm any race into doing something they were against nor did we lord what we had over our younger siblings. No, what they were calling for was our death, for us to let them take our place and fade away with the rest of our older siblings. They thought we had lived for too long.

There were even some races that tried to enact our demise. They would gather in secret before launching an attack, their metal battalions battering down on an unsuspecting colony. Sometimes, they were even able to win a fight but one colony was all that they ever acquired. While the fear of extinction had separated us from our younger siblings, it had united us as a race. Death on a universal scale was no longer tolerated and retribution was efficient upon our foes. Those usurpers that survived only went on to say that, the closer human-kind came to death, the harder we fought back. We reminded our universal community that we were survivalists and survivors. We seemingly convinced them that we could not be killed and perhaps that we were eternal. No, not yet.

This was the state of affairs for many millennia. Humankind's presence was tolerated amongst the stars, still a part of the universal culture. We attended the same meetings and gatherings that required our presence, donated our supplies and troops without expectation of compensation, and shared a fraction of our scientific discoveries and technology, the things we believed would be universally beneficial. In turn, the same was given to us and humankind put all of it to use. The fear of universal death trickled down to the common human and efforts were placed against that fear. While we knew then that death came for everyone in the end, that didn't mean we couldn't prolong it. We found ways to extend life without sacrificing physical ability, growing to the age of 200, then 300, then 500, then 700, then a millennium. We became the new Methuselahs. Our younger siblings watched as we refused that ever-lingering limitation, letting out subtle sighs of relief when our long-standing diplomats and politicians finally passed away, and watched their young replacements with anticipation, wondering how long this one would last. It was a sign that we were still like them, bound to the inevitable.

They didn't know how deep our reputation ran within us.

There is no exact date to when human-kind looked up and saw the stars begin to die out in large numbers. Like a plague through a crowded city, darkness was sweeping through the skies and across all lines of sight. The end of the universe showed signs of arriving. We were still not ready. The once-great inevitability that our planet-locked ancestors had accepted became a startling reality human-kind could not ignore.

As our younger siblings had long wanted, human-kind withdrew itself from the universal culture. We pulled out all resources, troops and foreign bodies and gathered ourselves together into planetary clusters. We evacuated colonies and boarded ourselves away from our younger siblings. Human-kind focused solely on itself and its new line of inquiry. Research and technology investigated into new types of metal, things durable and strong enough to withstand the pressure of black holes and the heat of supernovas. Our younger siblings were all but happy to finally be rid of us and any attempt to contact us was met with pleas to go away and leave us to our work. No one noticed or recorded when our last encounter with another race of beings was. Human-kind was alone once again.

Time had no meaning when our ark was finally launched. It was our finest creation. Forged from the strongest metals we could create, it was built to sustain anyone who lived inside it forever. It was the size of a solar system and it had to be. The amount of technology to both store the collected history and knowledge of human-kind, as well as the life-sustaining machinery, the self-sustaining energy generators, and the remaining 333 billion population of human-kind required every inch of that size. The only flaw to it was that there were no means of holding everyone in a cryogenic state. The generator wouldn't be able to handle all we asked of it and the ark would've failed. We weren't going to let that happen. It was built at the farthest edge of what remained of our galaxy, directed out into an unyielding emptiness. Its purpose was simple.

It was built to last us past the death of our current universe and, with any hope, bring us forth into the next.

Once everyone was aboard, our long wait began. The fear of whether we would survive this long began to fade and was replaced with anxiety and boredom. We had spent nearly a millennium preparing for these moments and now found that we had no idea what to do with the time we had. We began to tinker and toy with the resources on hand, exploring the massive artificial gardens we had created for agriculture and the way we recycled everything, including our wastes. There was no safety of mind for dumping things out into whatever void was left out there. Everything flushed away was cleaned and redistributed or used for fertilizer. As for entertainment, the arks had a near-complete recorded history of human-kind's stories and digital media. Human-kind would reteach itself all over again, ready for the generations of people that would be born aboard the ark.

In fact, this was the first problem human-kind on the ark faced. With so much time and freedom, people found bedfellows far too easily and in surplus. Sex became a thing to pass the time and soon a wave of offspring were born from it. The appointed leaders of the ark, the engineers and crew who designed and were trained to maintain the ark itself, set the rules for population control. Though the ark was mighty, overpopulation was still a concern. Too many people at one time would only be a drain on the resources which, while built to continually renew itself, still came with a cycle. It was decided that only official couples would have children and then only one at a time. When the possibility of twins was brought up, it was resolved with a medical procedure that would reverse the cell division, ideally reverting to an only child. Though it was met with some outcry, the decision of facing either human-kind's ultimate end or keeping themselves under control seemed an obvious choice.

Millennia began to pass and human-kind settled into habit. There were few complaints and they seemed small in comparison to extinction. One was how the meat, all synthetic and mass-produced, lacked any taste of the real thing, none of the blood and fat and juices that came from cooking living things. The reasoning was that having any other animal life on the ark besides human-kind would only be a burden. Another was how only the appointed leaders were allowed access into certain areas, reasoned away by it being technical information that was unnecessary for the comfort of human-kind. Otherwise, life was calm and well and people grew more bored than scared anymore. To try and stay focused, they turned their attentions to either books, digital media, historical recordings, or to the health and education of the next generation. These ark-based children, who knew nothing of existence besides sterile rooms and empty hallways, were the main attraction for everyone who knew any couple with a child. Everyone found it imperative that these children know about human-kind, know about our great history and eternal legacy. For the first hundred years of this generation's life, we had them learning every single recorded word, from the earliest history of Earth to our first encounter with the universal culture to the day the ark launched. There was no motion to produce new culture yet. Human-kind wanted to bask in the glory of its past and prepare for it all over again when they could leave.

That peace and settlement could not last. In the year 1066 AE, "After the End," one of the older residents of the ark fell over dead. Those who had witnessed the scene were interviewed later and reported that he had clutched his heart and strained against the back of the chair he sat in. When they saw it, they didn't understand what had just happened. We had grown so comfortable and serene in the ark that his passing came as a reminder. We had not escaped that force. If anything, we were surrounded by it more than ever before.

We did our best to not panic. Like a flash, it had left us stunned in the aftermath and we tried to live as we had for the last millennium. Still, there was a mood that swept through human-kind. What they had once been content to learn through our books and recorded media, the younger generation began to ask their parents about why it was so important that the ark be built and why this man's death startled us. So, we passed down our instincts of survival.

We had taught our children of the true greatness of human-kind. So now we taught them of our ultimate nature.

When the man had finally been carted away, there were inquiries and demands to know what would come next. They all boiled down to a simple question: "What would happen to the body?" He couldn't be recycled like waste. He was a human, he deserved better than that. It seemed that the administrators had already foreseen this, claiming to have the foresight to think rationally even in stressful times, as they had in the ark's construction, and revealed a previously unknown part of the ark. A morgue, an enormous rotund space with every inch chilled to near-freezing temperatures, with which to store the bodies of those who passed on our journey. Preserving the dead was much simpler than cryogenically freezing someone and so it was deemed necessary. When we would finally land, we would properly bury the bodies, in ways that that had been deemed respectable in the times before the ark.

Yet, the administrators were not as rational as they thought or perhaps tried to hide it from themselves. In another millennium, the morgue was more than half full. Even the bodies of the administrators were stored there, packed away among countless others, while their children took their place. Soon, the first generation had died and the second took their place, the third generation beginning the same lessons and hearing the same centuries long history lessons that their parents had heard. In that time, there was still no trace of the next universe, no sign that our journey would produce results. We were still surrounded by oblivion with no end in sight and human-kind persisted in numbers. The morgue had failed.

So, instead of being shut down or scrapped, its purpose was transformed. In the year 2108 AE, as human-kind came together for their dinner, the first ark-bred generation partook in our first real taste of meat. We loved it. No one suspected a thing, only noting how much more sensual the food was for once in our life. It did more than satisfy and nourish. It excited and engaged our disused taste buds, only accustomed to bitter tastes and the occasional sugar spike. Portions were disappearing almost the instant we sat down to enjoy them. Children kept coming for more and more, begging and pleading for any way to sneak out a second portion, even a mere scrap. Not only the children, but the adults too. Everyone to taste the meat couldn't get enough of it. We never even bothered to ask where the meat could have possibly come from. Perhaps we chalked it up to some advancement in the culinary skill of the cooks or perhaps some lenience with the administrators over what could be used to spice the portions. After dinner, we found out that the administrators did have a hand in it after all but never in a way we could have imagined.

When the administrators announced what they had done, we thought it was a joke or some ill-advised prank. The current captain, the head of the administrators, was a stern woman but surely, she was capable of jesting with us? But no, she was quite serious. The loss of free space in the morgue was becoming a growing problem, one she felt had to be solved post-haste. So, she and the other administers had found a solution, one that freed space within the morgue and made use of the removed bodies. As they explained themselves to us all, they made it clear that this was not an action taken lightly. It had come after many years, possibly a century's worth of consideration, but she had decided that it was the best solution. She had even tried to seem self-sacrificing, the first of the cuts having come from the previous administrators, including her father, our previous captain, the ex-head of the administrators and the one who had introduced the morgue in the first place. She stood by this new form of human waste and disposal, citing the name of survival itself.

Her words left us trembling. We felt disgusted at first. Human-kind had not openly engaged in such an act since we were planet-locked and any revelation regarding it was considered taboo and repulsive. However, we had never experienced it. We had never had a line of comparison before within the ark, between the manufactured meat and the real thing. No one denied the difference, how we all clamored for more when we didn't know the truth about it. That truth, that point of origin, wouldn't change how it tasted.

From the time of her announcement to when the next dinner rush came, the ark was all talk about the new meals. Parents would send children away as we talked, wondering if we should go to the next serving of portions or could avoid it. There was talk of boycotting the meals and having them find another way to dispose of the growing bodies, if the morgue couldn't be used as one. We knew we couldn't throw them out of the ark, not while the fear of utter extinction still resided out there, as was believed what would happen if the doors of the ark were open too long as there existed nothing else outside. This wasn't like with space and airlocks. As long as there was the utter chance that even opening the doors would lead to the destruction of the ark, so long as there was only void, they would remain shut. There was even talk about overthrowing the current administrators, who were said to not have been eating the meals themselves and were either mad enough to incite this plan or cruel enough to inflict it under a populace that needed them, but none of it meant anything. It was the hollow venting of frustration, the adjustment of a new way of life. No one would ever try to overthrow the administrators. They were the ones who knew the secrets of the ark. Not even that, they were the only ones who knew how to run the thing, to utilize the scanners and equipment necessary to maintain the ark as well as look for anything outside. The ark had not been built with windows, for the administrators had feared the psychological effect it might have to peer out and see the void, so it scanned instead. Without the administrators, there would be no leaving the ark. Still, that was not what really kept us from moving against her. We didn't act because we believed she was right. So, when the time for the next dinner came, everyone slowly shuffled to where the dinner was being held, uncertainty still lingering over the new food.

What we had not expected was to see the captain herself, her presence broadcast on all the screens in the ark, already standing alone in front of the food dispensaries. She just stood there. She had been waiting for us. The children complained about her being there before them but we held them back, wanting to see what would happen. When she was sure that we were all watching, she made the order for a meal. It was a meal of mashed potatoes, a thin pea soup and a slab of the meat. We expected her to play around with it, to wait to taste of it, to show some signs of reluctance at the thing that could have once been her father. No, the first thing she did was grab her knife and fork and cut off a piece. She stabbed into it and raised it to her lips, our eyes watching every second of it in anticipation. She bit down and chewed and we heard the most satisfied hum we had ever heard. She swallowed and began to cut the meat up into other pieces, a smile on her lips and a blush on her face. She mixed it with her soup and potatoes, slowly devouring it as though it had been her first meal all day, and we agreed. The meat was unlike anything else. There was nothing like it. We watched her devour it until she was running her finger along the edge of the plate, sucking up any juice that remained off her fingers. Then, when she was done, she got up, returned the plate to be washed, and left, regaining her dignified posture and sense of presence.

That had solved it. There was no more hesitation. We scrambled to be the next to eat the food, to mix it just as our captain had done or simply swallow huge chunks of the portions. We told ourselves we did it in the name of survival. We convinced ourselves that this was only natural and that our predecessors would want this. We would live through them. It was the best that human-kind could do.

The mood of human-kind had changed once again. Though death was still feared, it was no longer seen as another failure. It was seen as more hope for the rest of us. The morgue ceased to be anything less than cold storage from then on. There were plenty of bodies to live off of, plenty to cook and heat up and sauté. Families were given rights to the first cut whenever one of their own was being served. When one of us died, instead of avoiding talking about their missing presence, their family and friends discussed what they might be served with and hoped for a hearty meal. There were even those that tried to skip ahead, that cut tiny portions of themselves and heated it up as a snack. When they were found out, they were admonished and disgraced. How dare they horde themselves away? How dare they act so selfishly, so as to keep from everyone else's chances?

This was the state of the ark for many millennia. Things remained as they always had, living, breathing, teaching and now devouring. Our second captain died a hero and a revered leader, her body treated as a delicacy on the day she was served and the scene of her child eating of her meat broadcast for everyone to watch. It became tradition for each new administrator to personally devour their parent for all the ark to see. This new way of life though was only to hearken new things.

In the year 10,871 AE, the only allowed child of a 10th Generation couple was born and he was named Jakobson. It had only taken the first glance from all those involved to know that something about the child was different. Even as an infant, he barely resembled either of his parents. Though only newborn, his skin was gaunt and a light tan. His fingers already seemed long and narrow and his eyes bulged from an already enlarged skull. Now, between the 8th and 10th generations, it was becoming increasingly common for the newborns to have some sort of small mutation. Perhaps they had an extra finger or perhaps they had heterochromia. Medicine and science had come far enough that anything too terrible could be treated and with a little gene therapy or surgery, we could be adjusted. The doctors gave no such chance to young Jakobson. Gene therapy on a newborn was unheard of and the doctors agreed to watch over the baby while his parents were to wait at home. When he was dead, they could try and petition the administrators for another child. So, the doctors tried to make the young baby comfortable and waited.

They waited for hours. They waited for days. They waited for a week.

When they went to check on him, they were shocked as Jakobson squealed when the light hit his eyes. It was a dry squeal, so it sounded deeper than expected of a baby, but it was a squeal nonetheless. Looking over the child, he was even thinner than before, nearly all skin and bones. The nurses admitted to feeding him rarely and even then only morsels, just something to make his supposed passing easier. It was only enough to feed a baby for a day, not at all a week. Despite the odds, he had survived.

From there, Jakobson, named Jakob for short, had a strange life. When he finally went home, his parents cared for him unconditionally. His mother especially loved on her baby boy, proud of his survival. She would brag on his behalf and tell about how able he was, growing up just as any other baby his age. People who knew the couple would gather around, marveling and wondering how such a child could last a week on next to nothing. Though he usually looked like he would fall apart at any second, he grew just as any other child did and eventually attended school just like other children. Those children that questioned Jakob about his strange appearance were reprimanded by their teachers, who knew of Jakob's story from word of mouth or from his parents. As he grew, his reputation continued to proceed him and popularity began to follow. Even as his skin continued to grow tan and leathery to the touch, there were still adolescent boys and girls who wished to kiss his shriveled cheek and fantasized about his rangy fingers grasping their naked bodies. Even as his skull continued to enlarge, sloping back and to the left, he was heaped upon with scholarly expectations and met with each and every one. Even as his body began to grow and his once spindly form doubled in size, bones and muscles pressing against his skin, both teachers and students watched in marvel as he pulled himself up the ropes and suspended himself in the air with his strength alone. He was the boy who seemed to be everything human.

Yet we who did not have the pleasure of meeting him were not so easily impressed. Word of Jakob spread through the ark as people continued to watch his growth. There was no teacher or authority figure to admonish us when we pointed out how unique he appeared. There were those of us who described him as disproportionate and misshapen, a body that had somehow slipped away from medicine and science to produce something so different. The most ashamed and removed of us even described him as inhuman. Yet none of us would ever say it aloud or admit thinking so to anyone.

His existence was proof enough of how fallible this claim was. He had survived, so he was human. To say otherwise meant to interrogate everything that they had sacrificed to make it this far. This was all it took to keep us quiet.

Still, Jakob's story had only just begun. By his 1st century birthday, reports began to flood in of new births, babes as malformed and suspected not long for life as Jakob had been. This time, knowing of Jakob's story, we embraced our bundles of joy and began to compare them to each other. When their mothers met with each other, a baby with two mouths would find itself in competition with one that had a third arm growing from their side. They were taught the same as Jakob was, heaped upon with the same expectations and, just like Jakob, met most all of them. In fact, we taught them to aspire to Jakob, as the true icon that he is. He was their forbearer, their advent, and it was true. Jakob had only been the first in what was to come.

Slowly and surely, these new figures of human-kind grew in number. Soon, entire classrooms of these children were being taught, each made special and unique by one trait or another. They followed Jakob in lifestyle, wanting to do right by us and human-kind. It is even said that Jakob visited the classroom in which his future wife was just starting to learn. By the time Jakob was 250 years old, the population of this special human-kind was a quarter of the population of the ark. There were fewer average human births. No one wanted an average human birth.

Not even the administrators wanted average births. In his middle-age years, Jakob and his family became good friends with all of the administrators. The administrators flooded his parents with questions, wanting to know what raising Jakob had been like and were eager to plunge any secrets from them that may have resulted in the miracle baby. His wife, Annabelle, had been given special permission to give birth to two babies, was the envy of many and lorded her status as the sole reason Jakob's line would go on, as far as anyone else knew. The captain himself was especially fond of Jakob. He would often invite Jakob over to his personal cabin to talk about the ongoing of the ship and various theories and ideas they had about ancient human-kind history, when we were still planet-locked. He would often insist they share a drink of alcohol, instructing his wife to come and bring them the glasses. She would serve it to him while wearing shirts with plunging necklines and skirts that displayed her supple thighs. Once they were thoroughly buzzed, the captain would often make the excuse of going to find a certain book for them to read over and discuss next time, going out to the ark's library to retrieve it. He would leave Jakob alone with his wife and not return for hours.

As the population shifted and more creative mutations began to emerge, our older members of human-kind, who looked more like our ancestors than the current generation, went to work trying to understand what was happening. We were not urged on by fear of our surroundings, for we saw nothing to fear. We were not compelled by duty to the rest of human-kind, for there was nothing to resolve. No, in truth, we acted with jubilation and enthusiasm. We were excited for the task, ready to put our minds into action, to shed the nausea and veil of boredom that left us stagnant. We had all the knowledge to toil over but none of the application. We were desperate for anything. We toiled for years upon years, excited for any one new piece of information or discovery, no matter how inconsequential. Gradually, the new generation took our place until it was not uncommon to run the tests on ourselves, just for the slightest indication of difference. At dinners, we would meet and discuss our findings, only ever stopping to tear and devour our meat, something we can never get enough of.

The day Jakob died was a day of mourning for all the ark. All experiments were halted and everyone watched their screens as those closest to Jakob gave some parting words on his life, words we had heard ever since he had been a child but listened to again. Through a single involuntary act, Jakob had paved the way for the rest of human-kind and reaffirmed that all important part of ourselves. Survive. When his body was cooked and prepared, people whispered and admired how his family ate of his body, his wife's mouth prying open from cheek to cheek, jaw unhinged, to consume and digest as much of her late husband as she could. His children, who were not born with mouths like their mother, ripped and cut the meat into bite sized portions, skewering it with their forks, or fingers in the case of his daughter, and tore at it with sharpened canines, all while the crowd silently supported them. His family later described him as tasting tougher than other meats but having an odd spiciness that was otherwise unknown to them from prior meals.

After that, little else happened. The administrators locked themselves away, focusing on their work of sustaining and watching over the ark, and we saw nothing of them for millennia. The body of human-kind continued to change, children looked less and less like their parents with every passing generation. They had to be reminded, when being taught our history, that those beings on the screen, all sharing a common frame, were our ancestors and, just like

we were doing now, they survived. Because that's what we were doing. We were surviving. As long as we remained, as long as our lega-
cies continued, no matter how chaotic or mutated or strange our
bodies became, we would survive. That was all that mattered now.
As long as we survived, little else mattered.

Then, one day in the year 10 billion AE, the ark shook. The
ship tilted and everyone was thrown about. The voice of the administrators, who we had almost begun to doubt ever existed in the first
place, came on and warned all of human-kind to lock themselves in
their rooms and watch their screens for upcoming news and information. We did as we were told, our frames shuffling as quickly as
we could into our rooms with our families and friends. We turned on
our screens and saw the faces of the administrators. Their time alone
amongst themselves had guided them. They were all cyclopes with
one white, filmy eye, frail forms strapped to their chairs to keep their
bodies upright. They drew our attentions to the video feed, warning
us to only focus on the center of the screen and not along the borders. We listened and watched. There, we saw a white, flaming ball
floating in the void. Our bodies and minds shook in the silence, unable to quite comprehend what was in front of us and being drawn
towards the black of the blasphemous void. Then the administrators
welcomed us to the beginning of a new universe, resetting the clocks
to the year 0 NU, New Universe.

With those words in our heads, all fear and anxiety about
the void was banished. There were certainly children conceived on
that day and the morgue was raided of multiple bodies in celebration. Human-kind had not known such happiness in such a long time,
not since before the time of Jakob's death. Our journey was halfway
done. We had survived the end all the way to the beginning. We
would live on again, in a new universe, and reestablish the greatness
of human-kind.

The generations continued. The administrators allowed us
to watch the foundations of the universe to be settled, the ark's machines finally able to process an existence outside itself. We recorded everything that we could, from the birth of the first stars to
the first recorded instance of a planetary body. It was all so alien, so
new, and so strange. We reviewed our histories, back when we had
been planet-locked. We remembered the struggles that had always
proceeded us. We remembered the battles and wars. Physical necessity wasn't an issue, the ark had proved that much. But co-habita-
tions with others was discussed. Human-kind had always been

hunted. There was always somebody out to kill us, to remove us, to stop us from living another day. The tide of favor began to turn.

I was born in the year 13 billion NU, and am said to be one of the last of the ark children. I grew from my mother's womb, tearing through with already sharpened digits, taking her life with me. My father assured me that she tasted succulent. I sometimes think I can taste her when I try to imagine the scene, father's jagged, misshapen fangs tearing through roasted flesh. It does not matter, for I am of human-kind. We are all of human-kind. There is nothing to us but human-kind.

As I grew, I heard us talking about the end of the journey and I listened to us. We had found a planet that had developed multicellular life. By the time we reach it, it will have a wonderful, horrid ecosystem. It will reek of life and death. We children grew excited while the adults shuddered. The planets would sprout civilizations again, alien worlds with their own agendas and desires. They will want to be rid of us again. They will want the extinction of the ark children, of their human-kings. Because of this, I have been tasked with writing this very message you hear now.

To whoever finds this, I tell you now. Don't blame us. We don't have any choice. There is nothing else we can do. If we don't, it would all have been for nothing. Do not stand in our way. We will not hesitate. Human-kind will survive, even if that means alone.

WRIGGLERS
By Chantal Boudreau

Maddy and Charley weren't sure what city kids did for summer vacation normally, but they were pretty sure it wasn't what they had in store for their cousin, Scotty. They had protested when their mother explained to them that Scotty's family would be coming to visit from the city, and that they would be expected to keep him company and keep him out of trouble. Neither of them liked the idea of some strange kid tagging along and spoiling the best fun of the year. They both vowed that they would still do everything that they would usually do and drag Scotty with them, whether he liked it or not. They weren't about to let city kinfolk ruin things for them.

The morning after his family arrived in the country, Scotty was waiting in the kitchen when Charley and Maddy came down the stairs for breakfast. They were drawn by the smell of apple cinnamon flapjacks and weren't anticipating their visitor so early in the day.

They weren't sure what to make of Scotty at first. He was quiet, which was funny, because Charley and Maddy had been led to believe that city kids were tough and mouthy. But Scotty didn't look tough at all. In fact, he seemed much more awkwardly uncomfortable than menacing. He was a little taller than they were, but thinner too, although not in any sort of lean muscular way. The slightly older boy was pale and his hair was a dull brown. Maddy thought he looked goofy too, because his teeth stuck out a little, emphasized by his big nose and small chin. The only thing at all appealing about him was his soft grey eyes.

The pair had also heard that city kids were lazy, and they hoped to sneak away that morning before they could be roped into babysitting their cousin for the day. Perhaps their mother suspected that; she was a cunning woman. She was watching and listening for them to rise, and spoke their names loudly to let them know she'd spotted them at the top of the stairs. This may have also been to prevent them from slipping away without breakfast . . . or Scotty.

The three children ate mostly in silence, Charley and Maddy staring at Scotty in unison, while he tried desperately to ignore their glares. He wasn't very good at disregarding them, so he instead began to take stock of them to distract himself. His cousins bore much different appearance than he did; their cheeks were rosy and their skins had already been freckled and bronzed by the sun of late spring and early summer. Their hair, otherwise a colour similar to his, had been altered by the same effects as their skin, sun-bleached with a dash of reddish-gold highlights.

"Can you swim?" Charley asked, finally breaking the silence as he started in on his third pancake.

"W-what?" Scotty stammered, startled by the sudden question.

"He said 'Can you swim'?" Maddy repeated with a smirk. "You know." She made dogpaddle-like gestures.

"Um, yeah. I can swim."

He had been picking at his food, unaccustomed to a heavy breakfast. The rush of nerves—from actually being addressed by the children—made his stomach do flip-flops, the pancakes seeming even less appetizing.

"Good, cuz me an' Maddy are meeting some friends by the little pier. If yer gonna' come with us, it'll help if you can swim. We don't wanna have to be watchin' in case you drown." Charley said this with enough of a sneer that Scotty was sure the boy had already decided that his cousin wasn't worth their time.

"Don't worry," Scotty reassured him, pushing his plate away. "I won't get in your way. You can pretend like I'm not even there. I probably won't even get in the water."

"Yer not gonna leave that are you?" Maddy asked, gesturing at the remnants of his breakfast. "Mom hates it when people waste food. She went to the trouble of fixin' it. The least you can do is go to the trouble of eatin' it."

Scotty felt cornered, their cool stares still locked on him. His stomach continued to rebel, as much from anxiety as from being overly full. He'd always had a sensitive digestive system and this situation wasn't helping any.

"Tell you what—I'll do you a favour an' finish those for you," Charley informed him with a snort, nudging an elbow at the uneaten pancakes. "But only if you agree to get in the water. Otherwise, our

buddies will think we have pussies for kin. Are you a pussy, Scotty?"
Charley grinned, with an edge of mocking maliciousness.

"Why don't you wanna swim at our swim-hole," Maddy demanded, with slightly more hostility. "If it ain't some fancy chlorin-
ated pool, it ain't good enough for ya?"

That was exactly the reason Scotty had not intended on going into the water. Unlike the pool that he usually swam in, there
were living things in the water where his country cousins swam. The
pier was by open ocean and there was a wide assortment of sea-life
making a home in those waters and along the sandy bottom. When
Scotty's mother had mentioned swimming there when she was
young, he had found the notion repulsive. Just the idea of slimy seaweed coming in contact with his skin made his flesh crawl.

"I'm just not used to swimming in the ocean," Scotty suggested, hoping to defuse the situation. "I hear that it's cold, and that
you have to watch out for undertow. I could stay here while you go.
I don't have to come with you."

Maddy wrinkled her nose at this as Charley began to shovel
Scotty's leftovers into his mouth.

"Oh yes, you have to come," she insisted. "Mom says we have
to take you with us, so you have to come. What Mom says goes round
here, so you're just gonna have to grow a pair and put up with the
water bein' chilly. Either you do it, or we'll do it for you. Charley and
I are strong enough to take you, especially together. We'll dunk you
ourselves if we have to. No one's gonna be able to say we're related
to a chicken."

Against his better judgement and upon threat of a beating
and dousing, Scotty put on his swim trunks and gathered up his
beach towel. Then he unhappily accompanied his cousins out of the
house. The morning air was brisk, but he could feel it warming. He
had a feeling the water temperature would be much worse. He noticed his cousins were wearing ratty old sneakers without socks, as
opposed to flip flops like him. He soon understood why. Their trip
took them through the smelly, squelchy mud of a sea marsh, and
then across a cluster of jagged rocks. The rocks kept catching at his
mud-sodden footwear and making him stumble. He could hear Charley and Maddy snicker every time he almost fell, as they sprang ef-
fortlessly from stone to stone, like coastal mountain goats.

They arrived at the little pier, an old construct that was severely worn by weather and littered with barnacles and seaweed.
The sun had turned the rotting wood a pale grey, and Scotty wondered if it was safe to walk there. There were already three people

and a dog standing atop the aged wharf, so he had to assume that it was.

"You're late!" shouted the largest of the three. He was a red-haired kid with freckles wide enough that they blotched together into one near-solid patch. He had the same taunting smile that Charley always wore.

"Yeah, what took you so long?" hollered the girl standing next to the redhead, almost half the larger boy's size. The dog beside her started to bark.

Scotty swallowed hard. The animal was only a medium-sized dog, but he lived in a building that didn't allow pets, so he wasn't used to them. This one seemed particularly high-strung and snarly, sort of like the kids it accompanied.

Maddy jabbed her thumb in Scotty's direction.

"It was slowpoke here. He made Charley finish his pancakes, so we didn't head out in time. We warned you we might have to take him with us."

"That's yer cousin?" the shorter boy on the pier scoffed. His skin was tanned a deep brown and his eyes and hair were black. He was thick—oddly muscular for someone so young. "Where'd you find him? He's as pale as a ghost. Looks like you dragged him out from under a rock somewhere."

"He's a city kid," Charley grunted, and that seemed to be enough explanation, as the others nodded and shrugged. The dog continued to bark.

"Shut up, Scamp!" the girl next to it snapped, and she leaned over, giving it a hard slap on its rump. Scotty cringed. The dog yelped. Then it tucked its tail between its legs and sat down, whimpering softly.

Charley and Maddy piled onto the wharf alongside their friends, but Scotty waited stiffly on the shore, not wanting to approach the dog and unsure how stable the structure was. The five natives chatted for a few moments about people and places foreign to Scotty, before they all jogged down to the end of the rickety wharf. They tossed their towels onto the warped planking, and then one-by-one, they fearlessly jumped into the frothy water.

"Get yer arse in here, Scotty!" Maddy yelled as she splashed at the red-haired boy, whom Scotty had heard them call Derek.

He hoped they would have forgotten about him, caught up in their own antics, but his cousins were keener of mind then he'd given them credit. Having him hover on the beach watching them seemed kind of creepy, plus forcing him into the frigid water would bring them some sadistic pleasure.

"Looks like he's too scared," the short girl, whom they had referred to as Fran, teased. She kicked her way over to Maddy. "Yer family have a secret yeller streak?"

"Scotty . . ." Charley warned, balling up a fist and glaring his way.

Realizing he was not going to escape what he saw as essentially a hazing ceremony, Scotty started to inch his way towards the water. He moved with trepidation, carefully kicking off his flip flops and flexing his fingers before easing his toes into the surf. From Scotty's perspective, it was like ice water. He shivered and pulled them back again.

"Dammit, Scotty! If I have to drag you onto that pier and shove you into the water myself, I will—and I won't promise not to bounce your head off one of the side-posts on the way down," Charley growled.

Scotty looked at the creaky wharf. Not only did it look dangerous, but on top of Charley's threat, Fran's dog was still skittering from one edge of the planking to the other. He didn't want to give the over-excitable animal an excuse to bite him. With a heavy sigh, he started into the water.

He hated the fact that all eyes were upon him as he shuddered and squirmed his way into the water. He stopped advancing once he was waist deep, hoping that it would be enough for his tormentors. They did seem to be satisfied with that and went back to their horseplay, but they would throw an occasional glance his way to make sure he was not trying to sneak back out again.

Scotty thought the whole experience was awful. The briny cold water lapping at his goose-pimpled skin was the least of his troubles. The most immediate problem was the seaweed. Scotty had hoped to avoid the slimy yellowish-brown globules, but even steering clear of the large clumps attached to rocks on the sandy bottom was not enough because smaller segments had broken free and were brushing past him on the water's surface. He held his arms up out of the water, his fingers curled in disgust.

He soon discovered that there was a second feature to the ocean he disliked even more. The seaweed at least was limp and its only movement was whatever the tide allowed. On the other hand, there was the occasional purposeful movement as something firm grazed one of his legs and then something else made subtle contact with his hip. Scotty bit his lip to avoid crying out, knowing it would draw more negative attention from his cousins. He could not resist, however, when he felt something creep into his swim trunks, into the crack between his buttocks, and then, to his great horror, wriggled up inside of him. It was a fairly gentle sensation, something he might have missed if he weren't tense and standing stock still because of his circumstances. He shrieked, quite loudly, and it echoed around the cove.

"What's yer problem now?" Maddy demanded, exasperated.

Scotty was flailing about in the water, trying to shake out what had just swum in. He began to hyperventilate, twisting, turning, and pulling at his swim trunks.

"Something . . . touched . . . me. It . . ." he gasped, still trying to dislodge his anal invader. Before he could finish his thought, little Fran interrupted.

"Of course somethin' did, you big baby. There's a million different types of wrigglers in the cove. There's eels, an' crabs, an' minnows, an' even bigger fish like mackerel." Her chubby little face took on a mean countenance. "Sometimes even schools of bluefish swim in close to the shore. Two summers ago, we weren't allowed to swim here because they were in close an' bein' nasty. They attacked an' ate Bernie Miller's dog. Worst than the dog fish that we spot now an' then. They look like little sharks an' have sharp little teeth." She wanted to scare him. She wanted to make things worse.

That was too much for Scotty. He scrambled back to the beach and out of the water. The girls' mocking giggles burned in his ears, but that didn't bother him nearly as much as the awareness that there was still something alive working its way up inside of him. Avoiding the pier and the dog, he instead scurried farther up the beach to a very large rock. He climbed up on top of it and sat there shivering and clutching his legs to his chest as he fought back fearful tears. Resting his chin on his knees, he ignored the other children's taunts and jeers. He felt faint, the blood rushing through his head and pounding in his ears. Every time he was tempted to believe it had been just his imagination, he felt a faint twitching in his gut that made him worry again.

His cousins and their friends eventually realized that their teasing was being completely ineffectual. Losing interest in Scotty, they returned to their horseplay. They squealed and splashed and pulled one another gleefully under the surface. Scotty watched where he was huddled on the rock. His stomach ached and he wished that he were back in the comfort of his home. He dried off quickly enough in the hot summer sun, but that wasn't enough to cure his violent shivers. Agitated, he could still feel that something wriggling at his centre. By the time early afternoon arrived and the children decided that it was time to head home for lunch, he had already crept away behind some boulders to throw up what he had eaten of their heavy breakfast, twice.

When they returned to the house, Scotty could not bear to even look at his meal, so Charley obliged him and ate his share again. He behaved as though he were doing Scotty a favour and that the awkward boy would be expected to eventually offer him something in exchange. After they had eaten, they started out for the door, planning on a second outing. Scotty did not follow at first, lying on the couch, clutching at his abdomen with his breath coming in tiny laboured gasps.

"Come on," Maddie said, tapping her foot in annoyance. "Quit makin' us wait."

"Go without me," he mumbled. "I'm sick."

He was staring at the ceiling trying to avoid meeting their gazes, but Maddy and Charley could see he wasn't well. His eyes were glassy-looking and although it was difficult to believe, he was paler than he had been earlier that day. That wasn't about to slow them down any.

"No way," Charley insisted. "We can't leave you here alone, an' you ain't ruinin' our fun by makin' us stay home an' play nurse. Stop bein' a wuss an' pretendin' like there's somethin' wrong with you just so you don't have to go anywhere. We're goin' to the clubhouse an' yer comin' with us, like we had planned. You can lie in the corner there just like yer doin' here, an' if you need to puke, you can go out an' puke in the woods. It's not like you ate anythin' for lunch"

"What if something's really wrong with me? It feels like something's eating up my insides. What if it's appendicitis, or worse?" Scotty groaned.

Maddy stomped over to her ailing cousin with a disgusted sigh and placed her hand on his forehead. "No fever," she declared. "If you had appendicitis, you'd be burnin' up. You just got a little stomach bug, is all." She reached down and grabbed his forearm with a firm grip. "Yer comin' with us if we have to drag you. Yer not gonna wreck our fun."

She gestured with her head towards Scotty, signalling for Charley to assist her. He flanked Scotty from the other side, grabbing him just as firmly. They pulled the weakened boy to his feet and started tugging him towards the door. Scotty tried to resist but he lacked the strength, being dragged along like a floppy ragdoll instead.

It felt to Scotty like they were walking through the woods forever. The entire time, his guts felt like they were on fire: a twisting, churning knot of searing agony. He moaned and slumped in his cousins' grasp, but they ignored his pleas to take him back.

"Quit whinin', you big faker," Maddy grumbled. "We're almost there."

Their "clubhouse" came into view, a makeshift shack that had been thrown together from broken down pieces of wooden crates and rotting pressboard. The rickety structure was old enough, however, that the damper sections of the pressboard were overgrown with moss. Scotty eyed it warily through his veil of pain. He was surprised that it had somehow managed to resist the elements until now.

Not releasing his hold long enough to open the door with his hand, Charley instead nudged it open with his elbow. He and Maddy yanked Scotty into the dingy interior of their clubhouse and literally tossed him into a corner. He lay there in a crumpled heap, panting and muttering something almost incoherent about the wrigglers chewing up his insides. Fran and Derek were already there. The girl stared at Scotty wide-eyed.

"Is he okay? He don't look so good," she observed.

An instance of doubt flickered through Maddy's eyes, with a hint of conscience. Then she shook her head and shrugged it off.

"He'll be fine. It's lie around here or lie around home, an' we don't want him spoilin' our day cuz of a little stomach bug."

They had only been there a few moments when Scotty began to throw up. It was mostly dry heaves with the occasional spatter of dark viscous liquid, but it quickly drew an aggressive response from his cousins.

"*Ewwwww!* Scotty, not here! We told ya—if you wanna puke, go out in the woods," Maddy said, pointing at the door.

The city boy, now white as the driven snow and sweating profusely, stumbled to his feet with Charley's forceful help and staggered out into the forest. They heard him gagging, whimpering, and crashing haphazardly through the brush before all was quiet again. Charley and Derek seemed nonplussed, going back to their regular activities of digging stolen cigarettes and pillaged alcohol out of their clubhouse hidey-hole. The girls stared at the small puddle that Scotty had left behind in disgust. Fran poked at it with a stick.

"There's pinkish goop in there," she remarked. "And is that blood?"

"Nah. Probably just strawberry jelly from lunch," Maddy replied, forgetting that Scotty had not actually eaten any lunch. "We'll have to let it dry an' then scrape it up an' toss it. Until then, we'll just have to stay away from it."

Their other friend, Allen, finally arrived and the girls immediately warned him away from the vomit patch.

"Yeah—it was Scotty," Maddy informed him. "You musta seen him on your way in."

Allen shook his head, as he took a seat beside the other two boys. "Nope. Didn't see no one."

"Aw, man! The little shit musta headed for home. Probably went to crawl back into bed. He better not let Mom see him. If he rats us out and gets us in trouble, I'll give him a pounding he'll never forget," Charley grumbled.

The five decided to forget the other boy for the moment, and proceeded with their usual badness, making sure they chewed wild mint and rolled in pine needles to try to disguise the scent of alcohol and cigarette smoke when they were done. Charley and Maddy's mother was a smoker, so she likely wouldn't notice anyway, her nose having become desensitized to the smell long ago.

Arriving home, Charley and Maddy seated themselves for supper. When their mother emerged from the kitchen with food, she glanced with a frown at the extra empty seat.

"Where's Scotty?" she asked.

Charley shrugged, but the more inventive Maddy offered an explanation for his absence.

"We had a long busy day. He was tired an' he wasn't feeling good. He skipped supper an' went straight to bed." She managed to say this with enough conviction that she had her mother convinced. The woman set aside a plate for their visitor, in case he made an appearance later that evening. But he didn't.

Charley and Maddy didn't think anything more of Scotty until the next morning, and then it was only to make a concentrated effort to slip out before breakfast, so that they wouldn't get saddled with their unsavoury cousin again. They made their escape successfully this time, and giggled victoriously all the way to the pier. They were thankful to have rid themselves of what they considered a burdensome pest. The pair splashed and played in their customarily boisterous way with their friends, no longer concerned that they might have to fend off embarrassment imposed upon them by their city kin.

Towards lunchtime, they started making their way back along their usual route home.

"There was an awful lot of wrigglers in the water today," Fran commented, as they walked. "It almost felt like they were squirmin' their way around in my swimsuit."

Charley, Allen, and Derek grunted in agreement. Maddy was about to say something herself when Scamp took a sudden interest in something and took off like a streak into the brush.

"Scamp! Get back here!" Fran demanded, and when he didn't obey, she started after him, with the other children following closely on her heels.

As they approached the area that Scamp circled excitedly, they noticed large quantities of flies swarming overhead. They also detected a very unpleasant odour.

"Oh, gross!" Maddy exclaimed, holding her nose. "I think your dog's gone an' found himself some dead animal."

As they advanced, however, they soon found it was no animal, but rather a very dead-looking Scotty. His glazed-over eyes were staring unblinking up at the sky. His mouth, left open in an agonized expression, was encircled with bloody spittle. His hands and the entire front of his shirt were coated with scarlet-tainted bile. He looked like he had been there for some time, the better part of a day most likely, as flies crawled in and out of his various orifices and small maggots were creeping across his flesh in places. And lastly, he was curled up in a foetal position, his fingers frozen in rigor atop his badly bloated abdomen. The swollen skin there rippled, as something beneath it moved, like unborn offspring.

Fran stepped back, her hand over her mouth, and started to cry.

"Oh shit," Charley said glumly. "We are in so much trouble."

The other children stood there in horrified silence, until Allen pulled a branch off of a nearby tree, and approached the fly-riddled corpse.

"What the hell's going on with his belly?" he asked, morbidly curious. Before anyone could stop him, he jabbed his makeshift tool's point into the distended mound.

The stretched skin split with little pressure, as if Scotty's intestines were trying to free themselves from his body. The bloodied strands spilled out, propelled by what thrashed about within them.

Several dozen tiny wriggling creatures, about the size of Scotty's thumb tip, writhed about in his glossy entrails and putrefying body fluids. They resembled tiny embryonic sharks, with razor-sharp little teeth that continued to tear through the dead boy's flesh. All five of the children turned away, with everyone but Allen clutching at their stomachs, gagging, and covering their mouths.

"What are we gonna do?" Maddy whimpered, imagining her and Charley being shipped off to some sort of reform school. It made her knees weak. She couldn't bear the thought.

"We tell no one," Charley insisted, his voice hoarse. "We bury him somewhere in the woods, and we tell people he left us at the pier to make his way back on his own, even though we told him not to. They'll figure he got lost, and by the time someone eventually finds him, they won't be able to tell how he died. Pinky swear?"

The five agreed, pinky swore, and set about brushing the little wrigglers free from Scotty's innards, stomping on them with their tattered sneakers. When they were sure the lot had been crushed out of existence, they each found some sort of handhold on the body and started dragging him off to the boggy area where they intended on burying him. Their limbs were numb and their stomachs ached.

As they stumbled away, preparing to dispose of the evidence of the damage caused by their cruelty, all of them had but one thought on their minds. Was it just their imagination, or did they feel a faint twitch in their gut . . . a wriggling at their centre?

LITTLE MONSTERS
By Ed Burkley

"Data log 23.005-B, entry 9. This is Captain Ezekiel Schmitt and I find myself no better off than I was at last entry. There is still no response from the outside . . . my hope of eventual rescue is starting to look bleak."

Schmitt swiveled around in his chair and peered out the cockpit window into the void of space. The ship was adrift; its propulsion systems severely damaged. To conserve energy, Schmitt had routed the power to the science laboratory and cockpit, leaving the rest of the ship inhabitable. The ship, in this auxiliary state, left the cockpit dark and the air thick with the taste of metal on the tongue. Only the blinking lights of the control panel illuminated the room, but even in this faint glow, the toll of the long journey was evident on Schmitt's face. Dark shadows nestled under his red-rimmed eyes. His face, now covered in thick scruff, was hollowed under protruding cheekbones.

"There is still no response to my distress signal. Given the distance of our mission and the last known coordinates of our ship login, I am not surprised by this. At present, I am the only crew member left on the ship . . . me and those damned *precious* cargo."

He and his crew had come in search of the weeds. That was what they had nicknamed them. Finding these specimens and bringing them back had been a major part of this mission. What they had found would make them all famous and possibly help stop the scourge that plagued people back on earth. At least that was the rationalization the crew gave for the reason they were risking their necks on this obscenely long voyage. Seven years max, that was the timeframe given. But it had taken nearly twice that and now in the predicament Schmitt found himself, there was no definitive end in sight.

He took a deep breath, exhaled, and then checked the navigation systems.

"The ship's coordinates indicate that I am still headed in the direction of home. But given my slow progress, I'm not sure which birthday I should expect to celebrate upon my arrival, my 48th or 100th. Or if I'll arrive at all . . . If I am able to reach a slipstream by chance, then I could go into cryosleep and have a somewhat lengthy life left to live when I return."

As he spoke, he rubbed the thick bristles on his jawline. "In the present state, it is just too dangerous to hibernate with no propulsion system and no one at the helm. Autopilot is too risky in this uncharted environment. All I can hope for is that someone picks up on my distress signal before I age too much . . . But I am beginning to worry. I have been able to ration out the water, but the nutrient bars have run out."

As he leaned forward in his chair, a sharp pain struck Schmitt in his stomach and he heard the incessant growl of his body's call for sustenance. He had not eaten in some time now. He was weak, dazed, and tried to think of anything else on the ship he could devour to stop this ache. Weak with hunger, Schmitt closed his eyes, but this rest would be short-lived. Suddenly the cockpit erupted with an alarm. He checked the console and saw it was coming from the science lab.

He left the cockpit and made his way into the lab to investigate. When he approached, the large glass doors to the room's entrance parted and Schmitt entered. He made his normal rounds, parading up one aisle and down the other. As he did, he scanned the numerous covered containers that were lined up on the tables like little soldiers, each housing a unique inhabitant. Some were green and gelatinous, while others were like living stones or ethereal liquid beings. Some floated in their fluid-filled containers while others tapped against their arid confinements, each a little monster.

As he reached the table in the far corner he noticed one of the containers was cracked. Leaning in for a closer look, he could see a bushy, green plant had spilled out of the crevice and was now growing all around the glass dome. Schmitt inquisitively leaned in to examine the thing and as he did, waves of color pulsated through the creature as it breathed, taking in air through its furry, verdant skin.

A shiver ran up Schmitt's spine as he stared at the iridescent monster. It was like nothing he had ever seen; a twisted mix of flesh and fantasy.

Before he could even realize what he was doing, Schmitt prodded the creature with his finger. The creature reacted, changing colors as it quivered and drew back. As he retracted his finger, he felt a rushing sensation surge up through his arms and down the center of his torso. It was almost as if, in the act of disturbing the weed, he had felt what it felt.

Upon this, the first thought that entered Schmitt's mind was, *This is it. I am finally losing my grip on reality.* But the thought that followed that one surprised even him, almost as if it came from something other than Schmitt, something more primal. *I bet that thing would be tasty!*

Without even thinking, he grabbed hold of the creature and plucked off a fuzzy appendage. The segment readily popped free of the thing, pulling was almost unnecessary. Without hesitation, he greedily shoved the piece into his mouth and as he bit down on the fleshy weed, a burst of refreshing fluid gushed into every crevice of his mouth. The taste was divine, a meaty cinnamon aromatic that overwhelmed his senses. No sooner had he swallowed than he began to feel the meal's nutrients radiate throughout his body, feel the fuel surging into every withering cell in his body.

That evening, when he had retired to the cockpit, space enveloped the ship and so too a darkened calm cloaked his consciousness and he drifted into a sleep that was the most peaceful he had experienced since he was an infant.

"Data log 23.005-B, entry 10. Captain Schmitt."

Schmitt was now recording his logs from the science lab. After his recent discovery, he had grown to feel rather comfortable in his new, more spacious living quarters.

"I have been able to stay alive," he continued. "Unfortunately, some of the cargo has died off . . . The cause for this is unknown."

As he spoke, he reached down and plucked off a purple, fleshy succulent from one of the weeds that sat nestled on his plate, popped it in his mouth, and slurped it down.

"All systems are fine," he continued after swallowing. "The ship is on course for an area of space where there is a potential for me to come across someone. I plan to bounce the distress signal off a rocky moon that should appear in a few weeks. Hopefully the signal will head in the direction of space colony Gamma, New Earth and someone will come for me."

Schmitt wiped the green juices from his mouth, and then added, "Captain Schmitt, end entry computer."

Feeling better than he had in months, Schmitt propped his feet up and leaned back in his chair. As he did, he reached into his pants pocket and felt a sharp burn prick his finger. "Ouch," he said as he pulled out his hand for inspection. He noticed a peculiar looking pattern had appeared on his index finger. As he turned his hand over, he saw the ornamentation stretched up his arm and then disappeared beneath his shirt. Concerned, he stood up and stripped off his clothes. The pattern was everyway, spreading out from his mid torso in a tree-like design that resembled veins. It almost looked as if his circulatory system was making its way up through his skin. As his heartbeat began to quicken from this discovery, he could see his teal-colored veins throb and quiver just beneath the surface. To add to the shock, the veins began to itch.

Schmitt started to scratch incessantly to no avail. As his fingernails dragged across his flesh, a viscous fluid poured forth in response. Schmitt started to panic and stumbled over to the hydration area near the weeds. He washed his arms, but there was no improvement; the fluid, now yellow in color, still flowed. Schmitt reached for a towel and as he did, saw the fluid retreat into his body and the torn flesh started repairing itself. *What is happening to me?* Schmitt wondered, half-terrified but also half-amazed. Abandoning the towel, he retracted his arm, but as he did, the healing process that began seconds before abruptly stopped. Curious, he extended his arm again and the wounds healed and the throbbing tentacled veins submerged back into his flesh.

"What the hell is going on?" he murmured to himself. And then, a sense of clarity came over Schmitt, an epiphany perhaps, one that had escaped him in all the excitement but now had crept out from his subconscious. His arm was positioned so that when he extended it, it fell under the rays of the ultraviolet lights, the same lights used to feed the weeds. Ultraviolet light was the cure for whatever was happening to him.

Schmitt spent the next hour taking down the ultraviolet lights that had been positioned over the weeds he had already eaten

and used them to build a standing light shower that was four emit-
ters high and three wide. Upon completion, he stripped naked and
stepped into the light, bathing himself in the luminous nutriment.
The sensation was cooling, fulfilling, energetic, and eventually the
tendrilled rash on his skin disappeared completely.

"Data log 23.005-B, entry 11. Captain Schmitt." His voice
was coarse and husky. Over a week had passed since he had consumed the weeds and yet he felt and looked better than he had since
he started the mission. He discovered that after taking one of his
light showers, he felt satiated, as if he had consumed a large meal.
And despite not eating, he hadn't felt hungry in days. Water, on the
other hand, he consumed in buckets, far more than he had needed
before. Plus, his skin had started to feel dry and scaly. Perhaps the
lights were dehydrating him, but that was a small price he was willing to pay.

"No response to the distress signal," he continued. "I am approaching the compact Eyro solar system. Its small sun has started
to illuminate the cockpit. I can't express how nice it feels to gaze once
again on a sun, even if it is not from my own system . . . Captain
Schmitt, end entry computer."

"Unable to comply," the console speaker responded.

Schmitt raised his voice, "End entry computer!"

"Unable to comply," it repeated.

Frustrated, Schmitt typed on the keyboard console, *code
44218: Captain Schmitt/ command error/ cause/*

In response to the command, the screen reported, *Voice not
recognized as Captain Schmitt*

"Stupid computer," Schmitt growled. "Well, it looks as
though I will be typing my data logs from now on," he said as he entered the keystrokes, *command /end entry*

Command accepted, the console typed back.

Schmitt no longer made log entries. As the days had progressed, his skin condition had gone from bad to worse. His body had

rejected its mammalian follicles and was now hairless. It had been days since he had worn any clothes; he found the touch of any fabric only irritated the condition of his new flesh. Worse yet, he woke this morning to find another perversion of his human form: he no longer had fingers. Each hand was now a fused appendage with only a thumb sticking out.

He spent most of his days in what had become his favorite part of the ship, the ultraviolet light shower. He found that it calmed him, strengthened him, and nourished him. Light and water; that was all he needed now. Standing now in the shower, his eyes scanned his naked body, his skin now smooth and leathery, dotted with small fissures. As he bathed in the soothing glow, his inner body seemed to move freely within the confines of his new outer carapace.

"I'm changing," Schmitt said to himself. "Each day I go on living, another horror is revealed to me. I'm not sure how long this will last or when this disease, if that's what this is, will finally be done with me." He looked down at his hands, now just two fleshy mittens. "All I hope is that the progression stops soon, so that when it's done with me, I will not be completely unrecognizable."

As he finished his lament, a dry cough tickled at the back of his throat. Gentle at first, then the itching became incessant. He coughed violently, struggling to breathe, and dropped to his knees. Then the coughing turned into a lurching fit as blood poured from his mouth and nostrils. *This is the end of me*, Schmitt thought as he vomited large chunks of flesh that spilled down onto the ship's floor, amassing in steaming piles of plasma and tissue between his legs.

He frantically spat the substances out of his mouth, trying to let fresh air in. But it was no use. Try as he might, he could not breathe. He dropped to his side, quivering naked on the floor as blood continued to leech from his nose and mouth. A gelatinous piece of lung tissue hung precariously from his chin. *Death,* he thought, *is finally here.*

Then as violently as it had begun, the spasms calmed and fluids stopped flowing. *Breathe, breathe now*, his inner mind instructed. But he could not. He tried to open wide his mouth to pull in precious oxygen but something wasn't working as he once remembered. He reached up to touch his face and discovered that where his mouth had been was now nothing but a smooth surface. His hands slid up his face to his nose and found that the news was no better there. His nostrils were gone, as if they too had joined in on the decision with the mouth to close off all access to the outside. But as he looked down at the remnants that were his lungs on the ground before him, he gathered that it made no difference anyway. He was out of air and any means of acquiring it.

As the oxygen ran out and carbon dioxide started to build in his blood, Schmitt's body seized and he felt a chill run throughout his entire system. The sensations of fiery goosebumps, of hot needles and pins, rushed from his head downward as his skin gasped, then breathed in life saving air. No longer did his chest pulse in and out the way it had all his life. Now, his whole body breathed for him, creating a rippling effect across the flesh as it absorbed the air.

Feeling weak but revived by his new fashion of breathing, he slowly sat up. As he did, a small tear fell from his cheek and onto the top of his hand. He reached up to wipe it as a drop from the other eye fell, then another. He had begun to weep, but not out of sorrow or despair, although he felt those things too. No, these tears were of something more ominous.

The fluid started to pour heavily and as it did, his sight began to fade. A tunnel of darkness closed in around him and all became dark.

What more, Lord? Schmitt screamed inside his mind. *What more must I endure?*

He tried to wipe these strange tears from his eyes and clear his waning vision. As he did he realized from the tears' viscosity that they were not tears at all. No, he had been weeping out his very eyes. The fluid from his eyeballs had burst and was now running down his face. As he dropped his hands in utter surrender, he discovered that one of the eyeballs, now deflated and detached from the optic nerve, had slid free from its socket and landed on his lap.

It was all too much for him to take. *I must end it all*, he thought, *while I am still able to*. He crawled to his feet and blindly searched the room with his hands, sweeping his arms over every table and countertop until he heard the thing that he was looking for hit the floor with a loud ping. *Salvation!*

He dropped to his knees and grasped the cool metal object. Clinched tightly in his awkward new hands, he brought the blade of the knife down deep into his left wrist. But something was not right. The expected warmth of blood flowing across his arm had not come. He dropped the knife and blindly felt the area of the incision, but it was dry and smooth, as if his act of self-mutilation had never happened. He retrieved the knife and quickly cut again, jabbing the tip of the blade in once, twice, three times. But when he touched the wounds he felt them self-suturing, all three cuts were closing along the path of the knife's butchery.

$$\times\times\times\times\times\times$$

Schmitt sat helpless in the flight chair of the cockpit. He had tried all manner of suicide, but nothing worked. He even tried to starve himself by staying clear of the ultraviolet light showers, but the resulting pain was more than he could have fathomed and it would have been too slow and painful a way to go.

Why won't you let me die you damn disease? his mind cried out silently from behind blinded eyes. *Okay . . . okay, I admit it. I'm sorry. I'm sorry I ever ate any of you fucking little monsters . . . um . . . I mean sentient beings. Believe me, I've learned my lesson. Truly I have. I didn't understand . . . but now I do. You're not monsters, you're just like me. Just please . . . I beg you . . . Have mercy on me. Just let me die.*

There was only silence. But then, in the still darkness, he saw a blinking light. *It must be my mind,* he thought, given that he no longer had eyes. He saw the light flash again, only this time it was brighter. He reached up to his eyes and could tell that something had changed. No longer were there empty sockets. In their place, a smooth, glassy optical plate had formed. And through it, light started to grow, allowing him to make out the most basic of shapes. Maybe this meant he had finally begun to overcome the disease and was reverting back to his former self. But what he saw next put any fairytales of a cure far from his thoughts.

As his vision cleared, Schmitt noticed that he now could see again, but not as he had before. He looked around the ship and took in the sights. Lights of various chromatic hues floated all around him. Outside the cockpit's windows he could see that the vastness of space was brimming with a cacophony of colors that were so bright and overwhelming, the concept of a 'dark universe' suddenly seemed preposterous. The entire universe was ablaze. Every planet and star was ensconced in their own jewel-colored coronas as they floated among an ocean of iridescence. It was as if the gates of heaven had parted and illuminated another world before him, a world that only the mind's imagination could procure and the flesh's optic nerve impulses could dream of creating.

The whole spectacle was so beautiful that for a moment, he pondered if his suicide had been successful and that he was actually witnessing angels from heaven's opened gates descending to claim him. But these gossamer forms were no angels, just common celestial events—planets, stars, dark matter—only now seen for the first time from infant, albeit not human, eyes.

Unlike those primitive eyes he used to have, these new eyes allowed him to see the entire electromagnetic spectrum. He could see everything from the waves of heat on the infrared side of the spectrum to the bright bursts of gamma rays at the other end, and all that came in between—

A loud burst of static erupted from the console's speakers, followed by a voice. "Come in . . . this . . . signal."

The distress signal, Schmitt thought as he was shaken back into the present.

"Come in science vessel BEM 7774," the voice in the speaker continued. "This is Captain Drexel. We have detected your distress signal and have located your position. We are on our way to help."

It's all over, he thought, *I'm saved!* He tried to respond to the call but in his current state, was unable speak. Then he reached for the computer communications board, but his fused hands were unable to type.

"Come in science vessel BEM 7774, this is Captain Drexel. We have picked up your distress signal and have located your position. We are on our way to help. Please respond."

The only thing Schmitt could think to do was flip the switch for the distress signal on and off, tapping out an S.O.S.

He waited, praying for a response, but there was no reply.

Seconds later, the speaker erupted again. "We are seeing that your signal is oscillating."

For the first time in a long time, Schmitt felt hope well up in his chest. *They will find a way to fix me,* he thought. *I'm sure of it!*

"Science vessel BEM 7774, we understand your communication. It's good to know you survived. We will be arriving momentarily. Hang in there."

Out the cockpit windows loomed an enormous space station. As Schmitt watched on, smaller vessels flew toward his ship and began connecting the grappling hooks. With one big jerk, he felt the tug from the lines as his ship moved toward the station. Moments later, the ship's small circular emergency door on the side of the cockpit opened.

"Are you all right in there?" a man in a green space suit said as he peered into the darkened cockpit.

Schmitt, so excited to see another human, forgot about his appearance and leaped forward to greet his savior. But when the man in the green suit saw him, he screamed and fell backward into the docking bay tunnel that linked the two ships.

Schmitt thought quickly. Seeing his old space suit crumpled nearby on the cockpit floor, he snatched it up and tore off the name-tag that read CAPTAIN SCHMITT. With identification in hand, he crawled into the docking bay. It was only there in the bay's full light that the horror of what Schmitt had become was now visible for all to see.

"Guards move in, move in!" said a man in a red flight suit.

Wait! Wait! Schmitt screamed with his eyes as he held out his nametag.

A man approached him from behind and four others followed, surrounding him on all sides, their stunning weapons raised high.

"No sudden movements," one of the guards said.

Schmitt did as he was told.

"Keep that thing here while I investigate," the officer in the red suit commanded and then stepped inside Schmitt's ship.

Inside, the officer saw the dimly lit glass doors of the science lab and when he stepped through them, a small scream escaped his mouth. The signs of violence—overturned tables, stained knife, pools of congealed blood on the floor—were everywhere. Startled, he took a step back and as he did, his boot slipped in the pile of Schmitt's lungs and he nearly tumbled to the blood-soaked ground.

"That monster killed them all!" the officer said as he stormed back into the docking bay, his finger accusingly pointed at Schmitt. "There is blood and flesh everywhere. It's a slaughterhouse in there! No one was left alive. That monster ate them all and spit them back up!"

I'm no monster! Schmitt pleaded in his mind. As he looked at the guards that surrounded him with his new eyes, he could see the infrared heat signature in their faces raise as their anger grew. Then one of the guards pounced on him, jabbing his stunner into Schmitt's back. Another guard followed suit, then another.

Schmitt fell to the floor in agony, screaming a silent wail that ricocheted in his skull. *I'm no monster! I'm human! I'm human!* he repeated to the men unsuccessfully.

Using a loop at the end of one of a long pole, one of the guards ensnared Schmitt's arms and then pulled him into a small containment room just inside the station.

I'm human. I'm like you. Schmitt pleaded as the guard released his arms, then closed the door and locked him inside. Overhead, air rushed in through the vents. As the thick cloud of white vapor enveloped him, he realized it was poisonous gas.

I'm human ... I'm human, Schmitt said to himself as he curled up in a ball on the cold floor. *I'm human. I . . . human. I . . . no . . . monster.* Schmitt's body took one last shuttering breath through his convulsing iridescent skin, then went limp and he was no more.

The door to the gas chamber opened and a guard entered. He reached down and took hold of the creature's dead body. As he dragged it out of the room, a piece of fabric that read CAPTAIN SCHMITT fell to the ground but he didn't notice.

The man pulled the creature into a room outfitted with medical equipment. He propped the heavy body onto the autopsy table, then exited the room to alert the doctor that the specimen was ready for examination.

High above the table, vents brought in fresh air and removed the old, stale air. Under the caress of their soft breath, a quiver ran across Schmitt's body and it began to pulsate. Small openings erupted from the corpse; tiny volcanos that spewed forth fine dust balls, producing a verdant cloud of powder that hovered above the remains. As the vents inhaled air from the room, so too did they whisk away the green particles into their mechanic lungs. Pieces of Schmitt, now spores, rushed silently into the darkness of the station's vents to impart his new form to the human creatures; creatures he had once thought himself to be, but now only thought of as little monsters.

TOM'S THUMBS
By K.M. Campbell

While the old couple slept, Malakai the demon eyed them in the dark. They disgusted him and were perfect for his needs. Three-thousand years of servitude was over and he was free of this half-life. He was ready to return to the full world and no one was left to stop him. He had outlived all his hated masters.

His last token holder had died with no heirs to pass the trinket that held Malakai's spirit and so the cragged metal returned to Malakai, granting his freedom.

He held the shiny nugget to his lips, licked it slowly, then rubbed it against his cheek like a preening cat.

"Let us play and flay," the demon whispered before tucking the nugget back into his soul, where he would never again be parted from it, no matter how much it hurt to hold onto, the blunted edges that pushed at his insides for release

He had been watching the old couple for the past few moons. He hated them. They rarely spoke to one other and struggled to even look in the other's direction. They abused each other with their silent hate and disappointment.

The old woman's wrinkled hand moved as he scampered up her body, no bigger than a mouse. Even her movements repulsed him, shakes that screamed of geriatric weakness.

They blamed each other for their own failures, their bitterness permeated every corner of their shack which smelled of piss and boiled cabbage. Malakai felt only inevitability at destroying them. After all, they had left the door open for him; all he would do was give them exactly what they wanted.

For the husband, freedom.

For the wife, the child she was promised.

Standing on the crone's right shoulder, away from the husband, Malakai rearranged his features to resemble a child, the hag's ultimate weakness.

"Mama, set me free. I'm so alone." Malakai's sharp little needle teeth emerged from his purple lips as he smiled brightly.

The old woman was infected with him now, she would never stop until she saved her little boy from the big bad monster that lay in the bed beside hers. And in return for his hard work, Malakai would receive a body that would fit the size of his soul instead of this tiny carcass no bigger than a man's thumb.

He trotted closer to the old man, licking his large calloused thumb, wrapping his arms around it and biting down hard enough to draw a few drops of food.

Malakai was hungry and the old man's blood was good. At least these country types ate well and tasted strong, and when the old woman made the poppet, this body would be Malakai's to do with as he pleased.

✗✗✗✗✗✗✗

Enid woke to the feel of tiny feet scampering up her body. Her hands jerked in reaction before she could stop them. It frustrated her, all this aching and shaking: it would only scare the child away. But what could she do? She was frail and old, no law against that, goddamn it all to hell.

She glanced toward Tom's single bed on the other side of the room. The floral comforter was on the ground, tossed aside by his nightly struggles with sleep. She could see his striped summer pajamas, old man's clothes, and his plaid slippers lined up just so. Everything about him screamed old and stuck in his ways.

He wasn't sleeping, she knew him well enough to know the difference in his breathing. He was lying still with his eyes shut, like he did every morning, waiting for Enid to get up and make his breakfast. Lazy old goat.

"Dead yet?" There was little of the humor that had made their marriage a success left.

"After you, my sweet," he replied, gruff with lack of sleep.

Enid clacked her false teeth into place and left the room. The tiny child was waiting for her in the kitchen and she gasped in surprise, clutching a hand to her heart and wondering if her body's aged pump would stop dead.

"You're really real?" she asked.

"Almost," Malakai said on a wet, wobbly, pitiful sigh. "I need the doll. Have you finished it yet?"

Enid hobbled to the cupboard that held her knitting bag. Rummaging inside, she found the doll she had been working on for the past few days.

"Is it perfect?" Malakai snatched it away, sniffing each seam and licking each stitch. "Perfect." He turned wide blue eyes to Enid. "It's perfect. You have done perfect."

Enid held the table to help her sit. Resting her chin on her hands to stare at the gorgeous little boy who so resembled a young Tom. "Thank you, child. I followed your directions exactly, and now you're here. Will you be able to become a real child now?"

"Yes. Just one more thing . . ." He allowed one tear to trail down his perfect cheek.

"What is it? I'll do anything. I promised."

"I need my father's body to complete my transformation, to be with you forever."

Enid blinked, becoming more enraptured with each glance at the perfect child. "All right. Just some skin, nails, that sort of thing?"

"I need flesh to become flesh. I must be made from the meat of my father."

"How much?"

"Not much. Just enough to fill the doll."

Enid lifted the knitted doll. It was smaller than her hand, with tan skin, blonde hair and blue eyes, just like Tom when they met.

"Tom's thumbs," Enid said, "I'll use Tom's thumbs."

Malakai clapped his little hands, "Perfect. Perfect. Thumbs and Plums. Soon?"

"Tonight. I promise."

Later that day, Enid got her chance. "Don't worry with lunch for me," Tom said. "I'm not feeling so well."

"Your stomach?"

"Yeah, looks like the doc was right. I don't have much longer, Enid."

"What do you want me to do?"

"Nothing, nothing at all. I'm going to bed. I feel like I might actually sleep."

"Why don't you take one of the pills the doctor gave you to sleep?"

"No, I told you. I'll be ending on a mountain of drugs. I want to go without them for as long as I can."

"I'll bring you a warm drink then."

"I don't think . . ."

"Just do as I tell you and don't be a stubborn old man."

Tom chuckled, "All right, Enid, don't get your knickers in a twist."

"Would be the only thing that's happened to my knickers in years," she grumbled as she stalked to the kettle.

The spiked drink put Tom into such a deep sleep he didn't even move as she took his favorite boning knife to his thumbs. She reminded herself that this was his penance for having brought home the disease that had rendered her sterile. This was the least he could do for her.

Afterward, she cleaned his wounds, dressed them carefully like a mother, cooing gentle words of apology. She doubted he would notice, he didn't seem to notice much anymore these days, and if he didn't like it he could go tell someone. There was another problem. Their lack of children had pushed them away from those that had them until they were solitary with only each other for company.

She gently washed the detached thumbs, waiting for the blood to drain away, soaking them in the kitchen sink, wondering how they had ever created anything. They looked so small and shriveled when she pulled them from the water that she worried they would not be good enough for her child.

Back at the kitchen table she dried them with complete devotion, careful not to miss a watery red drop, even going so far as to use the napkins she had kept "for good." Except there had never been a "good." So the tissues were old and perishing. With frustration, she threw them all in the trash, snatching out the white linen sheets she had been given for a wedding gift. Another thing to keep for good. Useless.

They continued to drip and seep for so long Enid was in tears, certain they would never be good enough. For once in her life she wanted to accept only perfection, not the ongoing faults, blame, and mistakes.

She left them in the sun, sitting beside them on a blanket for several hours to ensure the birds didn't come and snatch her treasures away. The thumbs resembled tiny ham hocks. There was nothing about them that made her certain they would produce life.

That night she wrapped the thumbs in one of Tom's unused handkerchiefs, one he had gotten from his mother and hidden away in the back of his underwear drawer. His private territory. She then slipped the small package into the doll. It slid in easily. More room left around the doll than she expected when seeing Tom's thumbs still attached to his hands.

She washed her hands, wondering if she should sew the doll up or leave it to await instructions from the child. Emptying the sink she mindlessly wiped at the discolored ring left behind from the bloodied water. She wondered what the child would be called? Would he look like her as well as Tom? Would he have Tom's calm personality or her erratic temperament? She hoped he had more of Tom. Her several breakdowns over the years making her certain she was riddled with demons in her blood. Remnants from her deranged family.

Behind her a small voice cried, "It's not enough!"

She spun with a sinking sense of dread. "I did what you asked."

"It's not enough, and where's the blood?"

"I cleaned it, I refuse to allow blood to drip all over my floor."

"I need the blood."

His blue eyes flashed to red and Enid stepped back, once more automatically clutching her chest, worrying for her aged heart.

"You're not real."

"I won't be if you don't do things right. Thumbs and plums. I asked for thumbs and plums."

"Plums?"

"His nuts, the seed. I need his seed."

Enid sat down, disgusted even though it sounded logical. "I refuse. You can't ask me to do that to him."

"His dirty plums destroyed your life, they took your chance of children. They stole my life from you. All I'm trying to do is give that back to you. Please help me give you something. Help me. Set me free. I was supposed to be born and it never happened because he cheated on you and ruined your life. He took my life from me. Do this for me if not for you."

That small pleading voice drilled at her brain. When she next looked up, the child was a stunningly handsome young man.

"Who are you?" She gasped.

"It's me, Mom. This is what I'll look like when I'm older. If you give me that chance."

"I can't," she wailed. "I'm not strong enough."

"Cut them out. For both of us."

Enid stared at him, in awe of his beauty, so like Tom as a young man.

"Will you stay with me?"

"Always. *Always.*"

"I'll do it."

"I love you, Mommy."

Tom came awake. Something was wrong. He felt sick to his stomach. He relaxed back into the dirty old pillow. The cancer had taken hold. It was eating him from the inside out like a horror movie monster. On a frown, he lifted his hands that felt hot and thick. They were wrapped up and something about the shape made his heart beat hard. His head was too fuzzy to put it altogether.

His bowels clenched in a familiar sickening way and Tom scrambled from his bed, frantically kicking aside bedding that should have been replaced years ago. Forgoing his slippers for speed, Tom stumbled to the toilet, terrified at the amount of blood he found when he flushed.

Clutching his stomach with one bandaged hand he steadied himself with a shoulder to a floral wallpapered wall (he had always hated floral but Enid never gave him any choice in decorating all those years ago). He found his wife seated at the table with a doll clamped in her hands, rubbing it against her cheeks and whispering to it frantically.

"Enid," He interrupted, "I don't feel so good, in my stomach. I might need the hospital. And something's wrong with my hands. Honey, are you listening?"

When she turned, Enid's eyes had that flat, long stare that showed she was in the thrall of another one of her delusions. Tom wanted to punch her back to life. After all these years, of enduring her hostility and her mental instability, when *he* needed *her* for once she was off on another one of her fucking breakdowns.

"Not now, Enid. Snap out of it. I need you." She bared her teeth at him and Tom's heart sunk further. She had returned to that one indiscretion that had almost broken them. It was strange that she had forgiven him all those years ago, yet when her mind wandered this is where she inevitably returned too. His one stupid mistake. He would never be forgiven and he berated himself for ever having stayed in this painful loveless marriage.

Stumbling to the phone he lifted the receiver, thankful he had always controlled the money so bills were always paid on time.

"What are you doing, Tom?" Enid asked in that far-off voice that made Tom rage.

"I'm calling an ambulance. I'm sick, Enid, real sick."

The call connected but Enid touched his shoulder and took the phone from him. Dropping it back into the cradle, she smiled, just like the Enid of old, the passionate, fiery woman he had fallen for all those years ago.

"I'll sort it. A taxi will be faster. You go get dressed while I organize everything."

Tom sagged a little with relief. "Thank you, Enid. I know you're going through something right now but I need you. Just for a little while."

"I need you too, Tom. More than ever before."

His stomach clenched again and Tom had to fight black speckling unconsciousness that threatened to overwhelm him. Stumbling back to the room, Enid followed with water and pills.

"Painkillers," she said, dropping them into his mouth.

The look in her eyes was a warning but Tom was all out of fight. He swallowed the pills and lay back on the bed.

That night Enid gave Tom more pills, more than she thought wise but enough that he would feel nothing and not wake up. Whatever her decision.

He was hot to the touch and she noticed that above the bandage that covered his left hand a hot line of infection was creeping into the light. She wondered if she should have boiled the boning knife she used? It was too late now. She sat on his bed for a long time with a small pocket knife. One Tom had been given years ago by one of the many customers he had entertained in his shoe store. It seemed sharp enough to do the job.

The little voice came from her dressing table. "What are you waiting for?"

"I can't do it."

"We've been through this. You have to do it."

"He's sick, he needs a doctor."

"He ruined our lives."

"How do you know all this?"

"I'm not alive because of what he did."

"I forgave him."

"I didn't."

"I cheated too." She gasped, never once having admitted this before. The secret that festered in the back of her head now tried to worm its way out of her mouth.

"It was too late by then. He infected you."

"I can't let him die!" She was crying now. Yelling with certainty.

"Then I will die." The small boy turned away but Enid saw that flash in his eyes again in the mirror. That glint of something more hidden behind the façade she wanted to see. Could this all be her imagination? She had lost her mind several times before but those times she had never hallucinated. She reached out to touch the boy but he backed away.

"Not until I'm real. Please." His pleading burrowed into Enid's brain, twisting into her exhausted nervous system.

It was easier to just give in than to fight. "Okay."

"Don't forget the blood this time," he said and scampered away.

"What's your name?" Enid asked his back.

He turned back on a grin, "I'm Tom Junior."

It had been a late night for Enid but the next morning she awoke with a feeling of dread and excitement.

"Today's the day," she told Tom who slept on, unaware of his new mutilations.

Noise in the kitchen had Enid sitting upright, hand to her chest. "He's here, Tom. Our boy has finally come home."

Tom surprised her into a small shriek then by saying, "He's not ours, Enid. He's trying to kill me."

"Don't be ridiculous."

"I need the hospital, Enid. Please . . ."

"For once, this isn't all about you, Tom. It's my time."

She shuffled from the room to find Tom more drugs and to meet her son.

On the kitchen table the small doll had come to life. It moved and jerked with life. "Help me," he cried.

Enid rushed to hold the small creature upright, it's squirming sickening and unnatural. She had been expecting a real child, not an animated doll. Her disappointment sparked, that overwhelming feeling that had travelled the road of her life on her shoulder, reminding her of all the things she would never be, would never do.

"You're still a doll," she said.

The thing froze. "Not forever. I will change with your love and devotion. Like any other little boy."

"But I don't have much time left."

"There is time."

"Will you grow?"

"I will become more like you."

"But will you grow?"

"Am I not good enough?"

"I want grandchildren like all those nosy women in the fancy units in town. I want to be rid of their pity and their dislike. I want to be one of them."

"You have what you wanted." The knitted eyes sparked into life, not the blue of the child in Enid's imagination but the fiery red she had glimpsed. "I'm a fucking kid."

"Don't you profane at me!" she roared, insulted to her very core.

"Then be grateful I have worked so hard for you."

"But I wanted a child, grandchildren. All you have given me is a midget and a sick husband. Two retards to attend to."

"This is what you wanted."

"I've changed my mind."

"Too late." The little creature snarled, small teeth breaking through the knitted wool. "You will attend me, crone, else your torment shall be ceaseless."

"Torment? You think I don't understand torment?"

With that she turned away and left the room. Malakai tried to move but the vessel his body was contained in was tight and slow. Until he became accustomed, until he learned to control a body once more, until this obscene shroud began to turn into a body proper, Malakai was trapped and at the hag's mercy.

"Mother!" he called, "Please come back. I'm sorry I just . . . it's been a shock finally being with you."

Nothing.

It was sometime later that Malakai heard the sirens. He saw no one because Enid returned to the room only to stuff him into a drawer, unmoved by his pleading, her lips tight with anger, the wrinkles deep, her eyes heavy.

With little else to do, Malakai waited, eventually falling asleep. Something he had not done for over three-thousand years.

When he awoke it was bright and hot. He was under a spotlight of some kind and could hear a strange frantic clacking noise, could feel an incessant dull tugging at his legs. His head was held down with a cold iron, he couldn't budge it.

He squinted past the bright light to see Enid frantically knitting, the wool coming from Malakai's new body.

"What are you doing?"

"Getting rid of you before I go to jail to finish my days. You never warned me cutting Tom up like that would send me to jail."

"How was I to . . ."

"He's dead you know. Infections, cancer, blood loss, old age. Whatever it was, I started it and I killed him. Least I can do is make sure you don't do it to some other weak-minded woman."

"You can't do this. I'm alive . . ."

"Not for long."

"You don't understand. I'm trapped in this material. I can't be killed least it is completely consumed."

Enid smiled. "Consumed, huh? How's a fire for consuming?"

"My base is gold. You could never put me in a fire hot enough. Please, you must let me stay. Take me to this jail with you."

"Like hell. I ain't going to jail. I'm an old woman. I'm going to Hell to meet my maker and atone for all my sins. I'll meet you there, you evil little monster."

"Fuck you, crone. Set me free. There is no way an old piece of shit like you can stop me now. I'll find another way into the world. I've come this far, there's no way back."

Enid stopped knitting.

"I think I can slow you down at least."

She picked the doll up, slipping out the back door of her horrible shack as the police turned into her road with screaming sirens. It was dark now but they would soon find her. That was not Enid's focus. Her focus was getting this evil little puppet to the house three roads over.

She had to take the backway, down dark, dusty streets, past howling dogs and hissing cats. Eventually she came to the right place, clutching her chest as the huge dog threw itself at the fence then shoved his huge head through a hole it had dug.

Without further comment, hearing the police dogs on her trail, Enid dropped the shrieking doll into the hole. The dog growled at it uncertainly for a moment then picked it up and swallowed it whole, the smell of blood permeating his mind.

"Enjoy that, you evil little shit," Enid said just as a police dog brayed at the other end of the road and a policewoman screamed at her to lie down on the ground.

Malakai waited inside his precious stone. All his earthly trappings were gone by the time he left the dog. He was picked up by a bird and dropped into a nest. The bird either died or didn't find a mate as the nest was never used and it took long years for the twigs to rot enough for the stone to drop from the tree.

A young boy found the gold nugget, thinking it just a strange stone, he put it in his pocket and took it home. His life would never be the same and the voice in his head pushed him to many things he would otherwise never dream of. He even swallowed it once, interested when it re-emerged unchanged.

Malakai was patient. He would wait for the right time. He had nothing but time.

FAMILY DINNER
By A. Collingwood

I started with my left calf, for Uncle Terrance, because he was always a little too concerned with my legs, if you know what I mean. That was an easy cut, the tendons basically made to be severed by my big knife. It only took a little trimming, and then I had a nice-looking steak, with enough left over for Aunt Maggie, as well. I was only ever an afterthought to her, too. My sisters, Jordan and Miranda, got the left thigh, because they always wished they had thighs as slim as mine, and constantly put me down for whatever eating disorder they had just heard about from their model friends. The hard part there was slicing the strands of muscle just right, to keep the shape. Dad got my right bicep, because he expected me to carry the family's secrets. Mom I wanted to give a pectoral, you know, right over the heart, but what can I say? I wanted to keep my tits looking nice, even with my new role in life. Call me shallow if you want, but these bitches cost me an arm and a leg. No pun intended. So I gave mom my triceps, because it was convenient.

When the cutting was done, I had them help put the meat in the fridge and ease me into my shiny new wheel chair. It's great, one of those get ups that can be driven at up to ten miles an hour with a fun little joy stick.

It had taken longer than I thought to chop myself up, not because of the pain—I had already been through infinitely worse than a little nipping and tucking—but because skinning human flesh is more of an art form than I had imagined. So, being behind schedule, I didn't have much time to wash up and get ready. No doubt my family would all arrive early. It was the least they could do to try to catch me off guard. No doubt they would all have knives and poison in their pockets to finish the job, too. Of course, none of those little toys mattered anymore. Not with Hell in my blood, like it was.

The thing is, one of them, if not all of them, is behind my murder. Naturally, I'll revenge myself on the whole lot. You see, I am the golden daughter of a family of monsters, and now they are all about to be reminded why they had wanted me dead in the first place. And, they are going to be taught what a mistake it was to send an ambitious young woman like me to Hell. If my family had a motto, which we don't, it would be "take everything you see." Boy, have I seen things now.

I've seen my body burning as my soul fell through the horrible black void of Limbo, straight into the deepest circle of Hell, where the truly wicked burn at the Devil's feet. And I've seen so much worse, with only my rage and my greed to see me through.

When my suffering began, I begged. Not for mercy, but for vengeance. When the churning, shapeless beast ripped away my skin every morning for his breakfast, I begged him to take my sisters too. When the Goat came to toss me into his cauldron of acid every afternoon, and cook me to my bones, I pleaded that there must be enough room for my parents in there as well. And when the Fallen came to beat out my confessions with a burning whip every evening, the only words from my mouth were my qualifications to serve.

Eventually, they listened. Liked my attitude, I suppose. I was brought before Hell itself—the thing Catholics foolishly call the Devil, but make no mistake, he *is* Hell—and I was made an offer. I would be sent back to the world, at the moment of my death, to claim my kin, and be made an entry level demon. All I had to do in return was forward Hell's agenda, until the Angels came to punish me, as they are wont to do. Then, I would be on my own. Not terrible odds, if you think about it.

I won't tell you how Hell entered my blood, so that I could poison my family. I'll tell you everything else, but I won't tell you that.

Dinner was a joke, and only I knew the punchline. My family gushed about how relieved they were to hear I was alive, only an hour before my estate was distributed amongst those vultures. They all could fake a smile so well.

Let me tell you a little something about my family: they all are as evil as I am. They raised me after all. Good story? No? Let me add a little tension then. I was raised by some very wealthy people, whose greatest joy in life was amassing more wealth, by any means necessary. So guess what they wanted in the family? No, not a cigarette company CEO, we already have one of those. They wanted a lawyer, one who they could count on to cover up all their dirty little secrets. None of them, not even my own mother, knew how much like them all I really was. But I think they figured it out when I started blackmailing each of them with exactly the information they wanted me to hide. It did not take long for me to reach my untimely end after that. I thought I was ready; I had paid top dollar to the best security companies—both legal and clandestine—but I guess even protection can be bought out.

The beauty of my family is that none of them trust each other, and seldom disclose anything that will leave them vulnerable. I doubt any of them knew that everyone else was being blackmailed too. I'm certain that none of them admitted to having me killed. Of course, they will all have their suspicions. One of them had done it, and now whoever did it was enjoying a nice lobster bisque at my expense, while discussing the variety of their grief, and what a miracle it had turned out to be when my death turned out to be nothing but a clerical error.

After the appetizer dishes were cleared away, the help brought out the main course on silver platters.

"Steak Tatar," I said, leaning back in my wheel chair at the head of the table. Beneath the blanket on my lap, my exposed bones itch. Everyone dug in, and I smiled.

The changes happened slowly, at first, as Hell's poison moved from my blood to their bellies. Words slipped from boarding school precision to mumbles. Skin itched around the collar, and it suddenly felt much warmer in the room, for them. Teeth chopped through the raw meat with more ease every bite. When my father scratched at the back of his neck, he did not notice that his nails were longer, and sharper than they had been when he arrived for dinner. When he dug them into his itchy flesh, they drew blood. My mother was the first to lose her vocabulary entirely, raising her glass, smiling, and letting out a beastly growl rather than a "cheers." Everyone else raised their glasses, laughing, unconcerned. Teeth peeked out from beneath bloodied lips, as they became proper fangs. My dear Aunt Maggie grabbed her chunk of my calf with both hands and began cramming it into her face. If some part of any of them realized what had happened, what was happening, they showed no sign of caring as they all became cannibals.

I felt changes occur in me, too, as the conditions of Hell's contract were met. I did not have to suffer anything as grotesque as the rest, of course. After all, it was they who were to be my Hounds, while I was to be their Master. I was transforming into something far more appropriate. Oh, but I would hate to ruin the surprise. Let's just say that you will find out when you meet me.

When it was finished, the beasts before me looked nothing like my kin, nothing like humans, but they were fearsome. And they had become my slaves.

I have brought Hell to my family; next, it's Hell on Earth. And we are just the perfect bunch to see it through.

THE ITCH
By Stuart Conover

Matt couldn't stop scratching his hands. They had been itching for days, the blistered red skin turning to scaly scabs within minutes, demanding to be scratched. He wanted to cry but had no tears left to shed. He couldn't even keep his hands hydrated enough as is, let alone room for there to be tears.

He didn't even want to think about how bad his feet felt or looked.

"Mathew Warner," the receptionist finally called out.

It had felt like hours. Glancing down at his watch, there was no way that it had only been twenty minutes.

Standing, he tried to ignore the flakes which fell from his hands. He was sure everyone else in the waiting room was staring at them. Him. Freak.

What normal person would let themselves get into this kind of a position?

He slowly followed the nurse back to room 3. The only room Dr. Markow had met him in for the year he'd been going here. A new doctor for a new town seemed like a great idea but this coastal paradise had been anything but kind to him.

Sick within weeks of arriving and a skin condition shortly after. At first, he had thought it was eczema or even foot, hand, and mouth disease, but it soon proved to be neither.

"What seems to be the problem today, Matthew?" the nurse gushed through the smile that never left her perfect face. Like she wasn't revolted by the sight of him.

The doctor had diagnosed him with a rare skin disorder after a multitude of tests. They had tried a variety of treatments so far and yet, nothing. He stressed that the latest was the key.

"It's my hands," he mumbled, "they've gotten worse. The ointment Dr. Markow prescribed isn't helping at all."

Maybe he should go back to Chicago. Find a real doctor. Living on the coast had always been a dream of his but this was a nightmare.

"Well let's get your vitals and I'll take a quick look before the good doctor is available. Can you hop on the scale for me?"

Sighing, Matt slipped out of his shoes and emptied his pockets. Every ounce counted, though he knew he couldn't hide the fact that he was out of shape. Sliding his hands into his pockets he stepped up on the scale.

"Mmmhmm," she said after making some adjustments. "You can step down now."

He was off the scale before he even had a chance to look at what it read.

"What was the damage?" he said as he slid back into his loafers.

"187, you're down 8 pounds. Good job!" she gushed.

He had mostly stopped eating since the last appointment. He couldn't seem to make anything without shedding flakes of skin into it. Even when he wore gloves.

Who had to wear gloves just to eat?

"Now," she was suddenly inches from him, with a look of almost hunger in her eyes, "Let's take a look at those hands, shall we?"

He couldn't keep her gaze and started to look down but didn't want her to think he was staring at her cleavage and slowly started to pull his hands out of his pockets. When he had first started coming here, a quick admiring look down her blouse was a welcome distraction but these days looking at any of the women in town could only creep them out.

Before he could take them out the door opened.

"Matt. It's good to see you. Beth, that will be all."

"Yes but," she clicked her tongue in frustration, "yes, sir."

The resignation of having to leave filled not only her voice but her posture as she slowly walked out the door and closed it behind her with one last look at Matt.

Poor freak is what she had to be thinking.

"Attractive, no? Smart too, but far too ambitious and curious for her own good. It's nice to see you again, Matt."

Nodding but not looking up he blurted, "they aren't getting any better, Doc."

"Well you've only been on this new ointment for a week and I've told you it can take two before it really kicks in. Let's get you out of those socks and shoes and let me see your hands and feet, son."

The shoes were kicked off and Matt slowly brought his hands down to take off his socks. Each moment flecked scales everywhere. When his socks came off it was instantly obvious how much worse his feet were. The skin was pale, cracked, and scales almost didn't do justice to the serpentine pattern that was now etched into his skin.

The inside of his sock was full of flakes. He shuddered at the thought of putting them back on.

"They hurt. Everything hurts. Every time I move it hurts. It didn't used to go up to my knees."

Biting his lip to hold back tears he let the doctor examine him.

"Hmmm, yes, things are definitely coming along nicely here."

"Nicely?" he spat out. Anger filling his voice and for the first time he looked up at Markow. "Nicely? I can't go out in public. I can't go to work. I hurt. All. Day. Long. What do you mean 'nicely'?"

His toes curled and pain blossomed over his face as he couldn't help but going back to scratching.

"Things are coming through to its natural course, Matt. You don't have much longer to worry about this little infliction. I know it looks strange but I promise you that it will all be over soon. That scratching isn't helping either."

"It's getting better? How is it getting better if it hurts even worse? If it itches all the time?"

"Sometimes the pain means healing. Sometimes it means things are changing. Right now, your skin is doing just that but it'll all be over soon. The ointment will help this along quickly and you'll be good as new. From what I can see here, I'll be honest, things are coming along nicely. Just go home, have dinner, the nutrients will help too, rub in the ointment, and get a good night's sleep. You won't be better by morning but I promise that when you wake up you'll have an entirely new outlook on life."

Clenching his hands to not scratch them, Matt nodded.

"Thank you, doctor. It didn't seem like it was getting any better."

"I completely understand. You've got a condition that is rare and when it seems to be getting worse you have every right to be concerned but get on home. Tomorrow will be a whole new day. Believe me, you won't know what hit you when you wake up!"

Walking out of the office he pulled an app up on his phone to arrange a ride. While waiting he pulled up another to order food. Specifically, a steak sandwich. He ordered extra meat and instead of fries, he side ordered a hotdog as well.

With gloves on he felt he could keep the flakes out of it. His stomach rumbled at the thought of something to eat and for the first time in days, he was hungry.

Not hungry.

Ravenous.

Protein with a side of protein seemed like just the thing too. Craving meat, he almost added a second sandwich to the meal before he realized his eyes had to be bigger than his stomach. Besides, his ride was there. Hitting order, he climbed on in and tried to keep his hands out of view of the driver.

The poor guy was going to have to vacuum before his next pickup.

Once home it wasn't long before the grub arrived and, donning a pair of gloves, he scarfed it down. He tried not to notice that the scales were coming out over the top of the gloves.

Or that they seemed to be spreading farther up his arms.

He chased his dinner with a rum and cola, followed by three more.

The doctor's high hopes had rubbed off on him.

The food lay heavy in his stomach. He stood and the alcohol went straight to his head, passing the buzzed feeling he was expecting, the room spun. At least he didn't feel the pain for once. Stumbling to the bathroom he laughed.

If the doctor was right, he should wake up feeling better. He stripped out of his clothes on the way to the bathroom. Not even noticing he was leaving them strewn about his apartment. He turned the light on in the bathroom and winced.

A bit brighter than the kitchen had been. He looked in the mirror as he was unscrewing the top of the ointment bottle. Dark circles were engraved under his eyes and he almost felt like his face was breaking out.

Nope. Not going to pay attention to that. There was no need to add insult to injury at this point. He rubbed the ointment into his hands. Up to his wrists, up to near his elbows before realizing how much of his skin looked infected now.

Nothing to worry about. Things would be better in the morning. He rubbed it into his feet and the scales were up to his knees now. He added another dose for good measure. Really trying to rub it into his skin.

Laughing, he tried not to think of what he would have done with lotion just a few months back in the privacy of his bedroom but that thought quickly soured. He was far too disgusted with himself now to even think about that.

Looking in the mirror again, his eyes were slits. He needed sleep. The rum had hit him harder than he had been expecting.

Maybe that should have been his escape to sleep all of the last month.

No matter.

Things will be better in the morning.

Trying not to rub any of the lotion off his feet, he walked on the sides of each and toppled into bed.

Naked already as he knew he wouldn't want to touch anything, he clenched his hands together and tried to keep his legs off the bed as much as possible.

Not the most comfortable way to lay down, he thought as he drifted into the darkness of his mind.

Waking up, it was still dark out and his head pounded.

He should have had water before going to bed.

All he needed was a hangover on top of everything else.

Matt's eyes flashed open. There wasn't anything else.

Flexing his hands and toes, there was no pain past the thundering in his skull.

Markow had been right!

He was better. Running his hands across each other, they didn't feel sore at all. They felt dry. The feeling in his fingertips felt dulled.

Flexing his feet, they didn't hurt either.

He reached down and the same dullness was there.

With how dry he felt it would probably be a good idea to get some moisturizer on, and a glass of water. Or five.

Grabbing his phone, it was 3AM.

He shakily stood up, head pounding the entire time, and made his way to the washroom. Filling his glass with water he wondered if he dared to turn on the light.

The pain would probably be unbearable through the hangover.

He had to see though.

Closing his eyes, he flicked on the light and winced.

With eyes closed it was too much.

Sighing, he waited for them to adjust as he had more of his water.

Finally, he cracked them open and the glass fell from his hand.

The face in the mirror. He shook his head and tried to avoid the pounding.

A trick of the light. Looking down he clenched his fists.

No longer painful. He was enraged. Angry and on the verge of crying.

This wasn't right.

Matt looked in the mirror again and the creature that looked back at him was covered in scales.

Specs of skin were falling away, peeling, under it was. . . .

The scales were covering his body. All the way up his arms now and up through his neck. They didn't cover his belly but a green hue was shining off them.

What had happened to him? This couldn't be real.

He needed to call someone. 9-1-1. A doctor, something. He needed to get out of this town.

Matt's phone started to ring.

Dr. Markow's office.

"What have you done to me?" he hissed.

"Matt, Matt, Matt. Son, I've made you better. I told you that waking up today you would have a whole new outlook on life. You've been chosen, son. Now you need to come home."

A flash of movement and Matt was pushed to the ground. His hands were cuffed behind him and a bag pushed down over his head.

"We're here to take you home, son," rustled a voice behind him. Cold and inhuman. "Welcome to your better tomorrow."

THE BLIND ASSASSIN
By Damien Donnelly

I don't remember what happened before, no clue as to who I was, what I was, but afterwards, everything that happened afterwards is a completely different story, because when you open your eyes after death, you discover a whole other way of living.

Tick tock, tick tock.

There is darkness mostly; she left me no eyes to escape the blindness but I can see when I want, when the need fills me. I see shape in sound and smell. These are my senses now, she left me those. Guilt, regret, remorse, those weaknesses have no part in what I've become. I'm no longer accountable to the standards Men hold as law. I am beyond law and now, as I'm technically dead, I'm beyond Man.

Tick tock, tick tock.

"I remade you, better than before. You were a drunk, a drug addict with no direction. No one gave a shit about you. You would've died one day, I just gave that day a name. You should be grateful, I've given you something greater than life; indestructible, eternal death among the living," she declared that day, the first day of my everlasting existence, as I realised the horror of what she'd done. I wasn't human anymore, this was true. I would be unbeatable, also true. But she hadn't given me eternal death, it was eternal damnation.

I recognised her voice from somewhere before death, a sound bite on TV, a ranting about experimentation, radiation, creation; bringing heaven to earth. "I'll build a world that will never need creation again, all will be eternal," she'd bragged. I remember that. I'll always remember that. She won't, not anymore.

Tick tock, tick tock.

When I first awoke, to her restoration, I felt no pain at all, that came later, when I came to understand what she'd made of me. She was my Frankenstein, she'd remoulded me from her miscreant mind. "Without sight you'll see much better," she whispered to my naked form, strapped to a gurney, as forceps wrenched my eyes from their sockets. "The tongue just teases you with taste," she insisted, "this'll teach you to taste from within," and she snipped the tongue from my mouth with a blade, severing it from service with a single slice. Afterwards, she stitched it to the back of my neck, to remind me of all that was now behind me.

I was not a body of blood anymore, my veins had been drained, dried out like taunt twine that tore through my flesh from the inside out. My innards had been expunged, discarded, floor fodder for vermin to devour and they did, nightly, as I lay there, a monster metamorphosing. In my chest, empty of all organs except my heart, a machine of amorality maintained me, pumping a self-sustainable liquid through the little that remained of me; limbs that had been ravaged, a hand severed and replaced with a scythe, legs hacked at the knees, mounted on metal spikes while my manhood was slit, sliced, and stuffed with the slithering tongue of a serpent, still hissing. I was a despicable demon, an envoy of evil, a punishment for a world that had dismissed her dreams of total autonomy as nothing more than an inhuman, unjustifiable, godless existence. I was her retribution. She believed I'd bring them all down for her but she misjudged who was master. A monster knows no master. A monster needs no master. Monster *is* master.

Tick tock, tick tock.

Monster let her believe she had control while she trained me, taught me to walk, to hunt, to appreciate the divinity of my own damnation. Monster appeared grateful to his creator and her darkness, monster acted thankful to his creator and her inventiveness until one day when monster stabbed his spikes into his creator's feet as she leaned against the wall, smiling at the completion of her own genius. Monster smiled as his scythe slit her from nipple to neck and his one remaining hand reached inside her and disgorged the heart from her blood-bathed body before her face even had time to register fear. Monster left her there, in her darkness, in that heartless body, further fodder for the vermin who'd already begun to sniff her out.

That was four years ago. I can finally admit I'm grateful for her. I've lived more in death than I ever could in life. I don't need food or drink, don't shit or sleep. I exist as if every day were the first, do you understand? Can you understand me now, now that I'm standing behind you, so close that your skin prickles with fear as I sliver my scythe around your neck?

You came looking for me, didn't you? Foolishly searching the shadows for the monster you thought was myth. Well, now you're truly the fool because this monster is no myth, nor a white knight. I am the Blind Assassin, devoid of compassion. She removed that from me when she raided my body of blood and being. Do you hear the ticking clock? *Tick tock, tick tock.* It's inside me. It goes where I go. It counts down humanity while I continue on, slaying it. I feel nothing for you people anymore, nothing. And in a moment, you'll feel nothing too.

And he was right. In an instant, blood spewed from the gash in the human's neck and splattered onto the glasses that covered Monster's eyeless sockets and down onto his tongueless, grinning mouth as the clock continued counting. . . .

Tick tock, tick tock.

He'd killed his creator but he couldn't extinguish the desire for revenge that she'd transplanted into his useless, still beating, eternally damned heart.

FLESH

By James Dorr

He woke with the feeling that he should become fat. He did not know why yet.

Perhaps it was in a dream—he had had dreams lately. Wicked, ugly dreams, dreams of shadows. Shadows that coalesced into—he did not know. . . . *Zombies*, the thought came. But then he laughed.

Zombies?

He had been seeing too many movies. Too much cable TV. He could afford that, the time to watch TV, to go out on evenings and drink and dance till dawn, beyond the dawn if he should wish to. To drown the zombies, the shadows, the. . . .

Well, *what?*

And if they would not drown: It came with a clarity surpassing nightmares, that cold, bright morning. The sun streaming through his townhouse windows, his bedroom carpet dappled with winter light. That he could *insulate*—

He could afford to.

Much like a house could be insulated from the weather—his body his own house—he could add layers and layers to it. Fat. Skin. Muscle. Tendons and blood, covering bone-frames, beams and rafters, and overall softened, warmed, smoothed, protected, by layers of white flesh, spider-webbed in pink. Pink capillaries—the darker red of veins. Neurons and arteries. Fingernails. Body hair. . . .

He could afford it, to eat to build such a house. Was he not wealthy?

The company he owned, when he went to the office—he did not have to unless he wished it—unless he was bored—swarmed with drone-like people waiting to see him. Venture capitalists, as he was, begging for money to use for some new project. Most of these failures, but he knew how to bail out when needed—always just in time. To take the profit. And so he had grown rich.

Yet *still* they begged from him.

He shouldered his way through his outer office—so many supplicants—waving to Ms. Ransom, his receptionist. "Anything interesting?"

She looked up and smiled, as she was paid to do. "One kind of odd one." She handed a folder to him as he brushed by.

Inside he opened it: *PATENT PENDING*, the top sheet said. *AN EATING MACHINE.*

And the dreams came back to him.

He saw them, the shadows, thin, wraith-like, approaching. Long, bony fingers extended like claws. Reaching, prodding him. Trying to touch his heart.

Fingers six inches long. . . .

And he awoke, screaming. Ms. Ransom calling in over the intercom, "Is everything all right?"

Him answering, "Yes," and that he would be going out for the rest of the afternoon. And thinking. Thinking. *Six inches of fat, that would just about do it. Make it eight to be sure. Most fingers, he knew, were only three-and-a-half, maybe four inches long at most from webbing to nail-tip, but even allowing two inches extra for fingers he saw in dreams, eight inches should do it.*

Outside he shouldered his way past a Salvation Army bell ringer, past bums and trolls and tramps huddled together for warmth on heat grates, past better-dressed tramps importuning for money for this, for that charity. A light snow falling.

And it occurred to him: Christmas was almost here. And he . . . they must have thought *he* was Santa Claus!

And he laughed, *ho-ho*ing as they shrank from him, he still thin then but already laying plans.

An eating machine, eh?

So he would become one—an eating machine, himself—rich desserts, candies, meringues and puddings to follow down thick steaks. Obscene, heaped mounds of soft mashed potatoes, cone-shaped like women's breasts. Sucking, devouring.

"Patent Pending," indeed! he snorted.

And he dreamed of zombies still, but not so often. And always wistful zombies in some way, still reaching out.

But now at a distance. . . .

And as the weeks went from December to January to February he dreamed less. The distances, when he *did* dream, increased also—he calculated it once one morning, having still screamed when they had surrounded him in a sort of ragged circle within *that* night's dream, but, seemingly, could approach no nearer: So many inches for each new pound, or fraction of a pound. In kilograms and feet.

That afternoon when he went to the office Ms. Ransom no longer smiled.

Nor did he give her a raise when *that* time came, when winter became spring. Rather he luxuriated within his flesh—three hundred pounds of it if he weighed an ounce! His bathroom scale could no longer measure him. Clothing he bought in special stores now, not minding spending money as long as it was spent for some *thing*. Not frittered or given.

His body was too wide to fit in his mirror.

And as he expanded, his eating machine stock expanded also—he marketed it as a novelty item despite its inventor's wish that it help invalids gain needed nourishment, and, as such, it had soon become a fad. A sort of gag present that wealthy people gave to one another—a toy for the idle rich—and paid top money for.

Which meant that he sold his interest—just as the fad peaked. His timing impeccable, just as it always was. He made a *fortune*, as spring became summer. Himself his own kind of eating machine now—he could not stop himself even if he wished to, which he did not *yet*. He gloried, rather, in what he had become, four hundred pounds of him as June became July: His body not a house now but a temple, a grand cathedral! Walking rarely, rather keeping to air-conditioned cars.

Hobbling, really, when he *must* walk outdoors.

Screaming, the dreams came back. But now not just *dreams. Or, rather, he became more sensitive to them.*

When he did have to walk, still there were homeless, no matter how insulated his body became to others. Still bums who slept on grates, scrabbling for handouts, as if the rising heat—even in July—were somehow *their* homes. Just as the flesh was his that rippled on his frame, *heave-ho*ing itself in waves as he waddled imposingly from car to office—Ms. Ransom had quit by then—on the rare times that he *went* to the office.

From office to restaurant, where he now dined alone.

Ms. Ransom had said that he disgusted *her. Which was another layer he added to his insulation.*

His distancing himself from. . . .

Well, from what?

He took up farting. To relieve the pressure when such was needed, so more food would fit in.

From, outside, the zombies. The flesh-eaters, just as he ate flesh himself to pack on more calories.

Even in summer, as sweat rolled in rivers down his smooth, soft skin, even now lolling in air conditioning. He had a driver now for his car, the beam of his hips taking up a whole back seat.

Until even his driver said that he disgusted him. That he would drive no more. Leaving him, in darkness, outside a supper club where he had just eaten, just gorged, just filled himself almost past bursting. But it was not so far that he could not *walk home himself, now with a cane to assist in his waddling. Or was* this *part of his dream?*

He was not certain. He never was sure these days. At night he saw shadows, waking *or* sleeping. The sleep-shadows still somewhat keeping their distance, but growing ever bolder. Surer. As they surrounded him.

And the day-shadows, the ones when he woke: *These* were the shadows behind his own eyelids.

His facial flesh had by now puffed his eyes nearly into pigs' eyes—squinting, nearly shut—so corpulent had he become in his eating, as June passed through July. July became August. He *loved* himself for it.

But now, now the walk home. If he were *not* dreaming. He squinted, he felt his way, one block. Two blocks. His cane skidding under him. He looked up to see a sign, some indication—to know which street it was that he should turn on.

The street light was broken.

And shadows surrounded him. Wicked. Ugly. The ghouls and the zombies. The nights he lay, sleepless.

Screaming!

As, finally, he reached home. Air conditioning. The door shut behind him, sideways scrabbling down the entrance hall, barely squeezing through. Until he erupted into his kitchen.

Reaching, struggling. The stove.

The icebox.

"A small snack, perhaps," he said. Speaking just to himself. "Something for the flesh. To help meat stick to bones. Insulation needs fueling, after all—that's what they say. Corpulence needs to *grow.*"

And, as he reached, his own fingers touched yielding flesh. Soft, just as his was, but slippery from rotting as, his house and kitchen dissolving into a mist—perhaps he never having arrived there *except* in a hopeful dream—shadows became real. Kitchen knives clutched in hands, long and bony. . . .

And he knew the why of it—at long last now the why? *Of dreams and nightmares. Why he should have awakened, so long ago, one winter's morning feeling he* must *be fat. Cut from the world outside, safe in his flesh-fortress. Succulent. Juicy.*
And who had been guiding whom?

As, ignoring the screams of his flesh, the fingers extended to foot-lengths and more to carve their paths through it.

A NORMAL SON
By Spinster Eskie

I never truly felt that Jake belonged to me. I pushed him out and breastfed him, and cuddled him when he cried at night, but I always felt separate, more like a caretaker than a mother. Jake's father was a one-night-stand in Santa Cruz. He was Portuguese and barely spoke a word of English. I met him while travelling with my girlfriends and looking for a good time. When I found out I was pregnant, I was angry with myself, but I wanted children. I wanted Jake.

He didn't speak. He stared blankly at me when I would sit, sobbing into my hands on the floor because I couldn't afford the gas bill or because I felt stuck, drained, and useless as a parent. Sometimes Jake would mimic my crying noises, but he didn't hug me, didn't say "Mommy I love you, everything is going to be okay." I often worried that I was doing more harm than good by trying to raise him by myself. I had no experience with autism prior to my son. I had been a spoiled party girl. I liked to drink. I liked sex. But I was not one to take on responsibility or educate myself through research. When Jake was diagnosed, however, I knew I had to understand autism if I was going to seek help for him. What I wanted was for him to be fixed. I didn't want him to have autism. I wanted Jake to be a normal, happy boy.

Jake went to a public school that had a program for children with his disability. I had sought to get him into an intensive school for special needs, but with the salary I made on waiting tables, I had to take what I could get. The program at Colby Elementary wasn't bad. They cared a lot about Jake and wanted to see him get better. They gave Jake a sentence book so that he could communicate his needs with pictures, but Jake continued to mimic his teachers rather than express his own intentions. If an adult gave him a magazine to look at, he would hand it back to her using the exact same gesture. If an adult wrote the daily schedule on the white board, he would stand up next to her and rewrite the same thing with the same handwriting. The positive, his teachers would say, was that Jake had the ability to learn. The negative was that almost every action of his was a repetition, rather than a natural inclination.

The extent of Jake's ability to imitate was fully disclosed to me when my parents bought him drum lessons for his seventh birthday. Jake tended to mimic beats with his hands when I played music and we figured he would enjoy learning an instrument. But to his instructor's surprise, Jake needed only one lesson to figure out how to play. He calmly watched his instructor teach the basics, and then observed as the instructor combined the techniques to show off an elaborate array of complex rhythms and crashing sounds. In a matter of seconds, Jake was able to copy the instructor's every move and follow along seamlessly and without mistake. This also occurred when I brought home a how-to-draw book. Jake spent hours at the dinner table drawing each example from the book, with such perfect detail and flawless color and line, that one would think a machine had made the copy.

Jake's skills were limiting, however. Once he knew how to draw the Eiffel Tower, he could do it again, but if I asked him to free draw something like flowers or a smiley face, he would not know how to do it unless I drew the image first. And even then, his artistic skills would only be as good as mine, with shaky lines and a simple cartoonish quality. Jake's talent was not in music or in art, but in mimicking with literal precision. He was a mirror, a shadow, but his talents didn't stop there. As my son got older, he exhibited other strange behaviors that would puzzle even the most trained professional in the field of autism.

I was called at work one day and told by a police officer that my son had gone missing at school. When I arrived at the school, Mrs. Lopez was visibly upset. She told me that she had counted every head twice, when the group had come in from recess. A boy named Victor had pushed Jake on the playground, and continued to be menacing toward him when recess was over. Mrs. Lopez then put Victor in timeout and when she turned to comfort Jake, he was gone. I was screaming at the teacher, trying to understand how a child in her care could just up and disappear like that. Mrs. Lopez was ashamed and apologetic, but I was in no state to be forgiving. I could have killed her.

"We're doing all we can, Ms. Bonet," said an officer. "Nobody saw your son leave the building, so chances are, he's still inside the school."

The principal and several police officers searched the school for hours and questioned every staff person available. I stayed in the classroom, calling everybody I knew to see if he had wandered to any of their houses. Then, just as I was about to go home to see if possibly Jake had returned there, I saw eyes staring at me from a heap of blankets on the floor and then blink. Jake wasn't under the blankets, he *was* one of the blankets. His body had flattened and contorted to look soft and wrinkled. He folded and crumpled like polka-dotted fabric and was lying with the other patterned blankets in the rest area by the bookshelf.

It terrified me to see Jake's body bend in such a position, all scrunched up like laundry, but Jake had always been alarmingly flexible and his skin tone often changed with his emotions. When he was a baby, he'd go red when he needed to be changed or fed and ghostly white when it thundered outside his window. I had Jake checked for anemia but the doctors found nothing wrong with him. They said that his skin tone was simply translucent enough to show blood flow, and that his emotions would most certainly affect his coloring. But now I knew that Jake's ability to mimic also was an ability to disguise himself. He could stretch his back, flat and straight to look like a table. He could puff himself up, and go lumpy and fat while watching the clouds pass by.

"Don't do it anymore!" I told Jake at breakfast one day. "Never mimic again!" I grabbed Jake's face and forced him to look into my eyes. "Do you understand me?" I asked him, "Never ever make your body mimic again!" Jake, of course, did not respond, and I could only hope he was receiving and processing my message. I didn't want Jake to be different. He was an outcast already. I didn't want anything to further segregate him from a normal childhood.

When I was pregnant I had dreams for Jake. I wanted him to be successful and handsome. I wanted him to be my best friend and the one guy I could count on. But I couldn't count on Jake. I was afraid of him and afraid for him. If his talents became known, he'd be tested more and possibly taken away from me. I had no idea how to relate to my son, but I loved him. More than anything, I loved him, and I wanted to protect him. So, for me, Jake stopped making shapes and colors, but there were occasions when he'd unintentionally slip.

For his tenth birthday party, Jake played limbo with his friends from school. The other parents and I were in the kitchen, discussing articles we had read about autism and its cause. Even among other parents with autistic children, I felt like an outsider. At this point, I looked beyond a parent's head into the living room where the kids were. The stick was lowered four inches from the ground and Jake flattened himself like a pancake and glided beneath. Most of the kids were impressed and gasped with awe. However, one child threw a fit and had to be restrained by his mother and removed from the party. Thankfully, most of the parents assumed the outrage was due to poor sportsmanship, but one child asked me how Jake was capable of making himself flat. "He's just very flexible," I explained to the little girl and hoped that the incident would be forgotten.

At my friend's engagement party, I met Cesar: a fuzzy bearded, older gentleman with a drooping nose and thinning hair. Physically, Cesar was not my type, but he bought me a drink and displayed a friendly, kind disposition. Anyway, I was thrilled to be drinking, and even more thrilled that I was at an event that didn't require dragging my kid along. Jake was with my parents. He was usually with my parents when I wanted to get fucked up, but there were days when I couldn't help but be fucked up in front of him. Booze was the one luxury I allowed myself. I didn't style my hair anymore or shave, or go out dancing with the girls. I didn't date because most men would have nothing to do with a single mom, let alone one whose son was autistic. I couldn't remember the last time I had sex, or even had the energy and desire to masturbate, so when Cesar approached me, I put no faith into the possibility that he might be braver than his predecessors.

"You don't want me," I slurred over my cocktail, "I'm a basket-case. My life is a mess, my son is a mess. You wouldn't just be dating me. You'd be dating my baggage. You'd be dating my fears, my insecurities, and my sadness."

"Why are you so sad?" Cesar asked unexpectedly and I considered the question long before answering.

"I'm sad because my son doesn't love me like I love him." I don't think I had ever said it out loud before then, but it was the truth. Jake did not like to be touched. He reacted nervously when I tried to hold him, and he would pull away when I kissed him. Over the years, Jake learned to mimic gestures of love, but nothing ever seemed organic or from his heart. He didn't want to be with me. He wanted to be elsewhere. I'm not sure how I knew this. I just did.

Jake didn't like Cesar coming over all the time. He would blend into the walls, just so I wouldn't be able to find him for supper. But I needed Cesar to be around. I needed to feel adored again and I needed the financial help—and I needed the emotional help. So I asked Cesar to move in after a month. Living with us, it didn't take Cesar long to realize that Jake was a strange anomaly. Jake would come into our room while we were making love and silently watch us until we'd notice him. The first time it happened, Cesar yelled for him to get out and Jake ran into his bedroom and pulled himself up to the top shelf in his closet, using his stretchy, elastic arms and legs. Then he squeezed himself into the small, enclosed space and hid from us for an hour. Sometimes, Jake would mimic Cesar's affection, and would pat my bottom and sensually massage my shoulders. I'd have to explain to him the difference between the love of a son and the love of a boyfriend.

I figured it was only a matter of time before Cesar would pack and leave, but he wasn't giving up so quickly and was determined to somehow connect with Jake. I thought the man to be crazy. I'd been trying to connect with my son for eleven years.

When Cesar took Jake to the aquarium where he worked, something triggered in the young boy. He was clearly enthralled by Cesar's store. He studied every fish, every seahorse, every bizarre creature that gracefully twirled and danced within their wet, restrictive, habitats. I could tell how badly Jake longed to shapeshift and become one of the animals, but he knew better than to do it in public and he also knew I'd ground him if he tried. Yet, Cesar was instantly motivated to strengthen his relationship with Jake through their common interest. He brought home books on marine-life and Jake would lose himself in the pictures and would run to me and show almost every page with the most enthusiasm I'd ever seen him express. His eyes were wide and his skin would reflect the bright, tropical colors of the fish in the books, and then Jake would turn to me and his chin would drop at the recognition of my disapproval.

When Cesar brought home a reef tank for Jake, my son's typically serious face faded to reveal the most endearing, gigantic smile, and my heart ached. He could not take his eyes off the fluttering fins and the beautiful, majestic corals that decorated the glass. Although his obsession was a concern of mine, Cesar kept bringing home more books and documentaries on various aquatic species.

Then one day, Cesar and I caught Jake climbing into the tank, feet first, with his legs stretched like his bones were made of rubber. Most boys Jake's age would not have been able to fit into the shallow glass rectangle, but Jake contorted his body just so. He elongated himself and puffed up his malleable flesh, to fit like soft jelly in a jar.

"I want that fucking tank out of here!" I shouted at Cesar after we had dug Jake out of the freezing, sticky salt water.

"What's the problem, Maryanne? He likes that tank!"

"That's the problem, Cesar! He likes it too much! He wants to be a fucking fish! He can barely control his body!"

"I think he's a special boy with a gift!" Cesar said to me.

"He's a freak! And you're encouraging him to be a freak!"

"Why shouldn't I encourage him to be who he is?"

"I want him to be normal!"

"Well, he's not normal Maryanne! And all the therapy and all the sped classes in the world aren't going to make Jake a normal kid! Love him for who he is!"

"Get out!" I screamed and I tossed him one of his shirts from the closet. "Get the fuck out of my house!" I threw another shirt at him, and another, and began to cry as I piled Cesar's clothes onto the bed. Cesar did not move and I stomped outside the room to find Jake listening from the hallway. His skin was red and he pleaded to me using only his eyes. I didn't know what to say. I went to hug him, but he recoiled and went back to his room.

Cesar and I managed to make up that night, but I wasn't ready to fully let my guard down. I was still pissed off. Not so much at Cesar, but at myself for being the shitty mother I was. Cesar's words hurt deep, as I honestly couldn't say for sure what it was that I loved about my son. I'd spent eleven years feeling uncomfortable and disengaged from him. I was jealous of Cesar's ability to appreciate Jake's abnormalities and even understand them on some level. I watched mothers on the playground getting hugs and kisses from their sons and I felt only self-pity and resentment.

"Let's take a vacation," Cesar suggested to me. "You're overworked and overstressed. What this family needs is a good getaway." I laughed at the idea of a vacation. I hadn't taken one since my trip to Santa Cruz when Jake was conceived. But Cesar had some cash stored away, and said he wanted to take me and Jake to the coast for sunshine and a relaxing dip in the ocean.

"You mean you want to show Jake the beach," I said, mildly irritated by Cesar's persistence.

"Yes, I do," Cesar replied confidently, "and I want to see you in a tiny, tight bikini." He kissed me and rubbed my thighs and I remembered Jake's father looking me up and down on the beach.

I was twenty then, and skinny, and my breasts overflowed in a bikini that barely left anything to the imagination. We drank banana daiquiris and briefly conversed. Well, I talked. He nodded. Then we made love under starlight on the dunes. The waves made a haunting melody that echoed through the vast, open space, and the Portuguese man between my legs fucked me into oblivion. His long, smooth penis filled me up and his fingers stimulated me through some kind of suction method I couldn't quite figure out. I was drunk and things were hazy, so I just laid back and enjoyed orgasm after orgasm.

During the car ride from our home in Arizona, Jake read his marine-biology books and kept looking out the window in anticipation of the sea. When, finally, the Pacific Ocean emerged from the distance, Jake bounced and rocked in his seat. "Jake, calm down!" I demanded as his excitement intensified the closer we got. Cesar pulled into a parking lot by the shore and Jake banged on the car door to get out. "Christ, Jake, settle down!" I yelled, assuming he was having an anxiety attack from the road.

"Let him out of the car," Cesar told me.

"I don't think that's a good idea right now. He needs to calm down."

"Maryanne, listen to me. Let him out of the car now!" I opened the car door and Jake undid his seatbelt. Then he bolted past me and toward the great, blue ocean.

"Jake!" I called out, chasing after him through the hot, gritty sand. "Jake, stop this!" But he would not listen. He kept running as fast as he could and I ran after him, breathless and panicked. Finally, I caught up with him and grabbed what I thought was his hand, but a slimy, smooth tentacle slipped from my grip.

"Let him go!" Cesar shouted, holding me back.

"Jake!" I cried, reaching out, and I watched as eight slimy, limp tentacles appeared from beneath Jake's shirt and his body collapsed as he reached the water. An enormous wave then flushed over my son and he was gone. I was in hysterics now and kept calling Jake's name, even though I knew he couldn't hear. I ran into the water, fully dressed, and Cesar had to drag me back to shore and keep me suppressed under his weight.

"He's okay!" Cesar assured me. "He's going to be okay. He's home." There was a comfort in Cesar's words, but I still wouldn't accept them. Home was not the cold, lonely sea. Home was his bed in his room, in our little house, where he was loved and missed. I never saw Cesar again after that. He believed he had done the right thing, but he took my son from me, and now all I could do was wait, wait for the day when Jake would return. I quit my job and moved to the shores of California just to wait for that day. And every night I'd visit the beach and gaze out at its brilliant, sparkling mystery and hope that wherever Jake was, he was happy.

GAS MASK BABY
By Santiago Eximeno
Translated to English by Alicia L. Alonso

> *Child*
> *Do not ask me*
> *To decide*
> *Cause it's me*
> *Who can tell you*
> *How hard it is to live*
> **Embryodead: Wumpscut:**

The children pile up over each other. The bodies form a mountain of trembling flesh. Those at the lower positions can hardly breathe. The ones on the top move and shake, but they can't detach from the group because the rest of them hold them down. They hold them down firmly with their hands, imprisoning them. No one can break the mountain of children. And they're alive. And they breathe.

Maria knows this. She knows her son is there in the mountain, among the bodies of thousands, hundreds of thousands of other children, some teenagers, some newborns. Since she arrived, they haven't stopped crying.

There are other women by the mountain, a whole handful of them. Trembling and crying. Pulling the arms of children that aren't theirs. Climbing the mountain, stabbing the faces of sobbing babies with their stiletto heels. The women don't speak to one another. *Mothers,* thinks Maria. Mothers just like her who came to retrieve the child they lost. Because, in one way or another, they have all lost their child and come here to get their child back.

Here.

In Hell.

Maria covers her face with one hand. She can't stand the stink emanating from the mountain of flesh. Somewhere, someone has lit a fire, and the smell of burnt flesh is unbearable. The mountain is actually a wall, a palpitating wall over twenty meters high, a wall that surrounds her and reminds her of the old university lecture rooms where she used to teach before the guilt, the goddamned guilt condemned her. She turns around and looks behind her, at the place from where she entered. It no longer exists. The entrance is closed, blocked by the piled-up bodies of teenagers. Of babies. Of children.

The stench lingers, as do the murmuring and the lamentations. The litany of tortured children. Why aren't they dead? Why do they persist on living here, on the other side? Maria was always told that, no matter what politicians proclaim, mothers decide. But it seems that it's not so. It seems that the decision whether to live or die always belonged to the children.

Maria holds in her hands a map she was given at the entrance. The map is written with the blood of unborn children on the skin of elderly pedophiles. Typewriters were banned a long time ago in Hell. Maria holds up the map and peruses it, comparing it to the mass of howling flesh that festers, moans, and screams in front of her. She asks herself if the red circle dissolving into tears of blood shows the spot where her son lay, or whether it's some kind of ruse, another pantomime designed to increase her suffering. She folds the map to one small square of palpitating skin and puts it back in her mouth. She holds it with her teeth, fearing the possibility of swallowing it. She would put it away somewhere else, but she's completely naked. That was the deal when she came here; that's what the demon that was black as night said to her.

"Take off your clothes. Get on your knees. Do it."

And she did, did she ever. Anything to see her son again. To expel from her mind all the guilt, all the memories crystallized into an empty university classroom, a sad look, words spoken without conscience:

"I'm not taking care of it. If I were you, I'd have an abortion."

With their faces covered by muzzles, the pregnant women wait on the other side of the mountain. She can see them through the smashed-up bodies if she looks closely between the thighs and butt cheeks, between the open spaces that the bodies cannot completely fill. The pregnant women pose like shop mannequins, and some of them have barcodes tattooed on their arms in black ink. Here, they are nothing more than part of the décor. Like the carbonized trees or the rivers of blood covered by barbed wired. Hell's scenographer is a son of a bitch.

Maria puts her hands on one of the bodies—a girl with curly hair who smiles while she howls like a she-wolf in heat—and starts climbing. If the map is right, she will find her son up there among fifty other expectant lactating infants, next to a small group of primary school pupils. As she sinks her feet into the flesh, feeling inquisitive hands and tongues exploring her belly and grazing her vulva, Maria asks herself how she will recognize him. Deep down in her soul she knows she will do so instantly, and the knowledge terrifies her.

Climbing is everything. Wrapped up in the howling, screaming, and gurgling, Maria climbs the wall of unborn flesh without looking back, oblivious to the other mothers, the pregnant women, the masked demons using their red-hot spears on the naked bodies of women and children. On everyone. And when she unknowingly introduces her fingers inside a mouth and the bite rips off the first phalanx of her pinkie, she screams. She screams like a fiend, but doesn't stop. She keeps climbing up, always up.

She doesn't want to reach the top of the wall of flesh. She doesn't want to see what's hiding on the other side, the bits that she could glimpse through the bodies. She doesn't want to see the men that look like mutilated blow-up dolls chatting by the river. She doesn't want to hear the cries of the blind teenage girls sitting in a circle around old women with their lips tied together. Hell is everything, and she wants no part of it.

I'm just passing by, she tells herself.

She knows it's not true. She knows that, even if today she manages to escape, sooner or later she'll be back.

Another step up the wall and, suddenly, she's facing a smiling child. She knows it's her son as soon as she sees him. His eyes, the curves of his lips. She doesn't ask him how old he is because she knows the exact answer: one year, six months, and four days. That's how long it took her to muster up enough courage to come to Hell for him. Because Hell is not losing your child. Hell is getting your child back.

"Mommy," says the boy.

Maria loses her balance and nearly falls. But she doesn't. She holds onto her son's body as she screams and cries. She pulls him towards her, trying to extract his smashed flesh from the wall of bodies waiting for the mothers who aborted them to return for them. Some of them have faces covered in wrinkles; they know for certain that their mother will never come. Maria pulls with all her might, fearlessly. And the boy's body slips out little by little, centimeter by centimeter, while the other unborn children open their hands to set him free.

"Mommy," repeats the boy.

"I'm here," whispers Maria. "I'm here."

Going down is a feverish madness. The hands of a hundred failures hold her up, encourage her. They don't retain her, they just help her descend back down to the barbed wire floor. The hands treat her gently because they already know she's a mother, a real mother, the kind of mother who will give up her own life to get her lost child back.

Down below, women smile at her and try to touch her. Maria cradles her son in her arms and moves away from them, terrified. She doesn't want to think about how long their children have been trapped in there, waiting. Like so many other children who live there for eternity, in the wall of flesh while, oblivious to their reality, their mothers go on with their lives and forget. Forget.

There is a door, and it's open. Maria crosses it. She has returned. Sitting behind a desk, the demon is waiting for her.

"You'll have to fill out the form. Give the boy to the midwife so we can prepare him."

Maria trembles like a leaf when the parody of a woman whom she assumes is the midwife comes to her with her arms wide open. The stench of her withered and open body makes her gag, but she knows she must be obedient and silently gives her the boy.

"Mommy," he says, but there is no reproach in his voice.

The midwife displays her body shamelessly. It's completely covered in festering sores. Her extreme thinness and her black skin are a striking contrast with the healthy look of the boy. Maybe that's why Maria wants to scream when the thing she takes for a woman gently, very gently, puts the gas mask on the boy's face.

"He needs a name," says the demon, before showing Maria a series of documents. "And you need to sign all these papers with your menstrual blood."

Maria nods. A castrated man with shaved skin covered in cellophane gives her back her clothes. She gives him an imploring, begging look as she sinks the quill into her body and signs sheet after sheet after sheet of paper.

"Tonight, we'll go home," says the demon while she gets dressed, "and we'll take the man."

Maria nods. That's the payment. It's only fair. Her clothes feel scratchy. She can't take her eyes off the boy and the gas mask stuck to his face like a second skin.

"One year, six months, four days," says the demon.

"Yes," answers Maria.

She can't think of anything else to say.

"Fine," says the demon. "You'll go back, then. Good luck. Enjoy every day. In a few years, we'll meet again."

And then the midwife gives her the boy and everything goes dark.

The classroom is empty. There's no one there. Only her, with her son sleeping in her arms.

"I'll take care of everything," whispers Maria.

She shuts her eyes and caresses the gas mask covering the boy's face. Then she unbuttons her blouse and lets the creature find her breast and feed.

HUMAN BODY
By Balázs Farkas

"Thus the human body is considered an interloper, not being part of creation, the pillars of the world aren't strong enough to carry it. It should be unable to step into the great lake, which is the origin of all life. Even daemons stand before us puzzled by our presence, under-standing not how we are able to see, walk and create on this plane, we can only hope in the graciousness of the lotus. Hiding the higher knowledge and the true size of the cosmos from us was a merciful act, the wisdom of Tindalos."

(From the Fifth Cryptical Book of Hsan.)

It's a wonderful day for Péter Tabán.

He's standing in the house he'd inherited, staring at the mouldy walls, the battered bookshelves, the unmade bed. He's look-ing at the cobwebs on the ceiling and jammed windows.

Later, he's pacing around in the kitchen. He can smell spoilt food, cheap detergent, and the stench of death. He flips the switches to check if they're still working. He's thinking about the old lady who used to live here, whose name he hadn't known at all. At least not before he received the letter about the inheritance.

He's trying to deal with the fact that at only twenty-six, he's now a proud owner of a house. Maybe he could sell it. Or he could move here, away from the city. This is a tidy little village after all. He's got plenty of options.

He might not be an expert when it comes to architecture, but still he knocks on the walls, squeezes the door frames, opens and closes the doors. It's a good house. By no means big, and there will be plenty of work to be done, but it's all right.

Then he exits the house to the backyard, observing the unused pigsty and the neglected garden. He's about to leave when in the toolshed he finds the human body.

And from this moment on, it's the only thing that matters in his life.

The woman in the mayor's office is typing annoyingly slowly. It's almost unbearable.

"Your name again? Péter . . . Tabán?"

"Yes."

He glances behind his back. Through the window and out onto the street.

It's in the car. The human body is in the car.

Covered in a blanket, on the back seat. It's there. He found it, it belongs to him now. When can he get out of here?

"Your mother's maiden name?"

Reluctantly, he answers all questions. None of this matters now. The inherited house? It doesn't matter. He himself doesn't matter anymore. Nor his personal data. Nothing makes sense anymore.

The human body is in his car now.

As the woman is reading the instructions aloud, Péter is tearing off little pieces of skin from his fingers. His feet move involuntarily and he starts sweating.

They should let him go now. What's all this for? He has other things to attend to. He has a task now. He can't just leave the human body alone.

"For fuck's sake now!" he snaps.

The woman glances up from the monitor, from behind her glasses.

"Come again?"

"Nothing, it's just . . . it just occurred to me that . . . that I have to . . ."

The woman waves her hand.

"You shouldn't worry. We're done here. We'll send the rest of the documents through mail. You can call me, you know my number, right? I'll have to check with the mayor as well, if you decide to move here . . . some time in the future."

It's almost like the woman was scared. The words themselves didn't give this away, but her look. It's like she wanted to get this matter over with as well.

"Uh-huh," Péter says. "Can I go now?"

The woman shrugs.

"Can't see why not."

As Péter hurries away from the mayor's office, and as he's nearing his car, he grabs his phone, calling Krisztina, his girlfriend.

"Don't come over today," he says. "Still more paperwork to do ... I'm sorry, really, but at least I've got the house."

"All right," Krisztina says. "So, what's it like? Is it nice?"

"Nice ... real nice, but listen, we'll talk tomorrow, I'll tell you everything. Got to go now. Bye!"

"Uh, bye."

As he's talking to his girlfriend, some kind of inexplicable nervousness takes over him. As soon as he puts away his phone and he sits behind the wheel, he calms down. He can breathe out now.

Then he turns back, slowly, staring at the backseat. Under the blanket, the human body occasionally makes a sluggish, faint motion. That's all it can do.

"We can go now," Péter says. He stares at the blanket, wetting his lips. "Everything will be all right. Everything will be all right."

He's struggling to carry the human body upstairs. It's not that big, but a bit heavier than expected. It's still covered in the blanket, but it's stirring more intensely.

Péter chooses the stairs. He just has to climb two floors.

He has a horrible premonition. What if somebody sees him? What would they say? Or worse yet, what if somebody wanted to grab the human body from him?

For the first time in his life, Péter Tabán feels like he could kill somebody. If somebody asked him right now ... if somebody would stand in his way. . . .

Before he can finish the thought, he arrives at the door of the condo. He's fumbling with his keys. He can hear voices from the back end of the corridor. He glances over there, but sees nobody.

A door lock rattles somewhere.

They mustn't see the human body.

He holds it to his chest with his left arm as if holding a child while he struggles with the lock with his right hand.

A door opens.

Now Péter can't tell where he is. He's feeling dizzy; his sight is blurred.

"No," he groans.

He pushes his weight against the door. It gives way.

"Oh my God. Oh my God. Oh my God."

He steps inside the condo with an inhuman speed and closes the door behind his back. He tosses his keys somewhere. He runs towards the bedroom, to the bed. He doesn't even take off his shoes.

If his girlfriend would see this . . . if his *mother* would see this. . . .

But nobody sees him. No one should see him.

He hurries to the bed and lays the human body down, taking off the blanket.

"We're home," he mumbles. "We're home. It's okay. Everything's going to be all right."

Now he can study the human body for the first time. So far he hadn't done so, didn't even think about it.

Péter is convinced that the human body is beautiful.

It is perfect like this. It has no legs, nothing under its hips—but it doesn't need legs, if there's somebody who can carry it. Its skin is smooth like an infant's. Above its hips there's the torso, without a navel, without nipples. You can't tell if it's male or female, it's simpler than that: it's *human*, it has to be, it's the prototype of a human being, its most perfect, cleanest body. Its two arms end in elbows, nothing below them—but why would it need hands, if there's somebody who could help it? And that head, that perfect, regular oval form, is not ruined by hair of any kind, *nor a face*. The whole skull is just covered by skin, fair, smooth skin.

Human body.

It moves its head—turning that emptiness where the face should've been—towards Péter.

It's thirsty, he ponders. *Why couldn't I think of this before! Who knows how long it had been lying out there alone!*

He runs off to get water. He is not thinking. He moves in a hurry. He doesn't want to leave the human body for such a long time. He returns with a glass of water.

He hesitates at the bed, looking at the human body. What's he supposed to do?

But of course, he knows. He has always known.

He kneels beside the bed, dips his fingers in the glass, and with wet hands, he caresses the faceless head of the human body. The water drops are glimmering on the clean, smooth skin.

The human body turns its head eagerly.

"Yes," Péter says.

He dips his hand in the glass again, wetting the rest of the skin on the limbless torso. The human body moves, its muscles tense under the skin.

"Easy . . . easy . . . good."

Péter doesn't take notice of the fact that his own mouth is open, and a line of drool appears in its corner.

"Good."

He caresses the body with his wet hands.

Suddenly, a sound comes from behind the faceless face: a hollow moaning.

"You're going to tell me your secrets," Péter whispers hopefully.

And the human body tells him its secrets.

Péter Tabán has a terrible day.

He's been sitting for almost six hours in the office of the car dealership. He's crunching numbers, sweating, hoping that his boss doesn't return.

He was late this morning, almost didn't show up. In the first hours, he's been growling at customers, so his boss sent him in here to work on the computer. He's been doing that since.

Until this moment, the place hasn't seemed real. Now the contours are becoming stronger; the door, the chair, these are right here, they are so real, he could almost touch them. This is where he works after all, this is where he makes money.

He doesn't understand what's happening. Why was it so hard to leave his home?

And it comes back to him. The human body.

He's confused. *Did that really happen? Impossible!*

He's thinking hard. What kind of foolishness is this? Could such things be? And if so, why would he bring home a body, why would he care, why wouldn't he be able to leave it behind?

He's becoming nervous.

I'm gross, he thinks. *Never, never again! I'll have to get rid of it.*

His phone rings. He jumps in his seat, almost having a heart attack.

"What!" he yells.

"Huh, easy now! I thought I could call you."

Péter buries his face in his hands. He wipes the sweat off his brow.

"Krisztina . . . I'm sorry, I'm just . . . having a stressful day."

"Okay then," his girlfriend says. "I just wanted to ask if we're going to meet up this evening. I assume you've finished with your things."

"Hmmm? Oh! Oh . . . yes."

"When can I come over?"

Péter is startled by the question.

The human body is still lying on his bed. He's trying to remember what happened last night, but everything is confusing. His last solid memory is leaving that inherited house. And then. . . .

"No, don't come over," he mumbles.

"What?"

"I mean . . . I should be the one going to your place. There has been a . . . uh, I don't know, I made a mess, everything is wet in the house now . . . uh, accidentally."

"*What?*"

"Never mind, just . . . I'll tell you everything, but can we meet at your place this time? It's closer and I should . . . it would be better to meet up as soon as possible, I just need you."

"Uh-huh. Okay then, but I hope this house will settle the question of moving in together. I'll be ready when you're done."

"Of course. I lo—"

Silence.

Péter is staring at his phone.

Ripples appear on the table in front of him. It looks wet.

Péter closes his eyes.

He's looking around in Krisztina's condo as if he'd never seen it before, peering in every corner, fearing that somebody might be hiding here somewhere.

They eat dinner. Then they sit on the couch, watching a movie.

Péter has a vague feeling that all this might be fake. Staged. He's trying to remember who he is, who Krisztina is, what this place is, and what that matter was with the inherited house. From time to time he touches his own face.

"You must have had a really stressful day indeed," Krisztina says after the movie.

"Yeah, I guess . . . you know, everything happened so fast. It's weird. I mean what kind of person am I if I don't even know my own relatives? Like . . . absolutely nothing!"

"Don't overthink it. You got yourself a house, *bam*, just be happy about it."

Krisztina is smiling. Péter hopes that he's smiling too, but he can't tell anymore.

They start cleaning up.

While Krisztina is in the kitchen, Péter notices that his sense of time has completely changed and that he couldn't describe this feeling with human terms. Time didn't go faster or slower, it was completely off the hinges. Events happened, but independent of him, or rather, they went through him.

His eyes fix on the wall, on a picture of a lotus flower. He feels like years would go by in an instant.

In the next second they are in the bedroom, drinking champagne.

"I figured we could celebrate."

Péter is unsure whether Krisztina said this before opening the bottle, or she's just about to say this.

The alcohol is mercifully dampening these feelings.

They cuddle. They get undressed.

They make love.

The skin of the girl is smooth. . . .

Smooth.

Imperfect, fake, not right.

He thinks about the human body. It's now impossible not to think about it.

Péter and Krisztina lay in the bed, staring at the ceiling.

"I'm sorry," Péter says. "I . . ."

"It's okay," Krisztina says.

XXXXXXX

Péter Tabán is kneeling beside his bed, looking at the human body, struggling with his tears.

"I wasn't thinking," he whimpers. "I'm so sorry, I won't . . . I won't see her again! I'm sorry, I will never leave you alone!"

He came home at night; it's almost four in the morning. Soon he'll have to go to work. He thinks about his boss, the cars, the spreadsheets. . . .

The human body stiffens.

Péter screams.

"*No!* It's not important! I don't have to go! It doesn't matter, going to work, it's . . . no!"

His speech begins to fail resembling any words; he's now just bending over the human body with open mouth and closed eyes, trembling, drooling, crying, he can't even breathe. He's bawling like a little boy.

"Muhsorrysorry muh I-uh, I'muhsoooo . . ."

His tears and drool hit the skin of the human body. It's muscles twitch under the skin. The human body is turning its head again. There's a deep groan coming from it.

"Yes."

He's still sobbing, but he wipes off his tears. He pulls a napkin from his pocket, blows his nose, then he throws the napkin away, somewhere in the corner of the room.

"Yes, I'm listening. I'm listening now."

The human body is calming down. It lays perfectly straight and still. So peaceful. So beautiful, incredibly beautiful. The skin on the non-existent face is becoming softer.

"Show it to me," Péter whispers. "Show me."

A small opening appears on the skin where the mouth should've been. This too resembles a mouth, but it's small, lipless, and there's only the void behind it.

"We're all children of the stars," Péter mumbles. "Nothing matters. I'm insignificant."

The mouth of the human body is growing wider, like a demented grin.

A small tongue appears in the corner of that mouth, slipping forth carefully from behind the faceless skull, then slides all the way out like a venomous snake, reaching the chin of the human body.

Péter is looking at these events hypnotized.

"You're going to tell me your secrets," he whispers.

There's a deep, guttural moaning coming out of the mouth of the human body.

Péter reaches out to touch its tongue. It wriggles, its saliva making his fingers numb.

He doesn't need any fingers, he doesn't need his hands, because. . . .

Darkness encompasses him immediately. He can only see the faint light of the distant stars. They tell the origin of the human body.

Show it to me. Péter's thoughts echo in the void. *Show it to me.*

The human body complies.

It's showing him places and times long forgotten by the cosmos, worlds created with unfathomable geometries, Promethean temples, scorching suns of dying planets, metallic graveyards, slimy waterfalls, human bodies praying to trees.

Péter Tabán is the happiest man in the universe.

In the following weeks, he's breaking contact with everyone.

At first he's telling petty lies, coming up with small excuses. He promises his mother to visit her the next month. He tells his boss and his girlfriend that he's ill.

And then he doesn't bother anymore.

A couple of days later, Krisztina breaks up with him.

Then he receives a call from his workplace that he's going to get fired.

He has no recollection of most of these events. He can remember his usual answer, though.

I don't care.

There are moments when he does actually care. He wakes pondering. He could end all this. He could leave the human body behind. He could break its spell on him. He could get it all together. It's not too late, is it?

And then he realizes.

Why would he do that?

The human body has shown him that this mortal life, all this ... this is nothing. Why would he return to it?

And still, these ponderings come in the rare waking moments of the trance, then disappear again. Usually when he's walking to the grocery store, collecting things for himself and the human body. If he'd walk long enough, he'd question everything. But not for long.

After all, the human body is there for him. There's nothing more important than this.

Now he's walking to the grocery store again. His phone rings. It's that woman from the mayor's office. He's confused.

"What kind of papers?" he asks.

"You didn't get them?"

It's like waking from a long dream. He squeezes the phone to his ears. In his other hand, he's holding a grocery bag. He looks around. He's heading home. Home to. . . .

What the hell am I doing here?

"Hello?"

The phone.

"Y-yeah. I guess I got them. I remember the . . . I remember the postman."

"This is great, Mr. Tabán, but I'd like you to send them back with your signature. Have you visited the land registry office?

Land registry.

Péter wets his lips.

Saliva.

"Not yet," he confesses.

A long, audible breath.

"Could you come in please sometime?"

"I don't think so," he whimpers.

"What?"

"I'll try . . . hey, can I ask you a question?"

"Yes."

"Can you tell me something about the former owner of the house? I mean what happened to her?"

"Mrs. Kántor? I don't know. Her son disappeared. He used to live with her. They were arguing all the time. I'm not sure. After his son left, the woman didn't show herself that much. She was old and weak, natural causes, they said. The son was declared missing, therefore the next person in the succession line was his brother and your . . ."

"Yeah, I know all that. I guess. I can understand it. What did you say, should I go to the office?"

"That would be great, we still need to sign some of the . . ."

"I'm coming then," Péter says.

He disconnects the call.

He's just standing there, holding the grocery bag.

No.

He should go home. There's no other way. The car keys are in the condo.

Hesitantly, he turns.

"Or I'll just go in this direction," he says. "As far as possible."

A family passes by. They all stare at him, then walk away more promptly.

"Ah yes, I'm talking to myself," he mumbles. "Also, I haven't had a shower in a couple of . . ."

He realizes.

"Holy shit, what the hell am I doing here?"

No. It has to stop.

Never again.

"Never again," he speaks out loud.

He doesn't remember how he got back to his bed. He doesn't even care.

He caresses the human body.

"It's all right. Everything's going to be fine."

The human body looks sloppier. The skin is greyish.

"What I give you is not enough. Far from it."

The tongue in its mouth is moving flaccidly around the lip-less crevice.

Time is shifting as the trance begins.

Somebody's been ringing the doorbell, and he can't tell for how long, nor when this is happening.

Péter Tabán struggles to get up. He feels the drowsiness of every human being who has ever lived in the world. He shambles to the front door.

He opens it.

It's that woman from the mayor's office. Not his boss, not his mother, not his ex-girlfriend.

It's just somebody whom he met only once.

It's all I'm worth.

The woman is ready to greet him but suddenly she grimaces, probably noticing his smell.

"Well what is it?" Péter groans.

"Do you remember me? I'm Bianka Sallai. From the mayor's office in Zalarév?"

"You're asking me?"

"I'm telling you."

Peter shrugs.

"You never told me your name, so whatever. I don't know."

Bianka Sallai sighs impatiently.

"We're going to sign these papers right now, and we're going to the notary immediately after that, and then to the land registry office. We have to close our quarterly paperwork in the office. We just cannot wait any longer. We don't usually go to other people's homes, so consider yourself lucky."

"Okay. You want to come in?"

"I intend to."

She then goes inside and sits at the table in the kitchen.

Péter realizes what kind of a mess has been building up in this condo. Dishes are piling up, the trashcan full.

The woman is chattering endlessly.

"We're dealing with multiple towns from the region, you see, paperwork is a nightmare, and uh . . . could you please open the windows? You should let in some fresh air more often."

Péter stares at the woman, observing her for the first time. She's a bit obese, probably because of her sedentary work. Her face is pretty, and her ring indicates that she's married. She made her hair wavy somehow, but she's not wearing any makeup.

Péter opens the window.

As they are signing the papers, a weird noise emerges from the bedroom, resembling the awful bleating of a dying goat.

They both stiffen.

"What was that?" Bianka asks.

"Nothing," Péter says.

And again. Even louder than before.

Péter closes his eyes.

No.

"Could I just . . ."

"*No!*" With all of his strength, Péter slams his palm on the table. The woman flinches. "It's none of your business!"

Bianka presses her lips together, pushing herself back in her chair.

"I'm sorry, but everything you're doing is very suspicious."

She stands up, starting to walk towards the bedroom.

Péter shakes his head, pacing in the kitchen.

"No, no, no," he mumbles. "It can't be. She can't see it!"

Bianka steps slowly in the direction of the bedroom.

She yells inside: "Hello? Is anybody there? I can help you! Please answer me!"

"No," Péter grumbles.

He glances at the countertop. At the bread knife. The woman disappears now in the bedroom.

A few seconds later she speaks out loud:

"Oh my dear God . . . good heavens . . ."

Péter doesn't feel like thinking too much, and time is shifting again. Now he's standing right behind the woman, grabbing her hair while she's screaming, holding her head back, exposing her neck right above the human body.

It's perfect, this is how it should be.

Just a small motion.

Blood covers everything.

Everything.

Worlds, universes.

Multiple orifices open on the skin of the human body, on its chest, on its shoulders, on its head, everywhere. And from every small hole, fast moving tongues emerge.

They lick.

They feast.

Péter lets go of the woman. He lowers the knife.

He just stares blankly at the bed, that forest of tongues. They are ravenously licking, lapping up all the blood.

"Oh yeah, Bianka Sallai," Péter says. "I guess you're right."

Not a single drop of blood goes wasted on the bed or the carpet. It just disappears. Drop by drop.

"You're right, you're right," Péter says. "We should go soon enough."

Before the bedroom disappears to reveal the most secret, hellish landscapes of the cosmos, and before the strongest trance begins, Péter Tabán says:

"We have to go to that house!"

The human body is screaming ghastly screeches in the backseat of the car. Like a pig getting ready to be slaughtered.

"I don't care!" Péter growls at it.

That's it! It's shown its true nature! The bastard!

"You won't fool me again! Never!"

He's flooring it, speeding through the night, on the highway through the woods of Zala county. Péter feels rapturous with wakefulness and clarity.

"I've wasted my life, and what have you given me? Nothing! It was all a lie! The whole thing, a big fucking lie!"

That misshapen abomination on the backseat is squirming vigorously on its swollen tentacle-like tongues, its shrieking only punctuated by spasming, retching sounds.

"Drown in your own filth!"

Soon they'll reach that house where it all began.

It's his after all. According to the papers at least, if that even matters. The house belongs to him now.

And so does the Gate.

The human body, or whatever it may be, is now completely turned inside out. It's full now, gorged. It doesn't need anything right now.

It doesn't need Péter Tabán.

Now it's the other way around.

Péter Tabán needs the creature.

He stops the car in front of the house, opens the door, and grabs the wallowing monstrosity by one of its tentacles, pulling it out of the car.

It screams with thousands of mouths, likely waking everybody in the village.

Péter drags the body to the front door, kicking it with all his strength, finally getting it inside.

"I've had enough of you!" he yells. "You're full now, aren't you? You can't get hold of me now, you have nothing! I've got you now! *Show me!*"

Dogs are barking in the neighborhood.

"*SHOW IT TO ME!*"

He grabs one of the tentacles forcefully, his fingers sinking into the slimy flesh, dragging the creature deeper into the house.

He closes the door behind him, and locks it. He wipes his hand on his clothes while flicking the light switches frantically in the house.

"Where is it, huh? Where is it? I will find it, you disgusting lying worm!"

He ransacks all the drawers, looks into the larder, then glimpses under the tables.

Finally, he steps into the kitchen, pulling out the drawers there too. Suddenly he stops. He stands there with an open mouth.

"Well, look at this."

He finds no utensils. Just alien, weird items. Small idols. Notebooks, papers.

And a book. Its title can be read clearly. *De Praestigiis Daemonum.* And another book, but its cover is battered; so he can only make out a word: *HSAN*, and a Roman numeral: V.

He grabs the books, throwing them one by one at the creature in the living room.

"What's this? Huh? And this? What are these? Who reads shit like this? *You think normal people have anything to do with this crap?*"

Normal people.

He can't remember what a normal person is anymore. His mind is clear now, so he can recollect more and more memories from the last days. New memories: he realizes he met multiple times with Krisztina, his boss, even his mother.

He remembers now what he has said to them. They weren't his own words.

He feels dizzy for a second and grabs the doorframe. He shambles to the living room. He gains new strength, standing before the creature. He yells at it:

"*You make me sick! You hear me? You fucking worm, you destroyed my life! I want some purpose now! SO WHERE IS IT?*"

The creature is whimpering powerlessly. Pathetic.

The dogs are barking outside. They seem irate.

"They're coming for me, right?" Péter says. "They're calling the police. I have to take responsibility."

He's rubbing his temple, then he glances around, frightened.

"I didn't even find you in the house!" he says. "I know where the Gate is! I know where you came from! *You can't even walk!*

He drags the creature into the small toolshed. Where he found it in the first place.

In the distance, he can hear the sirens, but he doesn't listen. Maybe it's just his imagination. He's still got time.

"Show me," he says. "Come on now. We're here, are we not?"

He touches its walls, searching for the light switch. As soon as he finds it, he flicks it.

But there's no light. At the flick of the switch, reality is no more.

The creature shows it to him.

The walls of the toolshed fly away in the void. On the stark black texture of space, billions and billions of small purple symbols appear, like stars.

"So this is the place," Péter nods in agreement.

He doesn't dare to admit that he understands nothing.

The creature suddenly rolls away from his feet, and with unexpected vigor, it runs away into the darkness on its wounded, fat tentacles.

"*Hey! HEY!*"

All those shining symbols are fading like the stars at the end of times.

Only darkness remains. Péter is frightened, he looks around puzzled, unsure what to do now.

There's a single source of light in the distance in this wide darkness.

It's calling for Péter Tabán.

"Yes," he whispers.

He starts running with his hands held before him.

But his running slows as soon as he notices that he's knee-deep in water.

Péter Tabán stands before the glimmering lotus, where he finally learns all the secrets of the universe.

He sees the birth of time itself, he witnesses the end of all things, he experiences all shades of entropy, he lives the lives of billions of people, he can see civilizations rising and falling.

He embraces time, space, their abhorrent gods, becoming one with them.

Becoming immortal and eternal.

He touches the lotus.

He can feel infinite happiness.

And then he realizes it's all but a fraction of a second.

A scam.

He'd open his eyes to see where he is, but he realizes that he doesn't have eyes anymore. Why would he need eyes after seeing everything the universe has to offer?

He'd stand up to flee straight away, but he stumbles: he doesn't have any legs anymore. Where would he go after travelling through the endlessness of the universe?

He'd raise his arms to push away that horrible lotus, but he already knows: he has no arms anymore. If he'd done everything man can do, why would he need them anymore?

He can feel himself falling to the floor of the tool shed, with a *thud*.

Blind, silent, without limbs.

He wants to scream.

But all he can project is a faint moan.

Péter Tabán is no more.

Police officers who yell in the distance searching for him have no idea where this murderous madman is.

One of them tells the others a lie:

"No, there's nothing here."

Minutes, hours, maybe even days go by.

Then he feels the touch of hands. He twitches.

Yes, he thinks. *Yes, you. I'm going to tell you my secrets.*
He is now being carried away. Somebody whispers to him:
"Easy. We can go now. Everything's going to be all right."
The human body relaxes with gratitude.

FRESH FACE
By Tarquin Ford

Some are legion, and some are single. An individual demon hopped on the eyes of cockroaches in the mulch of the flowerbeds surrounding the house on 1387 Glen Usher Drive, a two-story suburban home on a cul-de-sac. The mulch hid rot, mildew, and natural decomposition in the beds, where small lives ended in pain and despair.

The front door of the house opened, and a man came outside to stand in his yard and smoke a cigarette. His glassy blue eyes stared at the flat expanse of the night sky, starless because of the bright lights of a nearby automobile dealership. The end of the cigarette glowed. The demon leaped to the glow and luxuriated in the heat of the burning tobacco. The man flicked the cigarette away, but not before he inhaled the demon.

The man so recently possessed by the demon was Ronald Bright, also known as Ronny, a man who often annoyed others with his eternal cheerfulness. Ronny hiccupped a couple times after inhaling the demon and then padded inside to wash the odor of the cigarette from his hands to avoid offending his fastidious wife at bedtime.

To a demon, the mind of a man like Ronnie Bright appeared as a complex construction of ropes, lines, and tackle connected by knots, pulleys, and blocks, all stretched taut with optimism. The demon plucked at a rope tentatively and then began to jump up and down on some lines, attempting to work some slack into the system.

Ronny Bright looked toward his wife, Linda Bright, who sashayed about the living room in a pink nightgown, making a show of straightening knick-knacks. She had taken her contacts out because her eyes felt scratchy, so she wore her glasses.

The demon yanked on a rope in Ronny's mind, and the man said, "Linda, those glasses make your eyes look tiny." Linda, whose parents were both born in Korea, resented such remarks about her eyes and was shocked by her husband's racism. She threw a small pot containing a favorite African violet at his head. Ronny ducked, but the flower pot struck him on the cheek.

The force of the blow to Ronny's head almost knocked the demon off his perch on a line, but his claws held fast. With a fight in progress, the demon saw an opportunity to do some real harm. He flew from Ronny into Linda's mouth.

The mind of an angry woman was far more comfortable for the demon than the mind of an inherently cheerful man. It was smooth machinery bathed in hot oil to him, a race car and a hell of a ride. The demon shifted Linda into a higher gear.

Linda strode toward her husband and slapped him on the same cheek that had sustained the impact of the flower pot. The demon leaped from Linda and landed in Ronny's nose, where he slid inside until he caught hold of a length of rope. He pulled the rope with all his strength.

Ronny shouted, "Get away from me, bitch." He put his hands in front of his face to protect himself from Linda's blows. Her arms were a windmill with open palms, and then she slammed the heel of her hand against Ronny's throat.

The struts and halyards of Ronny's mind slammed into one another. Chains and lines tangled. A counterweight fell with a crash. Sensing that the entire structure would collapse in seconds, the demon leaped from Ronny to the floor, knowing his work in Ronny's mind was done.

Ronny made a fist, and Linda quickly put her arms around him to prevent him from beating her. The couple fell to the floor. Ronny bashed Linda's nose with his forehead, and it began to bleed. Linda called out, "You bastard." The demon picked up a bit of grit from the floor and leaped into the woman's ear. He threw the grit into the rapidly rotating machinery of Linda's rage.

Ronny broke free of Linda's grasp and tried to rise from the carpeted floor. Linda grappled his legs, and Ronny fell again and hit his head against the fireplace. A rope in Ronny snapped, and he lost consciousness.

Bleeding profusely from her nose, Linda rose from the floor. She felt light-headed, but the demon shifted her once again to a higher gear and pressed a turbocharging button on her dashboard.

She stopped tottering and steadied herself on the mantle over the fireplace.

Linda dragged her unconscious husband by the legs from the living room to the kitchen. With demon-enhanced strength, she pulled his limp form from the floor to a chair. She grabbed her portable electric mixer and used the cord to tie Ronny's neck to the rungs of the chair. Ronny awoke and began to choke. Next, she gathered the coffee maker, the toaster, and the blender and used the cords of those appliances to bind Ronny's hands and feet.

With Ronny tied firmly in the chair, Linda reached into a cabinet under the kitchen counter and took out an electric frying pan. She plugged the cord into an outlet and turned the dial to medium high.

Pulling a boning knife from the rack by the stove, she turned to her choking husband and carefully cut deeply around his face. After separating a portion of the skin from the muscle underneath in accordance with the instructions whispered to her by the demon, she pulled hard and the face peeled off. Her husband tried to scream but was choking so violently he could not. He thrashed in the chair, but the cords held fast.

Linda flicked a pat of butter in the pan and then dropped in the bloody face of her husband. The face sizzled in the pan. From the refrigerator, she took a link of sausage and put it into the mouth of the frying face. Next, she broke an egg into each of its eyes.

The demon now stood on the bridge of Linda's nose and inhaled the buttery aroma in ecstasy, for there is nothing like a fresh face. *Mmmmm.*

MEET THE WIFE
By Ken Goldman

"Life and death are one . . ."

— Kahlil Gibran, The Prophet

Five words served as Liam Weston's introduction to the shapely young woman seated at the bar. Although unable to hide a tinge of desperation in his voice, his being middle-aged had the advantage of his not caring a whole lot about proprieties. Drink in hand, expressionless and straightforward, he offered one hell of an ice breaker.

"Hello. My wife is dying."

The blonde didn't seem to know whether to laugh or just turn her back on another lounge creep. Instead, she sipped her wine and attempted a smile as if guys said this sort of thing to her all the time.

"Hello, yourself. And that has to be the shittiest pick-up line I've ever heard."

An honest response. This was good. Liam wanted honesty. It saved time.

"Pick-up lines are for kids. My wife *is* dying, and I need to get laid tonight. Simple as that, Miss-whoever-you-are. Looking at you, I'm thinking we're not talking about wining and dining here, so forgive my directness. Feel free to correct me if I'm wrong."

Leaning close from her stool the woman whispered, "Are you a cop? The law visits this little bistro, you know, and entrapment is their sport. A girl has to be careful."

Weston felt no need to whisper back. "I'm an accountant. CPA licensed to kill, agent Double-O-Zero."

The joke was lame, meant more to stoke himself than to impress the woman. She offered another smile, wider this time. "Then you're not wrong, Agent Zero. Screw the part about dining, but I *could* use another cabernet." She extended her hand and he took it. "Dee Dee, but the second Dee is for show. Call me Dee. Short for Diane. And you're . . .?"

". . . Going to order you one cabernet so I can get your pretty little ass out of here reasonably sober." Weston gulped his gin and tonic, clearly anxious to prove a man of his word. He pointed to the woman's glass for the bartender to refill, turned back to Dee. "I'm Liam . . ." Hesitating with the surname, he decided he had no reason to share that information. This episode would be one-and-done, your basic wham bam, assuming the Viagra kicked in and he remembered how to perform this little slam dance with a stranger.

"Just hold on for a moment here, Liam. Some information before we close this deal, if you don't mind. For one thing, I don't come cheap, if you'll pardon the expression." She added a whisper, "And I don't take Visa."

Weston understood that for many of the women seated inside this tavern it was a seller's market. Reaching for his money clip, he gave proof he was not a man who worried about starving. Studying the roll of bills, Dee smiled her best one yet.

"No exchange of cash right here, Agent Zero, thank you very much. That's for the amateurs. Are we talking about an hour or the whole night?"

"We're talking about as-long-as-it-takes. I'm forty, so you won't exactly be riding the mechanical bull. But I've no problem going with your all-night rates." Weston put down his drink and turned serious. "It's been difficult for me—Dee, is it? I mean with my wife's dying and all. I've been faithful for almost twenty years, excepting the occasional pay-for-play. It's important you know that."

The woman took a demure sip from her glass, her fingers toying with its stem. "Cancer?"

"Pancreatic. That's the worst kind, and not pretty to watch. She hasn't got long."

Another sip. "You love her, of course."

"My Melanie was a remarkable woman before the illness. But a man has needs, you know."

Dee's grin spread to her eyes. "Oh yes, I know all about a man's needs. More than you would believe, Liam." Her hand secretly slipped to Weston's thigh, the woman's long fingers inching upwards, stopping just short of home plate. Gulping the remainder of her cabernet, Dee's eyes met his. "Are you staying nearby, or would you prefer I provide the accommodations?"

No streetwalker-type back alley fellatio-on-the-fly from this girl, no needle tracks in every available vein, and she showed some class, even if it were minimal. Liam knew he had chosen well. "My home is maybe twenty minutes from where we're sitting. It's in Glenn Echoes."

"Your home? I'm thinking, a comfortable little cul-de-sac in a picket fenced suburb filled with soccer moms and designer dogs?" Dee's brow knitted. "That's not usually where married men prefer to take me, Liam. You've heard the expression about shitting where you eat?"

"Yes, I should explain that part. See, Melanie and I, we have this arrangement, something we decided together would work for both of us, considering our circumstances. She's a very understanding woman, my wife. In fact, tonight—it was her idea I come here."

Dee's knit brow returned. "More and more curious. Well, it's your dime, Agent Liam." She finished her cabernet and offered her hand. "Shall we?"

It was that easy.

The man's home did indeed have a picket fence, complete with the neatly trimmed lawn and a small rose garden. The flowers could have used more tending, but Liam's dying wife probably had no time for horticulture. Once inside the foyer Liam flicked on the lights, and Dee saw no evidence of children (or even a dog) having been in this home. Maybe the kids were grown, maybe the dog had died, but she doubted it. This place seemed built for two, the textbook cozy cottage of Mr. and Mrs. Dull. Dee would have felt no surprise had her host yelled out "Honey, I'm home!"

No photos adorned the mantel or walls, no cutesy poses of a younger and more virile Liam with the Missis rollicking on some beach during happier times. True, sometimes people were camera shy, but Dee doubted that possibility here. Some people just wanted the world to leave them the fuck alone.

None of that mattered. This was business, after all, and backstory was unnecessary. Helping Dee with her coat, Liam gestured to make herself comfortable on the couch. He didn't offer a drink, but this wasn't exactly a date. Saying nothing, Dee decided she would take her cue from him, although silence lingered for several minutes. His attempts at clever banter over, the man's increasing awkwardness was almost endearing. But mostly it seemed pitiful.

"My wife, she's upstairs. Melanie never leaves her bed anymore. Pancreatic cancer is painful and spreads fast once it's metastasized. She's pretty much incapacitated."

Dee got halfway to a compassionate smile. "My mother died of breast cancer. I always worried that I might have the same—well, we hadn't been speaking anyway." She stopped herself. Small talk like this hardly seemed conducive to the night's scheduled activity.

Liam's eyes fell on Dee's ample breasts, but his attitude toward them seemed more clinical than lascivious. "A young woman has to be careful. I assume you've had regular exams, haven't you?"

No barstool Lotharios had ever thought to bring up mammograms, most certainly not during business hours and, why would they? Dee shrugged it off, wanting to get the night's activities underway.

"I'm fine, Liam. My girls are healthy and ready to play. Here, you can see for yourself." She unbuttoned her silken top before her host could utter a word. At this particular gambit she was proficient, but she refused to go braless because that wasn't who she was, screw the accessories (or lack of them) of her profession. "Would you like to undress me yourself?" Sliding closer on the couch, Dee didn't really give her companion a choice. She knew some men needed a little push to get things started, and those that did proved pretty quick on the trigger. She expected within the hour she would be on her way with cab fare.

"No children at home?" Liam asked. "I mean, sometimes women in your profession—"

"Do I look the maternal type? Besides, babies smell funny."

Liam said nothing and slipped the silken garment and bra from Dee's chest, staring at her tits like a child seeing his first rainbow. He quickly shifted his eyes to the floor. Dee had to smile. "It's okay to look at my tits, Liam. You're paying for them. Speaking of which . . ."

"Oh, yes. Of course." He held out his billfold, and Dee plucked out several of the larger bills, stuffing them into her long-strapped handbag.

"So, where do we do this, Liam? Right here?"

The man took a moment, then shook his head, his eyes drifting to the stairwell. He sounded almost apologetic. "Not here. Up there."

As if on cue, a woman's voice called from the bedroom. More croak than speech, the sound sent an ice floe along Dee's spine.

"Lee-ammm . . . Leeeee-ammmm . . ."

The voice had the disquieting effect of fingernails scraping a chalkboard. Dee needed a moment to compose herself. "Your wife sounds strong for someone who—"

"Leeeeeeeeeee—aaaaaaaammmmmmmmm . . ."

"She wants me with her." Turning to Dee, he offered his hand. "This is difficult for me. I would like you to come, all right?"

"I'm not sure that's a good idea." Actually, Dee was sure the idea sucked. The request was ghoulish, and she could picture the bedroom scene if she went.

Hello, Mrs. Whoever-you-are. You're looking very . . . yes, you're looking . . . well, actually, you're looking shitty, lady, really shitty. Now, if you'll pardon me, your husband has paid for my services for the rest of tonight, so I imagine we'll start with the customary blowjob. . . .

Liam's hand remained extended ridiculously before he allowed it to drop. Did he really expect her to smile at his dying wife, then adjourn to another room to fuck her husband's eyeballs out?

"Please," he added.

Apparently, Liam did expect it. Dee was no stranger to things kinky, although tonight's request rose quickly on her list. As she had told the guy earlier, it was his dime, and what he had asked wasn't as bad as the request of the good-looking family man who, weeks earlier, had paid her to pee on him. Strange requests were an occupational hazard. Dee figured fuck it. She wriggled back into her top, leaving the bra on the floor while again telling herself business is business. Running both hands through her hair, she took a deep breath. Trailing Liam, together they climbed the stairs.

The bedroom door remained open, the room dark until Liam hit the switch. Stepping inside revealed a sight more sickening than Dee could have imagined. The wife—Melanie—lay immobile in bed like a corpse, which was what she might as well have been. In the dim light, she didn't appear very old, maybe she even was young. But the cancer had deteriorated her, and she had gone beyond pale to colorless. Bed covers littered the floor, and she appeared dwarfed by the large bed while completely exposed, except for the filthy nightgown she wore. Veins spidered in all directions like thick tributaries, and she seemed covered with leaking sores. She could have been one of those glass figures used in med schools where every vein and artery showed on the outside. Maybe she was pretty once, but no trace of beauty showed now. Worse than the sight of her was the smell. Her decayed flesh reeked like putrefying liver, the stench of dying flesh withering right off the bone. Dee half expected to see maggots dining on that flesh, and she forced herself not to gag.

"Jesus . . ." The word simply slipped out. "I'm sorry, Liam. I can't—" She turned to leave but felt the man's hand on her arm.

"I know how terrible my wife appears. I have to admit feeling the same revulsion myself. I'm sure you'll understand when I say it will seem a blessing when she dies. If there were any way I could be the one who instead—"

"I think I want to leave. Look, I'll give you your money back, okay?"

Liam reached into his billfold again, pulled out several large bills.

"Stay. Please."

Placing his hand on Dee's shoulder, Liam must have seen her as the proverbial hooker with a heart of gold. Sighing, she stuffed the bills into her panties. She noticed another bed, a small cot a short distance from the wife. This guy must have loved his woman enough to sleep close by (but not *too* close!), even while his loving Melanie slowly decomposed before his eyes. Dee sat on the cot, thinking how Melanie's reek seemed ripe enough for the woman to climb into her coffin right now.

"That smell . . ."

Liam's eyes remained on his wife. "You get used to the smell. After a while a person can adjust to almost anything." He turned to Dee. "That's why I'm going to ask you to do something for me. I wanted a woman tonight who might understand what would seem an unnatural request to others who lack your—"

"—My experience? I have my limits too, Liam, and I think I'm pushing the boundaries right now." Seeing her host's expression, she softened. "All right. Fine. Tell me what you want me to do."

"You have to do it with me here. Mellie wants to watch us fuck, and I promised."

Liam's expiring bride seemed one kinky lady, all right, but Dee felt committed now. She told herself she could handle the wafting stench if she had to, and if Liam's smelly Mellie wanted to gawk at her husband's pumping party from across the room, well, then. . . .

"Fine. Right here on your little cot in front of the little woman." Dee removed her top again. "Let's go . . ."

"No, not here." He pointed to the large bed in which his dying wife lay. *"There. With her."*

His words took a moment to register.

With her . . .

[. . . in his own wife's fucking death bed . . .]

Threesomes were common in Dee's business, and often she even enjoyed them for the sheer creativity of the experience. Whether the third party were male or female never mattered, but sharing a bed with a nearly cadaverous third, this was unchartered territory and she doubted her stomach could handle it.

Liam added, "I'll double whatever I gave you."

The dying woman shifted in her bed, the first sign of movement she had shown. She pointed a trembling bony finger at Dee.

"Your name . . . tell me . . . what is it . . . ?"

"What?"

". . . your name . . ."

Forcing herself to speak, Dee felt her mouth go dry.

"It's—well, it's actually—I'm Diane. Or Dee. Whatever."

The skeletal finger found the husband.

"Tell her . . . tell her you . . . tell Diane you . . . promised . . ."

Dee whispered to Liam, "Your wife isn't rational, you know. Her mind, it's probably gone."

"This is what Melanie wants. You being here—with me—this is for her. She *needs* this! I'll give you whatever you ask, okay?" He didn't wait for Dee's answer, instead led her to the bed where his wife lay. The stench of her rotted flesh kicked in worse than before.

Another heavy sigh, then Dee removed her skirt. She lay naked trying to avoid looking at the woman. Liam turned off the light before removing his clothes. The bed had ample space for the three, but Melanie sprawled on half of it, what was left of her. The husband climbed into the bed, forcing Dee to slide closer to his dying woman. Dee thanked Christ for the darkness. She could do this . . .

. . . but I'll keep my eyes closed, closed tight. That horrible stink, I'll manage that and I'll perform like I always do, and I'll be worth every penny, your best E-ticket ride ever, and you can take that to the bank, Mr. Liam. . . .

"Have you a condom?" she asked.

"No need."

"It'll cost more. Another fifteen hundred."

"I'll pay."

No rules of etiquette applied when a man purchased her for her services, and Liam wasted no time reaching for Dee's tits. His hands were sweaty, but she knew the guy was nervous. She recognized the familiar moan of the man's pleasure. It didn't take long.

Dee managed her own moan, well-rehearsed but believable. "I'll make you feel good," she whispered. Reaching for his manhood, she knew he needed a little work. "I'll make you feel very good, Liam. In fact, give me a minute and I'll make you feel fucking wonderful." Lowering her head to his thighs, she took him inside her mouth. Not allowing the man's dying wife to kill a decent hard-on, Dee put her hand and tongue to work. The man's erection sprang to life, and she squirmed closer, squeezed out of her panties and quickly squeezed him inside her. Liam spilled himself within seconds. He grunted and rolled off her.

Another fifteen hundred for under five minutes. Worth it at half the price....

"It's all right. Really, Liam. We can try again in a little—"

An icy hand stroked her shoulder. The chill took Dee out of the moment. Melanie's bony fingers were on her, all over her.

"Touch ... me ... too ..."

Liam whispered, "Do it. Touch her. Hold her."

Another fifteen hundred ... give you whatever you ask....

Dee said nothing, took a very deep breath, and reached tentatively to the woman, uncertain where her hand ought to go. She touched the withered arm lightly. Its wilting flesh felt like she had grabbed hold of a human bone. Two skeletal arms embraced her, pulled her close. The ragged nightgown opened, and the woman's naked cold flesh felt waxy and thin like a badly fitting garment. Dee couldn't tell whether the woman was moaning with pleasure or gasping for air.

"Ahhhhhh ..."

Dee's gag reflex kicked in, but she managed to shove it back inside. Somehow, Liam's wife gathered enough strength to pull her closer. For one awful moment she worried the woman's fragile bones might snap with the slightest pressure.

"You're—You're hurting me a little," Dee said, but this only caused Melanie to hold her more firmly. "Liam, she's hurting me ..."

The husband no longer lay alongside her. He stood motionless in the shadows, watching them. Dee tried to pull herself from Melanie's grip, but the spindly arms held fast. Now she felt concern for her own bones.

"... tighter ... yes ... tighter ..."

"I can't breathe! Liam. Tell her I can't . . ." Pressed against cold flesh Dee heard a liquid slurping sound, like water belching down a drain.

"I'm sorry, Dee. I'm really very sorry . . ."

(FUCK!)

The sensation felt almost like being swallowed, but no, not like that, more like. . . .

URP!

. . . that sound, as if. . . .

. . . downdowndown. . . .

. . . it felt more like parts of her. . . .

(Shit! Shit!)

. . . like her own guts were being absorbed!

URP!

". . . so sorry . . ."

When consciousness returned, Dee realized she remained in bed. She had no idea how much time had passed, but it was still dark and she felt weaker than she had ever felt in her entire life. Worse, she ached as if every cell in her body had declared war. Managing to raise her head, she saw Liam standing over her.

"You're awake. That's good."

She attempted to speak but managed only a sickening gargle. Liam shook his head. "Don't even try. You're very ill."

"Ughh—mmm . . . Ummmm"

Dee's face contorted. Her eyes opened wide. Liam must have known those eyes were searching for answers.

"These ritual things can be tricky. You see, I do love my wife very much, so much that I . . . well, I'm afraid I'm not very good at explaining this."

Another voice, a woman's, spoke from the other side of the bed. "Perhaps *I* can do that. Hello, Dee. I'm Mrs. Melanie Weston, Liam's wife. We've met, quite literally, in a matter of speaking."

The woman was standing at Dee's bedside. Dee stared at her until some focus returned. What she saw took a moment to comprehend.

Here stood a significantly healthier Melanie, maybe a good ten or fifteen years older than her own twenty-four and not quite as fresh faced and firm in body, but one hell of a lot better looking than the woman she had seen in the bed she herself now occupied.

"My Liam hates when I use these spells, but I really had no choice and—how do I put this? My husband's seed inside you was necessary. It's the stuff of life, you see."

Taking his wife's hand, Liam bent to speak close to Dee, who lay beneath a pile of filthy bed covers. He whispered, "I *am* sorry, you know, but we do what we must. I mislead you, I'm afraid. You see, my wife, she never was really dying."

Melanie added, "You can't die when you're already dead, Diane."

Through her agony, Dee forced herself to understand.

Liam had practically said it. He had wanted his wife to die, because. . . .

. . . because . . . ?

['My Liam hates when I use these spells . . .']

'These spells.'

And now Dee understood. There could be no other explanation.

Mrs. Melanie Weston had not been a living woman who was dying; she was a dead woman who required a healthy young woman (like her!) to return to life. That, and something else. . . .

'. . . my husband's seed . . . the stuff of life . . .'

Can't die when you're already dead. . . .

And here she was!

Melanie spoke low. "I suppose I should thank you for your sacrifice, Diane. Your cancer will be quick. A few days at most, I promise you that."

Dee pushed herself from her pillow, held her hand before her eyes. Her gnarled fingers could have belonged to someone already dead, while her chicken-skinned arms dripped crimson goo and seemed to barely contain enough rotted flesh to cover them. She could only imagine what had become of her face, but she really didn't want to know.

"*Unnnnnghhh . . . uggggggghhhh . . .*"

Had she been able, the sickly woman sprawled on the bed would have screamed her lungs out.

Different tavern, different part of town. Liam Weston knew he had to be careful.

His Melanie had enjoyed a brief three months' respite from death. But malignant cancer cells never played fair, and again she had faded fast. Those tumors were insidious little bastards, all right. Once inside you they made themselves at home, feasting away at your innards until nothing remained. Even with the most successful spells, cancer was still part of you. The black arts provided relief, of course, but they had their limits.

The young woman seated at the bar was raven-haired. Blonde, brunette, ginger, it didn't matter. She was beautiful, and Liam required little else, although that was more Melanie's wish than his. He loved his wife, and until his own time came, he always would love her.

The long-strapped pocketbook and the purple ass-tugging mini gave the woman on the barstool away. Here sat a working girl, no doubt about that, and her type often moved around a lot. This was good. As he watched her sip her wine, Liam could tell the woman was clearly on call. He gulped his drink and approached her.

"My wife is very beautiful," he said.

"How lucky for you," the woman answered and returned to her wine glass.

Liam had to smile.

"Yes, but—well, you see, I'm afraid she's dying . . ."

MADMAN ACROSS THE WATER
By James Harper

Greg Emmanuel hated Christmas music. He hated it down to his reptilian brain stem. And, while he knew this made him a pariah, he couldn't help it; he was, after all, a music lover.

Coming off the Beltway to the access road that led to the Lanham IT industrial complex, he fumed as one of the songs he hated most played in his consciousness, an incessant blather that threatened to drive him to a rooftop with a sniper scope to take out his frustration and anger on the idiots surrounding him who hummed these musical pieces of excrement during the season. He found it maddening that his XM was insufficient to locate a stronger, better tune to eradicate the melody now ensconced in his head.

The insipid nature of the lyrics, the banality of the music and the sheer dearth of variety near about drove him insane. This created an earworm hell for him during the last six weeks of every year when the inexorable parade of dreck launched itself into his brain to take up residence with the steadfast determination of an indefatigable wood tick.

He knew, deep down in his secret self, that he could not reveal this fact to any; the cries "Oh, how can you say that?" and "But you have no holiday spirit!" would swoop upon him like a winter eagle scooping up a late December river trout. So, his mere daily self never complained aloud, never griped at the drivel that came pumping out of the retail store PA, never showed his bottomless contempt. But he knew it, he felt it; he hated Christmas music.

Still brooding, he pulled into his private parking space at the lab, the remnants of the abominable "Winter Wonderland" echoing through his sleep-deprived and under-caffeinated mind, the steadfast earworm attached to his cerebellum as a blood leech might host on a feral boar. Thinking to break free of the odious tether before leaving his Lexus, he switched off his dictation handheld to listen to a piece by Borodin. Perhaps that might expunge the wretched ditty to a well-deserved bubblegum doom.

After several minutes of the March from *Prince Igor*, he exited, the erasure complete. He moved to cross the few short steps across the lot to the entrance of the EmmanuLabs front doors, then through the foyer to the hallway and entered the lobby. Jamika greeted him with her usual bright "Good morning, Dr. Emmanuel" before motioning for him to step closer to her.

"Your interview is in the Potomac Conference Room," she said, tilting the crown of her head in the direction of the room.

Fuck, he thought. He had forgotten all about the appointment. His preoccupation with the current research coupled with the brutality of the traffic during the holiday season, along with his natural neglect to check his email for calendar alerts, had all conspired to cause him to overlook the engagement.

Looking into the glass-walled conference room, he saw a woman, her back to him, scanning her phone. He turned to Jamika.

"Right," he said. "It was supposed to be 10:00; I'm only a half hour late."

Jamika frowned. "Doctor, it was scheduled for 9:30."

He stiffened. "Well, let her know I'll be in shortly." He marched toward his office, taking off his coat as he walked.

("Ase's Death" *Exquisite*)

Minutes later, he entered the Potomac with his broadest, most charming smile. He thanked his good sense to wear his best black Anderson & Sheppard that day, along with a hand-sewn silk tie. "Good morning," he said, stretching out his hand to hers. "Gregory Emmanuel."

"I'm very pleased to meet you, Dr. Emmanuel. I'm Jennifer Davis." She handed him her business card.

As he sat at the head of the conference room table, he glanced at the embossed card that read *Quantum Field*. Pocketing it, he said, "Sorry for the delay. I got caught up in some late developments."

She switched on her tablet, sliding it to a point midway between them. "I understand," she said. "Shall we get right to it?"

"By all means," he said, nodding. He held out his hands to indicate his openness and welcoming manner.

"All right." She consulted her pad of questions. She looked up at him; her eyes smiled a wry glint. "I ask the same first science question at every interview. It's off the record and strictly meant to break the ice."

He didn't know how to react. "Um, okay," he said.

"So jet packs: when do you think we'll have them?"

Jet packs? What? Her smile broadened, letting him know she intended the question as a joke. *She needs new material*, he thought. He indulged it.

"Well, as you well know this is completely out of my field. Engineering and rocket craft and the like. I know only of the fuel/weight problem that hasn't been cracked and that, even after half a century, no one's been able to push through it."

She jotted her notes. "Still, I'd say we could have them in next decade."

"Really? That's very interesting." She wrote another note.

Looking up from her pad, she said, "Doctor, it's no secret that your firm, the leader in the field of genetic regeneration, has come on some hard times of late with SEC filings and lawsuits for patent infringement. Do you think that your latest effort to prove dissipation-driven adaptation will put this in the past before the litigation can get a decent head of steam?" She looked up from her pad in anticipation.

She's pretty, he thought. Not in a classic way, not in a wow-I'd-like-to-bang-her way, but in a wholesome, Midwest upbringing sort of way.

"I have no doubt," he said with authority. "The nature of the important work we're doing will have a sustained lasting impact on medicine and health for generations. It's a completely new direction that will provide an unlimited number of subsequent breakthroughs for years."

"That makes it seem groundbreaking. Sounds like what you're doing is either epic or foolhardy based on the cryptic way you've framed those statements."

"I assure you, Ms. Davis, they are more along the former lines than the latter. We here at EmmanuLabs rarely engage in the less-than-extraordinary. The work we do has always been for the greater good; always to benefit mankind.

"What we are attempting to prove; what we've been calculating all these years, is the proof of a fundamental, hitherto unknown and undetected force in the universe: the hinted at, but largely unresearched, dark force."

"Dark force?"

"Yes, what my partner Dr. Gorton and I have theorized, indeed, what we've been devoting our lives toward, has been establishing a basis for a fifth force, a dark force, if you will, that lies beyond the four we know.

"You see, the four known forces of the universe: electromagnetism, gravity, the strong force that holds atoms together, and the weak force that governs radioactivity, all do very well at explaining the vast bulk of what we can account for in physics. But it's that one percent, the tiny fraction that remains unexplained that we think the dark force shows. We think that, once we prove the existence, once we can show results that verify quantitatively the dark force, we will have the answers to a myriad of mysteries that have plagued physicists and scientists for decades."

"Centuries even."

He looked at her then allowed another curt grin. "Yes, indeed. We feel that the search for dark matter and dark energy is insufficient. In fact, we think that without this research, without first establishing the existence of the dark force, the other two cannot be found. In addition, I believe its discovery will unlock a host of problems physicists, and indeed all of science, have grappled with for generations."

"Fascinating." She typed on her pad with a new alacrity. He thought he had won her over. She put her finger to her lip, then asked, "But surely, Dr. Emmanuel, the research you're conducting can't be done in a vacuum. How is it that no papers have come out of this? Why haven't we seen documentation on the work you've done to show the foundation of this project?"

"That, too, is part of the plan. We expect that, in the next few days, perhaps within the week, we will be releasing all the work in one fell swoop." He allowed an internal laugh at the term.

"So, while the search for dark matter and dark energy is consuming the scientific community now, do you think that your research will crack the code, so to speak, to help open the door to the other efforts?"

"Indeed."

"But, doctor, I'm still not getting why all the secrecy. I don't understand why you've kept it under wraps for as long as you have."

"Well, part of the reason, you understand, has come out of previous experience, particularly those witnessed by Dr. Gorton." He let the statement stand as it was. If Davis had done her homework she would know about the embarrassing debacle Gorton had suffered at his last position.

"So help me connect the dots for my readers. What's the link between the dark force and your goal? By that I mean, how does this fit into health research? And, in explaining that, how does one connect it to the funding you receive?"

"Good question." He shifted in the leather-bound chair. "We believe that, when we can find the evidence—even peripherally—of the dark force, it will affect all of science going forward." He leaned toward her for effect. "Think about it, Ms. Davis, were you to prove the existence of gravity, would that not change the entire landscape of the discipline of science?"

Davis returned his look. Then she went to her next question. He lowered his estimation of her intelligence. She just didn't get it, he shrugged. She, along with the vast majority of the human race, didn't comprehend the monumental impact his work would have. With an ironic mental smile, he realized that even his partners had no clue, really.

"Ah, I think I understand," she said. The balance of her questions delved into the boring, almost preposterous nature of obtaining funding and meeting government standards and regulations. He answered with politeness while avoiding yawning at the dullness of it all. He gave himself a figurative pat on the back.

Half an hour later, she stood, saying, "Thank you for your time today, doctor. I think I have quite a bit to work with here."

He allowed himself a broader smile. "You're quite welcome, Ms. Davis. You will be sending me a tear sheet, yes?"

She blinked then said, "Yes. You'll be getting a copy of the file I submit."

"Very good." He left the Potomac, reaching into his pocket for his phone as he crossed the threshold.

("O Fortuna" *Brilliant*)

As he pulled it out, his phone blasted out "Aragonaise." It was Gorton.

"I'm ready for our meeting." When Emmanuel said nothing, he added, "You're late."

"I had an interview. You'll be pleased; it was with *Quantum Field*."

"Oh, really?"

"Yes, I'll tell you all about it when I see you." Hanging up, he marched through the lobby past Jamika to his car outside. By arrangement, Gorton kept his lab separate from Emmanuel's, at a facility lying on the other side of the lake that served as a decorative hub in the Lanham Maryland industrial development EmmanuLabs occupied. While it took an extra fifteen minutes for them to meet whenever they needed to get together face-to-face, Emmanuel considered that inconvenience a small price to pay for the secrecy the distance offered.

He dialed into a late Mozart symphony as he drove to Gorton's lab. As he steered the Lexus around the tree-lined road surrounding the lake, listening to the majestic orchestrations that only a certifiable genius could create, he thought about his partner then cringed at the necessity of their deal. His disgust for Gorton was only matched by his contempt for his sanity. There was no doubt about it, Emmanuel thought, Neville Gorton was one crazy fuck. Unlucky for Emmanuel that Gorton's brilliance in the field of biophysics was unmatched.

A quarter hour later, he entered the lab. He walked straight to Gorton's shop.

He shook his head as he always did when he saw Gorton. The man had no taste in fashion or sense of style whatsoever. He wore a Promo Uomo that hung on him as pajamas might, the cheap fabric serving to make him seem out of place with the sophistication an advanced laboratory demanded. Its admiral blue color, coupled with his short haircut and wildly out-of-date quarter-inch wide moustache, gave him the appearance of a fugitive from a 60s spy television show and not one that did well in the ratings. A mere five-foot-five, he would never confuse anyone for a formidable specimen, but, one would think that he could at least dress well.

"Neville, good morning," he said.

Gorton turned to see that he had entered then returned to his task. He seemed intent on studying the graphs his computer screen displayed. "Oh, hello, Greg. How are you?"

"What does the current analysis indicate?"

"Well, we're making the progress we'd hoped for. It looks as though the math has been borne out. If everything else goes forward as swimmingly as these results, we should achieve actualization in the next few hours."

"You must be kidding," Emmanuel couldn't believe it: too good to be true.

"No, have a look at the data," he took a step back away from his bench. "Structural organization is there, once we begin the process we've outlined, it'll only be a matter of time—and, I think short time—before we get the results we're looking for."

Emmanuel took a step to look at the screen. He clicked through the graphs and spread sheets to examine the material; leaning over to study the results. At least, on the surface, it looked as though Gorton was correct. The results indicated that they were not only on the right path, they had been dead-on correct from the start. These findings would bear out his theories and, although Neville had no idea, augment the secret research he had been conducting on the side, without Gorton's knowledge. A sudden irrational fear gripped his heart as he felt the urgent, eager need to leave Neville to pursue that hidden agenda.

Stepping away from the terminal, he said, "This is excellent. Very good. Send this to me immediately." He bent over the monitor as he typed for a few minutes. "But in the meantime, let's get to it, shall we?"

Gorton blinked. "What?"

Emmanuel sighed. "Let's conduct the trial."

"Now?"

"Of course."

"It—it's too early. I've only just confirmed the research."

Emmanuel shifted his weight from one foot to the other. He expected this resistance. His timetable, however, needed acceleration, especially if he wanted to meet Lambert's schedule.

"Nonsense. The work's good. I've examined it myself. Put it together. Given that we've been making progress by building the equipment all along, it shouldn't take more than an hour or two, right?"

Gorton sputtered and coughed. Typical. "I—I think more like a half day."

"Fine. Get it done. Let me know when the test is ready." He walked out of Gorton's lab to call Lambert from the lawn out back.

He sent a FaceTime request as his shoes touched the soft grass behind Gorton's building. From here, across the lake, he could just see the EmmanuLabs building, its sharp gables and multi-colored brick edifice a source of pride to his sense of architectural taste. Standing on the back lawn, the ground sloping downward and away from him toward the edge of the lake, he admired the structure of the lab, even as he congratulated himself on the good sense to build it by the water. No other physics lab that he knew of had a grander location.

His phone chimed. "Hello, Peter."

"What do you have for me?" Emmanuel let the rudeness stand. As always, he tolerated Lambert's impoliteness, knowing that the man, steeped as he was in the application of theoretical physics, was incapable of mastering the art of tact or diplomacy.

"We have the research completed."

Lambert raised an eyebrow. "Really?" He moved offscreen a moment. Emmanuel grimaced at seeing the movement, his irritation at the ubiquitous act ameliorated by the convenience of the communication. Lambert said, "This is far ahead of schedule."

"Not really. I'm sure you remember me telling you that we could easily meet the early ends of our date estimates."

"Yes, yes," Lambert said, quickly moving onto other, less taxing matters. "When can I have the calculations?"

Looking down at his phone, Emmanuel sent the email as he spoke. "I'm sending them to you now. We'll be conducting the trial immediately. This afternoon, in fact."

"This afternoon," Lambert said, the tone in his voice already disinterested, his focus on studying the data. "I'm sure you know what you're doing."

Emmanuel congratulated himself for not responding with "Of course I know what I'm doing." Instead, he stuck to the point of the call. "Get back to me as soon as possible with your results. I want to act on this tonight."

"Tonight? Yeah, no. I don't think that's going to happen."

"It will." He smiled as he headed into a softer direction. "I know you can do it, Peter. Get me the calcs by eight, then I can use the data this evening."

Lambert said nothing. He loomed over Emmanuel's phone like an image in a carny funhouse mirror, his face warped and distorted. "I'll do the best I can."

"I know you will." He disconnected.

("Appalachian Spring" *Invigorating*)

Hours later, after Gorton had put together the equipment to move forward with the trial, Emmanuel sat in the lab, drumming his fingers on the metal table to his side.

At the center of the arena-sized building stood a cube constructed of titanium and two-foot thick glass, its configuration and size resembling the sort of transportation device one might see in a horror movie where atoms of humans and insects get exchanged in the kind of things-go-horribly-wrong plot so popular with screenwriters and filmgoers. Cables as thick as his arm and pipes wider than his thigh protruded from the block as steam rose from vents from all sides, the liquid nitrogen used to cool the chamber that housed the particles coalesced with the air in the lab.

This portion of Gorton's lab, about the size of a professional basketball gymnasium, was restricted to techs and those working on the project at hand. Only that handful knew the true purpose of the experiment: to prove the existence of the dark force.

Emmanuel felt his pride swell as the squad of scientists bustled around him throughout the room. He stood at the threshold of perhaps the greatest breakthrough since Penzias and Wilson. He grinned at the thought of receiving a call from Stockholm.

"We're ready now, Dr. Emmanuel," a tech said. He stood by where Emmanuel sat. Emmanuel tried to recall his name. Was it Oliver? Oscar?

Standing, Emmanuel said, "Very well. Proceed."

"Osman?" Gorton called. The tech turned toward him. Gorton said, "I want you to finalize the checklist. Then proceed in twenty minutes."

"Right." He scurried over to the far side of the lab to run the programs as instructed.

Gorton approached Emmanuel. "Well, Greg, this is it. I think we're about to see the fruition of that plan we started all those years ago."

Emmanuel thought only Gorton could ruin a moment like this with base sentimentality but then, thinking it further, he decided that most people would probably feel that same need to make a time like this sanctimonious. Emmanuel hated that kind of sensibility, he considered it soft thinking.

"We're ready to proceed," Osman announced.

Gorton said, "Very well." He motioned for Emmanuel to join him behind the four-foot glass window in the next room. There, they could witness the operation in safety. Gorton leaned toward the PA mic to say, "Proceed when you're ready."

The techs went about their assigned tasks, each following the protocols Emmanuel and Gorton had innovated. Emmanuel watched as the team went through the established guidelines with care. He smiled inside; it was not every day that one opens the door to a new science.

Osman stood at the main console in the lab. As the project manager, his function was to scan the area for the emergence of new particles and the patterns of force as their appearance would prove the data. While some argument had gone forward on the safety of such a role, in the end, it was decided—by Emmanuel—the need surmounted the unproven low risk.

Osman signaled the tech who responded with starting the centrifuge. A low hum filled the room as the particle beams came to life. Within minutes the hum grew to a roar, the floor vibrating as the machine awoke. Osman pressed the keys on his keyboard then looked to where Emmanuel and Gorton stood.

"We should see results in the next few moments," Gorton said.

As if on cue, a field emerged. While Emmanuel watched on his monitor, the data showed a region of space move out of the centrifuge, growing into the lab where the console stood. Emmanuel looked to Gorton; this was not the result they expected.

"Neville—"

"I know." He leaned toward the mic again. "William, get out of there."

Osman went to move but could not. For some reason, he could not make his feet work; they remained stuck to the lab floor. The field grew. It looked like a dark cloud of empty matter, a pocket of negative energy that spread as smoke might consume an atmosphere. Out of the console and into the room, Emmanuel could see the field emerge from the centrifuge, its black space seeping out of the mechanism and spreading throughout the lab. It touched Osman.

Osman stood frozen as the field encompassed him. His face alarmed at the peril, his feet remained glued to the floor of the lab. Then he screamed in pain, Emmanuel had never heard such a cry, a bellow so blood-curdling, his own bowels loosened as he listened to it. Osman flayed his hands above his head in helplessness, his lower limbs unable to move. He opened his mouth wide, his jaw looking as if it dislocated to allow a leering gape. His tongue protruded like a vibrating node of flesh. Then his teeth slammed together cutting his tongue it into pieces.

Emmanuel watched as Osman's feet, then his legs, began to change, to transmute into a substance that somehow looked like stone and water. In some fantastic manner, Osman's matter, the atomic structure of his being, was altering into another form altogether different than anything known.

The change in his body marched upward, from his knees, up his thighs, to the core of his body. As Osman screamed over and over, the transformation progressed, making his appearance unimaginable: a rock in one second, fluid another.

Then his whole form went up in a blaze of red. In what seemed as though he had turned to plasma, Osman became a pillar of liquid fire, as if a solar burst were conducting with the matter made of an ocean current. Emmanuel shook his head in disbelief, either his senses had deserted him or those same senses had no capacity to comprehend the events unfolding before him.

Then Osman turned inside out.

Slowly, without pause, the internal organs within his body exuded through his skin which cracked and split to accommodate the blood-splattering eruption. Emmanuel saw Osman's guts, his liver and intestines protrude then explode from his form, the walls painted with the red gore of Osman's everted body.

At least the screaming has stopped, Emmanuel thought.

Osman's structure, in parts frozen as ice, in others burning and smoking, dispersed about the lab in an explosion that rocked the foundations of the building. For long moments, the walls trembled and the ceiling collapsed, dropping concrete and plaster to the floor as the structure quaked. Emmanuel and Gorton held on to the ledge of the window as it too shuddered against the earthquake that shook the lab building.

Gorton yelled over the noise of the building tearing itself apart. "Shut it down!" he cried, "Shut it down!"

A tech hurried to the console, standing over it in bewilderment. Looking from one monitor to the next, Emmanuel watched as he saw his goal. Seconds after typing into the keyboard, the tech stood to look over in Gorton's direction.

But the room continued to shake. Osman, now a mere smear of organic material that changed back and forth from water to fire then to stone and mist, had spread throughout the lab in a thin coating of matter, the color shifting from red to black to green then brown.

Emmanuel stared at the carnage even as the quaking slowed. The thing that Osman had become was still alive. It still held consciousness, its eyes showing intelligence and awareness, even if an awareness couched in despair. The head that had grown to the size and shape of a watermelon moved about in anguish as the new being that was Osman looked from one person to the next in an effort to seek an end to its suffering. The plaintive expression on what had become his face at once pathetic and horrible.

Then, in an instant, it melted. The whole of Osman's form disintegrated into a pewter-colored pool of loathsome fluid that smelled of harsh chemicals and dead matter. Seconds later, it steamed into a billow of noxious vapor that burst into the room like a thundercloud, thrusting toward the ceiling then roiling through the space, the air near toxic with its stench.

A tech reached for the exhaust vent. Switching it open, the vapor that once was Osman was sucked out of the lab, the cloud siphoned into the outside.

Minutes later, as the last of the field and cloud exhausted into the atmosphere outside, Emmanuel took a deep breath. *At least that was over*, he thought. Gorton went about the effort to check on the techs, making sure no one else had been hurt, but, more importantly, determining that no one could wage a lawsuit as a result of what happened to Osman. Emmanuel commended himself on hiring only lab techs with little or no family, and all singles, none with spouses. Always thinking ahead.

He leaned over the computer terminal before him to type. He sent the raw data from the experiment to his personal mainframe across the lake. There, he'd study the information to ascertain the error that caused Osman's transmutation, although, he felt he already knew.

He spoke into the mic, "Neville, I'm going back to my lab." Gorton, intent on the mop up, merely gestured at the announcement, not even deigning to look up or acknowledge. Shrugging and with a wave of his hand that would do Elizabeth II proud, he turned to walk out of Gorton's lab.

("Also Sprach Zarathustra" *Stirring*)

As he stalked the hallway to his office, he slowed his pace so as not to appear too anxious. *No need to tip my hand*, he thought. Still, it took every mental restraint he could muster to slow his speed.

Sitting at his large oak desk, he switched on then typed his passwords. As the system woke, he considered indulging in a whiskey to celebrate. This was, after all, the ultimate victory he had sought for the past five years. He deferred. Alcohol breathe, even during the Christmas holiday season, would seem very bad form indeed to the underlings in the lab.

He spent another three hours reviewing the data from the lab experiment before he called Lambert. His thoughts returned to the bottle of Glenlivet in his drawer as he waited for the chemist to pick up. Lambert's voicemail came on the line.

After listening to it, he said, "I need you to call me now. I'm sending you Gorton's results; they're exactly what we were looking for, in line with what we anticipated. You know what this means. So, get on the process immediately, using what I'm sending you along with the other data. I want the device finalized immediately. I'll be over there in an hour."

He pressed the red button on his phone to lean back in his armchair. Staring at the corner of his ceiling, he thought about where they were. It seemed too good to be true. They had achieved all the results they had projected, all the numbers had fallen into place with the calculations to an extraordinary degree, unprecedented in his career.

Lambert's research, coupled with Gorton's would unlock human immortality by proving pre-biotic self-replication. Gregory Emmanuel had just verified Jeremy England's theories.

He went for the Glenlivet.

("The Blue Danube" *Sublime*)

That evening when he went to Lambert's lab, he again pushed the scan button on his XM receiver, hunting for a tune that would wipe out the awful "Rudolph" that ran through his centermost thoughts. Unable to find even the most rudimentary decent strain, his curses echoed within the car's brocade interior.

As he stormed toward the concrete building that housed Lambert's facility, he still muttered curses as the tune played on an unending loop. He realized that, at this point, it was hopeless: until and unless a stronger song played or his mind became absorbed by more attention-grabbing information, he was lost to the clutches of the reindeer song.

After passing through Lambert's laborious security procedures, Emmanuel let himself into the lab. There, he went to the device they had constructed together, a console roughly the size of two household freezers. It was capable of converting the energy Gorton had tapped into earlier that day. The data Emmanuel had sent earlier, coupled with the swath of material Gorton collected, would allow Emmanuel to prove his real, secret theory, the one he had wanted to prove all along, the one that he kept from all the others: that life was immortal, that death could be prevented when dissipation-driven adaptation self-organization was employed.

In Lambert's lab, he went straight to the worktable to examine the device Lambert had fabricated. A compact generator connected to a laptop, it would project the field that killed Osman into the room without the horrid results that led to the tech's tragic end. Emmanuel had no intention of duplicating that. He switched the device on as he allowed a smile to cross his lips. *This will change everything*, he thought.

So thinking, he turned on the amplifying device that would change his life seventy seconds later. The field would give him immortality. Using the dark force and reducing its essence into such a field, Emmanuel had unlocked the mechanism that causes death. He had broken through the barrier that makes all living things die.

A pathetic shamble of his former self, Gregory Emmanuel now looked in the mirror to witness what he had become. The skin across his body had peeled from the muscle; in some cases from the bone itself as the tissue had rotted away leaving portions of bone poking through to the surface at his elbow, hip, and cheek. His scalp, too, had decayed to the point that only wisps of his fine head of good brown hair remained, the rest gone.

The skin that did remain had coarsened and had become brittle like the parchment of the Dead Sea Scrolls, its color as dark and chestnut as those ancient treasures. The orbits of his eye sockets had grown more pronounced as the skin around them had receded, making his eyes look as though nothing held them in his skull, the whole of their structure visible from nearly the optic nerve to the pupil. Blinking had become a remote memory. The bones of his fingers, especially the ends, protruded through the nails and tips so that, in their stead, white points of calcium extended out of his hands.

Walking awkwardly and robotically, his gait had taken the aspect of a cartoon stick figure whose ability to locomote suffered from the lack of any fluidity in musculoskeletal motion. He looked as though every step he took would cause him to collapse in a pile of cascading bones and limbs.

And he stank. The smell that rose from him made even him nauseous, the foul, fetid odor of decomp laid on and around him as the stench of a carcass lying in the sun for days, the putridity of his body an all-consuming rank. What was left of his face had become a visage of horror straight out of a SFX artist's portfolio, the bone showing and his lips having rotted to reveal teeth behind what was once his winning smile, the mark of a successful and famous American entrepreneur.

He knew now that his calculations were wrong, that his research had not, in fact, unlocked the mechanism that caused death. He had merely lengthened the time death took to come about, to take over the essence of the living. He had become a living corpse, a man whose death lingered in its execution.

Karma, he thought, *karma had its way with everyone.* It was something he should have recognized during his youth in Camden County.

As he sat dying, as he thought his last thought in the pain of ultimate decomposition, Jose Feliciano's "Feliz Navidad" sprang into his mind.

MANTIS
By Kourtnea Hogan

The pink carpet was sickly and stained from years of god-only-knew-what kind of liquids. Though luxury wasn't exactly what people were paying for when they checked into Carpenter Motel. The dingy lighting and dark wallpaper made it seem like the set of a B horror movie and Jacob was shocked that the woman had agreed to come with him in the first place.

He'd bought her a drink and rubbed against her under the pulsating lights in the club, running his mouth along her neck. When he'd asked if she'd wanted to leave she'd merely moved towards the door, barely acknowledging that he was following her. When he'd asked if she had come with friends she had raised a perfectly shaped eyebrow and given him a half smile. When he'd asked her name, she shook her head and whispered in his ear, "It's better if you don't."

He'd told her that he had come alone and she had smiled, looking at him from beneath long lashes.

The motel was out of the way and he'd worried that she had thought something was wrong as they drove down old country roads to reach it.

"I'm not afraid of you," she had said with no trace of humor. Jacob hadn't liked the way she answered, but he liked her, or the way she looked, enough that it didn't matter.

"Is that so?" he'd asked as he bent over to gently bite her neck at a stoplight, trying to lighten the mood. She let his hands wander over her body and laughed, the vibrations tickling his lips.

She grabbed his face, her fingers wrapping tightly around his hair, and whispered in his ear, "You're the one who should be scared. Green." Then she bit his earlobe and released his face.

He was confused by the last word until there was a loud honk from behind him. Blushing, he slammed down on the gas, the car jerking forward.

She opened the door before the car had even stopped, wheels still crunching gravel.

"I've been here before; I'll get us a room." He watched her walk to the office, admiring the long spiral of blonde hair that bounced down her back, hips swaying slowly as though she knew he was watching.

Once he could no longer see her he ripped open the glove compartment, throwing papers on the passenger side seat in search of a condom. He'd heard somewhere that you shouldn't keep them in your wallet, and the idea of the woman being here enough times to be able to get a room so easily both excited and frightened him.

He turned to see her standing beneath the vacancy sign, red light caressing her pale skin. She held up a finger, key ring dangling from the tip. He shoved the papers back into the glove box and met her halfway.

She must have noticed the apprehensive look on his face, and lightly slid her delicate fingers down his torso and to his beltline to reassure him. She smiled and bit her bottom lip and his excitement overrode his fear.

She led him to the last room on the first floor, shooting coy looks over her shoulder to make sure that he was still following. And he was. How could he not? He ran a hand across her ass, the nearly white hair tickling the top of his hand. He reached his hand forward, pressing himself against her as he followed her hip bone down between her legs. She stiffened as she put the key in the hole and his hand quickly rose to her stomach.

"Eager?" she asked as she turned the knob. He blushed and released her entirely, his mind occupied with semi-serious thoughts of just going back to his car and more serious thoughts of punishing her for embarrassing him.

But the door had opened and she had disappeared inside, not bothering to turn on the lights, and he'd come too far not to follow. He turned on the lights, taking in the unappealing layout with the very appealing woman lying on the bed in the middle of the room. It was shaped like a heart and he bit his lip so he wouldn't laugh, his hands shaking slightly as he took off his jacket.

She sat up suddenly, fingers reaching around his belt, pulling him closer to her. He laughed nervously at the unexpected touch and nearly tripped. She offered a half smile, only one dimple this time, and began to unbutton his pants.

"I, uh . . . do you have a condom?"

"Don't worry about that," she said, hands still working on his belt.

"Are you sure?" Thoughts of her with other men in this same situation flooded his mind.

"The things you are worried about are things you don't have to worry about with me," she said, her tone calm, but her voice thick and insatiable. Still, he pulled back slightly. "Don't you want me?" she asked, big blue eyes blinking at him.

He pushed her back onto the bed, hands gripping her hips roughly. "Take off your clothes," he growled in her ear, all nervous energy morphing into confidence. He kissed and bit her neck. He became nearly intoxicated with the sweet floral smell that he couldn't believe he hadn't notice sooner. It made his need for her deeper, no matter how cold she acted, and he reached his hand under the tight material of her deep purple dress.

She returned his kisses, her tongue reaching deep into his mouth, before she sat up and pushed him back. "Undress me."

He shoved his pants down and ripped off his shirt, throwing it across the room before kneeling on the bed beside her. She turned around slowly, moving her hair to the side, back perfectly erect. He struggled with the zipper and she rubbed his thigh lightly.

"No rush."

He blushed again, having vacant thoughts about choking her, as he carefully pulled the zipper down the rest of the way, revealing a beautiful pale back. He pushed it off her arms, kissing her shoulders before she pulled away. She lay on her back, hips slightly elevated. He struggled slightly to pull it down as it clung to her hips and thighs. He threw the dress on the floor and ran his fingers across her naked torso and legs, wondering if he'd ever felt such warm skin before.

He climbed on top of her, the floral smell nearly suffocating him, forcing its way into his mouth and nose. He buried his face into her hand, pulling it free from its ponytail. She groaned and moved below him, hands pushing on his shoulder, pushing him down.

"Slowly. Use your hands," she whispered, voice husky. He didn't need to be told twice, finally warming to her cold demeanor and demanding tone. He kissed down her stomach and legs, letting his hands run the opposite way.

She tensed at his touch and closed her eyes, head rolling back into the pillows. He took it as a good sign and continued, letting his free hand run up her stomach and to her breasts, leaning his body into hers. The smell was even thicker now, but it was so pleasantly mixed with her noises and it made him feel lightheaded in the best way.

Her noises were getting higher and he pushed in deeper, hoping that he could soon be inside of her when he heard a thick popping noise. He ignored it, assuming that he'd popped her legs or back and refused to embarrass her by drawing attention to it as she had done to him.

She gasped and threw her head back and he put his hand on her stomach, applying extra pressure. The smell was so strong now that he was sure he would pass out, but he couldn't stop, even as he realized that he wasn't hard anymore and that his hand was soaked. He looked down and saw a small pool of blood forming below her.

"Oh," he said dazedly, hands working without him. "Are you okay?" he asked, thinking about stopping but unable to do so.

Her noises got higher, inhuman, and the popping noises flooded the room. He willed his hand to lift from her stomach and she slammed it back down, his hands leaving a red mark on her pale skin. Or was it from him? He watched the red spread across her torso, a deep purple line running straight down her middle. He followed the line up her throat, his eyes struggling to focus.

He thought he saw her bottom lip begin to split as the noises grew sharper, blood dripping lazily from the sides of her mouth, falling into her hair. He thought about pulling away and making sure she was okay but he felt himself falling into her instead.

He looked down to see his hand going deeper into her as her body began to split in two. He wanted to gasp and pull back, wanted to ask her what drugs she had given him but the smell was making him weak, invading his senses and destroying his willpower.

He watched the hand that had rested on her stomach disappear inside her with a sickening wet noise. He groaned, watching her body convulse beneath him, unable to tell where she ended and he began. He sank lower into her, coming closer to the slit in her middle.

He tried to pull back but her hands rose to his head, fingers running lovingly through his hair. She pulled him closer to her, grotesque face rising to meet his, wetting his lips with blood.

He felt an immense pressure on his arms and looked down to see the wound closing like a sinister mouth, teeth made from jagged bits of bone serrating his skin. He pulled back as hard as he could, barely rocking backward. His hands snapped off at the wrist, bloody spraying across her, soaking her and the bed.

He fell forward, wanting to cry out, unable to understand why he couldn't feel the pain. She pulled him into her, spreading her legs and running her fingers along his spine. He could barely feel his skin against hers, could barely feel her body reopening. But he could feel it and he tried to push himself up, bone digging into the bed. Her arms and legs wrapped around him tighter and the smell got stronger, canceling out the copper smell of blood.

A wet sound issued from her mouth as spit and blood hit his face. Distorted cooing noises as she focused his eyes on hers, running her hands lovingly through his hair. He could feel the heinous mouth of her body open wide around his and she seemed to laugh as she lowered his face to hers, their bodies melding.

CICADA
By Carl R. Jennings

First of all, I want you to know that I'm not crazy. I need you to believe me or this entire conversation will be pointless. There was a time that, were I in your position, I would believe that the person sitting across from me was, just by that statement alone. But I say this now in perfect confidence of my own sanity.

Scratch, scratch.

For several months now I have been hoping to come upon a person who would believe me. The story of how I came to be in this position, and begging a complete stranger to listen to me, is a horrifying prospect but, thankfully, it will not take long. I won't steal any more of your time than is necessary.

I suppose I want to talk about it so badly because, if I have just one person believing me, then maybe I can believe myself. I was no different than you once, not this filthy, scarred creature that you see sitting before you: finely dressed, well-kept, college educated, with a comfortable job, and all the world working in my favor. I believed, in my arrogance, that I could live like that forever, perhaps get married and have children, start a family. The normal things that a person with a mundane life wishes for. Mundanity is often used as a negative term when describing someone's life, but it isn't until things are truly strange and so unusual that the mundane becomes a blessing to be hoped for.

I was rudely awakened from my dream life when I had my car accident which, I suppose, is the proper beginning of this tale. It was one of those in which nobody was to blame but nature and my own haste.

It was late and the roads were wet from the rain that was falling. It wasn't even as if it was a bad storm, just a light summer shower. I was on my phone which, I know, was a stupid thing to do; the advertisements about the dangers of texting and driving are hardly impossible to miss.

What happened next was so fast that it's blurry even to the scrutiny of memory. An animal of some kind, a four-legged bastard of a beast, darted out onto the road. There it stood, frozen with fear, staring at bright, on-rushing death. By the time I had noticed it, it was far too late for me to stop, even if the roads had been bone dry. Inevitably, I hit it.

The car slid off the road and, I was told, rolled several times before hitting a tree. The only thing I knew after the terrible sound of crumpling metal and crunching plastic was waking up in a hospital bed to the beeping and whirring of machines—there wasn't even time enough for me to feel pain which, in retrospect, I'm grateful for.

There was not a part of me that seemed to be left undamaged. I tried to lift the bed sheet to look at my body, to see myself, but I couldn't move my arm. When I tried, a grinding, sharp pain prevented me. I glanced over blearily and saw that it was in traction. As my vision solidified I saw that not only my arm, but both my legs were elevated by the complicated system of bright white straps and pulleys. My head felt as if there was a weight pressing down upon it and, when I tried to move it, I found that my neck was in a brace, forcing me to keep still.

That moment, not the crash, represented the pinnacle of pain and misfortune for me in my life; no other hardship that I had endured—bad grades, the loss of a grandparent, disappointment at my favorite football team's score—came close. Little did I know that my vocabulary of pain would, very shortly, expand in ways that I could scarcely have understood at the time.

Scratch, scratch.

A blue surgical scrub-wearing nurse came through the little privacy curtain that sectioned off my half of the room. It wasn't long before she noticed that I had regained consciousness. I asked the classic question, the obvious one that people in these moments always seem to ask first.

"How long have I been out?" I said.

"Just a little more than a week," she replied. Her tone was reassuringly dismissive, as if a week without consciousness was something that happened all the time and was nothing to get excited about. As practiced and professional as she was, it didn't work on me.

It would have been less frightening if she had said I had been unconscious for months or years. In that time things would have changed drastically, beyond my control, and well-wishing friends would have kept my bedside table supplied with fragrant flowers and colorful get well soon cards. I could have started life anew.

As it was just more than a week would mean that the paperwork at the office would have built up until I would have to put in hours of overtime to catch up, I would have to deal with the insurance company, and many of my friends and family would probably still be unaware of what happened to me, meaning I would have to contact each of them personally and tell the story over and over. Just a week unconscious would be exhausting.

The nurse took readings off the machines and from my broken body. "The doctor will be in soon to talk to you," she said and closed the curtain behind her as she left.

The definition of "soon" seemed to have changed in the short time that I was out. I lay in my bed, staring at the wall and its digital clock. Time moved agonizingly slow. The only thing to break the silence and monotony was the rhythmic beeping of the hospital's machines.

And, strangely, the chirruping of a single insect on the wall opposite my bed. Two long chirrups, and then a pause, then two more, all with a regularity that was nearly mechanical. It appeared in my audible perception suddenly—as if I had been hearing it for some time but had only just became aware of it.

Scratch, scratch.

I thought it was strange that a bug could make it into such a starkly white and sterile room. That it just clung to the wall without moving only added to the eerie sense that grew the longer I stared at it.

Just when I began to think it would never move, a sudden buzzing flutter of wings brought it to the cast on my leg. Closer up, I could see it in greater detail. It was a dark khaki color with burnt orange blotches on its back that were themselves speckled with black. The wings were large, transparent and lined, sweeping down over and beyond the length of its body. It sat there, making its drawn-out chirruping, and seemed to stare at me through its red, bulbous eyes. Somehow it seemed as if it was considering me, sizing me up. I realized that after the fact, having experienced what I have now.

It began to scratch at my cast with spindly, delicate-looking legs. I tried to shake it off but I couldn't move my leg enough to startle it. It scratched with a concentrated intensity until it had scraped away a thin layer of the cast, throwing up white dust in a small cloud around it.

It was starting to become scared—there was no telling why it was doing what it was doing or how far it would burrow into my cast. Its small body dug feverishly and started to disappear beneath the surface of the cast. I called out for a nurse again and again, and in increasing desperation, but none came.

Now completely obscured by a mound of shifting white dust, I could feel it touch the skin of my leg. It used its preternatural strength to start tearing through my flesh.

The pain was like ripping needles; its movements were tiny but relentless. I screamed, again and again, until my room echoed, but still no one came to save me. Blood and pieces of skin flew out of the hole that it had made in the cast in wild, almost celebratory throws, turning the white dust and the bed sheets red. I soon had no more voice to scream with—it felt as if I tore something in my throat—but still I tried anyway, thrashing in the traction but no more able to move than before.

I felt it meet the bone in my leg. That's when it stopped. Over my cracked and strangled voice still feebly calling out for help, I could hear it chirruping again.

Scratch, scratch.

Suddenly the curtain around my bed was open and an older man in a white coat stood there, looking down at me and calling out my name. I looked back at him and tried to point to my leg with a bound hand, nodding toward it with my head. He looked down and looked at me, confused.

"Do you have an itch?" he said, "Casts do that sometimes."

I looked down at my leg and the cast was whole and unblemished, not stained with blood and ripped pieces of my flesh. I stammered and found that I could talk.

"There was a bug . . .," was all that I could get out. My voice was shaking too badly. The doctor smiled reassuringly.

"It's just a bad dream," he said, "I don't want to alarm you but you've been out of it for more than a week."

He explained the severe extent of my injuries, how lucky I was to be alive, and the amount of physical therapy that I would have to endure. I tried to listen to him but my eyes were drawn back to my leg, as if I was expecting the insect to reappear at any moment.

What happened didn't feel like a dream; I felt the pain in my leg as it ripped pieces away; I felt the spindly legs and bullet-shaped body squirming inside me. Now it didn't even twinge.

After he finished talking the doctor gave me a fatherly pat on my shoulder and left through the curtain. I looked around the room, as if I would see another insect flying around now that I was alone, waiting to repeat the process, but the air was as empty and sterile as the rest of the room.

The walls and machines were unblemished and unoccupied as if, moments ago, diligent sanitation staff had just left.

I began to relax but as I did I thought I heard a muffled but nonetheless unmistakable, chirruping noise.

Scratch, scratch.

Before I go on, I have to thank you for staying through the story this long. Most people make an excuse and leave by now. That's if they're polite. If not, then they just leave. Just to warn you, from this point on my story becomes even stranger and farfetched. It's almost certainly going to test your mental endurance. If you're up for it then I'll continue.

Physical therapy was long and painful, but that pain was nothing compared to what I experienced the first day I woke up. I had almost convinced myself that it had been a dream like the doctor said—it wasn't as if there was any evidence of what I thought had happened nor had I had any incident, no more chirruping, since then. My body strengthened and healed as much as would have been possible.

The day came that I was to be discharged. I called a friend of mine and they brought a bag of clothes for me to change into, after which he would drive me back to my apartment. Poor Aaron. If I had known what would happen to him, what I would do to him, just later that night, I would have walked home.

Aaron waited outside of my room while I dressed. As I stiffly put on my jeans I couldn't resist another look at my leg—the one that

I thought the insect had bored into—and, truthfully, I inspected my leg each chance I got since the cast was taken off.

The incident was so real to me that I could still remember the pain that the bug had caused; the sensation of a foreign body beneath my flesh and muscle; how it had nestled against my shin bone.

I finished pulling on my pants, zipped and buttoned them, and made to stand up. That's when it happened again: a faint chirruping, only this time it was muffled. I looked around desperately, hopefully, for another insect, an innocent and mundane one, which had somehow managed to find its way into my room.

There were none.

I almost ripped my pants to pieces in an effort to get them off. When I did I looked at the skin of my leg, the place where I had seen, or thought I saw, the insect enter me. It was still smooth and unblemished but the noise was certainly coming from that spot.

Fear and panic gripped me. It had happened after all, it was real, and that thing was still inside my leg. I scratched and beat at my skin in an effort to get to the bug inside, to make it stop its maddening noise. I must have shouted out because Aaron came running into my room. He asked me what was happening but in my panic I could only point at my leg and whimper. He pushed me back down onto the bed where I thrashed to get at my leg. He quickly pressed the button by my bed and summoned a nurse.

One came rushing into my room and made the natural assumption that I had somehow re-injured myself. She injected a pain killer into my arm and I calmed down, but became too woozy to tell anyone about the insect. It didn't matter at that moment, though, as the chirruping had stopped.

I was given another X-ray and Aaron and I waited for the results. It showed, as I knew it would, that I had healed completely. I stayed quiet about what had really happened. It sounded ridiculous, even to me, now that all was silent. I was cleared to leave again long after night had fallen, the waning drug-induced stupor was still strong enough to help me along to sleep.

I don't remember the journey home, or Aaron putting me into my bed, but that's where I woke up. I looked at the digital clock beside the bed. The bright red numbers told me that I had only been asleep for a few hours. I was thankful I was awake, though—I felt that I had slept enough for one lifetime.

A shadow moving across the light that shined beneath my closed bedroom door told me that Aaron was still there. We had taken care of one another while drunk many times, and he didn't seem to be treating this incident any different. No doubt he had found the pillow and quilt in the hallway closet I kept for those occasions and was preparing to stay all night.

My thoughts turned to all the people I had to notify of my return. My phone was lost, destroyed in the accident, so I lazily rolled over to find the little black address book that I kept in my bedside table. I got as far as opening the drawer and wondering if Aaron would let me borrow his phone in the morning when I heard it again: the muffled, drawn-out chirruping.

I froze in my rummaging. Chemical-induced sleep had blissfully allowed me to forget about the insect and its residence in my leg, but the last shreds of morphine were chased away when I heard the noise yet again. This time I didn't bother to look around my room—I could recognize the sound well enough now.

I struggled out of my jeans and looked down at my leg, but again there wasn't even a lump to tell me where the insect was. It was then I felt it move—a tickling, itchy scrabble against my bone. In my mind I saw tiny, frail legs pressed down by red strips of muscle trying to find a purchase on my shin bone in order to move. And move it did, slowly climbing toward my knee; the tickling, itching sensation marked its progress.

Scratch, scratch.

I scrambled in the drawer of my bedside table for something to help me scratch the maddening itch. I soon found what I was looking for: the box that my parents had given me for Christmas several years ago. I opened it and took out the ornate gold-colored letter opener within. The blade was dull, but it was at least four inches long and the tip was more than sharp enough.

I scratched at my shin. The chirruping became more frantic, the insect began to move faster toward my knee. I broke the skin with the tip and blood dribbled in a thin line down my leg. There was no effect, so I scratched harder. Skin peeled away in small strips. Pain blossomed and wilted in a red pulse with each drag across my flesh. I shouted out, tears streaked my face, but still I had to scratch.

Aaron came rushing in just as I felt the insect reach my knee. I tried to dig the tip into my knee cap, trying to pry it off. To Aaron, the scene must have looked like madness: me, lying on my bed in my underwear, blood and strings of skin covering my leg.

He ran over to try and wrestle the letter open away from me. I'm not entirely sure, even to this day, what happened in those tense few seconds—him desperately struggling to take the opener away and me struggling just as desperately to hold onto it. I know I was shouting about the insect beneath my skin, now moving toward my thigh in a trail of itching and long chirrups, but that's all I could be certain of. He was deaf to anything but his attempt to, as he saw it, save me from myself.

During the struggle, somehow, Aaron was stabbed. I immediately smelled the foul scent of feces and urine as his bowls were perforated by the dull blade. I looked down and saw that it had slid in to the faux ivory hilt. I let it go, Aaron's blood covering my hand. The insect had fallen silent again.

Aaron fell backward and hit the floor with a hard thud. He made no noise but only clutched at the letter opener protruding from his stomach with a terrified expression, blood and other fluids pouring down over his groin and across his legs.

I wanted to help him, I did, but it was then I felt the insect inside me reach my thigh. It started chirruping again. I furiously scratched at it, but my fingernails were not enough. I dashed past Aaron lying pale on the floor. He reached out a pleading hand to me but I couldn't stop—I had to help myself first or I wouldn't be able to do anything for him with the distraction.

Scratch, scratch.

I stumbled into my kitchen and opened a drawer at random. Inside, digging through large spoons and other currently useless instruments, I found a cheese grater. I took it and rubbed it hard against the skin of my thigh, where the subdermal itching was now intense. It shredded my skin; blood dripping onto the floor in a patter of thick red drops.

The itching and the chirruping stopped just as suddenly as it had started and clear thought became possible once again. Recent memory rushed back in a tide of black horror. It felt as though my stomach contracted into a small wrinkled ball. I dashed back into my room.

Aaron was lying on the floor where he fell in an expanding puddle of his own blood. It had soaked into the carpet and turned it almost black. He wasn't moving; his skin was ghostly pale.

I panicked. My friend was dead on the floor of my bedroom and potentially at my hand. I grabbed my jeans and frantically pulled them on. The blood of my self-inflicted injuries soaked them immediately, turning them purple in large patches. And, to my eternal shame, I ran.

It's not something that I will ever forgive myself for, leaving Aaron to bleed to death on my own floor. If I had only been able to get the insect out of my leg, he might have been alive. But I could not allow the police to arrest me. I doubt they would believe me, and I would be thrown in jail or worse: a mental hospital. I'm not insane, I know it. Something that feels this real cannot be in my mind.

Scratch, scratch.

At first, a few weeks after the incident in my bedroom, I tried to talk to people, to get help. I hoped that I could find a solution to my problem while still avoiding the police. A life of poverty and homelessness would be bearable if only I could get rid of the bug that still remained resolutely inside me. People would only hear the first few sentences of my story before rushing off—I still wore my blood-soaked jeans, now crusted in a deep brown. They drove most people away.

Life, of a sort, continued on the street. I took shelter where I could—beneath overpasses or in deep doorways—and rummaged food where I could find it—from dumpsters outside restaurants or trash cans on the sidewalk.

I begged for money, but that only took a small part of my time. Most of my time was taken up trying to find things that would help me remove the insect inside my body. I quickly wore my fingernails down scratching myself, but dumpsters and abandoned lots were full of things to use instead: rusty food can lids, broken knives and corkscrews, the sharp edges of chain link fences, and many other impromptu instruments.

The bug remained elusive, moving all over my body seemingly at random. Nothing worked to force it out, or take it out. If you'll look at my arm here—let me pull up my sleeve—I tried to do a rudimentary surgery to remove it once and for all. I waited until there was a cloudless, sunny day and peeled my skin back to find the thing that was blighting me. My screams echoed down the alley and off the buildings around me as I cut open my flesh with a piece of broken glass.

It was all for nothing, though: I passed out from blood loss before I got too deep into my arm. But, on the plus side, it was the longest sleep I've had—most times the bug starts its incessant chirruping and itching when I try to sleep.

Scratch, scratch.

I've given up trying to get it out now. I'm resigned to it staying in my body until it determines that it's time for it to leave on its own—bursting out of my skin like . . . like a cicada, I suppose. I'm sure it will hurt enormously but I'll take it if I can be free of the blight of its occupation. Still, I cannot resist scratching at it when it acts up. It's an unconscious reaction now. Most often I'm not even aware that I'm doing it.

Scratch, scratch.

Thank you for listening to me this whole time. It helps more than you think to talk to people. Here, let me get you another drink before I leave; I've saved up enough money from begging to buy one at least. I don't need it for myself: I'm used to cold, half eaten hamburgers and the like now. What are you drinking?

Oh, before I get it, I have a question: are you using your fork?

Scratch, scratch.

TETANUS

By Chris Vander Kaay

You sit in an examination room in the emergency room, shifting back and forth on the crinkling paper unspooled from a roll at the top of the exam table across the soft Naugahyde underneath you.

You rub your jaw, pressing at the joint, massaging the muscle, trying to make your mouth open, but it still won't. You take deep breaths through your nose, try to remain calm. The doctor will know what it is.

You stare at the wall chart across the room from you that says, "Warning Signs You're Having a Heart Attack." You glance through the symptoms portrayed in tiny cartoon images. Whatever is wrong with you, it looks like it's not that.

You hear the click of the door and turn to see a doctor walk in the room. He smiles, but not at you, as he walks in the room. His eyes are on the file in his hands. His nametag reads Dr. Lync.

"Well, we can cross tetanus off the list of culprits that caused your lockjaw, Mack," Lync says to you, still not looking at you. "No fever, your blood pressure and heart rate are fine."

Lync sets the file down on the counter nearby, then finally looks up at you. The faux-friendly smile fades away, replaced with the sober, furrowed brow of a professional. He reaches over, sliding his fingers gently across your throat, the muscles in your neck, your shoulders. "The surrounding muscles aren't stiff to the touch. Hmm. Can you take your shirt off? I want to check some other things."

You pull your shirt off over your head, lay it on the paper roll next to you.

"Do you grind your teeth? Or clench them a lot?" Lync asks. *Not until my fucking jaws locked shut*, you want to say, but you can't, so you just shake your head no. Lync presses several spots on your chest, your arms. What is he doing? Looking for pressure points? But you can't ask.

"That rules out TMJ, then," Lync says, his face inches from your chest. "It might be soft tissue inflammation, but it's not exhibiting anywhere else." He steps back, rubs his chin thoughtfully as he looks at your body, then smiles as he makes eye contact again. "You're a bit of a mystery, Mack. Tell you what, while we're waiting for the blood tests, let's give you the once-over. See if anything stands out."

Lync pats you on the shoulder, pointing down at the shirt next to you. "You can put your shirt back on," he says, "but that's only because I need you to drop the trousers a bit. Not off, just so I can check your prostate."

You nod and slide your shirt back on. Lync snaps a glove from the box on the counter and slides his hand into it. The room is so quiet that you can hear the clink of your belt as you unhook it and slide your pants down. "Just lean up on the bench here," Lync says. "It'll only take a second." You turn around and lean down, your elbows crinkling the paper, it starts to tear under the weight.

"Just relax a bit," Lync says from behind you. You can feel his finger press into you firmly. "It'll be over soon. One of the first things we tell our patients during an examination like this—OW!" You tense at the shock, and you feel him pull his hand free.

You spin around quickly, grabbing at your pants to keep them from falling. You look at Lync, who is gripping his gloved right hand. The latex tip of the glove is torn and jagged, and his index finger is bleeding.

"What the f—" Lync says as he stares down at his finger. "Something bit or cut my finger." Lync snaps the glove off, and you both stare down at the wound. Squinting, you can see that the cut is actually a series of small punctuations, and you can see the half-moon shaped curve the punctures make across his fingertip.

"Holy shit, that's a bite radius," Lync says. He raises his eyes, looks at you in stunned silence. "Mack, what the hell is going on inside you?"

You button your pants, but don't bother with the belt. You didn't feel anything inside, nothing but his finger. There's nothing wrong with you, you know it, and you're not going to wait around and let people prod you. You hurry towards the door of the examination, throw it open, hurry towards the door.

"Orderlies!" Lync's voice echoes through the hall as you hurry towards the exit of the emergency room. "Grab that man, he needs to be quarantined, now!"

You fumble at the keys in your pocket, pull them free, and you can feel your pants starting to fall. The automatic doors slide open and you hurry through them.

Arms hook you around the waist, grab at your clothes, pull you back through the door. You want to yell for help from the people in the parking lot, in the waiting room, but you can only moan through your clenched teeth.

They drag you back into the examination room, Lync slamming the door behind you. You kick at them, try to pull your arms free, but they're stronger than you and trained to secure unruly patients.

"Get him down on the bench here," Lync says, ripping away the paper. The two orderlies press you down against the Naugahyde. One of them holds your head still, and you try to move, but he has you pinned in place. On the ceiling above you, you can see tiny, cute animal stickers, probably placed there for children to focus on when they're given shots.

You feel the pinprick on your arm, the rushing heat as whatever it was in Lync's needle spreads out underneath your skin. "Hold him still until the succinylcholine arrests his muscle contractions," Lync says.

Then you feel it taking hold. No pain, no sensation, but a growing fear inside you when you realize you're losing the ability to move. The rest of your body is as immobile as your mouth. You can feel the orderlies' hands release you, but you can't take advantage of the freedom.

"Okay, it's working, he won't move now," Lync says as he leans down into your face, peering into your eyes with a penlight. "Get his pants off." You feel the tug and hear the clink of your belt as they pull off your pants and drop them to the floor. "Find the OB-GYN foot stirrups. I need to get his legs spread apart so I can . . ." Lync's voice trails off.

It feels like someone's hand is on your penis, moving it side to side, but you can't look down to see. You know it's not that, though, because you can see Lync and the orderlies staring down at your waist, unmoving, eyes wide.

"Why is his . . .?" the fatter orderly says, pointing at your waist.

"That's not an erection," Lync says, tilting his head, looking closely. "It's distended and moving. Is there something inside the urethra?"

You feel it, suddenly, awkwardly. It feels like you're urinating, but it's not liquid coming out. A thin tentacle, a pale-yellow tendril, snakes out of your penis, lashing around in the air above your body.

"What the hell is—?" The fat orderly's words are cut off when the tendril wraps around the orderly's neck. He struggles against it, coughing and wheezing, pulling against it. You can feel your body rock with the violence of the struggle.

"What do I do?" the thinner orderly cries to Lync. "It's choking him!"

Lync grabs the tendril and pulls hard, but it won't release the orderly's throat. You watch Lync vanish from sight for a moment, and when he comes back into view, he has a scalpel in his hand.

"Get that clamp," Lync says to the thin orderly, pointing to the counter across the room. "As soon as I slice the tentacle, the stump of it will probably retract back into him. When it does, I want you to clamp the tip of his penis so it can't come back out, okay?" The thin orderly nods, grabbing the clamp.

Lync pauses, turns to look you in the eyes. You can't say anything, and he knows it. He nods at you and turns back to the tendril. He grabs hold of it, swipes the scalpel across it. You watch as the two feet of tendril go limp and unravel from the fat orderly's neck. The stump of the tendril snakes downwards and out of your vision.

As the fat orderly stumbles backwards, gasping for clear breaths, the thin orderly tightens the clamp on your penis. You feel the pinch and the stab, so sharp and clear that you want to scream. You can't activate your vocal chords, so the scream goes nowhere but through your head. You try to reach up and pull it off, to clench your fists, to shove them all away. You can't.

Lync leans down into your face again, and then you feel his fingers against your throat, pressing to find a pulse. "It's contained now, whatever it is," Lync says, turning to the orderlies. "Go to the next room, have Hanson look over both of you. I want this door locked from the outside while I continue my examination." The two of them stare at him in silence. "Go! Get your neck looked at and don't come back in here until I call you."

The two orderlies file out of the room, and you can hear the metallic clack of the door locking. Lync looks down at you again, then turns and walks across the room. You can't see him, but you can hear the opening and closing of drawers, the shuffling of plastic and objects.

"Mack, I'm sorry," he says from somewhere on your right. "I don't know what happened to you, but I have to put you under. The succinylcholine keeps you from being able to move, and you couldn't talk because of the lockjaw anyway. The only thing that comes from you being conscious is that you're going to feel all the pain."

Lync walks back over, hovering near you with a syringe in his hand. "You're of no use to us conscious," he says, leaning down towards you. You feel the pinprick again. "Don't worry, I'll figure out what's going on."

You don't remember the moment you weren't looking at Lync anymore, the moment when blackness overtook your vision, all the sounds melted into a single low-frequency buzz and your awareness of your body was a distant dream memory.

You seem to remember someone telling you that when you're in a chemically-induced sleep, you don't have a sense of the passage of time, no awareness of yourself. That's not this. You do feel something, but what is it? Like trying to talk with a mouthful of honey, everything is muted, slow, runny.

And then, you're suddenly crawling back into yourself, feeling your mind start making connections back to what your eyes are seeing. The light is blinding, painful, but it's a welcome pain because it's the first thing you can remember feeling since the needle stick.

You blink. Whatever that medicine was, it has worn off, because you can move your eyelids. The light is slowly waning, but you still can't see the examination room clearly. You try to open your mouth, but it still won't open.

You try to turn your head, but it barely moves. It's not like your jaw, it's not frozen; it feels held in place by something outside, something restricting. The light starts to ebb, the room makes itself known.

It's not the examination room. The ceiling is different, the stickers gone, fluorescents blasting down on you.

"Sir, the patient is conscious, sir!" The voice is loud, barking. You can't move your head, but you shift your eyes over to the right, and you can make out the blurry shape of a man in brown, a white helmet on his head. You're almost certain he's holding a gun.

"Thank you, Corporal," says a voice from somewhere on your left, and you know immediately that it's Lync. You scan your eyes back and forth, but you don't see him yet.

Lync suddenly looms into your view, right above your face. "Hi, Mack," Lync says. "You've been out for a while now." The first thing you notice is that he looks different. His hair is shorter, cropped. Something is different around his eyes, too.

"It's been seven years," Lync says, bending his eyebrows up in faux-sympathy. Your breathing speeds up, and you know he must see in your face how confused and angry you are. "It's going to take you some time to adjust. You haven't used your eyes or ears for a good long while."

You try to reach up, to grab him by his smug face, to punch him over and over until he either dies or someone tackles you, but you can't move your hands, either. You're not paralyzed, you're immobilized.

"Your limbs are secured," Lync says, nodding. "Straps and bars. Don't fight them, you'll just tear your skin up." Lync leans in close, speaking quietly. "As you start to come around fully, you're going to notice some discomfort, tightness and pulling and localized pain."

As the words come out of his mouth, you can already start to feel it. Pressure, like lying at the bottom of a swimming pool, and small burning spots everywhere; it feels like someone is pressing cigarette lighters against every inch of your skin.

"So just try to focus on me for a moment, okay?" Lync says, standing straight up and circling around to stand right in front of you. "I'll try to explain everything." He pauses, then smiles awkwardly. "This is going to be harder to sum up than I thought. Let's see, how do I say this?

"Mack, your body is . . . well, we don't have a term for it. We've been calling you a nexus in the absence of a better term. Something about your physical make-up is a doorway to other places." Your body is throbbing, but you're focused on Lync's words, rapt attention. "The orifices in your body all seem to lead to someplace. In the time since we initially put you under, we discovered that the tentacled creature that grabbed James was just an undersea creature from either a distant planet or another dimension, and it somehow got pulled partway into the portal that exited out of your . . . well, anyway, when we sent a camera down your urethra, we discovered what was on the other end, besides the tentacled creature, was plentiful fresh water, more than we ever could have imagined."

Lync holds his hand up for you to see. His index finger, the one that was bitten, is gone now. He wiggles the cauterized stump back and forth.

"I had to have the finger amputated after it got infected from the bite," Lync says. "It was an oversized insect. A camera in your rectum showed a dense, forest-like environment, teeming with thousands of tiny creatures which we have been harvesting and using for medication, research, more things than we could have imagined."

Lync smiles at you, shaking his head. "Honestly, I can't thank you enough," he says. "You don't know what kind of changes the world has gone through, positive changes, because of you. There's no water shortage in the world anymore. We've found cures for Alzheimer's and muscular dystrophy."

Lync scratches his head. "I'm sorry to say we still haven't figured out what's going on with your jaw," Lync says, shrugging. "It's not medically related, we know that much. It's possible that it's the only portal in your body where whatever is on the other side knows about the portal as well, and they're trying to prevent anyone or anything from coming through to where they are. Frankly, though, we haven't spent much time trying to figure it out because we've been so busy making discoveries about all your other orifices."

You blink your eyes over and over, avert your eyes downward, towards your body. Lync watches you, confused, but then he finally understands.

"Right, of course," he says. "The pain I described and the restraints. Yeah, that's going to be the hard part for you to deal with, but you won't have to worry about it for long. Hang on, let me grab . . ."

He moves away from you again. "After the first year of exploring all the places we could go by traveling through all the holes in your body, we started wondering about the nature of your body," Lync says. "We wondered if all the places we could access through your ears, nose, anus, we wondered if those were the only ones we could get to." Lync walks back over, a small square hidden in the palm of his hand, the sharp corners peeking around his fingers.

"So we made a new one," he said, pausing to look at your face. The heavy silence hangs in the air, and then he finally continues. "We created a biopsy hole on your arm to see what would happen. And sure enough, it led somewhere. Someplace empty, vacuous, no light or creatures of any kind, but definitely some kind of place. So we kept going, kept creating small holes to send our miniature cameras into. Mack, we found so much; our understanding of the universe, of reality itself, has multiplied a hundred times over because of the strange nature of your body."

Lync fiddles with the square in his hand, and you see a block of reflected light pass across his face. He must have a mirror in his hand, reflecting the fluorescents back up at his face. Why does he have a mirror? What does he want you to see?

"So we monitor them all, send things through into the worlds with intelligent life," he says. "Bring things back here through tiny tubes to use for research, or in the case of the water, we just keep pumping it out and filtering it to send to poor and desert populations. And it's all because of you. Look what you're doing for us."

That's when he turns the mirror towards you, shows you your own face and body. Riddled with open wounds and sores, each one is kept open by clamps and wires, some with tubes going into or out of them. You look at your chest, pockmarked and spongy; you look like a porcupine covered in quills that curve and bend away from you, plastic and black, wires thick and thin, like the fibrous hairs on a fly.

It's not your face anymore, it's not your body. It's not you. You don't know what you're seeing, some kind of meat pile with electrodes sticking out of it, a mottled turkey carcass ravaged by a hundred thousand pop-up timers. You don't know what you are.

"I know, it's hard to take in, Mack," Lync says, lowering the mirror. "It's a lot to deal with. Don't worry, though, we're not going to leave you like this. And I'm not going to send you back to that horrible half-waking twilight you've been in all this time. You deserve something better, more final than that."

Lync disappears again. You search the room as best you can, but you still can't see him. "Of course, you understand that we can't stop utilizing your body," Lynch says. "It's too valuable. But I want to free you to whatever degree I can."

He steps back into your view, a syringe in one hand and an iPhone in the other. "So what I'm going to do is put you back under, just temporarily, so I can remove the higher thinking parts of your brain and get rid of them. All we need to keep your body functioning is the brain stem, so I'm going to end your consciousness instead of imprisoning it in here. It's the least we can do for you."

Lync holds up the phone. "I looked through your playlist on your phone years ago, and I noticed that you played the Johnny Cash song "Peace in the Valley" much more than any other song," Lync says as he swipes through your phone. "I want to play that for you, one last time." You see standing tears in Lync's eyes as he looks right at you. "Thank you for everything you've done." He presses play on the phone.

'*I'm tired and so weary, but I must go along, till the Lord comes and calls me away . . .*'

Lync leans down and slides the needle in; you can't feel the needle, not with all the holes and the wires and the skin damage. But you know he has injected something, because you can feel the world dimming around you again, blurring at the edges, losing its shape.

Lync's voice comes to you one last time, murky and poured through a sieve, but clear enough to be understood. "It will be better, I promise," he says.

The dark closes in around you now. In moments, the only part of you that is still fully you, the gray matter, will be sliced out and tossed aside. And your body will continue without you.

Maybe Lync is right. Maybe it will be better. . . .

GRUB
By Alexander Lloyd King

A final dinner was all he asked. *Sure,* she thought, *what could be the harm in dinner?*

Ellie and Billy Goldstein started out romantically enough, two science majors in chemistry, and whatever fondness had spoiled between them was still digestible in small amounts. Dinner would be tolerable, somewhat constructive, especially if it offered Billy a little closure. She already had hers. His name was Luigi, and he was a far, Catholic cry from a Jewish atheist who wore a lab coat with house slippers.

Before agreeing to dinner, Ellie knew their final meal would be different, though she suspected most of their evening would run its usual course: Billy would blare some computerized travesty of jazz or blues; the dimmer switch would be adjusted so the chandelier above the dining room table seemed little more than the faint glow of a jack-o-lantern row, a quixotic camouflage Billy began hiding behind, she suspected, when he became aware that his long hours in the cellar had robbed him of the good features he once possessed; and the table would seem an oval ghost under that cloth she loathed—an abhorrent draping which matched Billy's lab coat when they purchased it and had since turned a tarter yellow.

Ellie stood on the porch, dressed in her most casual of dinner outfits, waiting for Billy to answer the door and trying not to smile at the thought of walking away from that table for the last time, leaving the wordless noise and dim room and ugly cloth behind. She made a silent vow to never forget. It would serve her better to remember the decade of marriage in which her husband grew evermore complacent, spending increasing hours in the basement. She recalled the crawling feeling she got one occasion when she went down there and discovered that he used up much of his time in the glass room not experimenting but instead ogling his specimens, his eyes bulging like two fat white grubs as ants crawled across his hand. She would hold onto the degrading experience of living with an entomologist/arachnologist who wanted to touch his bugs more than he did his wife, a thought that had wriggled in the back of her mind each time those rare moments arrived when he meant to touch her sexually.

She was in the middle of that thought as Billy opened the door. Poised in the entrance, he remained quiet for a moment, seemingly perplexed.

"Are you cold, Ellie?"

"No."

"I thought you might be . . . the way you were shaking."

"I guess I'm a little cold," she lied, hoping to spare his feelings, then wondering if he still had feelings like normal people. She often considered the possibility that too much time around his little friends had made him just like them, a shell wrapped around a complex nervous system.

Except, in that moment, she could tell there was much more within his fleshy husk than a jamboree of firing neurons. His eyes might have been hidden behind glasses reflecting a streetlamp, but he was staring at her—into her, she thought, with those bulging white eyes of his—in a manner of almost telepathic inquiry.

"May I come in?" she asked, playing off another shudder as if cold.

He stepped aside.

"Certainly. You didn't have to knock. This is still your home, too, Ellie, or have you forgotten?"

She entered, and there it was greeting her: the overly-condensed rhythms of what Billy considered music, electronic clots with all of the humanity stripped away. Rendered to a fine point; that was how he liked any form of art. As the tune invaded her ears, she thought, *this is the same sound I would hear if I could hear a spider spinning its web.*

Ellie almost jumped when he closed and locked the door behind them. Never in their decade together had Billy ever frightened her. Given her the creeps, yes, many times. But it was like the difference between hearing a ghost story and having a supernatural experience. The first does not impose an immediate sense of danger; the latter does. She found herself leaning toward the second as he stepped around her and toddled into the kitchen with barely a nervous gleam on his balding scalp. It was a powerful inflammation of the surreal fear generated by nightmares, and it was her first time experiencing anything like it. For a woman who had been content enough to share the house with Black Widow spiders, there was something to be said about her sudden level of unease.

How Luigi's voice had boomed hours ago at the very idea of Ellie and Billy Goldstein reunited and alone.

"I don't trust you going over there!"

Along with his slight accent, his large hands, and his full head of hair, his inability to filter emotion was one of the many things she had come to adore about her lover. The more he cared, the louder he became. He was not a rational man of science, but an impulsive man of emotion.

"I've known Billy for sixteen years and lived with him for ten. He's far more dangerous to himself than anyone else. I think that's how he needs to heal. It's his personality—he turns inward. If a final dinner together can help him move on, it will help me move on." She ran her finger along the sheet clinging to Luigi's thick forearm. "It will help *us* move on."

"And how am I to forgive myself if something happens to you?"

"Trust me, and I mean this quite literally . . . Billy Goldstein wouldn't harm a fly."

Ellie forced herself back into the air of normalcy she had felt in that very house less than two weeks prior, before she finally broke the news to Billy that she was leaving him to live with the man she had been seeing behind his back for more than a year. It further eased her nerves to recall his reaction; it had been passive rather than angry, rational rather than alarmed, and in a way, slightly relieved.

She took a seat at the dining room table, disregarding the yellow-tinted tablecloth she hated as she tried to erase any sign of guilt from her face. Billy entered the room with two glasses of red wine and a goofy smile she had not seen since their college days. She thought that smile had been lost to his research.

"I've done a lot of thinking, Ellie, and I've really come to terms with what's happening between us."

Ellie accepted the drink, wondering by his chipper behavior if these were the first glasses he poured that evening.

"*What* is happening between us?" she asked, afraid to approve of their current standing without first hearing his understanding of it. "I mean, in your eyes, what's happening?"

Those eyes, glossy and bright, wiggled in their sockets. He raised his index finger and proclaimed, "A metamorphosis, my dear."

She took a deep breath, released it, took a large gulp, swallowed, sighed, and tried but failed to say something, anything.

"It's okay, it's okay. You think I'm hysterical. That I should be happy about you cohabitating and copulating with a man who exceeds me physically—a man you chose for primal and instinctive reasons—certainly appears a blatant and painful case of denial in the eyes of lesser beings. But I am not in pain." He thrust his arms into the air in a grand gesture. "I could even dance, because I have defied death, found a way to grant new life, and our metamorphosed relationship will do the same. We're almost imago, Ellie. To become butterflies."

She could not think of a good response. He read the uncertainty on her face.

"You must be unsure of your old friend Billy right now," he said, calming. "I should have begun by informing you: it finally happened."

Curiosity replaced her unease. IT, the same IT he spoke of so often. She had thought IT a metaphor for his big break.

"*IT*'s happened?"

"Yes, not just a breakthrough but *THE* breakthrough. Completion. Everything I've been working toward since grad school is finally coming to fruition. The long hours, the sacrifices—our marriage being one of them—and the derision I received. Even when no one said anything, my peers were mocking me among themselves. Even you doubted me."

"I'm sorry, I didn't mean to seem—"

"No! Don't you dare apologize, Ellie. My success is where our new relationship cocoons. Your unspoken judgment allowed me to make this possible. Ridicule was the leafy goodness I needed, *we* needed. I have you to thank."

He's just excited, Ellie told herself, and she couldn't blame him. She was excited, too, so much that the atmosphere no longer bothered her. Though he was behaving far more eccentrically than she had ever witnessed, and though her physical passions had long since died for the man, she felt she had shared much of the sacrifice it took for him to fulfill his ambition, and she felt pride in herself for standing by him at least an overwhelming majority of the time in which he worked toward. . . .

Suddenly, something he said before began itching in her mind like a mosquito bite.

"Billy? What did you mean when you said you defied death?"

"First, let us eat. I will explain as much as I can before showing you."

He returned to the kitchen with his empty glass and began carrying silver-topped platters (which he must have purchased specifically for the occasion, because Ellie had never seen them before) two at a time to the dining room table. She offered to help, but he refused, stating that many of the covered dishes were a surprise related to his special breakthrough. There were ten platters in all: five he set on the right side, her left, and five he set on the left, her right. Then, after fetching forks and silverware and plates and apologizing for his absentmindedness, he unveiled, one at a time, the five helpings of food on the right, her left.

It was indeed different than she expected. The meal consisted of fettuccine, salad, steamed vegetables, spaghetti, and breadsticks. Despite his excitement and declared appreciation of their "cocooning" relationship, the meal he prepared was basically saying, *I heard you're a big fan of Italian.* Billy's engineered irony was in the air, but neither chose to verbalize what would surely subtract from his momentous revelation. He seemed humble as he filled their plates and this time filled glasses with white wine, so she considered that his choice of cuisine was only subconsciously spiteful. Men like Billy Goldstein—their subconscious thoughts pupate and grow into larger things. At least the food looked appetizing, for once, under the hollow, jack-o-lantern-like glow.

A good way into their meal, Billy began staring at the platters still covered, the ones on the left, her right. Continuing to eat small bites, he started his great divulgence.

"Ellie, do you remember Gregor Mendel?"

She hated to break from eating. The food was delicious, distracting from the strangeness of the scenario. She didn't want anything to shatter her current state of peace. She wanted it to last her until she was miles removed from this dreamlike dinner, at Luigi's place and in his solid, grounding arms.

"Mendel was the man who cross-pollinated pea plants to discover dominant and recessive traits," she answered. "He's one of your earliest inspirations. You even tried to start that educational band in college. Was it *Gregor and the Peapods*?"

Billy chuckled. He was a puzzle master holding the last few pieces in his hands, looking upon them as a doting father about to send his children into the bigger world, commit them to the bigger picture.

"I find it hard to believe that a boy with such silly ideas could accomplish what I have. I guess I've done a fair amount of metamorphosing since then. But you have it right enough. Mendel's experiments started me down my own path. I began toying with cross-pollinating—*cross-breeding*—different species of insects and arachnids. You thought I was just down there for the last ten years playing with bugs, but I was playing with something smaller. Particles, my dear. I've even gone as far as to clone my insects, and even that pales in comparison to the grand scheme. You remember the time you found me in the glass room with the ants out, crawling across my hand? I was marveling because they were clones. I could not tell you that, then, but it was true. Start small, make big. That's my scientific creed."

"That's all wonderful," Ellie said, then attempted humor. "Just don't tell me you've created a giant race of ants we'll have to build sugar factories to satiate."

"Not yet, I haven't," he said, as if taking her comment seriously. "The point is . . . I could if I wanted to. I could tweak this, manipulate that. Ellie, I've discovered something far deeper than Higgs boson . . . I've discovered the true God Particle."

He reached for the still-covered platter closest to him and pulled off the top. Ellie saw what was beneath the silver dome and dropped her fork into a tangle of spaghetti.

Never during their decade together in that house, no matter how pleased he was with his studies, had Billy dared to bring bugs to the dinner table. Now he had. The platter, which he moved directly before him after scooting his plate aside, contained two glass jars: one with a small, wriggling maggot inside; the other with a large, fat grub. They climbed at their glass cells with horrifying inconsequence, although Billy was watching them as if they were two, united pinnacles of existence.

"Do you know what these are, Ellie?"

"The lighting's not the best, but I can see from here that one is a maggot and the other a grub worm."

"You're half right. I'll explain, and it will all make sense."

She doubted that, and she knew he could read her uncertainty, but his eyes gleamed—human versions of the grub in the jar—as he continued.

"If I was going to successfully crossbreed insect species, fire ants with carpenter ants, for example, then I needed to manipulate those subatomic particles into accepting the DNA of the other. It took me several years to figure out how to grow those potential offspring in a stable environment, and even then the results were less than successful. I had discovered this small concoction, but I was lacking a filter to initiate true birth. In other words, I had to find that particular *something* that would spring *nothing* into life. A womb. Then it occurred to me. If I could tweak these un-living particles into life, then maybe I could use any piece of detached life as fodder, an incubation system— turning decay into spontaneous life"

"And?"

"And it worked! I used mice to grow my crossbreeds of insects. I changed them with my concoction, and the results were profound. Any piece of flesh I cut from them would transform. Do you see what I've done, Ellie? I have turned death into a suitable condition for life and created hundreds of new species of insects. I have defied what every true scientist dreams secretly of defying. I have found immortality." He pointed to the smaller jar, the one with the maggot. "Guess where this came from."

"Do I want to know?" Ellie asked, shuddering at the thought of his mutilated test subjects.

"It came from *me*, Ellie. It came from *me*."

"Bi-Billy, please don't tell me you—"

"Not on purpose. It didn't occur to me that my concoction and inevitable exposure to it would cause a change in me. After all, it is not toxic in any way, so I went about my experiments with more concern that I might contaminate it than thinking it might contaminate me. I used what I thought were the necessary safeguards, but there must have been a hole in my preparations . . . or in my hazmat suit. Somewhere along the line I either inhaled or ingested the transformative agent, the one that springs life from death."

The guilt returned to her face, undeniable. "You're not sick, are you?"

His grin in response made him appear even more at home under the jack-o-lantern-like lighting.

"Far from it, my dear Ellie. I am immortal."

As hard to believe as his declaration was, she had known the man for sixteen years and could not recall a single lie. She hoped he was exaggerating.

"You mean immortal because of your discovery, right? Because you'll go down in history?"

He finished his glass, grabbed the bottle, and poured another. "I. Mean. Immortal."

"Billy, maybe this isn't the best time to talk about it. I'm sure you want to unveil your findings yourself, to a prestigious institution."

"Fuck prestige!" Billy yelled, which was uncharacteristic for a man who compared swear words to barbaric grunts. Also, he used to be obsessed with those great academic clubs, desiring acceptance from them. "I'm not simply immortal—I'm enlightened." He gave the maggot-jar in his fingertips a gentle shake, sending the little white speck rolling back and forth across the glass bottom. "I asked if you knew where this fellow came from, Ellie, and I think you're starting to realize, though it scares you as I can see that by the look on your face. When I was shaving a few days ago, I cut myself a good one." He paused only long enough to indicate a small, white bandage just beneath his chin and on his upper neck. Ellie, until then, had not noticed it. "I set my razor down and patched the wound with a snip of toilet paper. Then I went to continue. I was just about to rinse my razor under the faucet when I saw it, wriggling between the blades. When I first looked, it was still a small piece of flesh. By the time I got to the basement, this sample was a smaller version of itself now. Soon it'll be a fly. The blood was also moving. It was red, so it became chiggers."

This is insane! she thought. *He's insane!*

Ellie tried to stand but could not. The recent dreamlike sense she felt was more than mental. It was physical.

"You drugged me, you bastard," she slurred.

"I knew you would have trouble believing," he said in an almost apologetic tone. I just put enough in the wine to keep you still. I have no intention of tying you up, Ellie-my-dear. Trust me. Soon you will be free."

The music she associated with the sound of spider webs was in the background. He lifted the jar with the grub worm and eyed it lovingly as he stepped around the table and hovered above the four, silver-topped platters. If the maggot had come from the shaved-off skin of his neck, he was daring her to guess from which chunk of him the larger specimen had manifested. She did not have to guess for long. With a smile as sideways as spider fangs, he hoisted his right foot to the table, set the jar beside it, and used hands trembling with anticipation to remove his slipper.

Ellie screamed . . . or at least she attempted to scream. What escaped her mouth was as droning as the music. She saw exactly what Billy wanted her to see: the place where his pinky toe used to be, right next to the glass-sealed grub worm.

"I had to be certain," he said. "I had to know that the maggot born of my flesh wasn't an isolated incident. As you can see, Ellie, it wasn't."

"No," she said. What she had meant to say was, "*No, I don't want to see! Let me go!*" What he must have heard was, *"No, I don't believe you!"*

"You will believe me. I will show you. You never thought we would have children together, Ellie. Tonight, you'll understand how wrong you were. Tonight, we're going to make thousands of babies." He lowered his foot from the table and lifted the top of another platter to reveal a small hatchet. "I'll prove my findings as well as my love."

Watching him run his thumb along the blade in that dim, pumpkin glow, her bladder released. Piss streaming down her legs and the chair legs, she understood that Billy was in fact no longer a man. He was immortal, as immortal as bloated roadkill with maggots squirming beneath, eternal in its provisions of fodder for those flies-to-be.

He reached her, brushed her dinner plate aside, wrapped his left hand around her right wrist, and raised it to the table with what seemed to be lamenting affection. Tears streamed down her face, but she could barely feel them.

"No, no, no, no."

He gave her a sympathetic look that said, *this may hurt like hell, but it's necessary.* Then he pulled her hand until her wrist was taut against the table, raised the hatchet, and brought it down with a force she never knew he possessed. Even in a semi-numb, semi-paralyzed state, she felt a level of pain she never thought possible. It came again and again and again because the first few chops were not enough to completely sever her hand.

Billy moved surprisingly fast for a man recently downgraded to nine toes. He jumped to a platter and revealed surprise number three: a blowtorch.

Cauterize, she thought. It was the only word her mind could muster before she passed out to the sound of the torch lighting and, in the background, that horrible music.

When she started to wake, she felt Luigi's broad arms around her and thought, *Thank God, it was a nightmare, only a nightmare, I'm safe.*

A smile of relief was just starting to form when awareness and pain penetrated her mind, and she realized that she was not huddled in bed with her lover but sitting on a hard, wooden surface. The bed sheets she thought she felt were really that horrible, yellowed tablecloth dangling over her legs, and the sense of being held in Luigi's arms amounted only to the broad weight of the drugs still gripping her system. Worse than anything, the tingling pain she at first took for a limb fallen asleep began to amplify into a high voltage wave of pain.

She could also smell charring. Head still pressed against the table, she opened her eyes to see the stump where her right hand used to be. Farther down her wrist, a grotesque cluster of blisters peeked out from the edge of heavy-duty gauze.

He stopped the bleeding, she thought. *He wants to keep me alive, to torture me.*

Tat-tat-tat-tat. She heard the sound first before feeling its corresponding vibrations through the table, where her facedown head was pressed, unable to look up. Something was crawling across the cloth, digging in with legs sharp and heavy enough to resound through the fabric and make an instrument of the hard wood beneath. Whatever it was kept getting closer. *Tat-tat-tat-tat.*

It pattered over to her and paused a moment, as if preparing to strike. But it didn't strike. One of its tat-tat legs merely touched upon her scalp. Then another. Then another. It was climbing onto her head, sinking its spidery limbs into her hair.

Finally, Ellie found that she could move. She lifted her remaining hand and in a single, quick motion thrust it under the large tarantula and flung it off the top of her head. It landed on its back only a few feet away, still too close for her comfort, and emitted a squeal.

She summoned enough strength to lift her head from the table to the back of the chair. She then gazed down upon her recent assailer. It wasn't a tarantula, nor was it any other kind of spider she'd ever seen.

The thing writhing on its back still somewhat resembled her hand. The skin was there, marked with small, porous pox where black hairs had begun sprouting. The wrist and its laceration had swollen to a lively size, which at first seemed impossible considering there was no longer—or at least should not have been—any blood flowing to or through that appendage; then she recognized the shape it was taking—a thorax.

Her severed hand was transforming into a spider.

"Do you see?" Billy's voice rose from behind her. His arms dropped on her shoulders. "You were exposed to the agent, too. Now, Ellie-my-dear, we're both immortal."

"Bastard!" she cried, her adrenaline finally pushing through the drugs in her system. "It was in the wine."

"Not the wine. What kind of sense would that make? I put the drugs in the alcohol, but I put the agent over the already cooked food. Alcohol would quickly dissolve the agent's most pungent of properties . . . and they are pungent. Fast-acting as you can see by the sudden and dramatic change your hand has taken. Fascinating, isn't it? I haven't watched an entire human limb change until now. It's as if the latent particles of insect mass I've manipulated spring forth from our decay in the forms most sensible based on their sizes and shapes. How fascinating!"

The spider-hand kept twitching in transformation. Her former fingers, its legs, clawed failingly at the air for at least another minute before settling, stilling. The sound of internal tearing cut through the music as each finger began splitting down the middle. The manicured nails fell to the table in pieces as little climbing hooks sprouted from the tips of each torn phalange. All but the thumb did this; rather than joining the eight legs and making nine or ten, it folded under the palm, fixed itself there, and split into two, dripping fangs.

She gazed in horror as Billy stepped around her and approached the final platter still on the table (she figured the one she had not watched him reveal had contained the gauze he used to bandage her cauterized wound). Her shock escalated as he lifted the silver dome and revealed what had been squirming beneath this entire time.

Larvae.

Using its new legs, the spider-hand sprang to an upright position and tat-tat-tatted over to the pulsing mess of a meal, where it dove in with a display of gluttony most likely derived from its human origins.

"How does dessert sound?" Billy asked, placing the silver dome over the predator and its prey. "Our boy sure likes it! Relax . . . those larvae weren't from me."

"There's no way. It's a trick. You're deranged and playing a cruel trick on me."

"Does the end of your arm feel like a trick?" he asked, though he did not wait for her response when he could easily read it on her face. "I'm not a magician, Ellie. I'm an entomologist and arachnologist. Truth or trick, science or fiction—what seems more plausible derived of a man you've known for the better end of two decades?"

She tried not to let him notice as her eyes scanned the rest of the table. Except for the larvae-filled platter and the jars he first unveiled to her, everything else had been removed from that ghastly yellow cloth while she was unconscious. There were no knives or forks or plates. Billy was being cautious, and she understood that she had to be a thousand times more cautious if she wanted to get out of this alive. He may not have expressed interest in murdering her, but she had a feeling that he wouldn't view dicing her into tiny pieces as murder if those pieces sprouted antennae or wings or reanimated in some buggy form or other.

Closing her eyes, she listened to the still-playing background music, and she thought.

Her phone and pepper spray were both in her purse, which she had set on a decorative chair in the entryway. Although Billy Goldstein was a weak man, he was still a man—that was evident with the strength used to hack off her hand. And it was not as if she thought she had the luxury of waiting for Luigi's suspicious nature to kick in and bring him kicking down the door. Compared to other corners, the one she was most backed into was an intellectual disadvantage. As intelligent as she was, Billy's mind was more brilliant—genius.

She glared at him, at the smug, self-pleased look he wore. She wanted to complete the job that his countless, sleepless hours in his basement lab started yet could not finish. She wanted to peel any lingering sense of humanity off the front of his skull. She wanted the fingernails (of her left hand, obviously) to scrape bone. She realized in a rise of perverse glee that this was not the first time she had experienced such murderous tones toward the man. How many times had she looked through the monstrous magnifying lenses perched on his nose and imagined how satisfying it would feel to dig her fingers into those wet, white, grub-like eyes.

There it was! In her rage, Ellie almost overlooked the one major advantage she had over Billy: her eyesight. She did not have to carry out her fantasy exactly. All she had to do was remove, and preferably destroy, his glasses. Without his visual crutches, Billy was a few decades from legal blindness. Exposing that weakness was her best chance of survival.

Her attention returned to the tabletop, to the glass jars in which Billy's former pieces dwelled. They were close enough to grab. They weren't much, but they would have to do. Two shots at escape were better than none.

Wait for it, she told herself, a higher sense of awareness taking over. *His music is still playing, and he's bobbing his head to it. It's slight, but I can see it. Wait until that sound of spider webs lulls him into its comfortable trap. Wait until he doesn't see it coming.*

The cacophony of computerized coos continued. While it sounded disturbing to her, she figured Billy's take on the music was epic. To him, it was the sweet surrender of seraphs to his secular self-righteousness. It reached high, it dipped low, and it culminated toward that moment of climax when he would be fully enveloped, a fly in a web. Building, building, building, and then—

Ellie lunged, ramming her stomach into the table and knocking the wind out of herself. Having just barely wrapped her fingers around the maggot-jar, she tightened her stomach and pushed herself backward.

Billy's head snapped left, and he jumped at her. He was mid-air when the jar collided with his glasses. Neither jar nor lenses broke, but the impact pushed the frames into his brow with enough force to make them bounce away from his face. They did not come completely off, but instead landed on the tip of his nose.

He was still coming.

Without pausing, Ellie lunged forward again and grabbed the grub jar. This time, before she had the chance to lean back and send it at his head, Billy was on her, in her face, and she and the chair were on their backs. He wrapped his fingers around her throat, pressed them into any hollow spaces they could find.

"Don't harm my babies!" he growled.

Blackness flared in and out along the outskirts of her eyes, and she realized that the back of her head had probably struck the ground when he tackled her and the chair. She figured that trauma, combined with his full weight focused into a death-grip on her air-way, was responsible for the ecliptic flashes bordering her vision. Fortunately, she had one last chance, an ace up her sleeve—another jar in her hand.

He hadn't seen her grab the second one.

She gripped the glass container and could hear the almost inexistent sound of hairline fractures running through it. Then, with everything she had left, she thrust it into his right eye, shattering the jar and sending the frames still dangling from his ears, as well as the toe-grub that had been inside the container, to the ground. Blood from Billy's shard-shot socket sprayed her face and leaked into her eyes. He stood and began pacing the room.

"My babies! I give you my love! I give you the blessing of eternity, and this is what you give me, you bitch! You nasty, selfish, bitch!"

He stopped cursing her only when he heard something shatter beneath him. Billy's foot had come down on the first jar she threw at him. He dropped to his knees and began sifting through the glass.

"Where are you, little buddy? Where'd you go? I'll save you."

This was her chance to run for the door. Ellie struggled to her feet and began turning her body in the direction of escape, but she only made it mid-turn before a fresh pain, an itchy pain, erupted in her eyes and pitched her into the table. It was a soapy sort of sting—only, a thousand times worse.

Is it glass? she wondered. *I broke the jar above my face, so it must be glass.*

She looked at the tablecloth through pained, watering eyes, and that was when she understood the source of her excruciation. The red puddles she had mistaken for her blood, for they had previously been her blood, were shifting under the dim glow and had been for some time. A countless number of mites.

She remembered something Billy said earlier: "*The blood was also moving. It was red, so it became chiggers.*"

Blood became chiggers, and his blood had just gotten in her eyes.

She had started to push herself away from the table when his left hand seized her right leg, tripping her over her own force. Her entire body screamed as she hit the ground, and hearing that beaten howl, she finally understood the gravity of what Billy had done to her. She was an ant-hill in waiting, a hornet nest to be. She was a tick, and she was a flea. No matter what she did, if she escaped the house and attempted to resume a normal life, she would always be haunted by her own infestation. Menstruation, she shuddered to think, would be the birth of a thousand, tiny bugs.

She looked at him. Even in dim light and through a red-mist veil of mites, she could see what had become of his right eye. A jagged splinter of glass had penetrated and deflated it, and dead inside the socket, it had metamorphosed into a dangling grub worm. Finally, it was true; the man's eyes—at least one of them currently actualized as such—were now the white, wormy things they had always resembled.

He began crawling up her legs. The closer he got, the more she saw of his grubby gash. He too had a mess of chiggers crawling around the wound. Ants, as well, fiery-looking things, were collecting at the fresh lesion. They were even attacking the grub at center.

Immortality is a feeding frenzy, Ellie thought as his face hovered above hers.

Billy no longer seemed angry. Except for the few dozen arthropods gathered there, she had seen this look on his face many times, more so in the early days of their marriage. It was an unmistakable look; the same one he had always worn while running his insect-familiar fingers against her sex.

"I still love you," he said, leaning closer. "I did this for us. I love you, Ellie-my-dear."

Her left hand shot into the air, struggling to find any weapon, but all she managed to grip was the tablecloth. Billy's face inched closer and closer, until his lips were pressing hard against hers, his teeth were grinding against hers, and his tongue was wriggling on the insides of her cheeks. She bit down, but he wouldn't stop. He wouldn't stop, not even when his tongue landed in the back of her throat and began seconds later to flutter like a wood roach.

She tugged at the tablecloth, fighting despite choking. The remaining silver-topped platter, the one with the spider-hand and larvae inside, crashed to the ground behind Billy. No longer held down, the white-turned-yellow shroud she always hated slid off the table and fell over the two of them.

The music she thought might be an accurate depiction of the sound of spider webs being made filled her head, and then, after a few minutes, nothing.

It's okay, Luigi told himself. *She's okay. That freak probably just coaxed her into one last pity fuck. That's all.*

The thought didn't reassure him much, but he liked it far better than the other ones which periodically crossed his mind as he sat in his car across the street from the Goldstein residence. He knew what Billy Goldstein looked like, had seen him around town before, and the idea of an odd-looking oddball like him delivering it to a beautiful woman like Ellie gave him the same kind of phantom chill spiders gave him.

That's all there is to it—she fucked him a final time, and when that wasn't enough for him, he played on her heartstrings, coaxed her into staying the night. She wakes up a lot. I bet she'll wake up any second and realize her mistake. I'll count down from sixty, and by the time I'm done, she'll probably step outside, get in her car, and drive away.

Luigi didn't count more than ten seconds. He stepped out of his car, felt a slight chill, and buttoned up his shirt as he crossed the street. He reached the door and heard something; it was music, probably that electronic shit Ellie said her husband loved so much. Muffled through the walls, it sounded eerie, especially nearing three in the morning.

He knocked on the door and this time tried to wait a full minute. Other than the music, there were no signs of life inside. He looked through the tall, slender window beside the front door and into the dimly lit dining room (he had been in the house on a few occasions Billy didn't know about). There was something, some shape, lying under a sheet on the floor.

All he could think was: *Murder, murder-suicide, murder, murder-suicide!*

It skipped Luigi's mind to try the knob. He raised his boot and sent it once, twice, third time's a charm against the door. It splintered away from the frame, and he rushed inside, ripping his recently buttoned shirt open to throw down with whoever crossed his path and wasn't Ellie.

A *whoever* would have been fine. Luigi wasn't afraid of anyone. But as he approached the dining room's dim glow, he encountered a *whatever*. Above the arch to the dining room in a thick, almost silky web was the largest spider he had ever seen. It looked like a tarantula, only it was muscular and fleshy and whitish. There was also something familiar about it. He watched, transfixed, as it crawled on eight bony legs across its thick-laced web to greet another guest, a single trapped fly still buzzing. The absurdity of a tarantula spinning a web to catch prey did not occur to him until years later, when he found an article about the many new species discovered at the Goldstein house and tacked it on the wall beside other stories he'd collected.

His sight returned to the mass on the floor. Deciding that the spider was too busy with the fly to bother with him, he swallowed his irrational fear long enough to pass under the oversized arachnid. The tabletop was bare, and the form he was staring at, the form he prayed was not Ellie's corpse, was covered in what looked like the tablecloth.

As he continued to stare, working up the nerve to toss the shroud aside, he saw that whatever it covered was moving, bubbling up against the sheet in various, random waves. It looked like there might be two people moving. Luigi's mind went frantic at the thought of the Goldsteins reunited under the cover. He bent forward, lifted the cloth, and began reaching forward to grab whoever was on top. That's when something, a bee perhaps, stung the palm of his hand. As his other hand dropped the sheet to the side, he saw what had really been moving beneath it.

Luigi ran from the Goldstein house and waited until he was safe inside his own car to scream. He would never forget the sight: so many of them crawling over each other, attacking each other—a violent orgy of bugs.

MY LOVE BURNS WITH A GREEN FLAME

By Thomas Mavroudis

That Ted Howard put a single bullet though the heads of six women is only slightly less significant than the six bullets that passed through his own head, discharged by his own hand.

He remained standing, conscious, practically pain free, after six close range shots to the head; his head, the mossy ichor draining from the wounds, sealing them almost as they burst forth with hot lead. And even as the insatiable lust inside him continued to blossom as dust compressed into a gas giant, into a sun, Ted Howard decided to relieve his pain. It was a sickness wanted, tolerated, needed and so vastly abhorrent. A sickness so unlike the pain suffered by the six women, and the greater suffering on the world, and Ted Howard didn't want to take that chance.

But bullets to *his* head—that just wasn't doing it.

The house in North Park Hill was not your standard Addams Family property; no widow's porch, no Victorian eaves or gables, no wrought iron fence. On the surface, it was a quaint brick pre-war bungalow on a corner lot blighted only by the dilapidated wood fence, dead grass, and faded remnants of graffiti.

The house was on the corner of the border street that used to separate the bad neighborhood from the worse neighborhood, and like many houses on this former battleground, was beyond the definition of a "fixer-upper." Almost every house on the block had been boarded up at one time or another. That was over fifteen years before.

All that remained of those days were a few survivors, families of pride and hard work, not tempted by fast cash schemes; families hardened to moral and civic responsibility. Yet, people from the suburbs were making a lot of money from neighborhoods like this, taking away the ghosts for cheap and re-building expensive dreams. People like Ted and Erin Howard.

The house was in better shape than most, and did not need to be entirely gutted. The floor plan of the main level was functional, with larger than normal bedrooms and a second bathroom. It was a perfect first home, and bound to double in value by the time Ted and Erin were ready to move farther south in the neighborhood and have children.

The challenge for the property was the basement. "This is where we're going to profit on this place," Ted assured Erin. Although it was finished, the basement was not, in Erin's mind, useable. The three great rooms were empty, dirt-littered, obviously unused in recent history, except for a few crushed cigarettes and pieces of beer bottles.

"Well, then that's your canvas, Ted," Erin proclaimed. "I can't wait to watch you design on a dime; or a penny—at least that's our budget for the rest of the year."

Weeks went by, and bit-by-bit, the house came together, mostly at the paint-stained, cracked, and sometimes bloody hands of Erin. Weekends went by and Ted devoted most of his time to the landscaping, a project Erin wanted to do together. It was late spring, but not so late that Ted couldn't start sod and new trees in the seemingly rich, semi-clay of the back and front yards. The first planting day, as Ted watered newly-mulched mounds of aspen bundles, the little lady from across the street hobbled down from her porch shaking her head.

"Ain't never seen no plants grown over there."

Ted smiled. He met her the day they moved in, but couldn't remember her name. She professed to be the neighborhood watchdog, and had watched the good and the wicked come and go. Overall, she was happy to see folks fixing up the houses.

"Is that right?" he asked, wiping sweat from his brow, taking a sip from the gardening hose. The old lady scowled at Ted's drink.

"Yep. That's right. See them bushes there? Ain't never seen them bloom yet; been on this corner since 1948." She pointed to the neighbor's spindly hedge, more dead than alive, that separated his front yard from the neighbor's.

"Well, maybe they just need some TLC? Maybe they just need some water?" It was the only detail next door that seemed unkempt.

"*Hmpf.* Maybe. But I ain't never seen nothing green, ever, over there. That's a fact. And I wouldn't be drinking that water neither." She scowled again.

"Well, what's your secret? Looks like you've got a pretty green thumb over there." Ted was eager to please the watchdog.

"My husband was responsible for that." She smiled. "He's dead now. Been dead for about fourteen years, but he keeps my garden real nice, bless his soul."

"Well," Ted said, "thanks for the advice. We'll see if we can get some greenery to pop up around this place."

"Good luck, honey. Don't drink that water."

Summer began, and the landscaping failed to even try. Ted was disappointed, but more than happy to finally retreat to the cool of the basement and the projects he had been talking about from the day they moved in. The basement was cool, but musty, more so than typical old basements. Ted couldn't focus, his mind distracted in a dank, mossy haze. He would sit on the upturned, brand new tool bucket, his back against cold concrete, methodically sipping cans of beer, and consider his failure with the dead dry sod and withered aspen sticks. It was like lying in bed, resisting the inevitability of going to an office, a desk, and a job one hated.

On a hot afternoon at the peak of summer, Erin called down, "How goes the masterpiece?" She promised not to set a foot below until Ted had at least swept and vacuumed. She never heard him perform either.

"Oh, you know," Ted answered, "I'm still mapping. I know you don't believe me, but there are so many possibilities down here."

"Okay, my sweet Morlock. But come up soon. We barely have two hours to get ready for Eve's."

"All right," Ted called up. "You better start getting ready. You shower first, there's got to be a leak down here, I think. I want to check it out."

Ted heard the water begin rushing through the pipes and stood under the area that, in the finished basement, would be the third bathroom. He poked the flecks of brown plaster around the edge of a moist crack in the basement ceiling. Searching for the greater leak, he peeled away a tiny bit of plaster and a large chunk of the ceiling fell through with a gush of soapy, warm water.

Ted spat the taste and grit of bitter almond and wood rot from his mouth. "Erin! Turn the shower off! Turn the shower off!"

"What?"

"Turn the fucking shower off, Erin!"

"Sorry," he heard her mumble through the floor when the water was off.

Ted came upstairs, still wiping his mouth with anger. "Well, shit. I guess we won't be using this bath for a while." Erin wrapped a towel around her hair and Ted, snapping another towel from the rack, stomped off to the other bathroom.

Ted and Erin left the party early, Ted complaining of severe allergies. "It feels like there's a squirrel's tail up my nose," Ted explained as they said their goodbyes. All night, eyes watery, face swollen, Ted blew his nose, trying to dislodge whatever was irritating his sinuses.

"Honey, are you all right?"

"I don't know," Ted said. "This is terrible."

"What the hell happened?"

"Well, I don't know," he barked, then backed off. "I think maybe . . . maybe, there was a mold or something in the floor." He rubbed his forehead furiously, pressed circles under his eyes.

"Maybe."

He closed his eyes tight. "This is just awful. I feel like shit."

Erin stroked his chest. "Well, don't go back down there. Okay?"

"Are you crazy? I've got to fix that shit. We can't just have a hole in the bathroom floor with water pouring all over the place."

"I know that, I'm not stupid." It was her rightful turn at bitterness. "Just get better first. Please?"

"I know. I'm sorry. It's just this damn squirrel in my nose." They both laughed and kissed each other goodnight.

Ted Howard was thirteen all over again. He and Erin did not suffer any marital problems. In fact, they had been frequently intimate for not having been newlyweds for some years. So Ted was surprised to wake from a dead sleep at the very moment of climax, Erin snoring soundly on her side beside him, and remember nothing of how or why. With certainty, his shorts were sticky and wet.

The following night when it happened again, Ted remembered the dream. He walked in a mansion with walls covered in lush oils of Victorian nudes. He was naked except for a black fur-lined coat. He attributed the dream to the anti-histamines that were no help except for knocking him into sleep. After the fourth erotic dream, he told Erin. She smiled, "That's a turn on. We're going to have to do something about that when you feel better."

Ted, expressing that he was indeed feeling better, had sex with his wife and he dreamed nothing. The sex was more intense in every way. He woke the next morning feeling rejuvenated beyond any rest he had experienced in his life, as though he had been reborn, fresh and new.

It went on like this. After increasingly extreme sessions awake with his wife, he slept deeply, undisturbed. But on the sexless nights, he dreamt. The dreams grew in length and detail every night. Other people were introduced, male and female and in-between, beautiful strangers dressed in leather and lace or gossamer rags, orgies in shopping malls and plaza fountains, sex on floating pillows, in submerged tunnels of luminous wine, Ted at the center, the master of it all, reaping and sowing.

It was the hot final day of August when Ted woke in the middle of a sexless night, first relieved and relaxed, then sickened with horror. He had dreamt of rape. Who it was, he didn't know, he couldn't see her face covered by a feathered mask. The memory of the dream was delightfully awful.

"Well, stud," his wife said, smiling, pouring a morning cup of coffee, "what kind of wild ride were you on last night? You woke me up."

Ted drank a slow draw from his glass of juice. "You don't want to know."

"Sick, babe. You're right, I don't want to know." She kissed his ear.

The dream troubled him all day.

At a late dinner that night, they argued over what to do with the basement. Erin insisted they forget about it; maybe hire someone to renovate later when they were in a better financial position. Ted disputed that they were losing money, would lose even more if they did anything stupid, but they hadn't even repaired the faulty plumbing. Dinner ended with Erin slamming—smashing some of— the plates in the sink. Ted fell asleep at the table, an empty bottle of wine by his hand. He woke to Erin pinching the skin on the back of his arms, a sweet, hot sting. "What the fuck are you trying to do? What's the matter with you?" He hung over her side of the bed, naked.

"What?" Ted rolled onto the floor, crawled into the corner by the bathroom.

"What's the matter with you?" she asked again. "Do you think you can just make up for being an asshole by trying to sleep with me? I was sleeping! Pissed, but sleeping. Then you come in, like a fucking bear . . ."

Exactly. Ted was dreaming he was a bear, walking like a man through the crumbled marble steps of a Greek amphitheater to a set of lily ponds below. In one of the ponds was a nude woman, bathing. Small white feathers covered her skin. She screamed when Ted, his fat and fur, crashed into the pond. She hissed like a swan.

Ted sat in the corner, shamed. "I'm sorry."

"Don't be sorry, Ted. Just don't mess with me like that. You started pulling my hair. Hard."

"I'm sorry," he said again. But he wanted to ask if they could still have sex.

Ted wanted sex every night. The lascivious thoughts eroded his days. Without sex, real cognizant sex, he had the rape dreams. He never told Erin about them, and when she began to ask if he was having nightmares now, he said yes. He raped someone, something, every night, and every day he woke tired and ashamed of his gross pleasure. His mood grew worse every day, and so every night, he and Erin would not have sex. When they did, he was still like the bear, his passion increased exponentially. And Erin grew colder, her desire for his passion lessening, until she was only doing it so Ted would not mistake her for some dream whore. She was almost becoming frightened.

Ted pushed too far again the night Erin made him sleep on the couch. She locked the bedroom door when she heard his body collapse on the furniture.

On the couch, naked and cold, Ted Howard dreamt. It was unlike any of the sex dreams he had had before. He was floating in darkness that felt like water. Electrical warmth surrounded him, pleasurably irritating his skin. He tried to touch himself and discovered he could not. Where were his arms? The concept of arms disintegrated. He wanted to laugh, but the sound he heard himself make was a squeal, a distant, feeble vibration behind a curtain of time. Was that really him? The concept of self exploded. A rush of colors bled from the darkness and what used to be Ted began to experience falling, a fall from the edge of space into the wilderness. The Ted-thing crashed, and fire, black and emerald, erupted from its crater. From this vantage, Ted-thing could see all angles: a sow with one hundred teats; featherless birds with song like a frozen rose; fish with gaping, hungry mouths that walked plains of sand; furry, muddy hominids clustered in furious orgy; black liquid stone that ebbed and flowed in the air; teeth-like beetles feasting on the remains of a blind serpent; wet electricity, an entire planet, pink and wet, pulsing—a squid, a jellyfish or. . . .

The sensation was like a flower blossoming, but the flower was the universe, and the universe was made of ice that became steam with the snap of a Cyclopean eye closing. Ted woke with a chiseled smile on his face, his hands and manhood bloody.

After the night he slept on the couch, Erin told him, "I think you need to see a doctor."

"Why?" Ted caressed her earlobe.

"Ted. Come on, there's something wrong with you." Erin pulled his hand away.

Ted smiled and tried to kiss his wife.

She backed away, said, "Ted, there's blood on the couch. What happened?"

His smile grew broader. "I'm all right." Erin imagined he was somehow drunk.

"Ted. Were you hurting yourself or . . ."

"Is that what it's called? I thought only church folks believed that kind of shit. Hurting myself, huh?" He stroked himself in his pants.

"Stop it, Ted. I'm serious! You're having these wet dreams every night..."

"Only when we don't..."

"Ted! Please listen to me. What is happening? I thought you were going to rape me last night."

Ted's smile folded. "Erin, I'm sorry." He grabbed her hands, lovingly pulled her to him and held her shoulders. "I know I've been a little aggressive lately."

"Ted, aggressive is kinky. You haven't been aggressive."

Ted nodded his head, a moment of cold clarity. "You're right. There is something wrong with me."

"Well, what are you going to do about it?"

"Don't worry, I'll think of something." He kissed Erin's forehead.

Ted Howard was no longer like men; his thoughts were truly consumed by sex only. He couldn't concentrate at work, began making the types of errors people make under extreme stress. His office encouraged him to take the rest of the day off.

"Yeah," Ted said, itching beneath his suit, already peeling it from his body as he stood up from his desk. "Good idea."

Ted's legs felt blurry as he walked passed row and row of ready-made office space, passed women he had seen almost every day. Most of the women he never noticed before, would never notice, and now, as he passed them, all he could do was think of how their sweat smelled, what their voices sounded like grunting and screaming, how their muscles looked flexed and contorted. Were they looking at him, wondering what he smelled like? Did they know? Did they want him? He managed to get to his car without incident.

Along and below the side of the highway, where Ted drove to and from work every day, were three gentlemen's clubs. Ted had been to Ruby's Gold just once before, not even for his own bachelor's party, but someone else's. The club was expensive and Ted was not looking for expense. Further along was Glass Kittens, really just a porn theatre and shop with a live pay-per-view parlor, the vintage peep show type with a blind that goes up and down. Ted did not want women under glass, although he had dreamt of it in the past weeks. At the end, where the service road bent off towards the rail yard, was a place simply called Fun. It was the club pregnant high school girls danced at, the club where high school boy's hearts were broken—a place where men became boys again. The club was all nude, eighteen and up, served no alcohol. Ted walked in the cool shadow of the highway, through buckled faux leather doors and into red light and heat.

Ted got home around four in the morning, prepared to detail his long-extended work day. There was a note from Erin taped to the television:

What the fuck Ted? You are such an asshole. Thanks. I don't even want to tell you where I am, but I will because I don't feel good and I think you should know. Please call me at Eve's. E.

Ted went to bed and slept for twelve deep, dreamless hours.

Erin didn't call all day and Ted didn't care. When he woke in the late afternoon, he checked the bank account to see how much cash he spent the night before. He couldn't remember.

The phone rang. "Hello?"

"Ted, where is she?" It was Erin's sister, Lynn.

"Erin?"

"Yeah, Ted, Erin. And where the hell were you?"

"Where?"

"Ted, look, did Erin come home yet? She didn't tell me where she went."

"Yeah. Yeah, Lynn, she's home."

"Are you guys talking?"

"Sure, she's pissed but . . . yeah, things are better."

"Well put her on."

"She doesn't feel well, Lynn. You should come over."

"Well, what's the matter, Ted?"

"I don't know. I better go."

After Lynn, what he did to her, Ted couldn't stay home. He packed a small bag and withdrew just enough cash to pay for a motel near Fun, leaving more than enough of the account for Erin to manage, at least for a little while. Soon he would disappear someplace, maybe Mexico, someplace where he could live as he had to now.

The girls at Fun soon became the contrary; the two he had been with were no longer extinguishing the sunburst flames of his desire. His cash didn't last long. He was half an animal, a reptile with the brain of Einstein. He was terrified of sexless sleep. He needed something new, something raw, something to keep the beautiful nightmares at bay. He chose Margo from his office.

Ted hadn't returned to work for almost a week. Surely Margo and all the office staff were aware of what happened. It made the prospect of the sex all the more searing. Ted knew where Margo lived, and hid there from early morning, waiting, shivering with want. It didn't matter that he could be caught. He felt protected.

Ted heard two voices from behind the opening front door: Margo and another woman he recognized from work. He smiled.

Later again, Ted was worried about the blood. Could someone trace it back to him? "Of course," he said to himself, snickering as if he told a joke. "Stupid blood. Ha!" At least he could sleep.

The next morning, Allie from Fun was at his motel door. In the shade she looked the color of algae.

"Ed, I'm sick. I don't feel good." She was nineteen, but could have as easily been fifteen.

"No? Oh." Ted was going to close the door.

"Can I come in?" the girl asked.

"Sure." Ted closed the door behind her and began to take his clothes off.

"No. Ed, I don't feel good. I can't do that right now."

"What?" Ted was erect and grinning. "Well, what are you here for? What do you want?"

"I think I might be pregnant."

"Oh." He pulled at himself, with more vigor at the word *preg-nant.*

"I don't know, my tummy feels bad and look," she pulled up her clean, white t-shirt, "does that look like a bruise to you? Do you get bruised when you're pregnant?" Her belly looked dirty.

"I don't have kids yet. We're waiting until we sell the house," Ted explained, scratching his cheek with his free hand.

"Oh," Allie said, a fluttering expression between a grin and a grimace on her face. "That's nice."

"Yeah."

"So, if I'm pregnant, I don' know what I'm going to do yet, but I wanted to let you know."

"Thanks." Ted reached out to Allie.

"Please, maybe later." `

"Oh, okay." Ted stood naked in his door and watched Allie walk down the street to work. He was tired.

He was fearful. Perhaps, he thought, one night without . . . it sickened him to think of a night without sex, the dreams were so much worse now, so much more exhilarating.

Ted lay in salty sheets, burning from a heat he created, more intense than the season outside. "I won't sleep," Ted screamed.

Was it sleep or something else? Suddenly or slowly, Ted was in the electric darkness. His body felt like a thousand bodies, his cry was a thousand sounds, he was traveling down a thousand pulsing corridors. Then a flash of white light, then light from a black sun, and before him wires, veins, vines, fingers, hairs, what was it that strug-gled in the black light? Nerves, dendrites, and holding the circuit to-gether, a fleshy nucleus, shaking, square and round, blacker than the anti-sun, radiating electric sex death heat.

Ted woke screaming, his manhood bleeding, and he knew. It was inside him.

What may or may not have been growing inside the six women Ted saved, he did not know, but save them he's sure he did,

all their bellies greenish black and starting to harden. It didn't matter where the gun came from. Ted couldn't remember anyway. Every
kill enflamed his desire more. Erin was the last. She had gone back
to their home, an animal seeking sanctuary for birth or death. He
fought the incinerating lust as best he could by trying to copulate
with the spent body of his wife. But the nerves, the tendrils at his
core sickened him with every touch of the cooling flesh. He had to
end it all before he could no longer resist the insatiable call to pro-
create.

　　He returned to the basement. The first bullet made a mess.
It nearly blew the back of his head off. Ted, in shock, turned to the
wall. The splattered black-green filigree disappeared into the pores
of the cement. Ted felt the back of his head; it was closing. He put the
gun to his mouth again and pulled twice. He put the gun under his
chin and pulled. "Come on, come on." He felt like crying, but he was
dry. Frustrated, he fell to the floor and putting the gun to his forehead, pulled. Ted sat up and touched his head. It was already closed.

　　The insidious need burned anew, Ted's spine drenched in
molten iron of passion. He needed to fuck. Every bullet was a tease,
a tickle amplified outside any sensation and he realized what needed
to be done. He remembered the last dream, the vision of the thing
inside him. It resembled, at its basest depiction, a human brain and
nervous system, inverted. Ted held the gun, and fighting the urge to
vomit or pass out, self-preservation quickly getting the best of him,
placed one final bullet in the empty cylinder. Ted Howard smiled and
mumbling some obscenity to himself, placed the gun to his crotch
and pulled the trigger.

THE FACE IN THE MIRROR
By Sean McCoy

It fell out a little at a time and then all at once. I ran my hands through my hair in front of the mirror daily, checking for clumps and flecks of dandruff and other telltale signs that I was losing my hair. My wife watched me and through all of this, nodded calmly, saying that I was fine, that I wasn't balding. That I had fine hair, not thinning hair. It was the product which made it look that way. I shouldn't use so much product anyway. I looked good as I was.

But I could see it. My hair had always been thick and my younger brothers, only a few years behind me, still had thick hair that they slicked back or puffed up at will, while mine had one or two styles that still worked.

I switched to an organic shampoo and conditioner and tried out different lather/rinse rituals and experimented with how often I washed my hair. I stopped using combs because I read that the teeth pull your hair from the root. Better to just use my hands. I cropped it short too. My thin hair was long and clumped together, revealing my roots and pale scalp. That was the problem. It wasn't thinning.

I was too fat to shave my head, I told myself. I'd look like an inflated ball sack. So I kept it short, close cropped. No product. Just a little hairspray. Maybe start running some more. I could always grow it out long again if my hair loss plateaued.

And then one morning when I got out of the shower and looked in the mirror I saw the first spot, the bald spot. Not at the back near my frustrating double cowlick. Not at the front either. My hairline wasn't receding.

My hair was falling out.

The missing clump came from the top left side, seven inches above my left eyebrow. Above the hairline, just a fallow blank spot with a few putrid hairs sticking out of my pink scalp.

I almost screamed.

I thought back to the night before. Had I pulled my hair out in my sleep? Or sleep walked maybe and shaved my head on accident? Was my wife playing a practical joke on me to calm me down or force me into making a decision about shaving my head? I raced through my memories trying to find a reason for the sudden bald spot.

The internet held no solutions either. It was something akin to the hair loss that many chemotherapy patients suffer, but it was localized to one specific, round spot. Alopecia, I heard, could be the problem. I saw pictures of dozens of men with perfectly symmetrical circles of missing hair dotted across their heads and I feared the worst.

When my wife came home I fretted about the spot for hours until she was sick of me.

"I didn't do anything to it and it's probably all this stress that's making you lose your hair. Stop messing with it. Shave it or leave it be."

We were short with each other all night but when I refused to take the hat off in bed she turned sweet and told me that it didn't matter to her. This was normal, even if it wasn't exactly normal, and that she loved me no matter what.

I told her it mattered to me.

The next morning the spot seemed to have grown more. To track its growth, I took a blue pen and marked a small spot that I thought only I would be able to notice. I was afraid that my wife would think I was paranoid.

I spent hours on the internet comparing anecdotal similarities and ruling them out or questioning the original poster further on long since dead threads. I checked my inbox every ten minutes waiting for a reply from someone who knew what I was going through, but nothing came back to me. Just an endless sea of confirmation e-mails requesting that I confirm my new membership to *eDocBBS.com, CareFriends.org, MaleHairAnonymous.net*, and a dozen other forums, newsletters, and sites that all claimed firsthand experience with hair loss. Or strange hair loss. Was it that strange? It happened to nearly every man on the planet.

The next day I saw that the spot really had grown. My tiny blue dot, once embedded in the ragged tree-line of my ever-thinning hair now stood alone on a fleshy hill. I showed my wife and she admitted, fine, I was right. I was going bald. What now? Was I happy now?

It wasn't that I was going bald that bothered me, but this was strange, wasn't it? I showed her my research on Alopecia and the pictures and posts by men and women who had been afflicted by it.

"Well if the internet says," she said.

I said something snarky and mean and she backed off. She told me to see a doctor or get a haircut, for the love of god, because if I was going to obsess over it, I should at least do something about it.

I resolved to see a hairdresser. No, a barber. A man who would know what I was going through. No, a stylist. A woman. Someone who had seen men try to hide their baldness before and would know a way to help me hide as well.

So I called a *Cheap-Clipz* down the street and made an appointment for the morning. I told my wife and apologized for how I had snapped at her. She was happy to hear that I was taking matters into my own hands, but I could tell she was still frustrated with me. We watched TV and fell asleep without talking about the spot any more.

In the morning, I felt refreshed. I had my solution: the haircut. Maybe my wife was right. Maybe it was just the stress. To prepare, I did my daily double-wash, first with the homeopathic remedy, a mixture of apple cider vinegar and soap, and then with the product I had ordered direct, *Restorox*. I let that sit for a few minutes, pretending to wash the rest of myself, while the subtle burn trickled across my scalp. I counted an extra thirty seconds on top of the 120 I had already counted in my head just in case I was counting too fast, and then rinsed it out. I could feel it burn in my eyes a little, but that was okay. The burn would go away. My hair could not.

At first, when I got out of the shower and looked in the mirror I was happy. The spot hadn't grown, I had marked it with another dot this time, just in case. But when I ran my hands through my hair, another clump came, this time on the right side, just above my ear. It came out quickly, as smooth as stripping the covers off a bed. As soon as I felt it tug I made a noise, terrified at what I had done. Unable to undo it. I tried holding it up to the new bald spot, pressing and holding the loose hair so it would reattach, maybe through osmosis, but instead, it fell in a dead mass into the sink. I flushed the clump down the toilet, immediately regretting it, thinking that it might serve some future purpose.

I called the hairdresser and cancelled my appointment.

When my wife came home I was sitting in the dark trying to sleep but unable to, afraid that the oils on our pillows had suffocated my pores and clogged up any chance of my thin weak hair getting through. When she asked about my haircut, I told her we needed new sheets. When she responded warily I showed her the new spot.

This time she had the reaction I was hoping for. This was too much too fast and for the first time I saw the fear in her eyes that I had, that something wasn't right.

She gave me a number to call and when the automated system picked up I left a vague message about scheduling an urgent appointment. I made sure to let them know that I didn't think it was life threatening but that I did think it was time sensitive and so to schedule me as early as possible. I made it known that I would be willing to come in early if the Doctor's schedule allowed.

We didn't fight about the hair that night. Instead I just slept on the couch with a fresh towel over the pillowcase and I took a shower right before bed without checking the spot for growth.

In the morning, I decided not to wash my hair at all. I instead put all my product into a grocery bag to show the doctor so that maybe they could decide whether my treatment, admittedly self-designed, was doing more harm than good. I had received no callback from the doctor's office, which I remedied right after brushing my teeth and seeing myself in the mirror again.

It wasn't another spot, it was seven. And they weren't all circles either. Some were patchy and oblong while others snaked around like crooked veins tracing a pale path across my head, dividing it like farmland. I wanted to cry.

I yelled at the nurse on the phone and when she didn't schedule for an appointment, I threw on a hat and drove to the emergency room.

They wouldn't see me in the ER for what now seems like obvious reasons, but I was so worked up that they sent me to a quieter wing of the hospital to see a doctor. A patient man who explained his procedures calmly, and promised to get to the bottom of things.

He asked me about my home life and my work, both of which I admitted were strained, but no more than usual.

He barely looked at my products though, and when I started in about my routine and the precise scheduling I did to ensure that my hair received round-the-clock treatment, he tuned me out completely.

What he recommended was cutting back on the care and just washing my hair every other day or so as normal. He did recommend that I shave my head for appearance's sake, to which I replied that I wasn't here for fashion advice, I had scheduled an appointment with a professional hair stylist for that.

He again ignored me, nodding instead to himself. He concurred that Alopecia was a strong candidate for the cause, but a trichoscopy didn't reveal any of the telltale "yellow dots" normally associated with the autoimmune disease. He took my blood work, but beyond that he couldn't really say. He sent my home with a sample of *Rogain*.

That night my wife gave me the Come-to-Jesus talk. After my unexpected trip to the hospital (and the bill it had accrued) she felt it was necessary to remind me that she loved me, and that aging was normal, but I needed to get on top of it, because it was getting on top of me.

"Neither my father nor my mother's father are bald," I told her.

"But it's happening," she said. "Here."

She handed me a pair of clippers and a towel.

"I picked these up," she said. "Maybe it's time. If the doctor took your blood work then I'm sure he can figure out a solution, but in the meantime, you can control how you handle this."

She was right, I had to admit it. She was always right. She sat me down in the bathtub that night and wrapped a towel around my naked shoulders and we shaved off what was left. Neck. Sides. Top. Everything. She gathered the clumps from the tub and threw them in a grocery sack before rinsing me and kissing my forehead.

When I looked in the mirror, I felt a small resurgence of confidence. I looked like myself but not myself. A familiar stranger. My wife hugged me and smiled and said I looked sexy and I thanked her for doing this and that I was sorry for being so crazy. She left the room to throw away the bag of hair and I inspected my new face.

She was right, it wasn't bad. I looked clean. As I wiped a stray hair from the back of my head, though, I noticed my right ear was curling in at the edges slightly more than normal. I had never examined my ears this closely before. And now without the hair to cover them up I saw them as lacking a little context and proportion.

I slept in our bed that night and my wife and I cuddled. We laughed a little bit about the strangeness of the days before and fell asleep in each other's arms.

I slept in the next morning for the first time in a week. My wife had already left for work and I felt content now to prepare for the day at my leisure, unafraid of looking at myself in the mirror. I showered, without product (God, how much was I really spending maintaining this illusion?), and again felt fresh and clean. Whole.

When I looked in the mirror though, I had a strange feeling, like my ears wouldn't pop. I turned my head to the side to inspect my right ear with the extra curl at the top from the night before and that's when I saw it.

My ear was gone.

Completely gone. A mangled bump where it used to be. I poked and prodded it, thumping against my temple and while I heard the dull *thunk* tapping against my skull, I couldn't place where the sound came from.

When 911 asked what my emergency was I was at a loss for words and yelled that they come over right away and that I was hurt. I took a picture and sent it to my wife via text and then called her, no answer.

When the paramedics arrived they couldn't find anything wrong with me and for a while they were paranoid that perhaps I was an amputee who had always been missing his ear and was per-haps reawakening to this fact in a state of confusion.

They questioned me for an hour and when I couldn't satis-factorily answer them verbally, I showed them numerous selfies and pictures from my phone, showing them dates and times of the pic-tures. And when finally, my wife called me back, her voice strained and terrified, the paramedics believed me and took me to the hospi-tal.

I saw a new doctor this time, though I could not tell him much apart from the last. He explained that they hadn't seen any-thing like this before. They kept me for days running MRIs and CT scans, interrogating me over and over. The curl of the ear in partic-ular was of interest to them. My wife sat by my side the entire time in a daze. When they asked her to recall, to the best of her ability, what the missing ear looked like she shrugged and said, "like the other one."

When they sent someone to talk to me about prosthetics, I knew the doctors didn't have anything. The questions stopped and instead only physical therapy remained.

Two weeks later, my wife guided me back to our car. She didn't talk on the drive home but sobbed silently. I couldn't hear her because she was on my now deaf side, but I caught a glimpse of her in the mirror. At home we tried to sleep in bed but couldn't and she took the couch, not wanting to disturb my rest.

I stayed up staring at the ceiling until I felt like I couldn't take it anymore and went to the bathroom to survey the lumpy mold that used to be my ear. The doctors hadn't let me look at it at all in the hospital, preferring instead to poke and prod me about the most intimate details of my day to day life. What did I eat and drink? What were my stools like? Had my wife and I engaged in any deviant sexual activities alone or with others?

There in the mirror I could see it. A crumpled mound like a flat raisin attached to the side of my face. I ran my fingers across it and it felt like a fleshy walnut. I couldn't believe this was happening to me. The hair loss of weeks ago seemed like nothing now.

When I turned my head to see my other ear though, I began to scream. I know because my wife ran into the bathroom and shook me. I couldn't hear it. My other ear had gone like the first. Dissolved into another membranous scar. I clutched my head and wailed. I could feel my wife's dull voice throb against my skull as she wrapped her arms around me. I felt her tears run down my neck and spine and we stayed that way until the ambulance arrived. I could only tell by the red lights reflecting throughout the house.

This time the tests took months, maybe longer. It was hard to tell. Functionally I was deaf but the doctors communicated to me the strangeness of my condition and their subsequent inability to diagnose it through a series of documents I was left to read alone. Along with my insurance's notification of their inability to cover said strange medical condition.

One night I had to be restrained and medicated because I was found bleeding from my skull wandering the hallways asking if I could hear now. If they could hear me. Or if I could hear them. It took three big orderlies to strip the bloody scissors from me and tie me down.

I read a lot and my wife and I wrote letters. In our last exchange she revealed to me why she had to leave. Not because of my condition, which she assured me meant nothing to her. But because the strain and strangeness had grown too much for her to bear. And should the doctors find any explanation or even a semblance of understanding, she would be happy to come and be a part of my care and my life.

I called her several times, knowing I wouldn't be able to hear her voice. But when I saw that she had answered I begged. Begged with my new voice, which I wasn't sure I controlled anymore, for her to stay. I never heard her response. But I did see the call disconnect.

After that and the insurance, the hospital bumped me to the curb and the cab dumped me back at home where I saw that all of my wife's things were gone. The bed was still there. The couch. The linens. The fridge was stocked with food. My hair product. And there was an unopened letter on the kitchen table that I decided I couldn't read.

The next morning, I needed to see what I had become wasting away in the hospital since the last season, afraid of my limp and weak body which had only subsisted on hospital food, which I hadn't eaten mostly.

Looking back at me in the mirror was my new. The stranger's face. Bald, with two grotesque protrusions on the side of my head, and now, a veiny patch of skin where my mouth used to be. I saw my jaw widen inside my face as a tormented wail echoed in my throat and tears welled up in my eyes.

I fell to the floor and crawled to the couch, where I doubled over and tried to scream and scream but instead only succeeded in smashing my head against the cushions over and over until they were soaked and damp from my tears.

The last time I looked, I had one nostril and one eye left. The nostril, I wasn't so sure of anymore, as I only felt my shallow breath wheeze through a flap of skin where my nose used to be. I used a hand mirror to check that it was still there occasionally, careful not to reveal the whole thing, lest it be stripped from me like everything else. The mirror now showed a craggy surface of broken and twisted skin, mutilated cartilage, and aborted features.

I had purchased IV fluids to sustain me and I spent most days in front of the TV running out the last of my savings on cable until that eventually ended as well. I never heard from my wife again. I never read her letter either. Afraid that after reading her farewell it would become too tempting to look one last time in the mirror and see nothing at all.

PORPHYRIA
By John S. McFarland

V iktor closed the elevator cage door in disgust. His friend, Sandor Bessenyei could not look at him. Sandor was pale and covered with perspiration from the fever he'd had all morning. He collapsed against the side of the cage as it started to make its way slowly up the mine headframe to the surface.

"I am sorry," Sandor mumbled. "I am too sick. *Èn vagyok a beteg.* I am too sick to work anymore." The black spot on the back of Sandor's hand and the one at the tip of his nose had been painful and distracting all morning. In the last hour, the one on his nose had gone completely numb and he smelled the metallic scent of his own blood when he inhaled. He struggled to redirect his attention toward his friend.

"*Én vagyok az egyetlen barátja.* I am your only companion here," Viktor said. "It's a harsh and unwelcoming world and you have to take whatever comfort you can, but it would seem you could try a little longer. Not everyone has money to live on. Some of us have to work. If you feel better a month from now they won't hire you back, you know? You quit now and you're done for in the mines, and no one else will hire Hungarians in this place. When your money runs out you're finished. In the meanwhile, I'm down in this pit with nobody to talk to."

"My money will soon be gone," Sandor said. "Regardless of that, I cannot work anymore. My strength has left me for good, I think."

Sandor felt ashamed, though he tried to hide a little smile. There was something very predictable, but oddly innocent about Viktor's resentful nature. Sandor knew, in spite of the visible symptoms of his decline, that Viktor would see his illness as abandonment and a personal inconvenience. Back in Budapest, Viktor had been an academic, a professor of Elizabethan literature at St. Stephen's until he was terminated for being "impossibly disagreeable." When the war started in 1914, he feared conscription into the army. He responded to a recruitment advertisement for able-bodied men to come to America and take jobs in the mines of the Osage Lead Company, asking Sandor, his only real friend, to come with him. To the disbelief of his family, Sandor agreed because he knew his friend expected it, depended upon it. His health had never been robust and though he quickly regretted his decision, he swore to God in Viktor's presence to never go back on his word. Sandor's wife had died of peritonitis the year before, the very week they had started reading Shakespeare out loud to each other in English. His grieving period was a short one, and knowing his friend could not function in the world alone, he sold his rare-books and documents shop and made the long and difficult trip with Viktor to the village of Ste. Odile on the banks of the Mississippi.

Sandor looked at Viktor meekly with red eyes that were, by the minute, growing increasingly sensitive and watery, as the elevator cage climbed up the mineshaft toward the afternoon daylight. Last winter his teeth had begun to discolor and darken, and his gums to recede from them, as the doctor predicted. Doctor Treves had examined Sandor four months ago and told him he had porphyria, a disease of the blood. He told Sandor he knew little of the condition, but recognized that his patient appeared to have both the acute and cutaneous types. Treves had read that victims crave blood to compensate for the deficiency in their own, and he advised Sandor to yield to this craving to keep his vigor and vitality from waning away. Treves said that Sandor would become weak and be unable to tolerate sunlight, that exposure to it would blister, scar and rot his skin, and that soon he may expect to start having hallucinations.

"I am sorry, Viktor . . . my friend," Sandor said. "I really can't help it. God is my witness, I am too sick to continue loading ore by hand. Should have quit months ago, and would have if not for . . . I was never really strong enough for this. I can't score-out in a single shift anymore. *Kívánom, hogy soha nem volt íde.*"

"Speak English! I, too wish I had never come here," Viktor nodded. "But here we are. I suppose you are blaming me for this."

They'd never had the elevator cage to themselves before. This was the first time they had ever left work after the usual shift change time. Viktor had waited for Sandor in the staging area underground as he spoke to the shift boss in his office and collected his final wages. By that time the early shift had finished and gone home for the day and the second shift had taken over, blasting tunnel to the west and southwest. With a war raging in Europe, the demand for lead had never been higher.

At the surface Viktor opened the cage door and the two men stepped out into the sunlight. Sandor squinted and shaded his eyes with his hand. He twitched in pain a few times, as he had done more and more recently, in a manner that seemed to irritate Viktor.

Sandor was careful not to pity himself in his situation. He did pity his friend though. Viktor had no love for himself and seemed to be naively angry at the rest of humanity because of it. Sandor knew how completely Viktor had come to depend upon him, even if Viktor himself didn't know. Very soon after his wife's death, Sandor became Viktor's only unassailable human contact in the world, and he accepted this as a responsibility he must uphold.

The volume Sandor had prized above all others in his bookshop in Budapest, was a late 16th century copy of Tyndale's translation of the Bible. The first time Sandor opened the book, his eye was drawn to Cain's disavowal in Genesis: "Am I my brother's keeper?" Sandor knew the phrase first appeared in Tyndale's translation, and when he opened the book, coincidentally, a second and third time to the same passage, and then dreamt about it that night, he was certain he was receiving a directive for his life and thinking. He spoke with Father Bartok at St Emeric's, who confirmed that Sandor had been given signs. That was why he had agreed to come to America and to take difficult and unpleasant work.

It worried Sandor that he could not make his companion understand how sick he was, and that he must inevitably leave this friendless man alone in a foreign place which, after two years, he had made no effort to adjust to. To press these facts upon Viktor would anger and upset him, and Sandor could not decide if he should insist, to his own satisfaction, that his friend understood what his doctors had foreseen or not continue to bring it up.

It was Saturday afternoon, the end of the work week. The two men walked east into town toward Tranquille House on Rouen Street, where they were boarders. From Sunday night until Saturday afternoon they shared a room there. After their shift on Saturday they gathered their things and boarded the train for a seventeen-mile trip west to LaMotte where Viktor had a room. Sandor's tiny house was a mile farther, in the woods near Gibson cemetery.

The train west was waiting at the station, and Sandor was glad he had not made them miss it. His legs had begun to cramp as

Viktor hurried him along toward the platform, and he had to walk even more slowly than usual.

The men seated themselves on a bench at the front of the coach. It hurt Sandor's legs to sit, and he was exhausted. As the train lurched away from the station, Sandor looked at the black spot on the back of his left hand, and noticed how much darker in general his hands had become from his disease, in recent weeks. And since mid-winter, fine hair had begun to grow in his palms. He knew if he were still home in Hungary, the superstitious country people he would see at the vegetable markets on Saturdays, would look at him with fear and suspicion.

Sandor thought of the appearance he must present to the world, and to Viktor, especially. His elongated, dark teeth, his purple gums, his gray skin streaked with darkened areas, his red eyes and the blisters and blackened spots on his arms and forehead, did not in themselves convince Viktor that his companion had not made every effort to keep him company down in the mineshafts and drift tunnels. Sandor smiled at the selfishness, and *innocence* of that.

Viktor shifted uncomfortably on the bench. Sandor noticed that his friend was looking at the black spot on his hand, and that he glanced briefly at his disfigured face. He could not tell if the expression on Viktor's face was one of disgust or pity.

"It's an unwelcoming world," Viktor mumbled. "I suppose we have to take comfort wherever we can."

"I don't see the world as bad as all that," Sandor smiled.

There were seven buildings on the muddy main street of LaMotte and only five of them were still in use. As the men approached Viktor's boarding house, a dilapidated brick building with a collapsing porch roof, Mrs. Hobbs, the landlady came out the front screen door.

"There you are, Mr. Suba." Mrs. Hobbs was a woman of forty who looked twenty years older. Four of her front teeth were missing. She had not seen Sandor for many months, and seemed a little shocked as she approached them. "I reckon you heard the news?"

"I heard no news, Mrs. Hobbs," Viktor said.

"Well, then, I'll tell you. America's a-getting' into the war. Your European war. Now we been dragged into it."

Viktor and Sandor looked at each other. Sandor thought it best to hide their elation from Mrs. Hobbs.

"I see," Viktor said. "I know it isn't good news to you, Mrs. Hobbs, but it will certainly end the war faster."

"What do we care how fast a war in Europe ends? It ain't our war!"

"Certainly," Sandor said. "We are sorry for that. Politics is an unhappy business."

"That ain't the half of it!" Mrs. Hobbs seemed determined to stoke her own rage. "It's gonna be a conscription. A draft. And you fellas, you foreigners, ain't a-gonna be in it. Our American boys hafta go fight your damned war while you Hunkies get to stay here a-workin' just as safe and sound as you please! I know you two come here to get out of it, now we gotta do your fightin' for you!"

"This great country loves the people of Europe . . ." Sandor began. His voice was weak.

"Well, it got nothin' to do with love," Mrs. Hobbs interrupted. "I don't love you people and I don't know nobody who does."

"I know it's just politics and national interests," Viktor said. He looked disapprovingly at Sandor. He knew Mrs. Hobbs well enough to know she resented anyone telling her how she felt or should feel about anything. "I don't know why my friend said that!"

Sandor smiled. "Love isn't something you know about, Viktor! We are upsetting you, Mrs. Hobbs. I will leave you both here. I am exhausted. I hope your son is improved."

Mrs. Hobbs' nine-year-old son, Vernon, had been sick for several weeks, coughing and pale, as had several other children at his school.

"You never mind about Vernon!" Mrs. Hobbs snapped. "I ain't the only one around here thinks you know more about these sick kids than any of us!" She turned suddenly and walked back to her house. Sandor watched her walk away, dumbfounded.

"What did she mean by that?" Sandor asked, but Viktor had turned away from him and was following Mrs. Hobbs back into the boarding house.

Sandor always enjoyed the walk from the train depot out to his property west of LaMotte on Saturday afternoons after work. The road out of the small town was a dirt path maintained by the county out into the oak woods, where it ended at an old logging road which wound past Sandor's small frame house. The house bordered the old Gibson Cemetery, and had been built for the caretaker just before the beginning of the Civil War. The cemetery had been abandoned for at least fifty years, and now, like Sandor's clapboard home, was nearly lost in the hardwood forest.

Halfway to the cemetery the road became almost completely overgrown with weeds and saplings. Just ahead of him, nearly hidden by a cluster of mayapple, Sandor saw a gray mound with streaks of red across it. A slight scent of decay blew past his face in a breeze and he thought for a moment he might vomit. He saw that the mound was the shredded body of an opossum, killed by a dog or coyote. The blood on the carcass was mostly dried, but some of it, deep within the wounds, glistened in the afternoon sun. He realized he was staring, transfixed, at the bloody flesh, and that he was imagining the salty taste of it. Abruptly he became aware that he wasn't imagining the blood taste. His gums had started bleeding again and his mouth was alarmingly full. Painfully, but almost involuntarily, he swallowed.

As Sandor had grown sicker, his appetite had changed and become limited. As he unlocked the peeling front door of his small house, he thought he might make himself a stuffed pepper or cabbage roll for a light dinner. He still had some Csabai sausage in his pantry, though what he really wanted, as he realized more and more lately, and as his response to the opossum carcass reminded him, was raw, bloody meat.

Since Dr. Treves told him he would crave blood as an effect of his illness, he had hungered for little else. He remembered having no particular taste for it before Treves diagnosed him, and he wondered if he was merely being influenced by the suggestion. "You are suffering from an anemia," Treves said, "and your body will naturally want to replace, from other sources, what it has lost."

Days ago, he had left a lamb chop wrapped in brown paper in his ice box. The ice was nearly gone and the chop was no longer frozen. He removed it and placed it in his sink. When it reached room temperature he would eat it raw. There was a half-bottle of wine in his pantry. He found a clean coffee cup in his cupboard and filled it half full.

Sandor sat at his small kitchen table and thought about his friend. The pain in Sandor's joints and mouth and skin was almost constant, yet he still thought mostly about the suffering of Viktor, loveless and alone in the world, except for their exasperating and one-sided friendship. Unlike Viktor, Sandor had experienced love. He knew what it meant to love another person completely, to the point of self-sacrifice and unquestioning immersion in the happiness of the other. When his wife Eva, finally died of her peritonitis a year before he left Hungary, though his loss was great, he was overwhelmed with gratitude that her suffering was done, and knew his relief was an expression of his love for her, and therefore right and just. He celebrated her passing with a high mass, followed in the evening by a glass of red wine and a special meal, a *pörkölt,* and he suspected that his neighbors on Hruza Street thought he was either insane or evil. He didn't expect anyone else to understand how grateful he was. He kept his grief a private and moderate thing, as Eva would have wanted.

Viktor had only had two brief flirtations in all the years Sandor had known him. Each lasted until they became an inconvenience to him, and he stopped investing the little effort he was willing to attempt, and the women lost interest. Viktor was teaching King Lear in his last semester at the university, and Sandor told his wife it was a sad irony that Regan's description of her aging father: "*He hath always but slightly known himself,*" did not inspire personal insight in his friend.

After the sun went down, Sandor stepped out onto his porch. In the twilight and in the dark, away from the sunlight that seared his festering skin, he felt a little more comfortable. He sat on his front step and sipped from his cup of red wine until his stomach started to burn. Tree frogs burred in the woods all around him and whippoorwills called to each other from the southwest and northeast. He thought how wonderful it was that these creatures could carry on their natural lives and tendencies in spite of human destruction and influence in the world. He felt he had entered a new phase of life: the last phase. His working years were over. He was destined to die in a strange land. Away from home, surrounded by unfriendly and disapproving strangers who resented him and his countrymen. He would live in this small wooden house, a hermit in the woods, until his health failed or his money ran out. Either or both would come soon enough. It made his heart ache to think of leaving his friend here alone.

He wondered what further suffering his disease would bring. Dr. Treves had given him no chance of recovery and he knew the longer he lived, the worse the pain would become. It would be bad for him to live too much longer. If he only had the strength to end his own life he could avoid a long and torturous decline. But he believed, he *knew*, as Hamlet did, that suicide is the gravest of mortal sins and if he committed such an act, he would never be reunited with his Eva in the next world. He felt a tear well painfully in his eye and suddenly he craved blood, the blood that seemed to calm him more and more as his disease progressed. He remembered the lamb he had left in his sink.

He went back into the house and tore the paper off the lamb chop. He bit into it, savoring its bloody piquancy. There was a hint of decay in its smell but he bit into it again and again until it was gone. He wiped the blood from his chin with a towel hanging over the back of his kitchen chair.

Sandor noticed that the black spot on his nose was no longer completely numb, but had begun to tingle a little. One of Eva's small mirrors hung on his bedroom wall. He examined his face in the fading light. The edges of the spot were damp and pink, and as he twitched his facial muscles slightly to test for sensation, the entire black mass fell from his nose, revealing the pink, triangular holes and septum underneath.

He looked at himself in disbelief and horror for many moments. His eyes filled painfully with tears and he began to sob helplessly. Why was God testing him in this way? Was not losing his wife and living for two years in this strange land in service to a friend trial enough for any pious man?

A loud crash and a spray of glass behind him in the front room caused his legs to collapse. Looking through the bedroom door he saw a damp mossy rock on his front room floor surrounded by glass shards. He heard the laughter of children out in the dark. Sandor made his way unsteadily to his front door. Three boys stood thirty feet away at the edge of the cemetery.

"Vernon Hobbs died!" one of the boys called. "And everbody knows you did it!"

"Everbody knows!" the other two boys repeated.

"You little hooligans!" Sandor shouted. "I'll get the sheriff on you! His wife is one of us!"

"You kilt Vernon," the first boy continued, "and Boyer in Ste. Odile and them three kids in Lesterton, 'cause you're a vampire!"

"A *vampire!*" the other boys echoed.

It took Sandor a moment to realize he had heard the boys right. "What nonsense!" he said. "Who put such nonsense in your superstitious heads?"

"Everbody knows!" the first boy went on. "Vampires is from Hungry and you're from Hungry. You're pasty and long-toothed and you cain't come out in the daylight. And kids is gettin' sick and dyin'."

"You ignorant yokels," Sandor interrupted. "Superstitious fools! You think you can cure sickness by putting knives under a bed or running chickens over people. You have to use medicine and go to the doctor!"

"Got a present for you!" the first boy said as he heaved a long string of bulbous shapes onto Sandor's porch. It hit the dry boards with a dull *thunk*, and flakes of skin particles floated down, jarred loose by the impact. It was a bunch of garlic. The boys ran off laughing into the darkness, toward LaMotte.

Sandor kicked the bunch of garlic off the porch. He stood for a few moments looking in the direction the boys had run. He knew they were repeating things they had heard their parents saying. He had seen mob violence before, back in Budapest. He had seen a mob drive Jews out of the neighborhood, and later, hang a homosexual man who was suspected of killing a boy. Sandor knew that fearful, superstitious people need scapegoats for their problems, and now he had come into their focus. To defend himself against these suspicions would be futile. In the morning he would cover himself against the sun as best he could, and take the train to Ste. Odile to see the sheriff.

Sandor went back inside and swept up the broken glass. He sat on his single kitchen chair. The fearsome and painful but essentially peaceful death he foresaw for himself an hour ago, was impossible now. He knew these people would never leave him alone to die in the dignity of isolation. He thought again about taking his own life, but knew, for his late wife's sake, it was out of the question. He suddenly craved the comfort of more raw, bloody meat. That would calm him down, but his icebox was empty.

A branch snapped outside in the dark. Sandor found his butcher knife in his sink and faced his front door. A footstep on his porch sent a stab of fear through his stomach, and he thought: "What will become of poor Viktor when I am gone?"

The front door opened slowly and Viktor stepped in, breathing heavily and out of breath. He was holding a large burlap sack.

"Viktor!" Sandor whispered. "What is it? What has happened?"

"The worst," Viktor said quietly. He seemed to not notice the hole in Sandor's face. "Mrs. Hobbs' son died and she has ordered me out of her house."

"I heard. Some boys came here . . ."

"I have no home, but now none of us do. No Hungarian is safe here anymore."

"What do you mean?"

"In Burley's Tavern in Lesterton today some Hungarians were drunk and boasting about how they could not be drafted into the army, how they would stay behind while the Americans went off to the war. They boasted they would stay behind and take all the mine jobs and take care of all the abandoned wives too."

"Oh," Sandor whispered. "Such stupidity in the world."

"A fight broke out, then a riot," Viktor sat on the kitchen chair and put the burlap sack on the table with a metallic clang. "They burned most of the Hungarian homes and loaded the families on a boxcar bound for St. Louis. Five Hungarians have been killed. So far. The word is they . . . the mob, will be heading out this way, to Ste. Odile, by morning. Maybe a hundred men. They want us all dead or gone."

"My friend, you must stay with me," Sandor said. "We will make our way to Ste. Odile early tomorrow. The sheriff, his wife is Hungarian . . ."

"I am so sorry I brought you here," Viktor interrupted. "For my own selfish reasons, I brought you here with me. A man so full of love as you are . . ." Viktor reached into the burlap sack and withdrew a straight razor, a bucket, and a heavy old revolver. He laid the things side by side on the tabletop.

"My God, Viktor!" Sandor said. "What is all this?"

"The gun is empty," Viktor said. "As you know, the company store will not sell cartridges to Hungarians. Hold it in your hand when the mob comes. Hold it up and they will shoot you. Quick and painless. Over in an instant. I told Mrs. Hobbs, that yes, you were what they say you are, and you are responsible for the children. They will be here sometime tomorrow when the train comes, and your suffering will be over. I wanted to be certain your suffering would be over."

"Viktor . . ."

"I would like to think I have learned something from you, though it may not seem so." Viktor set the bucket on the floor under his left arm. In an instant, he took the razor and slashed his left wrist. Sandor shuddered in horror as his friend lowered his bleeding arm over the bucket.

"No Viktor! Let me bind it!"

"Leave it alone, Sandor." Viktor smiled. "When Mrs. Hobbs threw me out of her house and told me the news, all I thought of was your wellbeing and how I could deliver you from this. It was a surprise to me, a revelation, that these were my thoughts at a time like this, but I of course knew it was only your influence. Only you! I thank you for that . . . that I hardly know myself at this moment. This will calm you as you wait for them. The blood will calm you, as you have said . . . as you wait for the mob." Viktor looked down at the quickly filling bucket and smiled a fading smile. "Thank you for never abandoning me."

Sandor felt his friend's forehead. It was already cooling to the touch. Viktor's expression had become bland and peaceful and unmistakably benevolent. Sandor smiled a mirthless, emotional smile, and was grateful to have deserved such charity, if he truly did deserve it: to have had such a friend, in a harsh and unwelcoming world.

THINGS
By Rick McQuiston

With great effort Chad heaved the corpse up onto the bumper and into the trunk, wincing at the heavy thud it made when it landed on the floor.

He wiped his brow with the back of his hand and took several deep breaths. He needed to calm down and reassess his plan. He still had to drive to the secluded location he'd selected (about fifty yards behind Melvindale Cemetery—a perfect spot because who in their right mind would trudge through such dense and mosquito-infested brush?), dig the grave, douse the body with acid, bury it, and then cover his tracks.

And all the while being sure that nothing escaped.

The thought sent a chill down his spine.

Chad looked at the still form wrapped in a blanket in his trunk. He felt a pang of guilt for having stolen the body, but what could he do? He was sure if he hadn't spirited it from the morgue slab something very bad would have happened. Something that would have expanded to engulf the town, and possibly, given enough time, the world.

He remembered the name on the toe tag: Joseph Delong; just an average guy who couldn't have been more than twenty years old at the time of his death.

How he wound up on a slab in the morgue didn't matter.

What happened to his body after he died did matter.

Chad closed the trunk and climbed into his car.

Dragging the body through the brush was not easy. Occasionally the blanket snagged a twig or stone and he would be forced to stop and dislodge it, all the while trying to keep the mosquitoes at bay. Fortunately, it hadn't rained lately or he really would have been in trouble.

At last he reached the spot he'd selected: a small clearing covered with desiccated leaves and sporting a natural depression that gave him a good head start with the digging. He gratefully dropped his burden and felt the burn in his muscles subside.

Chad doubted what he was doing. Was it really the right thing to do? Could he stop what would happen with some acid and a shovel?

He couldn't answer those questions but knew he had to try. The consequences if he didn't could be dire. Nobody believed him. Nobody cared. Not the authorities, or anyone at the University, or even his friends. Everyone said he was crazy.

But he knew better. He had seen things, things that shouldn't be possible but were.

After he caught his breath Chad raced back to his car to fetch the shovel and acid. Time wasn't on his side, and not because of the approaching dawn. He still had hours before morning broke. If he didn't hurry and dispose of the body it might. . . .

Pushing aside the thought, Chad grabbed his shovel from the trunk and the bottle of acid from the backseat floor. He held the acid up, studying the corrosive liquid in the moonlight.

"I hope you do the trick," he said to himself.

He then followed the same path he'd made earlier back to the clearing.

Wasting no time, he carefully set the acid down next to a large stone and began digging the grave. The blade slid into the soil easily, and within a short time he had a four-foot-deep hole dug.

Movement caught his eye.

Chad spun around and stared at the lump beneath the blanket. He watched it for a moment, its uneven contours creating shadows in the moonlight, but saw nothing.

"Chad, you need to get acid on that thing and bury it."

Heeding his own words, he continued digging.

When he was satisfied with the hole Chad tossed the shovel to the ground and turned to face the corpse. It lay there, right where he had put it, unmoving, inanimate.

He heard something growl in the distance.

He turned toward the sound, half expecting to see something charging at him, but there were only the tombstones jutting out of the cemetery grounds to be seen.

Chad stared at the markers. They reflected the moonlight back at him, casting an eerie glow on the scene.

Maybe I shouldn't have picked a spot so close to a cemetery.

A rustling noise behind him arrested Chad's thoughts and he turned to see the body moving away from the grave. The blanket it was wrapped in still covered it, but had become snagged on a rock and was slowly revealing its grisly contents.

But Chad was not surprised. In fact, although dreading it, he expected the body to become animated. It was only a matter of time before the things inside wanted out.

He only wished he could have used the acid and buried it first.

Mr. Joseph DeLong glared at the despoiler of his corpse with unseeing eyes. He sat up and the remainder of the blanket fell to the side, exposing his zombielike form to the night. His skin gave off a ghostly pallor and his arms twitched at his sides.

Chad recoiled from the sight. He could see the things squirming just below the flesh. They were innumerable, hundreds, perhaps thousands of the creatures using the corpse, somehow manipulating it like a marionette.

DeLong's mouth opened. Instantly dozens of writhing little beasts, multi-legged things with gnashing pincers where heads should have been, dribbled out of the grisly orifice and rolled down the chin, the neck, the chest, each and every one coated in putrefied fluids.

Then the torso split open. A veritable wave of movement spilled forth onto the ground. It gushed forward like an army of blind, leaderless predators, somehow working together to achieve its goal of securing prey.

Chad backed away from the horde, and reaching behind, managed to grab the bottle of acid. He then unscrewed the lid and flung the contents at the advancing mass. The caustic liquid splashed across the monsters, vaporizing hundreds in an instant.

But more poured out of the body. They spread far too rapidly to become contained, quickly oozing over the ground in an expanding perimeter that doubled in size every few seconds.

DeLong sagged more and more as the things emptied out of him. He became limp before finally collapsing to the ground, an empty husk, discarded after serving as a sanctuary for the creatures.

And under the cold glare of the moon the things engulfed the sole living person nearby, flooding into his body in a nauseous wave of unrelenting suffocation. They preferred dead tissue to incubate in, somehow reveling in the cold environment as opposed to a warm living one, but sensed many lifeless bodies close by, so instead focused on a means to reach those vessels.

Chad's body stood, and after grabbing the shovel, stumbled in the direction of Melvindale Cemetery.

THE FLESH GARDENER
By Jeremy Megargee

Y ou've heard of bug chasers, haven't you? Those odd ducks that engage in unprotected sex in the hopes of catching HIV. Offering up eager bodies and watering at the mouth, hoping a gift giver will plant that biological bomb inside of them.

I'm here to tell you that bug chasers are mere amateurs in the world of viral delights. Narrow is their vision, and mundane is their pursuit. If one is to poison a meat vehicle, then why not chase the most exotic of venoms? The self-inflicted ruin of a human carcass should be something bordering on a holy rite, and I've always believed that Eden is momentarily remade in the disintegration of flesh.

I suppose I am a gardener in that way. This pitiful form I call a body acts as the soil, and I plant little virus seeds deep within to cultivate growth. I study my own delicious decay. It is research, a diary of desiccation, and each festering petal sends a shiver of excitement traveling up the twisted ridge of my spine.

My experimentation is vast due to a genetic defect that I was born with. A severely compromised immune system with the ability to harbor multiple infectious diseases all at the same time. I'm a walking vat sloshing with internal horrors, and each one is like a trophy that I prize higher than any material possession. These viruses are my companions in the dark, and their blight is my reward.

I worship the collection, and it shows its love by slowly breaking me apart in the most excruciating ways. Are you familiar with the term "patient zero?" Think of me as patient infinity. I am not the first, but I make it my business to experience all the tastiest condemnations of the carnal condition.

I was a novice once in the long distant past, my garden of self-unfulfilled and barren of all sickness. Just a young butcher boy who had not yet learned how to wield the knife on himself, and it took a fascination with self-destruction to guide this lost soul to the path he currently walks. The masochist in me awoke late, but he awoke ever so *hungry*.

The garden feeds him well now. Each biological gift is like a nest of vines twining across a throbbing soul. I've had every kind of influenza, but such periods have proved lackluster. The snot oozes, the throat itches, and the head aches, but these moments are nothing, just appetizers for a gardener with my particular desires.

I had to search for something more, something real, something to rattle the bones and make the heart just a rotting little crisp that struggles to pump sluggish ichor.

My first experience with true viral glory came from the imported abdomen of a mosquito gut-loaded with Dengue fever. I ordered it from a forum on the deep web, and the Indian supplier was more than willing to provide for my eclectic request. I lapped at that tainted blood with a bone-dry tongue, and it was an immediate thrill to the taste buds.

The projectile vomiting came after. It spewed from my lips like a geyser of bile, and it mixed so wonderfully with the joint aches that practically bent all my limbs inward. My skin erupted into a magnificent rash, and as I admired it in the mirror, I couldn't help but think that it resembled a patch of swollen lilacs pushing up through the skin. That was the garden giving back. An affirmation that my green thumb has the potential to become smeared in the nastiest inflammatory goodies.

The fever boiled, but the strain was a weak batch, and soon this traitorous meat fought it off. Survival came as such a boring outcome. All that I planted began to wilt, and so the search for new seeds began.

I pounded my stubby fingers on the keyboard, made the proper connections, and soon a special package arrived from West Africa. It shipped from Niger, and it stank of fruity oblivion. I peeled it open with spittle dripping from the lips, and there it was, a crumpled little mummy just full to the brim with all things yummy. It was the dried remnant of a fruit bat; the wings curled around the torso and the eyes just sunken sockets long since devoured by insects.

This was the dish I'd been waiting for. The next phase in my garden of the flesh. A dead winged angel just fresh enough to pass on everlasting Ebola. I wasted no time opening my eating-hole wide, lips tattered and chapped, and I shoved the critter corpse down my gullet and chewed until my gums bled.

Bliss. Unnatural bliss. It took only days for the symptoms to ravage me. The shit gushed from my ass in a waterfall of putrescence. I felt my kidneys becoming nothing more than overworked lumps inside of me. I was weak as a kitten run down on the interstate, and no sustenance would take root in my stomach. All food came splattering back out as a partially digested stew, and it delighted me to see little fleshy pieces of organs floating in that river of wretchedness.

Ebola gave the garden life, but what might the gardener seek to invite *true* paradise? The great prize. The grand finale. The necrotic nectar to stilt the veins and core out the vessel. I aim to rot, to live as I rot, and only the most infamous infection will suffice.

I wiped clotted Ebola blood from my eyes to make one last order on the World Wide Web. I chose expedited shipping, because time is of the essence when a garden must be grown. It arrived in less than two days. It was wrapped in black silk with the prettiest bow, and I opened it like a child on Christmas Eve. My favorite toy waited for me.

A rusted syringe soaked for months in human sewage. It sang to me, a dirty ditty, and it promised to eat through my flesh with genuine enthusiasm. Necrotizing fasciitis waited on the sharp tip of that needle. Commonly referred to as flesh-eating disease, but lovingly thought of by me as man's most transcendent self-destructive experience.

I carved out a wound in the center of my forehead with a dull butter knife, and then I drove that syringe in deep and depressed the contents into the open wound. And like an addict after a long-awaited fix, I swooned back in my chair and waited for the fun to begin.

It's so quick. First the inflammation, the most beautiful shades of purple and black. Next the blisters to decorate, each one a pus-dripping miniature volcano. And then it started. The shedding of flesh in scarlet folds, bloodied lumps and chunks falling to the floor, pieces of who I am rendered into little more than messy plops against the linoleum.

I'm writing this memoir with the intent to document a demise that borders on the divine. Each scrawl of the pen leaves slabs of skin smeared against the paper. I'm a dripping red thing with a gleaming grin, and this is how all the best parties end. Deadened tissue splatters and stains, and how can I describe how sublime it is to feel your meat curdling from within?

So much irredeemable skin. It falls, we fall, and all turns to pools that I lick back up like a cannibal's gruel.

Brain black and broken, rhyming silly now. Fingers just skinned sausages. Hard to write. I've read that surgeons are supposed to cut away the bad flesh. I'll do that. I'll amputate the soft black pieces, and I'll revel in the rot.

This is all I've ever wanted.

The garden is in bloom.

EAR WAX
By G.A. Miller

"Dammit, now I'm completely plugged up again!"

"What's plugged up, honey? What are you talking about?"

"Oh, my ear. Damned wax again, completely blocked up."

Sara went to the bathroom, and returned with a small bottle, unscrewing the cap.

"Here, lean over and let me put some drops in."

Joe leaned over as far as he could, and Sara put in a few drops of the Peroxide solution to soften the wax.

"There. Let that work for a few minutes, then we'll use the bottle."

Joe grunted, thinking that the latest item he'd bought to try and win his lifelong battle against ear wax was about to get its trial by fire. It was basically a spray bottle, fitted with a short hose that accepted removable tips with even thinner hoses on them to concentrate the flow. He lifted his head slightly off the arm of the couch to hear what she was saying.

"Say again? Didn't hear you."

"How warm should the water be? I don't want to make it too hot for you."

"It said very warm, close to body temp, but not too hot."

"Okay, got it."

Sara came into the room with the bottle in one hand, and the small basin in the other. Joe sat up, took the basin, and put it on the side of his head, slipping the ear into the provided cutout. Sara sat beside him, and guided the small tip into his ear, squeezing the handle to squirt the water in.

"How's that? Is it too warm?"

"No, it feels fine . . . just aim high to try and flush from behind."

Sara continued squeezing, and started to see small clumps of wax flowing out into the basin.

"There we go, it's starting to come out."

Joe's eyes were tightly shut, and he felt something moving, shifting inside his ear, something too large to be in such a small place. The bottle held a lot of water, and the continued squirts were loosening, moving that overly large mass. It was stubborn, though, and held on. Sara had to pause, and empty the basin before starting again.

"Hang in there, honey. We're getting it."

The basin back in place, Sara continued flushing his ear, one squeeze right after another, keeping the flow as steady as she could. Joe felt a pop in his ear, and the mass moved more than it had before.

"It's coming, keep it going . . . you've almost got it!"

Sara glanced into the basin, and guessed she had a few more squirts before she'd have to empty it again, so she shifted the small tip, aiming more at an angle from above, and squeezed the handle again, open and closed, keeping the bursts of water steady, when suddenly Joe cried out as a large, dark glob plopped into the basin.

She looked at it, and it seemed to be moving.

"What the hell?"

Joe said nothing, his head down, eyes shut. As she watched, the mass seemed to change shape, moving on its own, not simply floating in the water. It stretched larger, thinner, and she clearly saw the outline of a face, as though pressing from inside the mass. It was only there for a split second, but she knew that face. Joe's face. It vanished, and the mass became still and lifeless.

She looked up, just as Joe raised his head, turning to look at her. His eyes opened, and they'd turned black, as though the pupils had somehow absorbed the entire irises. Tiny red veins surrounded the black centers, like spider webs capturing prey for the patiently waiting insect.

And then he smiled. There was no humor, no life in that smile, more predatory than friendly.

And then, Joe leaned toward Sara, as she dropped the full basin, with its now still mass of wax down onto the floor, spilling onto the polished wood surface. The small moan in her throat escalated to a full hearty scream as he closed the gap between them.

And then. . . .

THE FACE

By Kurt Newton

. . . scrabble . . . scrabble . . . hush . . . hiss. . . .

The man in the chair sits hunched over his desk. The small room is dark but for one reading lamp that casts a yellow cone of light upon the stacks of books, notepads and coffee mugs that litter his desktop. The man combs feverishly through the pages of the volume that lies open before him. Above, just beyond the light's reach, lie the foot-shadows of leather-bound volumes, some inscribed with arcane symbols—reference books for old world languages, recovered texts of lost religious manifests, and how-to guides for the practice of alchemy and the occult. He is a man of letters, a scholar, a professor at the local university, in fact. His name is Edwin Ellunder. Dr. Edwin Ellunder, Professor of Literary Artifacts. But to look at him, one would never assume such a title to be true.

He mumbles absentmindedly. His attention is suddenly captured by what he has just read. His arm reaches out; he pulls a jeweler's magnifying glass over the pages before him. He takes notes. He's getting closer. But the sounds come again, quickly quelling his sudden elation.

. . . scrabble . . . scrabble. . . .

He pauses. His ears pin back as he feels the presence behind him, hidden in the dark recesses of the room. *If only they could see him now*, thinks Edwin—his colleagues, the ones who whispered names like Ghost Chaser, Demon Hunter, and Dr. Demento under their breath when he entered the faculty lounge. Some had even suggested the University would be better served if he taught creative writing instead of his pursuit of "foundationless knowledge." Though hurt by their lack of professionalism, Edwin did not let their petty jealousies dissuade him from his curriculum—nor from his own personal and private research.

... scrabble ... hush ... hiss. ...

There comes a knock at the door.

"Edwin? For the last time, please come out."

Edwin's wife, Alice, concerned that her husband has been locked in his study for nearly three days now.

"I've told you before, Alice, I can't. Don't you understand?" he shouts to her.

"Why won't you tell me what's wrong?"

... scrabble ... scrabble. ...

Edwin cranes his neck toward the sound, his head obscured by shadow. The sound emanates from the far darkest corner, climbing toward the ceiling above.

"Edwin, what's that noise? Edwin, please! If you don't come out I'm going to call the hospital and have them send over a professional."

... scrabble ... hiss. ...

Edwin laughs. "Dear sweet Alice. You never understood my passions. You merely tolerated them. You believe me insane, don't you? Heaven knows I should be—putting up with your insolence all these years." These are Edwin's thoughts, but he speaks them aloud. Now that the barrier has been breached between the internal and external, the truth and the mask, it is much easier for Edwin to express himself.

"Edwin, you don't know what you're saying. You're not yourself. Please, let me help you."

... scrabble ... scrabble. ...

Directly overhead now.

A sneer of disdain touches the corner of Edwin's lips. Hot flashes of pain erupt. Blood trickles down his chin. "If you must, Alice. If you must ..."

Edwin leans back in his chair and unlocks the study door.

"Edwin? Oh, thank God." Alice enters and puts her arms out to embrace her husband, but he pulls away.

"Edwin, please? It's so dark in here. Why are you doing this?"

Edwin finally turns to face her. Light cascades across his features. "Because I can."

Alice screams and stumbles back toward the door.

... scrabble ... click ... pop. ...

Something falls from the ceiling above and lands upon Alice's face. Her screams are suddenly blanketed, her cries for help drowned in a liquid garble. She falls to the floor. In seconds, she lies motionless.

... click ... pop ... hiss. ...

Edwin reaches down and swings his arm as if to bat something away. "That's enough!" he yells.

The thing skitters off into the dark. Edwin pulls the desk lamp forward and angles its light toward the floor.

Alice's face is devoid of flesh and cartilage. Her barren white skull gapes ceiling-ward.

"Forgive me, Alice," Edwin whispers.

He turns and focuses once again on the manuscript. As he reads, the ancient Sumerian language becomes a miniature landscape of peaks and valleys. He speaks aloud the last line he deciphered.

"... ur-erech ah-kish tuttul el-eridu paddan-aram ..."

... the hairless face becomes an organ of great mobility. ...

Edwin breathes deep.

... scrabble ... hush. ...

He can smell his wife's blood and the residual fear that still clings to the study's stale air like cigarette smoke.

... scrabble ... scrabble. ...

He feels the power he has unleashed.

He closes the book before him and turns to face the dark. He clicks his fingers. "Hamath!" he commands. *Come.*

... scrabble ... hush. ...

"Hamath, azif!" *Come, now!*

... scrabblescrabblescrabble. ...

The thing in the dark crawls up his leg and trembles upon his knee. It awaits its next instruction.

Edwin leans over the tiny beast. His hands caress its contours—contours that mimic his own features, his own face.

"Shinar," he finally tells it. *Home.*

The face scrabbles up Edwin's chest and quickly seals itself back over its place of origin.

Edwin now sees the world in a different light, filled with brilliant blues and spectral whites. He sees a land of immense beauty and unimaginable horror. But mostly he sees revenge and retribution.

After a quick shower and a shave, he gets into his car and heads toward the University.

BATTLEGROUND
By Drew Nicks

France, 1916

As the skies unleashed another torrent from their gray depths, Captain Noel Chamberlain stepped out between the canvas flaps, lit a British Consul, and let the rain run over his bloodied apron. His hands shook as he took a second drag.

It had already been a long day and, while glancing to his watch, there was still much more to go. Serious injuries had been the norm all day, owing to the offensive Field Marshall Haig had ordered. Ragged stumps and spilled entrails. Gas burns and major blood loss. The severity of the wounds and the near constant need for expertise had left the surgeon exhausted. He gazed out into the muddy field that was now his life. In the near distance, he could see the ambulance drivers and stretcher bearers enjoying a quiet moment. Over the tumble of the rain, he heard them enjoy a laugh.

Lucky bastards.

"Captain Chamberlain?" the young voice called from behind him. *Lance Corporal Hedges*, the surgeon knew, *I hope you can handle this life.*

The surgeon dropped his cigarette in the murky mud and turned to face the fresh faced, blond, twenty-two-year-old who'd been drafted into this vocation. Captain Chamberlain coughed slightly before returning to the confines of the tent.

"Yes, Hedges, what is it?"

The scent of rotting flesh and iodine hung thickly in the air like a fog. Most of these young men would never walk out of this hospital. The ones that would, would never experience a normal life. For this, Captain Chamberlain felt nothing but sadness. The oldest man he'd treated that day was only two years older than his son. Or, so that soldier's papers had claimed. The surgeon had doubts about many of these boys' ages.

"The patient in bed fourteen has woken up," said Hedges. "He seems to be adjusting well to his new predicament."

Chamberlain looked down sullenly. The patient in bed fourteen had had to have his left arm and right leg amputated. The man's life had irrevocably changed in a matter of blood-spattered moments. Chamberlain and Hedges approached the sprawled figure in bed fourteen. Blood still oozed into the man's damp bandages. With a questioning eye, the soldier looked over the surgeon, who still wore his blood-stained apron.

"It hurts, Captain."

"You'll be all right, son," lied the surgeon. "We'll have some morphine for you."

Dejected, the soldier turned to face the blank canvas wall, grimacing as he did so.

Chamberlain leaned over to Hedges and told him to get the young man some morphine. When the surgeon was informed that their morphine supply had run dry, Chamberlain told him to wrangle some rum. The brave man did not deserve to suffer.

It was just after 22:30, and the exhausted Captain Chamberlain collapsed on his cot. He stared at the flickering lantern above his head, weaving to and fro amongst the surrounding shadows. It was stifling in his "private quarters." The only thing that separated him from his patients, and their snoring between bouts of agonized moaning, was a thick, muck-stained, canvas curtain. He shut his eyes, briefly, only to open them again. He cared not for what he saw behind those dark lids. Standing, he grabbed his British Consuls and lit one. He dropped the spent match into the dirt at his feet. He inhaled deeply and dropped back on his cot.

Fuck.

Suddenly, the alarm sounded and the rushing of feet was all around him. He got to his feet and threw his moist boots on. Pushing aside the curtain, Chamberlain spotted Hedges rushing for the intake area.

"Hedges!" called Captain Chamberlain. "What's going on? What's the situation?"

"Unsure, sir! Sounds like it was a gas attack on our poor lads. They're just being brought in now."

Without hesitation, Chamberlain grabbed his apron and field surgeon's kit. Before hurrying to where he was needed, he paused a moment and listened to the patter of the rain on canvas, and then rushed to the operating theater.

The horrors were evident immediately and the stretcher bearers still brought in more wheezing boys.

"What's the situation?" the surgeon quickly asked, while springing to action.

"Well, sir, it must be gas. That's the only thing it could be. When we reached them, the ones that were still conscious were coughing up blood. Their eyes were the strangest color."

Chamberlain listened as closely as he could while he worked on the first man. This soldier clawed at his eyes ferociously, between bouts of wet screeching. The surgeon tried to calm the frantic man.

"I know it hurts, son, but you've got to let me see."

The soldier continued to screech and claw. Chamberlain looked back to Hedges. His dutiful assistant stood wide eyed, silent and pale. Chamberlain knew this was Hedges' first experience with gas victims, He felt sympathy for his young assistant. Barely a man and being exposed to some of the worst atrocities known to man. He would weep for Hedges . . . later. Now, he needed the young man to be focused.

"Grab his arms, Hedges! Quickly, before he does more damage!"

Hedges did as he was told. He swept behind the screeching frame and firmly grasped the clawing arms. For the first time, the surgeon saw the cerulean shade of the soldier's eyes. Not just the iris. Both the pupil and the cornea had taken on this ghastly shade. This was like no other gas he had ever seen.

From the corner of his eye, Chamberlain saw the soldier two beds down convulsing and clawing at his throat. He stopped his examination and hurried down, Hedges followed close behind.

This poor soul couldn't make a sound. The surgeon knew what he must do. Dropping his kit to the dirt, he retrieved a scalpel. He instructed Hedges to, again, hold the man's arms. When Hedges had the arms secure, Chamberlain began the tracheotomy. He preferred to do these sorts of surgeries with anesthetic, but time would not allow this. As he made the first cut, one of the patient's arms came free and swatted Chamberlain's scalpel. He felt the razor-sharp edge slice his thumb. He grimaced with pain.

"Hold his arms, damn it!"

Hedges secured the arm again with shaking hands. In a few moments, Chamberlain heard the sound of air passing through the patient's new breathing hole. He sighed in relief and looked to the now breathing soldier's face.

The soldier returned the look with a malicious grin.

The surgeon continued down the line, providing what aid he could to these maimed soldiers.

At 01:30, Chamberlain slumped back into his quarters and drew the curtain shut. He fell on his cot and shut his eyes. Sleep took him away before he even felt the tingling in his thumb.

The following morning, Chamberlain awoke refreshed. He was uncertain how long he slept, but however long it was it had definitely done the trick. He stretched tired limbs and threw on his boots. Taking the prime opportunity before the work truly began, he snuck out of his quarters, past the rows of still sleeping patients and out the canvas flap.

When he was outside, he withdrew his British Consuls and lit one. The first inhale was like heaven. He felt calm wash over him. That was when he looked at the hand that cradled his cigarette. On his thumb, a dark hue had begun to form. Puzzled, he drew his thumb closer. On the tip, where he had nicked it with the scalpel, a blackish blister had formed. When he poked it, blue pus seeped from it and pain shot through his arm. So intense was the pain, that he'd dropped his cigarette in the still moist dirt. He returned quickly to his quarters.

After wrapping his thumb in gauze, he headed out to the Mess. Before he could start the day, he needed coffee and perhaps some eggs. That was if there were any eggs to be had. Rations had been in short supply for the last few months and he knew restrictions would become more drastic in the weeks to come.

Stepping into the Mess, he looked about at all the faces. Nearly all were emotionless. Men shoveled food into their mouths without really paying attention. However, in the back-left corner, a group of officers were sharing a laugh. Chamberlain ignored all those around him and walked to the meal line. Judging from what food he could see, eggs were entirely out of the question. He saw some misshapen loaves of bread and a vat of gray gruel.

So much for a real breakfast.

He took a few slices of bread and spread a little butter on each. Turning, he glanced about for Hedges. Through the sea of faces, he spotted his assistant. Hedges sat near the tent flap and uninterestedly spooned gruel into his mouth. Chamberlain sat down beside him.

"Good morning, Hedges. How are our patients doing today?"

Hedges stopped eating and looked down sullenly at his food.

"There's something not right about them, sir."

Chamberlain picked up one of the slices of bread and bit off a chunk.

"What do you mean? I know this is your first time with gas victims. The body does strange things when it's hit with that substance . . ."

Hedges shook his head.

"No, sir, there's something else wrong with them."

Chamberlain took another bite of bread and felt his stomach grumble. It felt like everything was curdling in his stomach.

"Well how do you mean?" asked Chamberlain, trying to conceal the nausea. "What exactly is wrong with them?"

"I went in to check on them earlier, sir. All of them have developed this blackish rash all over their bodies. I brought them all gruel this morning and fed them. Not a single one of them kept that food down. They all were retching the strangest vomit I've ever seen. It was the same color as their eyes . . ."

Chamberlain tried to stay focused, but his vision had become blurry. His stomach felt like a butter churn. He knew he wouldn't be able to keep up the calmness much longer.

"I don't know what kind of gas does . . ."

"Would you excuse me, Hedges?" Chamberlain quickly asked.

Without waiting for an answer, he stood on wobbly legs and stepped out of the tent. His stomach felt like it was on fire. He knew he needed to be further away to not draw attention. His shaking legs carried him an additional ten feet before he evacuated his stomach contents into the dirt. Relief washed over him. When the purging had stopped, he wiped his mouth with the sleeve of his uniform. He looked down at his puddle of vomit and stopped. The putrid concoction which lay in the dirt was a deep cerulean shade. He kicked dirt over top of it and returned inside the Mess.

The morning was full of extensive surgeries. Chamberlain performed several amputations and cauterizations, treated further gas victims, and reset many broken limbs. He had sat down at a desk and was beginning to fill out the necessary charts and paperwork when his thumb began to throb. Wincing with pain, he began to unravel the gauze. Each layer he pulled away, the strange cerulean fluid had soaked through. When he reached the final layer, the gauze was slick with the sticky, foul smelling fluid. His entire thumb had changed color. The initial slice was now oozing. Horrified, Chamberlain moved his paperwork and rushed around to find more gauze. Careful not to spill any of this bodily based infection on anything, he quickly rewrapped his thumb.

Chamberlain was terrified. He had never seen any infection spread like this before. He couldn't think of any diseases or virus that shared these symptoms. He left the desk and made his way to the intake ward. He needed to see if he could communicate with any of the gassed soldiers.

The closed section just off the operating theater held twelve patients. Three of these were the gassed patients the surgeon sought. When Chamberlain entered the room, an overpowering stench filled his nostrils. The room reeked of rot and the sickly sweetness of infection. The room was lit only by a single dancing lantern held high on a hook in the center of the tent. Yet this was not the only luminescence in the dank room. Shimmering from the floor, Chamberlain could see cerulean flashes. The flashes came from the corner where the three soldiers "slept." Chamberlain crept in close.

He couldn't explain what he was seeing. Tendrils, covered in small spikes, had burst through each of the three men's uniforms. These tendrils emitted the flashes. What confused the surgeon even more was that these tendrils had crept along the floor and had twisted and wriggled their way up beneath all the blankets of sleeping soldiers in sight. Chamberlain came to the nearest soldier and threw back the blanket. There he saw the tendrils had burrowed their way deep into the sleeping man in the next cot. The sleeping man did not seem to notice.

Chamberlain quickly tossed the blanket back over and turned to leave when he took a glance back at the gassed three. The one in the middle, the one who had smiled so maliciously at him, was wide awake and watched the surgeon with his glowing eyes.

"Hello, Doc."

Chamberlain stared in shock at the thing that was once a British soldier.

"You're probably wondering how long it will be before you too will be like this. Don't worry. It won't be long now. You'll need to feed."

"Wha . . . What?" stammered Chamberlain.

"You may not understand now, but you will in time. Our kind has lain dormant in the soil since time immemorial. Your war has brought us back. You will find your place amongst our hierarchy and you will help propagate our species again. We are of the earth and our time has come again."

Chamberlain could take no more. He dashed from the room and out again into the open air. Tears rolled down his face. When he wiped them away, to his horror, his tears had changed in color.

18:30 hours rolled around and Chamberlain finished composing his letter. He put it in the envelope and wrote "Hedges" on its bare front. He stiffly stood. His vision was blurred. The infection, or whatever it was, had spread down his arm. He knew he did not have much time. He pulled out the last British Consul in his pack and lit it. Forcing his rigid legs to move he made his way to the intake ward. He carried a canister of kerosene beneath his arm.

At 19:00 hours, the fire in the intake tent had been reported. The only time that week the skies had not opened into a torrent, was the night of the fire. While soldiers and ambulance drivers attempted to douse the flames, it was of no use. The fire burned too hot. The only thing they could do was to ensure that the surrounding tents did not also catch fire.

Lance Corporal Hedges cleared the tears from his cheeks. He knew, just knew, that his superior started the fire. There was simply no other explanation. He made his way to Captain Chamberlain's quarters. He saw the letter immediately. He grabbed it from its perch and tore it open. The words he read, made him question his superior's sanity:

Dear Hedges,

I know you wonder why I did it. This is to be expected. Those men were no longer human. They carried with them some form of ancient infection or organism. I can't be sure what it was, or is, but I know they must die. I too must go with them. Their being has crept into me as well. I cannot let this spread. The Hun is one thing, but something like this could destroy all of mankind. I want you to know Hedges, you were the finest assistant I have had in all my years. If you survive this war, and if the God above is a just man, you will go places. Can you please find my son and tell him that his father died an honorable man? His name is Pvt. Julian Chamberlain, First Battalion, Sherwood Foresters, Twenty-Fourth Brigade, Eight Infantry Division.

Thank You Hedges and God speed,
Captain Noel E. Chamberlain,
Royal Army Medical Corps

WHIZZ-BANG ATTACK
By Sergio "ente per ente" Palumbo

"I don't want to go in the trenches no more,
where the whizz-bangs and shrapnel they whistle and roar ..."
from "I Don't Want to Die,"
Popular WWI Song

It is well known that the earliest military uses of chemical weapons were tear-inducing irritants rather than fatal or disabling poisonous gases, and they were deployed during the First World War. The initial tries on both sides—the so-called Central Powers (the German and the Austro-Hungarian Empires, the Ottoman Empire, and the Kingdom of Bulgaria) against the *Entente* Powers (the French Republic, the British and the Russian Empires)—that had been eagerly put into practice turned out to be largely ineffective. Italy and the United States joined the *Entente* only later and other countries like Japan, Belgium, Greece, and the Czechoslovak legions were secondary members. The fact was that the small quantities of gas actually delivered were not even detected by the enemy soldiers in the trenches. Another thing that happened was that the chemical froze and failed to have the desired effect, as it occurred in January 1915—which was the first instance of large-scale use of the new terrible weapon—when Germany fired eighteen-thousand artillery shells containing liquid *xylyl bromide* tear gas on Russian positions on the Rawka River, in Poland.

Anyway, before the Germans could employ a deadlier gas as a killing agent, something else was waiting to happen while the war was increasing its fierceness on many bloody battlegrounds throughout Europe. Such a secret story, however, had never reached the media nor been told so far, and many would clearly deny that such events had ever occurred. But this is what I, now a very old soldier, already in my 100s, once told a middle-aged researcher working for one of those neglected or ill-reputed TV programs showing strange facts and weird situations that were never truly exposed to the viewers worldwide but could have changed the course of history. *Or perhaps even the life of the whole of mankind.*

Those occurrences were never broadcasted, for some unknown reason, and such accounts never got into the newspapers in the end, but the following is what I said. Believe it or not. . . .

The Western Front was the name applied to the battle zone in France, where the British, French, and Belgian troops faced the armies of Germany. Eventually the American forces would join the others on the Western Front. But there was an Eastern Front too, in Poland and down to Serbia, where Russian armies faced those of Germany and Austria-Hungary.

As a matter of fact, the Western Front was not the only theatre where the British army saw action during the Great War but it was by far the most important. After the battles of 1914, both sides held an entrenched line that stretched from Nieuport on the Belgian coast, through the flatlands of France, continuing through the wide expanses and into the high mountains, until it got to the Swiss border. The British held a small portion of this four-hundred-mile long line, varying from some twenty miles in 1914 to over one-hundred-twenty early in 1918. During the war, the disputed area that lay in that sector had been courageously held by the French Army. Its strategic importance made it the staging ground of a lot of bloody battles that had already taken place. But many more battles would soon be coming. . . .

The boundary of the front had remained almost the same until the present year, which was 1915, even though several thousand soldiers had died in other local attacks or *coup de main* operations. History shows that from the moment the German army moved quietly on August the 2nd 1914 to the end of the war, the fighting in that part of France never stopped. There were some short, quiet periods, just as there were more intense, huge-scale battles.

By the end of the fierce confrontation of November 22nd, 1914, the two sides were in siege warfare that included extensive use of underground tunnels, shelters and emplacements, counter-battery artillery fire, and mining (which was also used offensively). The continuous trench lines of the Western Front presented all army commanders with a serious problem: it had been proven that the way to win battles was to 'turn the flank' of the enemy (that is, to go around his position)—*but there was no flank on the Western Front, for either side!* At one end was the North Sea, at the other end four-hundred miles away, the Alps. So, the Front settled in for a long period of trench warfare.

The British army was still very much the lesser partner on land at first, and took part in many attacks of increasing scale as the army grew in size. Casualties were very high and little was gained in terms of territory; the British lost the main part of their pre-war regular army while being greatly outmanned and outgunned. It became clear that enemy positions could be broken into, but not broken through, without the deployment of much larger forces.

It was almost noon on the day in late January 1915 and the snowy, hard terrain wasn't very different from what it had been the previous day—apart from some bloodstains that covered portions of it and begrimed many carcasses of horses left dead on the ground. There had been a skirmish during the night when the Germans had tried to break through French defenses, but they had been stopped before advancing too far, as it had happened time and time again.

Well hidden in my hole, I, Claude Souillè, being a soldier of only nineteen, wore the so-called *capote modèle simplifié* whose color was simply known as *gris bleu anglais*, with the buttons on the right; and the characteristic *pantalon-culotte* of a common French infantryman of that period. There was a light *képi* on my head that allowed only a few short, dark curls to fall around my face. My rifle, being a reliable though heavy 8mm *fusil repetition Level 1886 M93*, was aiming apparently at nothing across the barren terrain. My hazel eyes kept watch for any movement in the distance, while the burden of the heavy equipment I had on—made up of a military knapsack, a huge *bouthéon* and my *outil individuel*—made me sink much lower than I normally would have within the hole, in order to keep my body safe. Actually, in 1914, uniforms, equipment, and tactics for the average soldiers had changed very little since the Franco-Prussian War of more than forty years before. Most of the troops had only recently put away their previous greatcoats and red trousers—as wearing such colorful trousers made men perfect targets on battlefields where machine-guns and artillery ruled, and those innovations in uniforms had only begun by the winter of 1914. In a way clothing had been poorly improved, and soldiers still didn't wear helmets yet. Such a useful safeguard was still to come for the infantrymen courageously fighting day by day across those battlefields where death could suddenly come from any direction.

My standard military unit was the *34th* Infantry Regiment (R.I.), which consisted of seventy officers along with three-thousand-four-hundred other ranks and was organized into three battalions. The young French soldier thought that, likely, their politicians hadn't ever witnessed any battles like these, because they hadn't done anything to try and stop them. Or maybe such terrible losses didn't have a particularly profound effect on their rulers' minds or on the Military's thinking either. Thousands of men like me, ill-equipped and poorly led, were marched off into some of the costliest battles France had ever fought. The Battle of the Frontiers and the fighting in 1914 alone cost their army more than three-hundred-thousand casualties.

It had been said many times that the French Army of 1914 was prepared for war: *whether it was prepared for a conflict like the Great War was another matter.* France had a general conscription at the outbreak of war, with men being called-up to join the army at eighteen and, on average, completing a four-year term of service. After being discharged from the regular forces, they were immediately placed on the reserve until they were roughly thirty-three years of age, and then they joined the territorials, often staying in until they were in their late forties. It meant that the average Frenchman was committed to military service, in one way or another, for most of his adult life. This was requested under common circumstances, but this war was not one of those, certainly.

I thought that, after that continuous standoff and all the casualties involved in the cruel fighting, both High Commands should have properly reviewed their offensive capabilities and decided upon what was to be their final, winning strategy. But things hadn't gone that way nor were they going to make strides towards a quick end in the near future, according to what soldiers—like me—saw in front of themselves every day.

On the other hand, many older officers had been overheard during meals saying that to finally beat them a sort of new Great Offensive would properly be launched within a few months against the British and French sectors. This was because the last infiltration attempts tried by the Germans using small, maneuverable units especially designed not to incur into time-consuming battles at some

strong-points—had completely failed so far, therefore more aggressive measures were sure to be used, sooner or later. Truth be told, I
had ended up by feeling very dejected over the course of the last two
nights in the trenches as the others had talked about what they had
heard. It was especially frustrating to discover that the resistance I
and my fellows put up every single day hadn't proved to be helpful
or decisive at all. Instead it would just force our enemies to deploy a
much more aggressive and bloody attack against our positions soon.

Some of my fellow soldiers said they had already experienced such offensives, being in the rear, and they well-remembered
what the few surviving ones among the advancing troops had told
them: while the sheer scale of the assault was staggering, the fear
most had was to be completely overrun, this way remaining entirely
alone within a zone that was already held by the enemy, with predictable consequences. Of course, there was also a worse alternative,
which was being shot—be it struck in the head or in the chest- and
immediately falling to the ground during the first moments of the
attack itself. That was a way to not worry anymore about the terri-
fying effects of such an offensive—*but the only problem was that you
were already dead at that moment*, so you didn't need to worry about
anything else at all, ever again.

Only a few small arms had fired at the French positions during the first part of that day. Then, all of a sudden about four o'clock,
the French were attacked with a massive artillery barrage. The
shells were coming in, hitting the trees and exploding, so the defending soldiers—who were spread across that small portion of the
front—were exposed to insidious tree burst shrapnel uninterrupt-
edly raining down on them.

After some time, before the French artillery started to retaliate against the Germans, sadly I was ordered to go out and cut apart
some large branches that had been knocked down during the
shelling. It was already getting dark, or perhaps it was just the smoke
that persistently covered the entire area that concealed the feeble
sun in the sky. The logs were to be placed over the foxholes of my
fellow infantrymen deployed nearby to protect from further shell
bursts. After leaving my main weapon behind and going about 100
yards towards the first carcasses of a few emaciated horses killed
during the previous battle, I got about four logs cut when I was almost shot through the face by a German rifleman in the distance, unexpectedly.

'*Damn!*' angrily I told myself and immediately hit the ground, trying to stay away from any further danger. After immediately turning back to my hidden position, I fell flat on my face in about fifteen inches of snow. My only thought was, *"When will it be finally over?"* But my sad conclusion was, *"Maybe never . . ."*

As another long bombing started again, everyone inside their strange, long trenches that stretched past my current position stayed in hiding—protecting their belongings and their guns. A powerful hit was heard very near to my hole, but it seemed not to have killed or wounded any of my fellow soldiers, as no cries or moans came from them. "*Just a Weary Willie . . .*," I told myself. That was a term our British allies commonly used for a German shell passing safely, albeit rather slowly, overhead. "Luckily no one got hurt . . ." was what I whispered—or so I thought anyway.

But things proved to be very different. *And unexpected, too.*
. . .

I really hated such Whizz-Bangs, which were high-velocity German shells—named for the noise of the fast flight and the subsequent explosion. I was highly-motivated to remain in hiding for the time being and so I started singing in my mind a familiar song from that period. As a matter of fact, I had heard the British troops repeating it for days, while they were together defending the area during the previous weeks. "*I don't want to go in the trenches no more, where the whizz-bangs and shrapnel they whistle and roar . . .*" and the rest of the popular music resounded in my head over and over again for some time.

While paying attention to what was going around my position, the dense mist was very heavy and visibility only about twenty yards, so I thought about some things I already well knew: our High Command knew that the enemies wanted to capture the *Creute* terrain (also called *La Caverne du Dragon*, or *Drachenhöhle*, as the Germans had named it), that was the last remaining French stronghold in the area. So we had to be ready anytime, whatever the cost, as any minute could be the Zero-hour when a bloody attack would commence.

Even though I was unable to know the whole story at present, from early 1915 onwards, German troops had invaded an underground quarry that dated back to the 16th century. During WWI, they had placed heavy weapons at each of the seven entrances, ready to breathe fire like a dragon. Soon, the caverns were said to have electricity, dormitories and even a cemetery. The walls of the cham-

bers in there were also said to be adorned with drawings and mes-
sages that were wartime propaganda. Strange to say, but both the
French and the Germans were going to live and fight some forty-nine
feet below the ground in the near future, starting in 1917. That was
what war on that front was going to be like in a matter of a few years:
moving in close quarters and under very harsh conditions. But I
couldn't imagine it at that moment, certainly, and really it didn't matter anyway.

There were some single insidious shots more, over my light
képi, and just after the noisy hit I had heard before—as soon as the
smoke caused by the shells began to dissipate and I expected that
the orders to attack the enemies could come very soon—my ears listened again for any voices, but I didn't hear the Germans speaking.
The chilly part of me that didn't want to remain in here any longer
was planning to slowly and quietly turn around and walk back safely
to the low terraced lines of the French trenches, when something re-
quiring my attention appeared, and I thought I had seen some movements within that unnatural mist. Then my eyes saw a fellow ally—
he was British given his uniform, even though he didn't presently
wear the characteristic stiffened peak cap that all the British soldiers
usually wore. He walked with a very pale look on his face, was moving at a very slow pace, and seemed to be lost.

The fair-haired tall man had the appearance of somebody
that truly lacked a freewill. Maybe the last hit had wounded him in
some way or he was just confused and unable to reason clearly. . . .
But there was something else that looked very strange about him, at
least according to my thoughts: he seemed to be incapable of speech,
but tended to make moaning and some very unusual guttural
sounds, which was increasingly strange. But another detail made
everything about that ally stranger and stranger: his very pale skin
displayed visible signs of desiccation, decay and emaciation—and
the expressionless, empty face was really frightening me now.

Then the British soldier started sniffing the air around him
and, as soon as another French infantryman of the 34th appeared
nearby, emerging from the same smoke that was slowly dissipating,
that one immediately turned to him and started running after the
soldier in an unexpected way. It didn't take him too long to catch up
and as he came nearer he grabbed him—*yes, it was exactly what he
did*—all of a sudden, his mouth moved feverishly toward the French
soldier who was caught by surprise and he didn't react on time. Soon
after, the British soldier's teeth started eating the infantryman's

skin, piercing his body as if that man was the main course of a tasty dinner. *Unbelievable, by any means!*

Apart from the complete unreality of the scene, the British soldier seemed to display an increased strength relative to normal humans, as if it had been set free due to the removal of normal neurological limits of muscle strength. And he didn't stop, he kept devouring the fellow French soldier's body! It was just as if an insatiable and endless desire to consume a living individual had become his only motive for existence!

I thought that I surely had to do something in order to stop all that, as I had to help my fellow infantryman, who was from the same military regiment I was. But what could I try? Then I saw before my own eyes that the cruel scene was still going on, and it was also becoming fiercer and fiercer, as the attacker was removing parts from the arms and the chest of his poor prey. So I made up my mind. Immediately I fired a shot, then another against the madman assaulting the Frenchman, hoping that the Englishman would cease his senseless actions finally. But nothing happened . . . there was no effect! *"What the hell . . .? What is going on . . .?"* I silently asked himself, while a sort of desperation started growing in my mind.

Why hadn't two shots been enough to wound the British soldier? I wondered about that, but I didn't have any explanation. The attacker didn't seem to have taken any offense at my shooting at him, nor was he in pain. He wasn't even crying, in spite of me targeting his chest, and that was really unbelievable! What man could not be affected at all by a *fusil a répétition* hitting him directly in the chest?

And now, what could I do? Where were *Le Service de la Santé* and its capable *pharmacies* and *infirmaries* when you most needed them? Why were there no superior officers around to tell me what exactly to do?

Then, another strange figure appeared nearby, coming out of the same smoke that was now very feeble and started quickly disappearing from the area. It was very easy to spot him and recognize his uniform, *as it was German*! But he didn't wear the outfit commonly used by the enemy for a frontal assault, as he looked to be a very dapper artilleryman, wearing riding boots, which were taller and of thicker leather than the common infantryman's jack boot, while his helmet cover didn't fit particularly well. He also had a three-section leather ammo pouch on his belt, a typical *pistolet automatique P 08* dangling in a harmless way from his waist, and he was walking at a very slow pace too.

Because he didn't stand upright, with straight legs and back, as common men usually did, the German seemed to be affected by a serious restriction in his muscle control, forcing him to move with an awkward shamble. His overall posture wasn't right, for sure, as he had knees and ankles which were bent at awkward angles, with a prominent lean to one side. His movements were becoming increasingly irregular, as he walked on. I didn't have any difficulty recognizing that his face and his skin displayed the same strange signs the previous British soldier had, which only made me even more afraid of the whole damn situation that was going on. *Maybe some new, strange, and terrible weapon was at work in that place and I was in the middle of that zone of unknown operations!* I had already heard of those first tries from the enemy and his own troops, too. I had heard how both sides had recently put into practice the use of gas and other deadly substances on the battlefields—but I had never witnessed such a terrible thing for myself, of course. And I wished I never had with all my heart, of course. . . .

As the British soldier seemed to have completed his bloody meal and left the few remains of the dead body of the unfortunate French soldier on the snowy terrain, the German approached, moving faster than before, just as if his nose had sensed something tasty in the air as well. As soon as he got to the corpse, he started licking the blood that begrimed the cold ground and then tried to satisfy his hunger by eating the few body parts still at his feet. Then, once those monstrous actions were over, he rose to his feet and stared at the other being who was nearby in an inexpressive way, without speaking. From his mouth only a strange moaning and some guttural sounds came out, exactly the same as the British soldier.

The two didn't attack each other, as if they were of a common alliance, in a way. *But they were enemies*, in reality, the first one being British and the other one a German! What was happening in there? Maybe they were spies, or traitors. But I immediately dropped that thought, as I had never seen spies eating other combatants nor individuals being hungry enough to devour corpses on the ground, and I didn't think they could be from somewhere else in the world, after all. . . .

There was a sort of brief, strange silence, while the seemingly empty eyes of the two strange men looked at each other, then something else happened. In fact, it was at that point that another French infantryman reached the same place, his uniform having some bloodstains on it. While he moved along he kept his right hand on his opposite arm, as if it had been hit and was wounded now, and he wanted to protect that part of his body. His approach was immediately noticed by the two pale figures who, almost in accordance, turned their heads to him and used their noses to savour the blood smell in the air, along with the reddish drops that were falling behind him on the white cover of the battlefield. Then they both moved together against the newcomer and tried to hurriedly reach him in order to accomplish their evil task. What surprised me the most was that the strange pale British soldier seemed to be acting in complete accordance—*or at least in silent agreement*— with the German artilleryman who was next to him.

The two appeared to be a couple of very unusual individuals, as their weird faces and their overall features didn't display any signs of intelligence. Everything about them clearly revealed that they weren't completely right in the head. On the contrary, those two soldiers looked like two madmen, without reasoning, with no ties to this world, at least not any longer. Right then they didn't even notice each other as both of them kept moving toward the new soldier, that fellow soldier of theirs, in order to attack him. *British soldiers and Germans working together?* That was really incredible; certainly something unexpected and unexplainable was happening in that place.

Then my attentive though incredulous eyes saw other people advancing at a very cautious pace, wearing huge gas masks: they might have been Germans but I wasn't sure at all, given their strange outfits. At least they weren't dressed in any uniform that I was acquainted with.

"What is going on?" being already very frightened, my mind wondered.

Then, suddenly, five, no, six other figures came out of the faint haze and all of them wore wide chestnut-colored protective suits. Immediately I recognized the suits now as the clothing scientists wore to prevent themselves from coming into contact with deadly liquids or contagious diseases. They reached the two pale soldiers who were still attacking the poor French infantrymen. They raised their hands and the heavy though thin metallic machines they had with them sent out a long controllable stream of fire. This flame was projected at an incredibly high rate of speed from those mechanical devices, causing the incineration of those who were their distant targets.

The thing that most surprised me at that moment was that they didn't die at once, as their movements continued even after the huge flames had engulfed their arms and legs. In fact, they didn't stop trying to move and walk until other men in suits came nearer and started cutting their burnt bodies in half using swords and other huge white weapons. They then continued to repeat this incredible process, over and over again. They didn't stop until there were only little pieces on the ground out of what once had been two living soldiers, formerly fighting on opposing sides.

I didn't have enough time to look at the whole scene, as another powerful blast was heard not too far from where I lay, and a lot of heavy smoke started filling the area again—so I kept myself well hidden in my hole. When it was finally over, all the men in suits seemed to have disappeared and not a single part of those cut bodies was still visible on the terrain, just as if they had never truly been there. Only the blood on the snow revealed that something terrible had occurred in that place, but all the rest of the evidence had been already removed and there were no other signs of what I had seen, or of what I thought my eyes truly had witnessed that day. . . .

For a long time, during the many terrible weeks of war that followed those unbelievable events, I wondered if what I had seen along the front was just a figment of my imagination, after all. Perhaps I had simply become mad in some way. . . . I also decided not to tell anyone for several years, until one morning, when I was in my 100s, finally I reported it to a journalist who was searching for fresh, strange material about the war—interesting though unusual stories from the few surviving veterans of WWI, for a TV documentary that was still in the planning stages.

What I, a former infantryman of the *34th Régiment d'Infantrie,* told him really amazed the reporter, but what surprised me was that I had finally found a way to reveal to somebody else what I had witnessed that day, without fearing that I would be considered a madman!

Probably the knowledge that my life was almost over once and for all helped me to make that decision. But I myself, Claude, was well aware that the story appeared deeply incredulous to my own ears while I was telling it to the reporter—the tale that nobody else had ever heard before.

Just a few days after the strange events occurred at the front, four generals of the Central Powers were lined-up along a wall and were staring in silence at the events that were happening in front of them. Past the wall was a long window that let them watch the lab on the other side, where two tall physicians were handling a weird emaciated man—or better, a pale moving corpse—tied with strong chains that didn't allow him to move too far.

The worried look on their faces showed that the minds of all the high-ranking individuals in there were troubled, and they had many doubts about what to say or what to think after seeing all that. The first physician, a slim blonde-haired Bulgarian of about 50 who led the medical team working in the lab, exited the main metallic door, and the tallest among the generals approached him. This was a middle-aged German with a traditional gold emblem on his typical field-gray uniform collar. He looked intensely at the doctor's bearded face where two tired blue eyes stood. "Anything new?" were his plain words, expressed in a low tone.

"No, sir" the other replied.

"So, you don't know yet what caused such a thing to happen . . ."

"Well, we're not entirely sure. Maybe it was simply that the gases we deployed during the battle weren't mixed correctly. Or perhaps some substances were added afterwards and they all reacted together in a weird, unexpected way."

"But what are we dealing with, in reality?" intervened a second general, a highly decorated Austrian, with two dark eyes on a strangely pleated old face with a light beard.

At that point, the blonde physician frowned. "Apparently, the victims appear to be creatures connected to some fabled, bizarre practices that are in use among the citizens of the Caribbean islands—at least according to common legends that local people there believe in. They call the men turned into such living carcasses—like the moving corpse we have tied down here in our lab— 'zombie', or something like that . . ."

"So how can they be here, and not in the Caribbean?" the first German general asked the man of science.

"And how can they be real, if we are just talking about legends?" the Austrian insisted, with two vivid, inquiring eyes that stood out from his exhausted features.

"Well, there is someone back at Headquarters that also suggested it might have been caused by a form of sorcery at work on the battleground."

The other high-ranking commander stared at the physician in return with a hard look. "But you don't think that, of course . . ."

"No, sir, of course not."

"So, what is it? Why did it happen?"

"Apparently the poisonous gas our units used during the test had some very strange effects on victims on both sides. It was an unexpected result, undoubtedly. It was just luck for our troops that some members of our medical team were already wearing their protective suits and masks in case the artillery malfunctioned.

"So, is this the only explanation you can give us about all that?"

"Yes, sir, it doesn't seem to have affected anyone else at the moment . . . but we're still examining every variable that could have affected the subjects."

"Any other details . . . ?"

"Some of the human features of the few victims we retrieved and we were able to bring to our labs for confinement—according to further studies—seemed to be very different, at first glance, and the natural wear and tear made the face almost a dead giveaway. Their eyes were filled with a white substance, partly obscuring their pupils, even though it didn't detract from their sense of sight. In addition, because they appeared to have lost all regenerative abilities, any damage to their face or skin remained permanent, along with any cut or bruise they suffered. Generally, those 'zombies' . . ." there was a pause as the bearded man of science pronounced that term and a heavy silence fell on the whole room ". . . in these situations looked like a slow, lumbering and unintelligent kind, but after a while . . ."

"Yes? Go on, please . . ." insisted the third one, a bulky Turkish individual who looked older than 60, in a characteristic tunic with tri-pointed pockets whose Red General Staff officer's collar clearly indicated his rank.

"A sort of hunger, for meat or fresh blood of other living creatures moving in the vicinity, especially of men and women, began tormenting them, becoming an obsession. That bizarre need completely seized their mind, or what was still left of it . . ." the physician added, being a bit embarrassed. "We're still checking out how this thing progresses, and we have some other volunteers to test."

"*What are you saying*?" the first German general objected at once.

"Stop it, immediately!" the fourth high-ranking individual ordered. "We can't handle this thing. How do you plan to put an end to their existence after creating others like that one?"

"As our medical team discovered at the time of the unexpected accident, the living carcasses can't be killed or controlled, but their body can be cut into little pieces, so that the remains are not a danger to anyone, even though they keep moving awkwardly."

"But you can't really reverse the process, once the gas reaches them . . ."

"No, and we still don't know why," the physician admitted, lowering his eyes.

"Did you find any way to kill them? Cutting their head and their arms off perhaps?" the Austrian commander asked.

"Not yet, sir" the physician said. "Actually, it seems that there is a sort of neural connection that continues even after the death of the common life functions of the subject. Most organs appear to keep working even when you remove the heart—thanks to some unknown means . . ."

"So, why would you do more testing on other people? *Why?* It's not something we are looking for, this is not the weapon we need to win this war!" the third general asked the leader of the research team.

"Headquarters ordered us to keep researching for a while, but they also told us to wait for your final evaluations and act according to what you decide, certainly."

"Any other important facts you need to give us, before we make our decision?"

"Well, there is something else that is interesting," the man of science said. "Reports indicated that some British soldiers affected by the poisonous substance started acting as one with our infected troops."

"*What?* Please, tell us what you mean, specifically," the tallest general cried out.

The physician nodded. "That's true. The victims seemed to be cooperating, in some ways, just as if they were all parts of the body perhaps. And they hunted for human prey together, to find and eat . . ."

"Some of our soldiers worked together with our enemies! During the war? This thing must not be repeated . . ." two generals stated together almost in a single voice.

"What do think we should do now? We could just seal them up somewhere, and keep studying their reactions and behavior . . ."

"*No way!* Just imagine if this outcome would spread across the battlefields. Just make them disappear, *immediately!*" the first general stated.

"And no one must know anything about it," another one added.

"We will follow your orders, sirs!" the physician nodded.

After that very delicate matter was decidedly resolved and put aside, the generals talked to each other for some time in rapid conversation. Then the German approached the physician and stared at him with an intense look on his face. "We thought you had something else to show us today . . . something that will help out our war!"

The Bulgarian immediately understood. "Yes, of course, sir. I can show you the great results we got just recently thanks to another useful substance our technicians have been working on. Please, follow me . . ." and that being said, he pointed to a long tunnel leading to the west wing of the building they were in.

After a short walk, the group arrived at another area of the structure and they stopped as the physician gestured to them. He then showed them another window along the wall, with a lone man on the other side, wearing only a long robe with a dejected look on his face. "There is this promising gas we are developing, which appears to be what we just need at present. The original substance is colorless, viscous liquid at room temperature. When used in other forms, such as warfare agents, it appears yellowish in color and has a strange odor resembling some rotting plants."

"So, please proceed . . ." the tallest general said.

"Now, please, just look at it . . ." the physician said. As the man reached a button, he pressed it and immediately a yellowish substance started entering the small room, soon filling it almost entirely.

As the first effects were noticed, the prisoner in the room tried to move to the door, that was locked of course, and then he started crying, beating against the window. It was obvious he was doing his best to break it or to create a way out, a safe escape to life. . . . But all his movements proved futile.

While the group on the other side of the window, the safe side, watched the cruel scene, some terrible minutes went on. And on. . . .

The skin of the human target of that gas blistered, his eyes became very sore and then he began to vomit. Such a weapon seemed to be able to cause internal and external bleeding and attacked the bronchial tubes, stripping off the mucous membrane. This proved to be extremely painful, as the poor man who tried to stand to his feet appeared to be constantly fighting for breath. His cries became strange whispers, saying that his mouth was closing against his will.

When all was accomplished and the test ended with the death of the prisoner, there were some words of appreciation among the high-ranking men. And their features appeared much more relaxed and very glad now.

"Better," the Turkish general added, while a large sneer appeared on his furrowed face. "Really, that is much better . . ."

The physician explained, "This is the most effective gas we have found so far. Our technicians are going to call it mustard-gas at last, in colloquial language . . ."

"Finally, we are on the right track," the German commander stated, happily impressed.

"This is a sustainable weapon. And please, let's have no more of those creatures who are half-living and half-dead at the same time!" the Austrian general smiled, satisfied.

THE ALWAYS WATCHING EYE
By Gary Power

"**W**hy do bad people make such good books, Uncle?"

Edmund Frankes looked up from his writing desk at the far end of the grand library and considered his niece's words.

"Perhaps because the colourful way they lead their lives?" he suggested.

"Hmmm," she mused, ". . . maybe."

Lilith, perched on a wide ledge, gazed distantly through the leaded light windows down onto the sprawling landscaped garden below. A light mist, like a vaporous sea washed over the rambling lawn and lapped gently against the towering walls of Cedar Lodge. In her imagination, the gothic mansion was an island lost in an ocean of clouds drifting above a world of insufferable ignorance and moral corruption.

She rested her palm on the hefty tome by her side. The sinewy cover was clammy and shivered beneath her warm flesh. A solitary eye stared back, weeping and bloodshot. The pages were cold and the print fading as though being drawn from the page. From a corner that had been bumped there oozed a fine trickle of blood.

"It's been too long; the books are ailing and the curator's not at all happy. The reading room is such a sad place to be at the moment, and it smells in there too, like something's died."

Lilith glanced anxiously towards the solid oak door of the anteroom to Edmund's left. Somewhere beyond came the sound of restless movement followed by a resonant growl.

"Have patience, Lilith. Matters are in hand; I believe we've found a perfect specimen. You'll have your book soon, and then the curator will be happy again."

Lilith, now in her twenties but possessed of childish exuberance, turned her haunted face in his direction and stared through silvery eyes. She looked so fragile, like a porcelain doll. If she fell, Edmund feared she would shatter into a million pieces. Despite the chill air, she was dressed in a gown so sheer that it left little to the imagination. He was forever warning her that she'd catch her death roaming the draughty corridors if she didn't wear clothing that was more substantial, and a little more appropriate. But Lilith was strong-willed and quite whimsical in her ways, just like her mother, an eccentric and free-spirited woman of French descent.

"*Deshabille . . . deshabille!*" she would shriek, much to her Uncle's bemusement.

"What will the book be, uncle? Something savage and cruel perhaps? Do you have any idea yet? Surely you must."

The news brought life and colour to her sullen face and infused the gloomy room with incandescent light.

"I think this time it will be an anthology, or portmanteau if you like. A collection of stories dredged from the depths of mortal despair. It will be our darkest work yet. I have a feeling the curator will be very happy with this one."

Evan Gore wasn't well. His thoughts were muddled and his emotions numb. Cigarettes and alcohol did little to abate his declining health but at least they tempered his festering contempt for the world.

He'd not been feeling himself ever since he'd moved into an allegedly haunted apartment, which was embarrassing, because Evan was also a notorious sceptic of the paranormal. His sneering attitude towards occult matters had been the cause of many a heated television debate. The tabloids thrived on his outspoken ways and cynical stance. His subsequent employment as an overpaid chat show host in which he ruthlessly mocked guests and their supernatural experiences made him an enviably rich man.

He celebrated his success by purchasing an apartment from one of London's most prestigious estate agents, Darkwood Estates of Mayfair. The deal for 3 Dakota House was completed live on his TV show when he famously declared that no building is inherently evil. The apartment had gained historical notoriety when the previous owner, Barnaby Wright FRSC, an eminent surgeon, invited four of his students for an evening of light-hearted banter—and then drugged and slaughtered them.

The scale of depravity exacted within those walls transcended the most extreme boundaries of human degradation, to the extent that there were even those who considered it to be the work of a deranged genius.

Having forced entry into the apartment, four bodies were discovered, two males, two females, stripped naked and bizarrely posed at a table as though in the midst of a joyful dinner party. Their dismembered limbs and heads had been randomly sown back together into obscene ragdoll creations of the human form. Their eyes had been gouged and in each empty socket had been placed a single rose, alternately white and red.

Barnaby Wright was found sitting upright in his bed, feasting on a platter of eyes. Calmly, he told the police that they'd been gently sautéed to preserve their texture and flavour, the liquid residue being deglazed to make a piquant sauce. "*The roses were a personal touch*," he explained as they pulled him from the bed— "*white as a representation of purity and red as a symbol of love.*" And then, with teeth bared he bit on one of the glistening orbs, rupturing the eyeball and sending a spray of vitreous fluid into the face of a young police officer.

He explained that his work, entitled "*the art of anatomy,*" was a celebration of the human form and that it signified unity and strength.

"I was going to put it on Instagram," he remarked nonchalantly to his incredulous entourage.

Barnaby Wright never came to trial. He slit his own throat in the back of the police car using a concealed razor and died haemorrhaging blood into the face of the same policeman that he'd covered in eyeball fluid.

Evan's introduction to the supernatural world was, at first, a subtle affair: nocturnal scraping sounds from beneath uneven floorboards; fragrant breezes in closed rooms; sobbing cries that lingered hauntingly in the air. His only confidant was Victor, an ageing concierge who seemed more interested in poring over lurid old paperbacks, the kind with semi clad women in peril on the cover and titles like, *"She Paid in Flesh,"* or, *"Born for Sin."* Victor was a simple man, happy to listen to Evan bantering on without paying the slightest attention, and that suited Evan fine.

While unsettled by the strange goings on, Evan still managed to convince himself that there was a rational explanation . . . until things became impossible to talk away. He began to catch sight of nefarious creatures moving about the flat. The glimpses were fleeting and usually from the periphery of his vision. The ephemeral manifestations came in three forms; one a wolf-like she-beast and another, by its sleekness and agility, more like a leopard or panther. The last gave him most reason for concern; a hunched troglodyte beast that watched from the darkest shadows. Its eyes burned in the gloom and its fetid breath made him gag. Usually he would see it in waking moments; it was as though the beast appeared only in times of vulnerability—when consciousness returned after heavy sleep, drunken binges, or coke-fuelled orgies.

There were two explanations, he told Victor who, because he was ensconced in his latest book, *D for Delinquent*, managed only a conciliatory glance. The first was that the apartment was indeed haunted and, by the nature of the manifestations, possibly a gateway to hell. The other was that he was simply going mad.

Victor's advice was to live with his ghostly intruders; better that than suffer the indignity of being branded a lunatic or even worse, a hypocrite.

The biggest irony was . . . Evan came to realise that he was clairvoyant as well.

Soon after the haunting started, he began to hear voices. One in particular took to the fore—the gritty tones of a man by the name of Harry Speirs—a discarnate spirit who quickly became Evan's personal guide to the "other side." Harry had fought on the Western front during the 1914-18 war. Injured twice, he eventually returned to the "frightfulness" at Fleurbaix as a war correspondent. He was killed in action after volunteering himself to report on a night-time raid. Married for barely a year and with a baby daughter back home in Reading, Harry's tortured spirit refused to let go of its mortal ties. What particularly amused Evan though was the way Harry would growl "allo guvn'or" whenever he wanted to make his presence felt.

Communicating with an ethereal lodger in his head wasn't something that came easily to Evan: the most obvious being, should he think a reply or speak it? Thinking it seemed a bit hit and miss; speaking aloud was more reliable but would appear odd in social situations, unless your name was Derek Acorah. What concerned him more though was just how much access Harry had to the thoughts in his head; some of them just lately had been a little . . . extreme.

"*I sees fings, Evan,*" Harry told Evan, "*Stuff like you couldn't imagin'. Been savin' the best stories for you. Gonna put 'em in your head so's you can write 'em down. Always wanted to write stories, I did. Now I can do it through you. Make you a mint it will.* Nine Lives, *we'll call it.*"

"Why nine?" asked Evan.

Harry scoffed at that.

"*. . . 'cause nine is the number of human discord. Cats 'ave nine lives and according to the Cabal, nine is the number of achievement. There's nine plains of the Chinese sky and the Greeks and Egyptians consider nine to be a sacred number. There's nine months of human gestation. Jesus snuffed it on the cross on the ninth hour an' then appeared to his disciples nine times after his resurrection. There's nine choruses of the Angels and accordin' to the Freemasons nine is the number of immortality. A stitch in time saves nine an' I'm sure you've been on cloud nine or gone the whole nine yards, Evan. Thrice and inverted it is the number of the beast, and in Dante's Inferno there's nine circles to Hell. You want more?*"

Evan raised his hand; he'd heard enough. He'd play along, for the moment. Eavesdropping on the dark side might even prove to be fun

"*. . . the best thing is,*" growled Harry, "*you're first story happened right here in this apartment when some surgeon geezer lost 'is nut an' fucked up a bunch o' young'uns.*"

In order to dampen media interest and exploit his new project, Evan made it publicly known that he was taking a lengthy sabbatical. His television was consigned to a skip, newspapers cancelled, and mobile unceremoniously cremated in the basement furnace. For the price of a bottle of scotch and an endless supply of sleazy pulp fiction, Victor became his own personal firewall to the outside world.

Harry helped Evan by bridging the intangible gap between life and death so that he might find himself more tales from beyond the grave. Consequently, the flat became a spiritual squat for those beleaguered souls trapped in a twilight world.

Immersing himself in such dark matters drew the attention of less friendly entities. He wasn't frightened though; such malicious activity served only to strengthen and focus his resolve. His sexual appetite, fuelled by rapacious demons, became voracious. The frequent visits by escorts did not go unnoticed by the residents of Dakota House and his demands became quite extreme. Screams of ecstasy might well have been cries of agony, not that anyone seemed to care.

As time passed so the nocturnal intrusions became even more menacing; furniture and ornaments hurled in Evan's direction became a daily occurrence. The incarnate visitors thrived on the shadowy darkness that surrounded him. Obscenities were whispered in his ear and the stink of things long since dead filled the air.

What followed next though took him beyond the realm of the corporeal world and possibly to the edge of his own sanity.

One night he was drawn from his bedroom by the sound of woeful crying emanating from the dining room. From the gloom of the doorway at the end of the hall he heard the brutal thud of what sounded like meat being chopped on a butcher's slab. Cautiously and with a racing heart, he approached the room, and by the flickering light of several ghostly candles saw four unclothed bodies slumped in chairs.

A large man donning a surgeon's gown was standing behind the trembling figure of a young woman, hacking at her shoulder with a large knife. Apparently drugged and in a state of paralysis, the girl whimpered, but her tearful cries were those of one resigned to a dreadful fate. The man continued in frenzied fashion until, with a resounding crack her arm was wrenched free of its socket.

"Welcome," uttered the surgeon calmly as he studied the dismembered limb, "come and wonder at my magnificent creations." The wretched souls sat about the table were barely alive. Smiling somewhat insanely, the surgeon moved on to one of his male victims and continued with his butchery.

"I see your adventure has begun, Evan. Believe me it is a glorious descent. I'm quite envious of the journey that lies ahead of you. Remember this my friend; for you there is no more right or wrong. From now on you live by your own rules, not those imposed by conceited hypocrites."

The surgeon hummed merrily as he continued his work. With one deft movement of a surgical saw he cut through the neck of his whimpering subject. The shrill whine of the motor drowned out all but the surgeon's demented laugh as he held the head aloft like a grotesque carnival lantern. With eyes still blinking and mouth contorted in silent scream, he turned his trophy so that it could see its own headless torso.

"It has been proven that consciousness remains after decapitation, as with the guillotine for example. The severed head could still see from the bucket," he told Evan. "Under such circumstances, the brain continues to function for anywhere up to a minute." He chuckled.

Far from being appalled, Evan found himself curiously aroused by the merciless slaughter. He had entered a world where desire was ruled by depravity, and he found it an exhilarating experience.

That night, when his scalp began to itch . . . by the light of a candle . . . he parted his hair and saw . . . there, just a few inches above his right brow . . . letters, as though tattooed on his skin.

And he found himself laughing like a man unhinged.

In glorious fashion, his book had begun. Not just in his head but indelibly etched onto his flesh. No longer was he imprisoned by the human condition, for this was a transformation of the most profound kind.

He celebrated the only way he knew—with bottles of vodka and copious amounts of cocaine snorted from the sweaty flesh of several hastily summoned working girls. Even by his own standards it was a marathon session of unrivalled debauchery and substance abuse.

He had been crashed out in an armchair for several hours when he found himself roused by movement in the room. Upon waking he saw a man, quite possibly just another manifestation, standing before him.

Evan was neither surprised nor shocked by his uninvited guest, but merely glanced at his watch and smiled as he gently drifted back into consciousness.

"I was expecting some more young ladies," he declared wearily, "my appetite in that department of late has become quite voracious."

"Sorry to spoil your plans," replied the well-spoken man.

Evan chuckled at that. "I think I was going to do something bad to them."

"I came just in time then."

"Full marks for getting past Victor."

"The old man on the door? He was fast asleep with a rather sordid looking book on his lap."

Evan chuckled at that, too.

"You seem familiar?" said Evan.

"Edmund Frankes, proprietor of Cedar Lodge Publishing. Creator of fine, limited edition books of the dark arts. Our books are a form of embodiment of the printed word; we like to call them living books. And to answer your question, we met on your show; you might remember that you were rather critical of my publishing business. A load of *airy-fairy bollocks*, was your exact comment."

Evan lit a cigarette, inhaled deeply and with a wry smile studied his mysterious visitor.

"The thing is, I've heard that you intend to write a rather interesting collection of short stories. If that's so then Cedar Lodge would be the perfect retreat for you to create what I am sure is destined to become a unique and incredible document of the afterlife, and one that we would be proud to have in our esteemed collection."

As far as Evan was aware, only Harry, his spirit guru, knew about the book, which intrigued him even more.

"So, who's been blabbing and why so interested in me?"

Edmund allowed himself an amused chuckle. The reason to him seemed obvious.

"You are not exactly discrete, Mr. Gore. You, a renowned sceptic of all things supernatural, suddenly consider writing a book documenting genuine stories from beyond the grave. A man who used to inflict such vitriolic mockery on well-meaning people? It is what I believe is termed a U-turn."

"Well, Edmund, it's certainly true that I used to be a cynical cunt. I'm just not quite so cynical these days, although deluded people living in cloud cuckoo land made my job an easy one, and I still believe that most of the guests on my show were exactly that."

". . . and therein lies the germ of a fascinating book."

". . . a fascinating book that might be better placed with the big boys?" declared Evan as he stubbed out his cigarette on the arm of his chair.

Edmund considered his reply and moved to the window. Tapping once on the rain-spattered glass, he made a beckoning gesture and then returned to his chair. Several minutes later a young woman entered the room, her clothes drenched and clinging. She wasn't wearing a coat. Just a thin blouse and skin-tight leather trousers.

Frankes shook his head in despair at Lilith's appearance. She was determined, it seemed, to catch her death of cold. But Lilith had studied her quarry and knew exactly what she was doing: an unfastened button and a tactical tease of flesh; a coy smile and decorous grin; and of course, the drama of a memorable entrance. She stood before Evan and rested the palm of her hand on the side of his face. Her stare, cold as her icy fingers, silenced him and sent a shudder through his body. She too shivered and then, with an expression of ecstasy on her bloodless face, uttered a blissful sigh.

Evan saw another place in that sultry gaze, a chimerical land blissfully disengaged from the world for which he had so much contempt, and for a moment he experienced a lightness of being that was as euphoric as an ecstasy high.

"What do you see?" she asked him.

Evan sighed and stepped back so that he could focus on her face.

"You know damned well," he told her.

Her priggish grin said it all.

"Take me there," he said.

Kissing him gently on the cheek she whispered, ". . . of course."

Several days later Evan was collected by a burly chauffeur driving a midnight blue Bentley Continental. The limousine slipped silently into the London traffic to the accompaniment of Chopin's Nocturnes. On the backseat in an ice bucket was a perfectly chilled bottle of Louis Roederer: 2000 Cristal Rosé, a champagne flute and an accompanying note.

"*Evan, allow me this divinely decadent way to welcome you to our world. Enjoy your journey and your passage to revelation. Yours cordially, Edmund Frankes.*"

There was also a small book that was surprisingly heavy. It was warm and trembled in his hands, as though it was alive. The inside front sheet was inscribed: *One of our early chapbooks to make your journey a little more fun. Lilith xx.*

". . . mad tart," laughed Evan as he dropped the book on his lap and opened the Champagne. "So where is Cedar Lodge?" he called to the chauffeur.

The large man shrugged his shoulders and grunted a reply in what sounded like a foreign language.

Reluctant to pursue what would obviously be a strained conversation, he slumped back into the sumptuous leather seat and let the swirling music wash over him like a warm, intoxicating breeze. With the alcohol starting to take effect, he opened the book, started to read, and promptly fell asleep.

He was rudely woken when the limo stopped on a deserted country road and, in a confused and compliant state, Evan was transferred to another vehicle. The wide grit road was eerily still and silent, the only movement being when a thick mist began to seep through the trees and envelop them as though aware of their presence. For Evan, the whole incident felt quite surreal and within minutes of being settled in the carriage he found himself once again overwhelmed by lassitude.

Torrential rain hammering against the carriage glass and a howling wind, like a banshee cry screaming in his ears, eventually roused him. He woke in a cold sweat, sprawled across the extravagant velvet upholstery of a carriage drawn by four furiously charging horses. A coachman, who sat on a bench to the fore of the vehicle, was whipping the poor beasts like a man possessed. They were hurtling through a scorched landscape where charcoaled trees rose from the black earth like the charred skeletons of cremated creatures. Clouds, blacker and more oppressive than any he had ever seen churned restlessly across a blood red sky. It was an insane scenario and although very "real," he couldn't help wondering if he was hallucinating. Seeing the silhouettes of rampaging beasts, raised on muscular haunches and roaming the surrounding woodland, chilled him to the core. Some were running and following the passage of the carriage, others just watched from the cover of the trees, piercing the darkness with fiery eyes.

The horses galloped frantically, urged on by the coachman who was whipping them with a manic ferocity and inflicting raw lacerations across their backs. With all his strength, Evan gripped the carriage door and strained to get a view from the open window.

A violent jolt sent him sprawling backwards across the floor, causing him to strike the back of his head against the carriage door. He remained where he fell, dazed and wondering where the madness would take him next. The pounding of heavy hooves on the sodden earth grew louder, as did the gut-wrenching howls of the forest beasts. In a sudden fit of panic, Evan pulled himself up and leaned from the window as though about to jump out. The coachman caught glimpse of him and gesticulated madly to move back inside.

"Get back in for God's sake, man . . . they'll have your head off in a second," he bawled.

There was a look of utter terror in the man's eyes as he lashed first at the horses and then at the massing monstrosities that were closing in on them. Evan retreated just as one of the beasts leapt onto the side of the carriage and made a frenzied attempt to force its way in. He found himself confronted by the bloodshot eyes and flaring nostrils of a slavering beast. Claws, like razor-sharp talons that could slice easily through human flesh, gripped tightly, leaving deep furrows in the wood.

The creature glared back and let out a hellish howl. Behind it, as though drawn by its rallying cry, a legion of similar quadrupeds swarmed forth from the depths of the woodland. Bringing the heel of his boot hard down on the creature's snout, Evan sent it reeling back into the savage wilderness, but not before it managed to inflict a deep gash in his left ankle.

In its place others followed and the carriage was soon shadowed either side by a baying horde of the rampaging beasts. The coach driver cracked his whip in an attempt to hold the hellish monstrosities at bay, but to little effect. In a fit of desperation, he lashed mercilessly at the horses instead and cheered when suddenly, the carriage emerged from the forest and onto an open road.

The beasts remained where they were, apparently reluctant to leave the cover of the forest.

Only when the movement of the carriage had slowed to a more sedated pace did Evan look from the window. With the forest far behind, they had ascended onto an elevated track that took them over a barren, swampy wasteland. In the distance were several pinpoints of light cast against a dark, foreboding sky. It seemed this was to be their destination.

As they neared what looked to be a large building of gothic design, the horses, exhausted and with steam rising from their sweat-drenched bodies, slowed to a gentle canter.

"Do you enter this place of your own free will, Mr. Gore?" called the coachman as they approached the gated entrance to the imposing mansion. Pulling the carriage up to a stop, he waited for an answer.

The question, although delivered with a degree of thespian dramatics, was apparently a serious one.

Perplexed, amused, and certainly not wanting to return through the forest, Evan replied emphatically that he was. The horses reared and neighed, reluctant to enter the grounds but a harsh whip to their bleeding rumps was enough encouragement to set them on their way.

They passed beneath an arched wrought iron banner suspended between two ivy clad pillars on top of which oil fires furiously burned. It was just after they had passed through the gates that Evan allowed himself a giggle of irony. "Cedar . . .," he muttered to himself. It wasn't Cedar at all. The iron letters spelled the word SEDAH as though in reflection. Observed from within the grounds it read HADES.

"Hades Publishing," he mused with a chuckle.

Frankes, it seemed, had a wickedly impious sense of humour.

"Welcome to Hell," Evan said to himself as they passed beneath the sinister sign and pulled up to the entrance of a grandiose gothic mansion. It was at that point that he noticed on the floor the decomposed remains of Lilith's chapbook. The cover was shrivelled and the pages fast becoming a putrefied mess. It was as though the book had become a withered corpse.

The coachman opened the door and beckoned him from the carriage, never once entering into conversation or looking him in the eye. As he lifted a small case from a wooden trunk at the rear of the carriage, and with darkness descending, he broke the uncomfortable silence and imparted a bit of friendly advice.

"I recommend haste, sir; it is far from safe out here after night falls."

With a nod that he would, Evan turned his attention to the imposing building.

A thick mist drifted down from the roof, descending like a ghostly veil and settling in folds at his feet. Suddenly feeling quite exhausted he stepped through the vaporous curtain and into a spacious entrance porch. The coachman seemed reluctant to follow and was, by his restive disposition, anxious to leave.

With his eyes fixed steadfastly on the upper floors of the building the man climbed back onto his seat and took up the reigns. The horses stamped and snorted impatiently. *What evil could the mansion contain that was scarier than returning through the forest?* wondered Evan.

With a whip crack lash of his whip the horses reared and the carriage trundled off into an enveloping mist, and for the first time, as Evan banged his fist on the sturdy front door, he wondered just what he'd got himself in to.

The door creaked on its hinges and a young woman with lustrous, dark hair, ashen skin and a sombre manner ushered Evan in. It was a moment before he recognised her as Lilith, the quaint young lady that he'd met back in his apartment with Edmund Frankes. She seemed different somehow, as though nervous of him, not the confident, sultry maiden who had so cunningly seduced him into leaving his apartment.

At first glance, she was a delicate creature but behind those eyes, there was a tough and resilient woman. The way she stared reached within . . . like inquisitive fingers probing and penetrating his mind.

"You've hurt your ankle," she said, "We'll have to get that seen to. After all, we don't want any blemishes on that lovely skin of yours, do we?"

Leading the way, she gave him brief instruction as to his stay, warning that to wander beyond the perimeters of the grounds would be a foolish and very dangerous thing to do. He couldn't help but think it sounded like a challenge. Meal times were announced by the resonant jangling of a bell but that evening, as an exception, food would be brought to him in an hour's time. Having shown him the dining room and library she took him to his bedroom on the second floor and sat next to him on the bed. Gazing deeply into his eyes, she told him:

"Beware of the Demon Bride; she wanders these corridors at night. She seduces men with her beauty and steals their souls with a kiss that sends fatal fire into their veins."

Evan couldn't help but wonder just where the line between fantasy and reality existed in her peculiar mind. With stern expression, and probably a little too patronisingly, he said that he'd met women like that before but nevertheless, he would heed her words.

His bedroom was a creaky-floored, oak-panelled room dominated by a four-poster bed. The décor was drab, the furnishings dark and the air tainted by the damp stench of mildew. Not quite the opulent interior he'd been expecting.

On his way to the bedroom he saw that there were others present, but they were timid things, avoiding eye contact and maintaining their distance. There was something quite feral about the way they used shadows and dark corners from which to make their observations. According to Lilith their role was to maintain the running of the sprawling lodge. To be seen and not heard.

For reasons he couldn't quite understand, Evan felt immediately at home. Stepping across the threshold had been like a homecoming. From the moment he entered the building it was as though the outside world simply ceased to exist. Memories of his recent past faded and trying to remember things took more effort than it should, not that it bothered him. Rules and regulations had no part in his life anymore, and nor did social etiquette. Here he would allow Harry's stories to flow through his mind and commit them to permanence.

For the first few days he slipped comfortably into a daily routine. No more itching or aching in his back. There were no alcohol or drugs, and yet he was happier than he'd ever been. Words and letters continued to appear randomly on his body, but far from being concerned he was ecstatic and wore them proudly.

By night howling winds and torrential rain would assault the fragile panes. Evan would bury himself beneath the lavish quilt and there he would listen to the ferocity of the raging storm with childish wonderment. When the storm made sleeping impossible he would sit upright with the bedding wrapped tightly about his shoulders and watch ferocious lightning storms as they lit up the savage land beyond the perimeters of the grounds.

On occasion in the dead of night, through a moonlit gap beneath the door, he would catch glimpse of the movement of bizarre nocturnal creatures apparently attracted by his insomnia. The long shadows of beasts with spidery limbs and snapping claws would reach into the room. Sometimes he would hear mimicked voices of Lilith or Edmund Frankes attempting to lure him out. At other times the sound of ribald women making carnal suggestions that surpassed even his own debauch excesses would tease him, pound his door . . . and he would find himself quite tempted to investigate.

One night, during a particularly violent thunderstorm, he woke to find Lilith in his bed. She slept in his arms and they fell into each other's dreams. By dawn's early light she was gone, and Evan was a spent man. He remembered asking who she was talking of when she had said, "they walk in darkness." She told him, ". . . the people from the books of course."

From that moment on he found himself inexplicably drawn to the vast library and would spend hours poring over the intriguing volumes there. He would sit in the same place, always facing the window so that he could gaze at the desolate beauty of the sprawling grounds and let his thoughts drift there.

Beyond the farthest fringes of the grounds he observed the forest through which he had travelled. Beyond that there existed nothing more than a hellish black void that instilled in him an overwhelming sense of desolation.

Evan would use the precious daylight hours to explore the extensive grounds; one particular day he discovered a lake on the far side of which was a memorial tower in the midst of an arboretum.

Gorse bushes with spiked thorns on which were impaled the bodies of small birds and field mice guarded access to the tower. To the rear of the lodge was a small graveyard for which he developed a particularly melancholic fascination. The gravestones were sculptured in the fashion of book covers and the inscriptions described those buried beneath as their authors.

Evan resigned himself to a simple daily routine with no agenda except for his indulgence in books and gathering morbid tales in his head. It suddenly occurred to him that since leaving his flat he had been abandoned by Harry Speirs. But that was of no consequence, and as the days passed by, so recollections of his former life became faded memories.

Evan woke unusually early one morning to find the door to his room wide open. There was a light spattering of rain against his window and a gentle rush of wind whistling about the frames. The air was crisp and he felt refreshed, his head clearer than it had been for a long time. His clothes had been taken and in their place what appeared to be a monk's robe had been left. Having had a breakfast of fresh coffee, oak smoked kippers and toast that had been left on the dresser, he made his way to the library as instructed. The spacious corridors were unusually quiet and blissfully unthreatening by day. When he reached the library, he found Lilith waiting for him. She was more attentive than usual as though excited by something. Taking him by the hand, she guided him deeper into the library, every now and then glancing back with a mischievous grin on her face. Eventually they reached the locked door of the antechamber and in silence . . . they waited.

Somewhere beyond the hefty portal there came the sound of restless movement. A fluttering at first, like a pigeon trapped in a small room, and then a stomping of feet and scraping of nails on a wooden floor. Someone or something on the other side was aware, apparently, that Evan was there. Playfully, Lilith pushed him forwards and the movement became more frantic followed by the sound of pounding on the door, but with such violence that Evan took a step back. Lilith laughed and, anxiously, Evan laughed with her.

"Turn the handle," she told him.

He did as she said, standing back as the dark space within sucked at the warm air.

The light was poor, but he could just about perceive movement in the background, like shadows cast against darkness.

"Go in," she urged.

Obediently, Evan took a few timid steps into the chamber.

Within the anteroom; there was an incandescent radiance like the flicker of a candle, but without any source. And the warm air was tainted by an aroma that he likened to that of a cheap brothel which, sadly, he knew only too well. There was also a feeling of great space about the chamber. Not just large, but massive, as if he was outside. From the periphery of his vision he could see there were immense walls of book laden shelves that extended far into the murky depths. But there was also restless, quivering movement on those shelves and he began to wonder just what Edmund meant when he described them as living books back in his apartment.

Set on a table before him was a large book that at first had the appearance of an antiquated bible. As he got closer he saw that the cover was striated with swollen veins that were gently throbbing. Even more disconcerting was what looked like the impression of small bones pressing against pliable skin. The mere act of touching the cover caused an explosion of images and words in his head. Stories within the living book were playing in his head and indulging him in a fantasy that was as real as the living, breathing world outside.

Lilith pulled him away and turned his face towards her own.

"Beautiful, isn't it?" she said excitedly ". . . one of our early works. A little primitive, but always popular with our clients."

Evan found it difficult to focus his eyes on her; her image was distorted like a shimmering mirage. Pulling gently at the buttons of her blouse and without once taking her flirtatious gaze from him, she took his hand and rested it back on the book.

"Slower, this time," she told him, "I can see it's starting for you. Free your mind. Breath slowly, deeply, and you'll enjoy the experience so much more."

The book beneath Evan's palm began to pound in time with his own racing pulse as Lilith continued to undress.

"Read me," she said to him, "like a book."

In the ambient light, he saw that Lilith's skin appeared to be mottled with bruises. But as she moved closer he noticed that the dark patches on her skin were in fact clusters of words. Beautifully inscribed prose covered every inch of her flesh. She turned slowly and brazenly, letting his gaze linger upon her. Her eyes guided him as did her fingers. She was a woman without shame, wallowing in his voyeuristic gaze as she explored the intimacy of her own body. But they were so much more than just words. They were images and sounds and odours.

The woman was seducing him—that much was obvious; but there was something more, there was a look of iniquitous evil in the way she stared. She sucked at a finger and then traced it across his lips. Her saliva was sweet to taste, like a fine desert wine. He let it linger on his tongue, all the time watching her and wondering how this bizarre game would end.

Lilith stepped away and in that fateful moment he saw that the writing had spread to his own body. Letters, like tiny insects, crawled over him, piercing the epidermis and burrowing and rooting into the deep layers of his skin.

"Your skin is parchment and your blood is ink," said Lilith.

"*Your skin is parchment and your blood is ink*," repeated the household workers as they emerged from the darkness that surrounded him.

The stories that were in his head were being transcribed onto his body, slowly at first but as the metamorphosis progressed so the writing became frenzied and his skin fell into folds, rolling and crumpling onto the floor like a typewriter spewing out pages of living flesh. He thought he was hallucinating, like one of his acid trips in the good old days.

At first he was quite euphoric, his eyes closed tightly as though in a state of ecstasy. But then the realization of what was happening hit him.

"What's going on?" he cried, looking around frantically before bringing his petrified gaze back to rest on Lilith. "Help me, Lilith, please," he begged, "Stop this . . . this . . . stop this now!"

Lilith stared back, unflustered by his appearance or his panic.

"'ello, guv'nor," cackled a familiar voice. "It's your old mucka Harry Speirs 'ere again." But Harry's voice was outside Evan's head, not in it.

Edmund Frankes moved into view with Harry's voice coming out of his mouth, like a living ventriloquist's dummy with rolling eyes and a manic stare. But it really was Harry's voice. It really was a dead man's voice coming from Edmund's gaping mouth with no articulation of his vocal cords or tongue.

Evan stared in disbelief, his mind struggling to make sense of things.

"Dear old, Harry Speirs," said Edmund having slipped back into his own dulcet tones, "One of our helpers from beyond the grave; his job's done now, he'll trouble you no more."

Fast becoming a broken man, all Evan could manage was a whimpering, "Why are you doing this to me?"

"A very good question, Mr. Gore. Firstly, I can assure you it's not personal," replied Frankes as though they were chatting over a leisurely pint. "Let me explain it this way. Committing words to paper has always been man's way of attaining a kind of immortality; and books are essentially a legacy of life, after death. At Cedar Publishing we have taken the process . . . a little further. I remember how you eloquently told me on your show that people like me were '*pissing away our lives.*' Well now, Evan, you are experiencing first hand just how we—*piss away our lives.*"

Pausing for thought, Edmund moved closer and stared chillingly into Evan's eyes.

"We take the publishing side of our business very seriously, Evan, and we do that very successfully. Here we commit our words not to paper or computer, but to flesh. Our clientele pays dearly to *experience* our books, and you are going to bring fresh blood to our esteemed collection. Interacting with our books is a particularly intimate experience, as you well know. The curator will be very pleased with our latest acquisition, and we love nothing more than to make our curator happy. And you get immortality in the bargain, so I guess it's win, win."

Evan tried to move but beneath the ever-expanding weight of skin and blubber all he could do was sway somewhat comically from side to side like an overinflated Sumo wrestler. No longer whimpering, he began to cry hysterically, like an inconsolable child.

"I . . . I'm famous for fuck's sake," snivelled Evan, "I'm a *someone*. People will come looking for me. You can't do this."

Speaking was becoming increasingly difficult as his tongue swelled and filled his mouth. Panic set in when he struggled to draw breath but Edmund seemed unconcerned.

"Oh, we're all a *someone*, Evan. And of course, people will wonder what happened to the immensely talented Mr. Gore, but like Richard John Bingham, 7th Earl of Lucan, or as you probably know him, Lord Lucan, you will disappear without a trace. Old 'Dickie' became one of our more popular books, you might be surprised to know. But then again, the man did have a very sordid tale to tell. Perhaps our biggest coup is a certain Mr. Adolf Hitler who, as the conspiracy theories correctly speculated, did not commit suicide but took flight from his bunker in 1945 and escaped to Argentina. Thanks to our South American contacts, he ended up here on our extraordinary shelves having undergone his own Kafkaesque 'meta-morphosis.' It can't be said that we lack our own sense of ironic humour. And the list goes on, Evan: 17th century navigator, Henry Hudson; aviator, Amelia Earhart; satirist and writer, Ambrose Bierce. Our global list of contributors goes back centuries. We even have a children's section," he grinned. "People can be so careless with young ones, but they do make the most wonderful books."

"Leth mee . . . goo . . .," begged Evan, "pleeth, juth leth mee goo . . . I wonth . . . tellth . . . aneebothee . . ."

By now his words were almost incomprehensible as he gagged and struggled desperately to draw breath through his slowly constricting air passage. His head was sinking slowly into the sweaty, quagmire of mutated flesh that his body had become. The stench was quite appalling as were the sounds of belching and flatulence as the contents of his bowels disgorged themselves.

Frankes ushered his household out and was about to make his own exit when he was distracted by the sound of shuffling feet. From the gloomy depths of the anteroom sauntered an old man in a shabby suit. He smiled briefly at Frankes and then with a look of obvious delight examined the quivering mass of blubber and bone that Evan had become. If ever Evan could express a look of surprise, it was now. His eyes widened and bulged as though about to explode from his face. He even managed a few strained words.

"Veeecctooor!" he blurted, and then with a look of bewilderment he turned his tortured stare towards Lilith and uttered, "Veeectorrr . . . consssseeeerge . . ."

"Victor Sauvage, chief curator, bibliophile and editor extraordinaire," corrected Lilith as she began her own retreat. Such a visit during the inauguration of a new book was indeed an honour.

"Oh, dear Evan, didn't you realise that Cedar publishing owns Darkwood Estates—you really should have read the small print. And Victor is our custodian of Dakota House, not just a silly old concierge, although he does seem to enjoy those awful old paper books. Barnaby Wright, the previous owner of your apartment was such a perfect specimen, but unfortunately, he lost the plot while we were working on him.

"And then of course you came along, and we couldn't believe our luck. Victor kept you under his scrutiny for a while, and here you are, approaching the final part of the publishing process—and so we will bid you *adieu*."

Evan, no longer a man, had become a grotesque malignancy of flesh and bone. A tidal wave of madness had washed over him and now he was drowning in his own visceral swamp. But he still, if it was any consolation, had consciousness and spirit, and would continue to for longer than he ever cared to contemplate.

It was early the next morning that Lilith returned to the anteroom. Evan's book, *Nine Lives*, was laid open on a presentation stand, ready to take its place on the shelves of the living library. Brushing her palm across its clammy pages, she squealed with delight. So much more than just a book, it was a living tome, born of flesh and possessed of life. A spine of human vertebrae; skin, crafted into the finest parchment pages; prose masterfully scribed in congealed blood. But what really sent a shiver through Lilith's trembling body was the quivering mouth that screamed so silently from the cover.

And the tortured, weeping gaze of Evan's always watching eye.

HOT FLASHES
By Jenya Joy Preece

≈⊙⊙⊙⊙⊙⊙⊙⊙⊙⊙⊙⊙≈

"**D**amn these hot flashes!"

Vi Matthews sat in front of the wide-open window fanning herself with a spiral notebook—even though it was the middle of winter and there was enough snow to build an entire city of snowmen with. She was burning up. Kenneth, her husband, turned from his nightly news report to look at his sweaty wife.

"Will you just shut the friggin' window already. Our gas bill is going to be through the roof this month because a you." It was Kenneth's job to bitch about the bills because he was the only one making money to pay them. This was about all he was good for, too.

"Seriously, I feel like I'm gonna ignite or worse, melt like a snowman in summer."

"Yur not gonna go in flames," he said, adding, "I wish ya would though," under his breath so his wife wouldn't hear.

Vi reached up to wipe the sweat from her face. She sat there fanning and wiping in just her bra and panties. Once upon a time Kenneth would have come and torn the set off her in urgency, but now he spent his free time watching the high-def plasma god. Taking in all the sights and sounds and in the process turning his brain into a sort of mush. Vi felt her bra strap slide off one shoulder. By this point she didn't care nor did she care what her piece of shit husband had to say about the bills. Sweat rolled down her spine in a long line that ended in the waistband of her undies. The band soaked up the liquid greedily.

The sweat made her face begin to itch from all the salty bits of body dew. She reached up and scratched at the center of her forehead. The skin underneath her nails felt foreign to her, but she went on scratching away, seeking relief.

She gazed out the open window at the snow and ice. She wanted so badly to jump into it and make angels, even in her underwear. Then she thought to herself, *it would be just my luck for all the snow to melt before I got cooled off and we'd have a lake in our yard.*

This thought made her laugh a little and Kenneth replied by telling her that she needed to shut up and to shut the window. She continued to ignore him.

Vi's upper lip began to itch much like her forehead. She wiped at it at first with her hand then began using her nails to scratch it. She felt the skin beneath as it stuck like clay. She clenched her jaw in worry. Her muscles were sticking now. She unclenched and her teeth felt loose inside of her face. She reached in her mouth and pulled out one of her teeth. They all wiggled as she grinded her jaw.

Oh, my hell, what's happening? she thought as she gently removed another tooth. She examined this one carefully then stuck her tongue into the gap where the two teeth had just come from. She noticed something odd. She opened her hand and began spitting tooth after tooth into her palm. Tears mixed with the sweat on her face. She knew that her age would catch up to her, but she didn't think that it would happen all at once.

She scratched at a small itch on her cheek. She noticed that there was a slight blemish on her skin so she picked at it, her nails digging into the flesh. She felt her face again making sure that she'd gotten all of it, but to her astonishment she'd created a hole in the side of her face. She shoved her tongue into the hole and could taste the salt of her finger. Her tongue expanded the hole.

"What the hell," she tried to say, but as she made noise, she felt a chunk of something slide into her throat. She swallowed hard, but the object wasn't moving up or down. She choked and wheezed, trying to get her husband's attention but the T.V. was much too loud for her to be heard over the reporter.

Her tongue was gone. She felt her breasts start to slide even closer to her knees. She couldn't explain what was happening to her. She was still dying from the heat inside her, scared and alone.

An hour later, Vi had grown eerily quiet. Kenneth noticed because her bitching had come to a halt. He paused the T.V. to check on her and take a leak.

"Damn it woman! I'm freezing my friggin' ass of in here!" He got up, noticing that his wife was missing from her spot at the window. Now he was really mad about the bill he would no doubt be paying.

He stomped over to the window, slipping and falling on his slightly frozen ass. There was something all over the floor.

"What in the name a . . ."

He stuck his hand into the muck. The dark red hues were nearly black under the dim light. He sniffed at it and a metallic smell wafted back to him. Then he decided to lick it to make sure that he was sure. It was blood all right, but where did it come from. His heart fluttered inside his chest. He got up from the floor and peered out the window onto the snowy lawn. There, with the notebook, lay the bones of his wife. Vi had melted like a snowman after all. He laughed to himself, shutting the window and going back to watch his beloved T.V. He knew that he could clean her up in the morning.

THE IMPLOSION OF A GASTROCRAT:
AN EXPERIMENT IN AUTOPHAGY
By Frank Roger

Clipping #1 (from a regional weekly paper)

As Mr. Laurent Malherbe showed up with a bandaged hand in The Paper Rose, the local pub where he's one of the regulars, all his friends and drinking buddies, including this reporter, assumed he had had an accident while fixing something at home. However, Laurent quickly reassured us there was nothing to worry about. The bandaged hand, he explained, was the result of an experiment he had embarked on after watching a TV programme about a man who ate light bulbs and bicycle parts. "You see," he told me over a pint of Guinness, "eating light bulbs and other objects usually considered inedible may appear sensational, but actually it's an act totally devoid of meaning. A man eating light bulbs is a freak, but nothing more. Yet the sight of this man merrily munching crunchy bits inspired me to attempt something more profound and meaningful. I decided to eat a fragment of my own flesh." He proudly lifted his bandaged hand and said, "I chopped off the tip of my little finger, scraped off the flesh, pulverised the bone and ate it all. This way my body swallowed a part of itself. Just think of the philosophical underpinnings of such an act. And, mind you, this was just the initial phase. The last few days I chopped off and ate a few more finger tips, and right now I'm thinking about tackling an earlobe or so. Be assured I'll keep you informed of my progress!" Laurent Malherbe then turned his attention to his Guinness and his friends, and engaged in heated conversation. I have this feeling we'll be hearing more from our dear friend in the near future.

Clipping #2 (from a national newspaper)

Mr. Laurent Malherbe, a forty-year-old man from the greater London area, is building quite a reputation ever since he publicised his bold plan to attempt an experiment never tried before in recorded history, to quote his own rather grandiloquent words. The man has been steadily eating parts of his own body, starting with the chopped off tips of his fingers, his earlobes, layers of fat and callus that were removed with surgical precision by himself, and other parts that were deemed superfluous and hence available for consumption—or perhaps bio-recycling might be a better term. Until recently, media attention for Mr. Malherbe's remarkable experiment was limited to a few regional and national papers, but his announcement of his next "Big Step" landed him his first TV interview. "It is my intention," Malherbe declared before the camera, "to remove one of my testicles and eat it. Each new phase in my experiment only serves to sharpen my hunger, if you allow me to use this exceptionally apt term, for bigger and bolder steps forward on my chosen route. I am currently looking into the possibility of having some of my internal tissue removed, and hope to eat as much of my own body as medically possible. I am curious about the limits of this autophagy, to use the term I coined for my endeavour. How much of his body can a human being miss? How far can I take this mind-boggling consumption of myself? What is the deeper meaning of this drive, this seemingly nonsensical ambition? Or, to put it bluntly: Can one eat oneself?"

Clipping #3 (sidebar from an in-depth article in a magazine)

"I decided to mount fund-raising campaigns after watching Laurent talk about his plans on TV," says twenty-nine-year-old Jennifer Sandoval, a London bank employee and active member of the recently founded Laurent Malherbe Appreciation Society. She is only one of the many men and women who chose to actively support Malherbe's bizarre quest for self-consumption. "I quickly realised," Sandoval confesses, "that Malherbe would soon run into financial troubles, which would cut off all his hope for success. I went out and found other people willing to support his wild plan, formed the So-

ciety and now we help keep Laurent on the road to his chosen des-
tiny. We think he fully deserves our unending support." Need we still
present Laurent Malherbe, the man who's nibbling away at himself,
and who looks prepared to continue nibbling until there's nothing
left to sink his teeth in—supposing he will still have teeth by that
time! When Malherbe chewed on fingertips and earlobes, he only attracted the local press, but now that his testicles and parts of his organs and intestines considered non-vital have been removed and
disappeared down his oesophagus, he is basking in full media attention. Not only did his grand dreams give rise to several fan clubs in
the U.K. and abroad, they also led to controversies and harsh criticism from conservative and religious milieus. Yet Malherbe seems
determined to continue his mission, especially now that his steadily
mounting medical bills are paid with the funds raised by his Appreciation Society and some of his fan clubs. "I feel more stimulated than
ever," he declared to us, "knowing that so many people actively support me, and put their money where their mouth is." Malherbe himself appears to have opted for putting his body where his mouth is. .
. . In his latest TV interview, he announced his plans for removing
what's left of his genitals ("completely irrelevant body parts in my
current life") and having his toes and left hand amputated. Will this
man go all the way? Will he swallow himself down to the last mouthful? Perhaps his next interview will reveal more. To be continued,
doubtlessly.

Clipping #4 (Letter from a newspaper's readers' column)

Why does every newspaper in the country devote so much
attention to this Malherbe nutcase? I would say there are more important things going on in the world worth covering. But no, a man
who eats his own penis is infinitely more interesting to the sensa-
tion-craving crowd, a man who's now wheelchair-bound after losing
his feet and lower legs to his insatiable hunger, a man who appears
willing to sacrifice anything to get his face on TV and on the papers'
front page. Please do not give in to this slip into tabloid-style sensa-
tion-mongering, and leave the coverage of this man and the mis-
guided souls active in his fan clubs to the specialised psychiatric
journals for whom this "case" may be of some scientific interest.

Clipping #5 (from a weekly paper's news roundup)

The media's current number one sensation, Laurent Mal-herbe, also affectionately known as "The Man Who Eats Himself," may by now be reduced to a legless man strapped into a wheelchair and constantly hooked up to a variety of machines intended to keep him alive after some vital parts of his body were removed, his busi-ness acumen seems to have survived his endeavours unscathed. Now that his plan to consume as much as possible of his own body has reached a critical point, and medical bills have surpassed the level that could be covered by the fund-raising efforts of his fans, Malherbe has sold exclusive TV rights to Sky Channel to cover his progress for a substantial amount of money—no doubt much more than his entire plan will cost. Firstly, this ensures his "experiment in autophagy" of reaching its completion, financial problems being the only possible barrier against success, and secondly it provides Sky Channel with a guaranteed audience of many thousands (mil-lions?)—and hence with advertising rates soaring to dizzying heights. The burning question, however, remains: How far will Mal-herbe take this mad plan of his? Will he, as his die-hard fans claim, indeed go "all the way?"

Clipping #6 (from a leading monthly magazine)

An interview with Laurent Malherbe

Mr. Malherbe, how would you describe your current condi-tion?

Malherbe: I feel great! No, of course, that's not what you wanted to hear. Let me put it this way then: I'm a man without legs, without arms, without private parts, without hair, without . . . well, let's just say I'm a man stripped down to his bare essentials. I am still fully alive, I am happy, I still harbour ambitions I'm itching to carry to their limits, I still have hopes and dreams, I have everything it takes to be a full-fledged human being.

But without all this medical equipment you're hooked onto, you would die within moments.

Malherbe: That's true, but isn't that also true for many handicapped persons who are yet considered full human beings? The fact that I arrived at my present condition on purpose is totally immaterial. A man is more than his mere outward physical appearance. My soul is intact. My mind vibrates as it never has before. My thinking is of crystal-clear lucidity. I am more convinced than ever that I chose the right path for my personal fulfilment. And I will walk that path down to its very end.

You still think you have not proven enough?

Malherbe: Have I proven anything yet? I've proven you can cut off a few bits here and there and wash them down with a glass of water, so to speak. The hard part is yet to come. Can I eat my lungs and survive? My heart? My brain?

Surely you cannot be serious?

Malherbe: Be assured that I am. To quote an old movie star who shall remain nameless, "You ain't seen nothing yet." I will indeed attempt what some still deem impossible, and continue eating body parts considered vital. I am determined to take this experiment to its very limits.

Will you go "all the way," as your fans keep chanting?

Malherbe: I will go as far as humanly possible. It will soon become clear exactly how far that is. No doubt it will be a lot further than people have assumed. My experiment will have tremendous scientific value, besides its profound ethical and philosophical repercussions. I hope I will have the time and the opportunity to convey all my thoughts and theories regarding this matter to viewers and readers out there.

Do you have any final thoughts to wrap up this interview?

Malherbe: Oh well, let me put it like this. My ambition is now foremost in my mind, pushing all other considerations into the background. It has become the focus of all my thoughts and actions, to the point that I no longer have any interest in what you might call a regular guy's worries and woes. In a sense I transcended that kind of existence. My ambition to eat myself has become my true *raison d'être*. I know very well that I've come in for some criticism in certain quarters, and I'm not deaf and blind to their accusations, but basically it doesn't matter to me anymore. What matters is my burning ambition, how to make my dream come true, and how to do that to-morrow rather than the day after tomorrow. To put it succinctly: I truly live for this all-consuming passion of mine.

Thank you for this interview, Mr. Malherbe.

Malherbe: You're welcome. I hope we'll meet again . . . be-fore the Last Supper!

Clipping #7 (from a national magazine)

Laurent Malherbe, once a curiosity happy to see his follies covered in regional papers, has by now become a regular guest in all national and even international media outlets, a caricature of man's desire to push his own limits and transcend himself, and an insult to the medical profession, all rolled into one. It could be said this is quite an achievement for a man who is, strictly technically speaking, no longer alive . . . depending on one's definition of life. Malherbe, who roped in vast amounts of money with the sale of exclusive cov-erage rights, subsequently hired a legion of doctors and surgeons to execute his "will," a term apt only for those who consider him dead, by all accounts a dwindling minority. Ever since the medical team known as the Malherbe Foundation started removing some of the vital organs of their patient (or their client?), as per his instructions, what remains of Laurent Malherbe's body is kept alive artificially, a near-empty hulk devoid of what is usually considered "life." Mal-herbe's growing hordes of fans, however, worship the man as if he represented God on earth, and applaud his every move, however posthumous. Is this man, as his fans claim, still eating himself, as highly paid surgeons remove yet more slices of quivering flesh and force them down a throat that is attached to a stomach and a reduced set of intestines, with a brain and a heart thrown in for good meas-ure? Or is this a joke perpetrated in bad taste, a scientific experiment gone awry, a waste of medical and surgical skills unavailable for more pressing needs? Needless to say, Malherbe's fans are unwilling to even listen to any criticism of their idol's progress, and hard cash appears once more to prevail over ethics and common sense.

Clipping #8 (from a Laurent Malherbe fan club magazine)

The most thrilling news is, of course, that the long-awaited moment is imminent: Laurent's body has once more been stripped of some of its parts (considered vital by the narrow-minded), such as his lungs and a large chunk of his brain. What's left of our dear friend, his digestive system, his heart along with a rudimentary bloodstream and a handful of braincells, is kept alive and fully functional thanks to state-of-the-art medical technology and a handsomely paid crew of doctors and paramedics. Dr. Gomez, who heads the medical crew, has confirmed in a recent interview that "nothing can stop Malherbe from carrying his ambitions to their logical conclusion. Modern technology will allow him, however unlikely this may seem at first sight, to eat his own last shreds of body tissue. For contractual reasons I am not at liberty to divulge any technical details of this procedure. But be assured that we will do anything necessary to achieve total success. Mr. Malherbe will definitely go down in history as the man who ate himself." Obviously, we will cover the final phase of this awesome experiment in extensive detail, complete with full interviews of all those involved. No other paper or magazine has the kind of access to reliable sources that we do, so stay tuned for further news. Preparations for a mega-"Eat Your Heart Out, Humanity"-party are already well underway. If this doesn't prove our unshakeable faith in the outcome of Laurent's big plan, then what does?

Clipping #9 (obituary from a national newspaper)

Yesterday Laurent Malherbe died in a private hospital in London. He was 41. Malherbe had become a national celebrity by eating parts of his own body, a bizarre habit which quickly grew into an all-consuming obsession. As Malherbe's rise to fame and fortune has been extremely well-documented, we need not repeat the details of his final year, which he spent devouring himself. It is debatable whether that is a fitting description for his condition in the last months of his "life," when he was hooked up to a battery of machines, a Frankenstein's monster in reverse, having its flesh and blood artificially removed and consumed until nothing was left. The video footage of the final phase of Malherbe's descent into his own digestive system, released shortly after his death, is rumoured to be "digitally processed," meaning that special effects-like elements have been added to the original footage. This is firmly denied by Malherbe's vociferous fans and followers, but observers less blinded by worship, and spokesmen of the scientific community in particular, harbour serious doubts about Malherbe's alleged success in "swallowing his own digestive system thanks to a cutting-edge technological sleight of hand," discarded as "tabloid-style pseudo-scientific gibberish" by at least one acknowledged medical authority. It appears rather unlikely that the complete truth about Malherbe's death will ever be revealed, considering the amount of idolatry (not to mention financial interests) among those who guard the facts as though they were sacred teachings.

Clipping #10 (from a published letter in a newspaper's readers' column)

Frankly, I fail to see what all the fuss is about. Does it really matter then whether or not some ultra-high-tech contraption was made allowing old Laurent Malherbe to serve what was left of himself by way of his own private Last Supper? All right, I admit I wasn't immediately convinced when I heard about this fabulous machine that broke down Malherbe's last strips of flesh so incredibly fast and raced these particles down his not-just-quite-vaporised-yet throat almost instantly that, strictly technically speaking, this procedure could count as "eating yourself completely." It sounds like pure hogwash, but even if such a machine was indeed developed and this process (a giant leap forward in "fast food!") was indeed applied to our ever-hungry friend Malherbe, what difference does it make in the end? Lots of money was wasted that could have been better spent, lots of attention was paid to a man out to immortalise his name through an act of unmitigated sensationalism (without any redeeming qualities), lots of people did their best to create or get involved into a hype that by all accounts ought to have been ignored for the cheap thrill of a media-saturated and money-driven society it was. As I said, I fail to see what all the fuss is about. Now that Malherbe is gone to Fast Food Heaven, can we please get on with real life? Thank you so much.

NO STRINGS

By Josh Shiben

"I've got no strings," muttered Evan to himself through gritted teeth as he hauled his heavy body roughly up the side of the metal structure. The song had been stuck in his head, on repeat, for days, just endlessly looping like an annoying commercial tune. "To hold me up." Sweat of the exertion dripped from his body, making it sheen in the baking Virginia sun. He watched as his forearm gleamed in the light, watched it ripple and distort as something inside him slithered just beneath the surface. It was one of the worms, or parasites, or whatever they were. He wasn't sure. It didn't matter.

Evan grunted and continued climbing up the ladder. His mouth was so dry. So thirsty. They used to hurt, the worms. He remembered the pain they'd caused as they stretched his skin and bored through him. He remembered the fear, as he lay there on the hospital table, worrying that some parasite was turning him into a human-shaped block of Swiss cheese. But then, the doctor had given him drugs and it'd stopped. The pain. The crawling under his skin. They'd assumed the worms had died, but now Evan knew better. Poisons didn't kill them. Antibiotics just drove them deeper into his body. They were still there—still hiding inside of him. Burrowing into the very core of him. But when they came back, the pain stopped. Evan knew why—he was getting used to them. He was numb. Even the thought of pain was fuzzy—he knew it was an unpleasant sensation, but like a blind man thinking of color, he could not summon any impression of it. Pain, like most other sensations, was something that had passed out of his life. It had become alien. He tried to worry about it, but all he felt was dry. Like a leaf in the fall, threatening to crumble to dust in the slightest breeze. He licked his lips and continued his climb.

"I've got no strings." He only knew the two lines, so he sang them over and over like a skipping record.

His hands were blistering on the rungs of the ladder, but he ignored them and climbed on. They didn't hurt, and he was too close to the top to stop now. It was so hard to climb with the heavy tools strapped to his back and his stomach distended the way it was; too heavy and awkward, and the writhing inside sometimes pushed him off balance. He had no attention to waste on something as trivial as blistering hands—he had to focus on gripping the ladder tightly, dragging himself up one rung at a time. Evan needed more water. He had to hurry.

He'd tried submerging himself in his bathtub, but it hadn't been enough. He'd just lay down there, watching as his breath bubbled to the surface, staring up through the ripples at the ceiling. He had drunk until he vomited the water back up, and then kept drinking, desperate for any kind of relief. After all of that, he'd still felt parched.

One summer, years ago, Evan had gone to the beach and gotten a nasty sunburn. But the burn hadn't hurt—it itched. The itch couldn't be scratched—it was under the skin, down deep in the muscle, and so he had paced his room in agony, thinking that if only he could cut the skin back, flay his chest and shoulders like a butchered animal, he might cure the irritation. That was his thirst now—a deep-seated, unquenchable itch, burning in his throat and mouth. It permeated every solitary cell in his body—his entire being cried out for water. He needed more than just a bathtub or a pool. He needed something drastic. He needed the impossible weight of thousands of gallons. He wanted to be buried in that crushing, impossible wetness—that black, freezing gulf, where even the sun cannot penetrate.

Evan had once seen a submarine flood in an old World War II movie he'd watched with his father. The hull had been breached by a depth charge, and the crew frantically sealed bulkheads to stop the implacably rising water from taking them all. As a child, Evan had stared at his ceiling, shuddering at the thought of being surrounded by the icy depths in that cold prison. He would lie awake, trying to exorcize fears of a black tide sliding up to consume him. Now, he fantasized about it. The icy cold grip of the water rising, promising more than he could ever drink.

He reached the catwalk, and with some effort, rolled himself onto the structure, where he rested only a moment before rising slowly to his feet. His legs were so weak and he was so heavy. He wondered-how much of him was still Evan, and how much was worm. Two-thirds? Half?

He looked at his bloated, bulging stomach, wriggling with alien mass, and considered how much it must weigh. He'd been fit before all of this. Not in great shape, but good enough. He would have at least passed for a healthy person. Not now, though. The lesions on his flesh and undulating shapes under his skin removed any doubt as to his condition. He wanted to feel angry, or sad, or anything about it, but couldn't seem to muster the emotion. The thirst outweighed it all. He moved along the catwalk, to the small ladder leading to the top of the rounded tower, and with some effort, began hoisting himself up.

"No foreign travel or anything?" the doctor had asked. Sitting in his hospital gown, looking down at his feet glumly, Evan could only shake his head "no." He'd never even left the state. He didn't have the money or the time away from work to go anywhere exotic. That was back when he still felt—the pain, the fear, the anger—it all bubbled up in him like a volcano. He was alive, then.

"Have you had any water that was maybe contaminated?" the doctor had tried. Again, he'd shaken his head. He only ever drank tap water—provided by the city, and purified by chlorine. The worms couldn't live in chlorine, could they? Tap water was clean.

Evan wet his lips again, and his tongue felt like sandpaper rubbing over a cracked and dried riverbed. With a grunt, he hoisted himself up another rung on the ladder. Some part of him realized he was dying, but he couldn't bring himself to be upset or bothered by the insight. The knowledge only gave him more motivation—better to receive this one last satisfaction than to die without it; a baptism to cleanse him, to wash away the wretchedness. It would bring relief. It had to.

"To hold me up," he whined out deliriously, his hands only two rungs below the edge of the structure. He looked down to see the tiny town beneath him, and briefly considered just letting go. The fall would certainly kill him—end this struggle in a splatter of worm-infested meat. But then, he'd never get his satisfaction—he'd die, never knowing relief. That thought alone was enough to spur him upward, toward the salvation only a few rungs above him. He tried to swallow, but his throat was too dry—his tongue felt like a burned piece of leather in his mouth, and he had to hold on tightly to keep from retching.

He pulled himself up the last two rungs and then clambered up on top of the hot metal structure. His arms and legs were weak with thirst, but with some effort, he hauled himself into the center of the circle. There was a round door in the roof, with a spinning handle on it that reminded him of the door of a vault. It was held in place by a simple padlock, and with a satisfying click of the bolt cutters he had brought along for just such a complication, Evan was through. His hands trembled with anticipation as he took the heavy crowbar he had carried up all this way and used it to force the wheel to slowly turn, unsealing the door with a metallic groan. He eased the door open, and was almost knocked backwards by the scent of chlorine that assaulted him.

When he'd first found out the worms were living inside of him, Evan had researched parasites. Now, as he looked down at the dark body of water, he remembered the Horsehair Worm. It repro-duced in large, freshwater lakes, but grew inside the carapace of crickets. Sometimes, it would grow to be nearly a foot long, coiled tightly inside the little body like a spring. The problem was that, in order to complete its life-cycle, the worm had to return to the water. The solution was simple—it would convince its host to hurl itself into a lake; the vessel apathetic to its own self-destruction.

Evan remembered reading about the Horsehair worm and wondering, how could something subvert an organism's drive for self-preservation so effectively? What did a cricket feel, when poised at the edge of the lake? He wondered, now, if it felt anything at all. Perhaps, only thirst. The thought almost stirred anger inside Evan's mind, but instead he gazed down through the open portal, and the feeling passed almost as quickly as it had started.

The water looked so calm and cool, and Evan was so thirsty. A soft drip from somewhere inside the water tower echoed through the door to Evan's ears, and without any more hesitation, he threw himself into the black water, mouth open and eager. His stomach ruptured when he entered the liquid, and Evan felt the tightness in his gut relax, as thousands upon thousands of worms fled the confines of his body for the cool freedom of the water around him. They spilled out of him, like flies fleeing a rancid piece of roadkill that'd been kicked, uncoiling from his belly like a disemboweled man's intestines.

The water tower echoed with the splashing of the worms as they undulated through the drinking water. Salvation choked Evan, pressing in on him from every direction. But he didn't thrash—he only opened his mouth as wide as he could. He'd finally found enough. He wasn't thirsty anymore. He'd never be thirsty again.

BABEL

By Ian Steadman

Ptolemia used to be known as a party planet. That was before things went south in '92 and it dropped off the map. No contact for over thirty years, then some bright spark had the idea of sending an expeditionary team to see what was left. I'm guessing the dancing girls are all long gone. I'm also guessing we're heading for a vast, hollow pit of nothingness.

"Welcome to Vegas, baby!" Maxi shrieks into the comm as we drop out of orbit.

That was one of its nicknames from back in the day. Others weren't always so polite. Preachers tried to convince us that its excesses were the start of the Second Coming, a modern-day Sodom. Given the way things ended, they may have had a point.

"What happens in Vegas, stays in Vegas—right?

That's Sarge. His name, not his rank. I guess his parents were on a military fix when he was born, which might explain why he's turned out the most gung-ho of us all. He's recently had a new graft added to his upper arm, insignia and rank molded into the musculature. We give him grief about it, but privately I think it's kinda cool. The only 3D augment I have is a slightly elongated trigger finger on my right hand. I had it done to meet the minimum physical requirements for the corps. Go figure.

Burnsie is the silent one. He has more augments than the rest of us put together: extra-wide kneecaps, protruding collarbones of an unbreakable polymer, a scary-looking bone ridge down his forehead. He doesn't say much but he scares the shizzle out of anyone we come up against. Sometimes we joke that he's more plastic than flesh and blood.

The ride is bumpy, but the landing's smooth. It's all sand out there. At least that hasn't changed. Burnsie once told us a story around the food-synth unit, about a desert planet so blasted with nukes that the entire surface turned to glass.

"Got anything on the readouts?" Maxi says, once we've all unstrapped and moved to our stations. "Something's wrong with mine, can't get a fix. Is that stuff out there breathable or not?"

"Nothing here," I say. "Get suited up, we're going to have to take readings manually."

Burnsie had his suit custom-made, to accommodate all his augments, but the rest of us just chop and change as we see fit. I think Sarge had mine last. It stinks of sweat and synthesized barbecue.

The sand outside is grittier than the stuff back home, rising and falling in gentle drifts. There's barely any wind to speak of. Ptolemia had a near-breathable atmosphere when it was colonized—one of the reasons why it was selected—but they were meant to have been running purification filters nonstop. Given the lack of any visible cities or dwellings when we flew in, I can't imagine that's been happening. If anyone's still alive, they'll be relying on personal filters or lung augments by now.

Maxi has been waving the gizmo around, holding the screen up to her visor from time to time.

"Okay, I think it's breathable, just. Not toxic, anyway. Maybe the filters ran for a decade or two after the collapse? Who wants to try it?"

Burnsie is first, as usual. There's the click and whoosh beside me as he releases his helmet clasps. He coughs, and for a moment we all think this might be the time, his last first breath on an alien world. Then I hear him growling over the comm.

"You can breathe it, but it stinks. Man, this place reeks worse than Sarge. I'd stay helmeted if you don't want to puke."

He still keeps his helmet off, though. Maybe he finally got those nasal augments he's always been talking about.

It's not entirely clear what we're supposed to do, now we're here. Look for survivors, obviously. That goes without saying. Beyond that, they just want to know what the hell happened. Before all the links went down and the planet went dark, there were all kinds of rumors circulating about this place. Weird alien drugs, year-long parties, augments that would make your eyes water. The last delivery shuttle dropped off sixty-two bio-printers, a custom order for whoever was in charge. Clearly they were either as high as a drone or physical augmentation was trending in a major way.

The rest happened so fast there wasn't time to do anything other than sit and watch. Explosions levelling the major cities. Armed militia chasing survivors through the desert wastes. Fires, screaming, a planet in collapse. Then all the news feeds went silent. The final message came two days later, via an old satellite, from an unknown sender: "Ptolemia is all one. Dead planet. Leave us."

There were the normal conspiracy theories—did they mean to say, "all one?" or "all gone?" who were the "us?"—but it amounted to little more than a mildly interested buzz. Business as usual: we wrote the planet off, worried about colonizing the next one. Sometimes the colonies thrive, sometimes they implode. We've learned that the hard way.

Sarge is already kicking at the sand like it's done something to offend him, and I'm about ready to call us all back inside when Maxi waves the gizmo at me.

"Come look at this. Maybe I'm going crazy, but I think there's something out there. A building. A structure. Something, anyway. We should check it out?"

I'm hoping she's got it wrong, but when she shows me the screen there's no mistake. We can't tell what it is from this range, but it's registering a footprint big enough to be a military base, or maybe a small city. Now I've seen it, we can't ignore it. Cursing our luck, I give the order to unpack the rover and wheel it out. None of us like using it—the seats are hard and cold, even with our suits on—but it's either that or spend the day wading through this sea of grit. This way we can be there in under half an hour.

I don't know why, but I let Sarge drive this time. Usually Burnsie likes to rip it up, but his helmet's off and I have a feeling that we might need someone more responsible at the controls. Call it intuition if you like. Burnsie moans in frustration as Sarge trundles us along at regulation speeds, while Maxi and I whoop it up to amusing effect. It's like a school outing, minus the teachers. All we need is for the food-synth unit to rustle up a packed lunch.

We first see it after about twenty minutes. It's clear that it's a tower of some kind, a spindle reaching a kilometer or two into the sky. Even from this distance it looks immense.

Maxi whistles. "Told you there was something. You think the colonists could have built this? There's nothing in the file, is there—not of this size. Who the hell builds a tower in the middle of the desert?"

Who indeed. I've examined the files front to back a hundred times on the way out here, and none of the registered structures were higher than a couple of stories. None that we knew of, anyway.

We're still getting nearer, and the detail is coming into view. It looks pieced-together, as if someone has assembled it from a pile of junk, the odds and ends of a wrecked civilization. What appeared symmetrical from a distance is gradually distilling into individual turrets and ridges, openings and what might be air ducts.

"Will you look at that?" This is Maxi again—she always did like to talk more than the rest of us. "Something this size . . . who has the time to make that? Or the manpower? I mean, the number of people involved in something this big—"

And then she stops. She's seen it. We all have. And we're still moving, drawing closer and closer faster than we can think, and that arm becomes two arms, fifty arms, a hundred legs, a thousand torsos.

Finally, Sarge brings us to a halt. We're only half a kilometer or so from the base of it now and we can see it all.

The tower is constructed of human bodies. Thousands of them, grafted together with untold augments—bones stretching from head to ribcage, tendons connecting wrists to ankles. I see two heads joined at the temples by what appears to be a section of intestine. I see a child, no more than two or three years old, emerging from the stomach of an adult male, suspended in the air by a narrow bridge of gristle. I see things I cannot—will not—name, until I can't take it anymore and I close my eyes.

Over the comm I can hear Maxi crying, Sarge cursing. Burnsie is close to silent, but even he is muttering under his breath. There's the sound of retching and someone's breakfast splatters against the inside of their helmet. My money would be on Maxi, but you never know. None of us truly knows how to deal with this.

It's Burnsie who turns us around in the end. Sarge is wailing now, his head in his hands, so Burnsie reaches over and wrestles the controls from him. My eyes are open but I can only stare at the floor. As the sands rush beneath me they blur into nothingness.

Back at the shuttle, we don't speak. We pack our suits away. Maxi rinses the inside of her helmet with the water jet. The rover is stowed. I find my hands are shaking, so badly that it's difficult to undo all the clasps. I know the others are struggling with it too.

It's Maxi who speaks first. Her voice is subdued, sitting quiet and heavy in the recycled air.

"How could they do that? I mean . . . why? I can't understand this, I can't . . ."

Burnsie fills the silence. "Did you see? At the bottom? In the sand? There were marks there, tracks dug into the desert. Like it had been moving. Whatever it is, it's dead now. But it wasn't. It *lived*. What could it have been like? Existing as . . . that?"

None of us speak. My imagination is conjuring answers but I don't want to share them. I don't want to poison anyone else's mind. We don't talk about this as we take off and set our course for home. We won't tell stories about it around the food-synth unit.

"What happens in Vegas, stays in Vegas."

I will not be including this in my report.

A POUND OF FLESH
By Edmund Stone

I should not have let her go. When she needed me most I, too stupid or prideful, let her slip into oblivion. She offered her skin for a canvas and I used it willingly. The perfect foundation for my greatest artistic achievement, a tattoo to rival anything I had ever created. But I went too far and twisted it into something abhorrent. Now I brood and the anger I feel only fuels my disdain; my memories of her are locked in my heart.

For two years, I've kept a tattoo shop on the edge of town, where most days I plan designs and troll the internet for inspiration. Lately, I've found the same designs lame; either some tribal circle or a letter-type tattoo. The people who enter my place are, by design, destined to ask for the same thing; some letters, typically in Roman typeset, to remind them of a date. Be it their child's birth or a date that reminds them of their anniversary.

I always agree to do what the customer wants, because any other response would end in no business. I would then have to resort to some other living. I can think of nothing else I could do that would bring the same money. There are others that produce tattoos in this city, but most say that my attention to detail makes me the most sought-after artist in the area.

But say what they will, a good tattoo always begins with the canvas. If the skin is lumpy, then the tattoo is harder to line up properly. When Aryn walked into my shop, I fell into a stupor. Her skin was the perfect canvas: smooth and free of blemishes. She had a color that would blend perfectly with any ink. I knew I could produce a tattoo that would rival anything I've ever created.

I've always dabbled in the occult; old symbols and hieroglyphics of the ancient world, things that have fallen out of context to the modern day. I have a wonderful collection of prints that I've spent years collecting. My plan was to incorporate them into a spectacular tattoo, given the right flesh canvas came along. The benefactor of this gift would have to agree to have their skin bombarded with writings and symbols that made no sense to the common person.

Aryn, perfectly suited to the task, had a trust in my abilities that bordered on fascination; I think she had a desire to tear an envelope that needn't be opened. In so doing, we unknowingly introduced an evil power to a new realm of possibilities.

She came to me from the urging of a friend. Her interest in the occult slightly mirrored mine, and our attraction was immediate. Aryn, an archaeology student and self-proclaimed Wiccan, more than willingly volunteered to be my canvas, when I explained to her what I had in mind.

Her beauty mesmerized me, with long black hair to her waist and dark eyes that enchanted the soul. She stood an even five foot seven; tall by a woman's standard, but only two inches shorter than me. Her legs were her most prominent feature: long and luxurious, a canvas that begged to be painted.

I'm not the best-looking man, and Aryn could have her pick of suitors. For some reason she wanted me. I have no explanation. Perhaps my art attracted her; the darkness I attach to it. But darkness made sense to her. She invited it, but never understood it. I only wish I had.

When I first introduced her to the idea of my illustrious plan, she couldn't contain her enthusiasm. Aryn jumped up on me, wrapping those million-dollar legs so tight, that my breath momentarily left me. It was settled, she would be the canvas, although she didn't know I planned it that way. We made love that night and talked afterward about the tattoo. It would take several days to accomplish such a feat, but Aryn didn't care. In fact, she couldn't wait to get started.

In the morning, I made coffee and began to go through my collection. I reached for an old box of supplies by my work table. I opened it to reveal a stack of prints, copied from old papers. I spread them out on the table and Aryn and I scanned the symbols to see if we could find a suitable design. Her eyes were drawn to an interesting configuration. It had two triangles and a circle that encompassed the perimeter. Inside, the head of a goat presided. She said it reminded her of Wiccan texts, but had not seen anything like it in her archeology books. There were symbols of unknown origin, at least to me, adorned inside and outside the circle. They were strange and I shuddered to think of what each of them meant. But the artistic expressions that abound in each symbol drew me in and captivated my soul.

Aryn stood leaning over the table in only a short silk gown that hung open slightly in the front, revealing one of her breasts. I marveled in her perfection. She caught me looking and grinned. Then she stood and released the gown to the floor. Her perfect form glistened in the morning sunlight that beamed in from the window. She placed her leg on the table and bent forward over it, as a ballerina would warm up before a performance. I studied that leg for a moment and anticipated drawing on it. Aryn, satisfied in the spectacle of my erection from the sight of her, only smiled.

I grabbed a roll of drawing paper and stretched it out the length of her leg. Picking up a pen, I started to work. I aligned the drawing on the paper in as perfect symmetry to the leg as possible. I would complete the tattoo in four parts, starting from the pelvis to the mid-thigh. Then work my way down until the design encompassed the entirety of the leg, from the top of the thigh to the ankle.

I drew feverishly, a man with purpose. Aryn had put her leg down, but still leaned up against the table, disrobed and apparently aroused by my work. She breathed heavily in my ear and whispered naughty desires she wished upon my person. I grinned, but stayed focused on my work. The symbols and pictures that she and I picked were prints derived from a book called the Necronomicon. This book claimed it contained spells to conjure the dead. I never believed such things, but thought the pictures very cool. The drawings were mostly bereft of color, but some symbols did contain a red and black tinge, although faded together. A drawing of a dragon devouring its tail caught my eye; an elaborate circle with another circle inside. A crude sketch of a tortured creature mummified and bandaged up to the waist. Its head uncovered and the chest splayed open with the skin pinned to the side. The entrails of the thing hung out and sprawled down to its feet.

In the space of an hour, I created a drawing for the basis of the tattoo. I presented the drawing to Aryn and it pleased me to see her face light up. She ran her fingers along the paper and traced the symbols and figures. She was so pleased, that she pinned me to the table and gave me no choice but to make love to her. Not that I minded, my love belonged to her and I reveled in our perfect union; she the canvas and I the artist.

I planned to start on the first part of the tattoo the next evening, after my last customer of the day. The insipid day dragged with laborious skin paintings of cartoon characters and a tribal band that made a man twice my size cry like a baby. I so longed to decorate Aryn's fresh skin. It consumed my thoughts to the point that my lack of concentration nearly turned a pink bunny into a greenish reptile. I closed the shop at my normal time and waited for Aryn to arrive. She left that morning to work a waitressing job in the city. It wasn't her favorite thing to do, but the tips were good, especially for a young beauty like her.

I prepared a small meal for the two of us, complete with white wine. When she arrived, Aryn could hardly contain her enthusiasm. Famished, she ate the meal hurriedly and after several glasses of wine, readied herself for the leg tattoo. I requested that she cover herself, as the distraction of her womanly parts may cause me to lose focus. I prepared my ink gun with the needle and laid out the supplies I would need. I began to work on my masterpiece.

Aryn never flinched, even though the work proved laborious. She stretched out and relaxed, as my needle hummed and embedded the ink into her skin; she my Mona Lisa and I her daVinci.

Two hours later, I finished the first part of the tattoo. I marveled at the creation and how Aryn's skin complimented the superb design. Star symbols, goat-like creatures, and unspeakable things from some unknown afterlife, sprawled down that perfect leg. I covered the fresh art with bandages to ensure no infection could occur. Aryn rose from the table and kissed me, long and deep; the same kiss that Leonardo may have received from his painted muse.

We slept that night, our bodies intertwined. We never made love, only held one another; the exhaustion of the previous hours had taken a toll. I for one tossed in my bed waking up on occasion; my sleep invaded by vicious entities. The creature I painted on Aryn haunted my slumber. I woke in a cold sweat. I considered the room and found nothing there. Just a crazy dream, I assumed. Aryn lay next to me, sleeping soundly with a silky sheet covering her naked body. She lay perfectly still, unaffected by my movements. I did notice a small twitch on her leg, under the sheet. It bobbed up and down and then stopped. The sporadic movement turned to a fluid one, like the locomotion of a snake, writhing under the sheet.

It journeyed up Aryn's leg and toward her hip, and followed the contour of her body, until it stopped just short of her breasts. My curiosity piqued, I felt compelled to pull the sheet back. When I did,

I saw something incomprehensible. The skin over Aryn's ribs distended out in a distorted fashion, and I couldn't understand why she wasn't feeling this, because as I watched in amazement, she lay still, sleeping, as though nothing was happening. The tumorous thing began to move again and I heard the skin, that perfect over layer that I painted the night before, begin to tear. The terror of the canvas being torn was more than I could bear! Trickles of blood produced small drips down Aryn's side. It pooled on the bedcover and still she slept. Her flesh ripped with ostensible audibility and a large splash of blood covered my face. I pushed back against the top of the bed, cringing with horror.

There it was, the flayed man looked at me, his flesh pinned to the side of his body; blood dripping from every orifice. He was the same size as I had drawn him and he had teeth that were chomping on Aryn's tender flesh. He considered me, then jumped for my head. My arms went up in front of my face, anticipating the death that followed.

But instead, I woke up. Lowering my arms, I looked around the room and then over at Aryn. She still slept, as quietly as ever. No part of her body had been harmed. My heart hammered in my chest and I trembled with goose-bumped flesh. I switched on the lamp sitting on the nightstand. Rolling over, I put an arm around Aryn, and pulled her close. She woke and considered me sleepily.

"You're shaking. What's wrong?" she said.

"Nothing, just cold," I said. I held her tighter and tried to sleep.

The next morning Aryn woke before me and made coffee. I couldn't get the dream out of my head. The flayed man still hung heavy on my mind. I had created several tattoos, but his was the first to ever mess with my head. She sat at the table when I entered the room, investigating her leg.

"I think it's healing faster than you thought it would," she said.

"Yes, I think you may be right. About the tattoo, I'm wondering if we should go any further with this." I said. Aryn considered this and turned her head to the side.

"What do you mean? I thought you were as into this as I was?"

"I am, but maybe the design should be different? Have you ever wondered what those symbols might mean?" I said.

"I've never thought about it before. I guess they are just random things, why does it matter?" Aryn said.

"I had a terrible dream last night, there were monsters and you were in it, and I . . ." my voice trailed off and I looked down at the ground. She came over to me and sat in my lap. She caressed me, running her fingers through my hair.

"There, there. It's all right, I'm here now and no monsters will get us. It was only a dream, no doubt brought on by fatigue, you've been working too hard," she said.

"I suppose you're right," I said.

"When can we start on the next part of the tattoo?" Aryn said. She kissed me and looked into my soul with eyes that held a need for something beyond my control. How could I say no to her? How could I possibly say no?

The next two weeks brought the same schedule. I worked in the shop by day and at night designed and implemented the tattoo on Aryn's leg. I feverishly labored to make every detail stand out. There were more symbols and a tentacled creature that wrapped the full of her calf. The text itself was printed in a way that started from top to bottom. I didn't understand the writings, but the design held true; a flawless structure of artistic achievement, laid out on that perfect leg. The canvas always makes the difference.

"I think I know what that says," Aryn said one time. "It says: To play with death is a way to invite Hell. I saw that in one of my Wiccan textbooks."

"You surely don't believe such nonsense, do you?" I said.

"No, don't be silly. I just love the design of the whole thing. Once it's done, I can tell everyone about that," she said.

After every new application, Aryn would make love to me with a new fervor. I responded in kind. But then, wouldn't DaVinci do the same? Is that why Mona Lisa smiled; anticipation or annoyance from waiting? Though Aryn proved to be a patient subject, she bent her fair share of frustration toward me.

All seemed right, until that fateful night. I should have held her tighter, I know that now. But life doesn't give second chances and what we sow can be reaped by the most unlikely benefactors. I should not have let her go, I know that now.

The tattoo was finished and my labors had proved extensive, but well worth it. We lay in my bed after an exhaustive sex-capade; Kama Sutra and forms of geisha. Things I never knew, but felt enriched to understand better. Aryn never seemed to tire, but this night she gave in to sleep. Perhaps some wine made that easier. I held her, closer than I ever thought possible, and felt her push her hips and buttocks close to me. There we were, a tangle of flesh that seemed endless; if only that were the way of it.

Sometime in the middle of the night, I felt a tug. At first I thought Aryn had another burst of energy and I would do my best to take her again. I would hope my stamina made a miraculous comeback. But this was something else; something entirely different.

"Why are you pulling at me?" she said groggily.

"I'm not, my love. I thought you wanted another go," I said.

Then she screamed; a bloodcurdling cry. I pulled back the blankets and couldn't comprehend what I was seeing. My creation had come to life! In every form of evil entity that existed in this and other realities! The flayed man chomped at her thigh and Aryn renewed her anguish. The tentacled creature rose from the picture on the leg to form as a three dimensional being before me. I reached for Aryn, but the tentacles pushed me back and set me into the floor. I landed on my backside and hit my head on the nightstand.

Aryn screamed again and though my head reeled against the pain and near blackout, I found my feet. I jumped back up to the bed and saw the dragon figure swirling furiously on her leg. Aryn was being dragged into her own skin. The flayed man gnawed on tender flesh and the tentacle creature pulled toward the inner part of her thigh. The monstrosity's appendages flailed about all around him, but three of the tentacles held Aryn tight and had no plans to release her. I grabbed hold of her.

"Darling, please hold me, don't let them take me!" Aryn cried. I held her and had no intentions of releasing. I then heard something, which caused my stomach to turn. Her flesh, that tender, flawless skin; the canvas I used and caressed over countless nights, was tearing, separating from the pelvis. Aryn wailed in pain. I held her though, and still held no thought of letting go.

"Don't let them take me!" Aryn howled with tears streaming down her face. "No matter what, don't let go!" she screamed.

I held her at the waist, but felt my grip slipping, as the leg continued to rip, making an unholy sound. All of the creatures were angrily agitating in the air around Aryn's leg. I tightened my hold, but to no avail; I was losing. I considered Aryn's eyes; full of fear and regret, much like my own. Why did we play with something neither of us understood? My fingers raked her side and dug into the flesh, drawing blood. My hands slipped to her arm. I tried to renew my grip, but lost it. I looked into those eyes, as I grasped her hand. Never had I wanted to hold something more. I needed her, but something from beyond desired her body. Aryn sobbed uncontrollably; her eyes pleaded with me, but I had no power in this struggle. I kissed her and lost the grip on her hand.

"No!" Aryn protested, and then began to disappear into the ball of ink that used to be her leg, her body up to her waist, completely swallowed; the dragon encircled her form. She clawed at the bed taking the sheets with her. I lunged for her again, but fire shot out of the dragon's mouth, preventing me from going any further. She disappeared into the vortex of dragon and ink-created monsters. The room spun with a spiraling force; several items floated in the air and vanished into the oblivion. Then a loud pop and it was gone.

There is nothing now; my canvas and muse forlorn and forgotten; the pain of her skin ripping, more horrifying than I could ever have imagined. I contemplated calling the police, but what would I tell them? This story is too fantastic; I would be locked up right away if I mentioned one part of it. I only have the sadness and realization that I let go. Aryn talked of inviting Hell, but neither she nor I believed that possible. I feel she may have gone there.

I've sat here for a week, trying to consider what to do. I've read and studied the prints, but can't figure out why they turned on her. I guess I know only one way to find her. I've known it all along, but was too afraid to admit. My Hell is hers and I accept it willingly. I place this gun to my head to take my life, feeling the regret that has haunted me. I will see you soon, my darling, in this you can be assured.

CONDITIONED APOCALYPSE
By Aric Sundquist

The police officer tells me to stay in my apartment. He's tall and muscular and grips a mean-looking tactical shotgun. He gives off an aura of entitlement, like all men in uniform do, and stares at my breasts as if they're a crime in progress. But I don't hide them. Actually, I do quite the opposite.

I lean against the doorway and stick my chest out and ask him if I can leave to go and run a few simple errands. He frowns and tells me that I can't go outside because the visitors are extremely dangerous. That's what he calls them—*the visitors*. I tell him that I call them *slithering alien shitheads* and he smirks a little at this. Then he says they're downright hostile and I should stay indoors for the time being.

I'm not really afraid of the visitors, so I feign some emotion and begin sobbing. It works beautifully. He takes a step closer and reassures me that I have nothing to worry about, that they will all die by the end of the week. Then he insists I keep out of sight and he'll check up on me later.

I tell him that would be great. And then I ask about his wedding ring.

He is startled, just long enough to cue me in on a lie forming on his lips. He says his wife died of cancer, just recently, and he wears his ring in her memory. Then he puts his hand on my shoulder and asks if I'm alone and if I have any weapons in the house. I tell him that I'm alone, that I don't like guns, but I do have a protector named Max. But all he does is take naps on the rug and beg for table scraps.

The policeman grins, because I'm an attractive young woman in need of rescuing. I bite my top lip and he gives me a weird look, so I switch to the bottom lip and play with my blonde hair and this time it works beautifully. I can tell I'm getting his blood pumping. I tell him to make sure to come back and we'll have a nice time together.

He agrees. He wants more.

The officer moves to the next apartment, a little flustered, he still eyes me up good. He knocks on my neighbor's door. Nobody answers. He moves to the next apartment and repeats the procedure, but this time he is greeted by an elderly woman wearing dark sunglasses and holding a potted plant that looks dead. I don't know her, and I don't care to know her, so I shut the door and try not to laugh.

Men.

Max comes to my side, unsure of what to do. Eventually he nuzzles my hand and licks my fingers. I hate being licked, but I keep my hand completely still. Licking is a sign of affection. That's what I want in a new pet.

I make sure to lock the door and wedge my desk in front of it for an added level of security. The desk holds my mother's antique sewing machine. It's heavy as hell and makes a good doorstop. Then I sit at my kitchen table and begin sorting through my remaining food.

This is what I have left: a couple boxes of corn flakes, four cans of expired tomato soup, a box of rice, and a half jar of crunchy peanut butter. That's it. Not great.

The electricity went out two weeks ago. And all of my perishable food went with it. That's when I discovered a set of empty canning jars while scrounging through the cupboards. At one point during my early college years I had wanted to make raspberry jam, but never got around to it.

So here they are—the empty jars. I use them to collect rainwater out on the fire escape. But what I really want to do is sneak outside and pilfer some of the untended gardens around town and do some canning. Or maybe set up some snares and catch a squirrel or rabbit to cook for dinner.

Thinking about food makes my stomach grumble, so I pour out a handful of corn flakes into a bowl and nibble on a few. I place some of the corn flakes on the floor and Max slinks over and gobbles them up in a second. I pet him behind the ear and he curls up on the floor and falls asleep. At least he pretends to fall asleep.

I dump out a second helping of corn flakes into the bowl right when gunshots go off outside. I hustle to the front window and peer through the shutters.

In the street below, a military unit weaves through a series of abandoned vehicles. They move on foot, with handguns and rifles and tactical vests. It reminds me of one of those ant farms—the kind with interconnected paths and tunnels. I cheer them on in silence, but I know what's going to happen.

I whistle to Max to come over and watch, but he doesn't move, just pretends to sleep on the rug. He hasn't been feeling good of late.

Outside, something happens. Figures slithering out of an abandoned garbage truck. They're not human anymore; they're in the process of changing. Tentacles swarm from craterous slits in their stomachs and resemble sea lamprey. It looks pretty weird, but it's actually kinda neat.

I watch the military men fire their weapons. They're winning at first, but the gunfire only attracts more of the creatures and the men begin suffering heavy losses. They retreat. A few survivors left behind start bleeding out. The others flee to a parking lot. Then more gunfire. And more screaming and dying.

By this time my eyelids are getting heavy and my stomach is doing cartwheels, so I lie on the couch and Max settles down next to me, more out of habit than anything else. I clasp his leash around my wrist so he'll wake me up if he moves, then I close my eyes and slip into the world of dreams.

When I wake up, it's dark, and Max's collar is on the ground, unclasped. I light a few candles and eventually find him trying to get out through the bathroom window. The window is nailed shut and won't budge. His bandages are bloody from pawing at the sill. He sees me and curls up into a fetal position and pisses on the floor.

It's useless. He just won't work.

I clasp the collar back around his neck and tighten it up. The spikes underneath the leather clamp down into his skin. I lead him from the bathroom to the living room and his whole body begins to shake, so I sit him back down on the floor and rub his back and try to calm him down, but he isn't having it. He lashes out and bites my hand. I take no offense at this; he's scared and the only thing he can do is retaliate.

Luckily, his bite isn't serious. I pulled out all of his teeth with a pair of pliers two weeks ago, when he first tried to bite me in my sleep. Shortly after, as just an extra precaution, I had him declawed, cutting off the first joint of his fingers and toes. Then I sliced his vocal cords with a razor. It's called *debarking*, in case you didn't know. I read about it online before the power went out. There was lots of blood. It drew ants.

Thinking back, maybe I should have done the procedures sooner. Maybe I should have done them when he first kicked his way into my apartment, full of lust and rage and his breath reeking of cheap whiskey. He was a wild dog back then. But not anymore.

I tased him and tied him up with an Ethernet cord, then with a pair of sewing shears, I snipped off his balls and fried them in olive oil. They made a strange popping sound in the pan, but didn't taste half bad. After that, he calmed down a bit. All pets are captors until they learn how to love you back.

That was also the day the lights first appeared in the sky.

Earlier that morning, a bunch of us climbed up on top of the roof and watched those strange yellow orbs swirl through the atmosphere. They looked like dying comets. I didn't know what they were—spirits maybe? People online kept saying the lights were possessing people and making them go crazy. But of course, we didn't believe them. And then we all went crazy thereafter. The whole world did.

We started killing each other off in record numbers. Cities burned. Everything reduced to rubble and ash within weeks. Then the change started with a select few. Supposedly, they were believers in some old god, and had given up their bodies as vessels for the yellow lights to possess. I thought it was all bullshit at first, until I saw for myself. Then I became a believer, too.

Or maybe I'm just imagining it all—all the violence and the lights and everything else. Maybe it's how we've always been, how we've always treated each other. I don't really know for sure, and I can't think too clearly anymore. My mind is slipping away. All I can do is think about food. All I can do is react.

As for Max—I'm going to give him a handful of sleeping pills. When he finally slips under, I'll place him in the bathtub and slit his throat. Once he's drained of blood, I'll cut off the pieces I can eat. I have plenty of canning jars left so it won't be a problem storing the leftovers.

The lights didn't possess him. They only drove him mad.

As for myself. . . .

Something stirs inside me, like a snake uncurling in the pit of my stomach. But it doesn't feel like one snake—it feels like a whole pit of them. Maybe they need to come out? Maybe I need to perform another procedure, but this time myself? One long incision down the length of my stomach should do the trick.

I ponder this and rub Max's head until he eventually stops whimpering. He pretends to go to sleep, but his trembling gives him away. Then I think of the policeman; he'll be stopping by soon, no doubt. It remains to be seen how a man of the law will fare on his knees and bound in servitude to something like me. Hopefully he'll be a better protector than my former neighbor.

But if not, it'll be fun housebreaking him.

LENGTH
By David Turton

Dylan Turner stood in his small, untidy bathroom, holding a tape measure against his small penis.

It had definitely grown. Maybe not to the naked eye, maybe only by less than an inch, but it was definitely bigger than it had been two days ago. He pushed the tape measure as far back towards the base of his penis as he could and stared down at the numbers on the yellow tape, which clearly read *1.8 inches* in large black letters. What had it been before? One and a half perhaps? He wished he had written it down. Determined not to make the same mistake again, Dylan made a note on his phone. *Tuesday 7 November 2016. 1.8 inches.*

✗✗✗✗✗✗✗

It had been three days since he'd seen the gypsy. Stumbling across the woman as he walked home through the woods from his local pub, she had known. The small, scruffy old woman had stumbled into his path in the dark and she had *known*. She had raised a gnarled, bony finger, pointed towards Dylan and said, "A darkness haunts you."

She pointed to Dylan's crotch. "Shame. Oh, great shame." She began to shake her head with genuine anguish. "Oh, great shame," she repeated.

"Look, I don't know who's told you what but I—"

She cut his words off by grabbing his penis, making him gasp. "No more shame. No more shame. No more shame. Grow! Grow! Grow! Shame will go. Shame will go! Dylan will grow and shame will go."

She let go and let her head roll back, the whites of her eyes flickering in her dirty, blackened sockets. Suddenly she released a bone-dry, bloodcurdling cackle. Her long finger rose once more and pointed at Dylan who stood quivering with fear.

"No more shame, Mr Turner. Dylan Turner will be shamed no more! Go and live. Go and conquer. Go!"

Dylan looked at the old hag. She seemed to be getting older, her nose large and swollen, her clothes were falling off her haggard, skeletal body. Her thin, grey hair fell around her shoulders revealing large patches of dry grey scalp on the top of her head. Her remaining teeth were an awful combination of black and yellow and her cracked lips were thin and pale. She was still cackling as Dylan pushed past her and ran the half-mile through the woods and into his house. As he ran he could hear her cackle become fainter and fainter. The little sleep he had that night had been plagued with dreams of the old woman. His penis tingled with the pain her bony fingers had caused, the long dirty nails had dug through his jeans into the soft flesh.

He had woken the next day feeling disturbed. *How did she know my name?* he wondered. *And the shame thing. About my dick...*
.

The size of Dylan's penis had been a source of depression since his teenage years. A micropenis was the technical term for it, something he'd learned after several private internet searches. At twenty-three years old, Dylan was still a virgin; he had never wanted to let any member of the opposite sex see where he quite literally came up short. And as a black man, he had to put up with countless comments from white people about the size of a black man's penis. He would just smile and feign an embarrassed look whenever these comments emerged, giving a non-committal laugh. But inside he was dying. How could the size of one body part affect a human being so much? A small nose, small ears, small feet. Even some kind of deformity. He would take all of them over his micropenis. He remembered with some pain the first time someone had seen it. He was thirteen in the swimming pool changing rooms and Billy Stephenson had pointed it out to the entire class. They had crowded round and laughed. He had glanced at their penises, each were at least twice the

size of his. Billy himself had what could only be described as an ele-
phant's trunk hanging out of his groin. Word had soon spread
around school; Dylan had a tiny cock. Of course, as teasing and jokes
tend to do, the joke soon died and people forgot. But Dylan had remembered. He had cried himself to sleep for weeks, and told no-one.
From that day on, not one person had set their eyes on his naked
penis; Dylan fully committed himself to ensure this would never
happen.

In his later teenage years and early twenties he had had
some relationships, but had always broken them off whenever
things got too steamy. He hoped he could find someone one day who
would understand. A woman who could look past his tiny penis and
fall in love with the man attached to it.

2.

Something was definitely happening. It had been a week
since the old woman had grabbed him and his penis had grown to
four inches. Dylan laughed as he looked at the yellow tape measure.
Had it been wishful thinking? Was he somehow measuring it wrong?
Or had the old witch used some kind of magic to make it a normal
size?

He stood opposite his bathroom mirror and looked at his
genitals. His flaccid, fleshy appendage hung over the testicles. *Below
the balls!* It must have been over a thousand times that Dylan had
stood opposite this mirror and something around the size of an
acorn usually peered back at him, nestled on top of a wrinkly dark
ball sack. But now what he saw was longer. It was *definitely* longer.
The old woman had put a spell on him *and his cock had grown*. It was
normal size. *He* was normal. Dylan stood to one side to view himself
from a different angle. His dick still hung over his balls. His head lay
back on his shoulders and he bellowed a loud, joyful laugh.

3.

The same night, Dylan lay naked on his bed, browsing the internet. He wanted to test his new-found confidence. Browsing the search engines, he came across listings for local escorts in the London area. He found a white woman. She was of large proportions and over fifty years old. She charged £40 per night for her "services." Dylan phoned the number and arranged to meet her in Tottenham at ten o'clock. He booked a local hotel, one of the budget ones where the workers look on with no judgement.

"Sandra" was uglier in person than the pictures on her website suggested, but that was okay by Dylan. With his confidence fragile, he felt that he would start with someone who would be grateful of his company. He kept checking his penis every few minutes to make sure it hadn't shrunk back to its original tiny form, that the old woman's spell hadn't worn off. It hadn't.

The sex with the prostitute was fast. Dylan was excited and didn't last long at all. But he left the hotel with a huge grin on his face. The woman must have seen thousands of penises in her working life and she had called Dylan a *big boy*. A big boy! Dylan couldn't believe it. He felt like a man for the first time in his life. He was no longer a virgin; a woman had seen his penis and not only thought it was acceptable but it was *big*. Of course, she might have said that to all the punters. And that was okay by Dylan, even if she did, the fact that she could say something to flatter him without it being sarcastic or ridiculous pleased him hugely. She had even bled slightly from his penetration.

Dylan returned home and went to bed. He slept a dreamless sleep with a huge grin slapped on his face.

4.

The grin remained on his face when he woke. But that wasn't all. He looked down the bedsheets at his naked groin. His morning erection stared back at him. To Dylan it looked huge. He jumped out of his bed and went to the bathroom, grabbing the tape measure out of the cabinet drawer. When he measured his now flaccid penis, he gasped, putting his hand to his mouth. Six inches. It was still growing.

Dylan punched the air and danced around his bathroom, his penis slapping against his thighs as he moved. He booked another prostitute, this time one slightly younger, in her late-thirties. She was pretty, blonde and slim with a pleasant face.

The sex lasted longer this time and again the woman commented on his size. This time though, something happened to disturb him somewhat. The woman had bled again but appeared to suffer pain.

"Sorry, it's too big and it felt like . . ." her words faded as she failed to complete her sentence.

"Felt like what?" Dylan asked.

"If felt like it jabbed me inside. Something sharp. Like a bite. It felt like something bit me."

5.

Dylan's penis continued to grow. Six inches became eight, eight became twelve and on the morning of 21 November, around three weeks after his encounter with the witch, it measured eighteen inches long.

People at work had begun to notice the long bulge in his trousers. Dylan saw women giggle and wink as he walked past them in the work café. He was struggling keeping it tucked into his trousers. Its tip went well below the crotch of his trousers and he needed to constantly adjust its position, such was his discomfort. He had slept with two more prostitutes. Both had commented on his size and both had bled. The last one had cried out in pain and thrown him out angrily, telling him he was a monster, that he shouldn't be allowed near women. Dylan didn't care, if anything, the prostitute's words had boosted his ego. She was *angry* at him for the size of his penis. It was something he could not have imagined before.

A woman sat opposite him as he ate his jacket potato. Dylan had seen her around.

"Hi, I'm not sure we've met properly," she said. "I'm Debbie. I work in the Accounting Department."

"Dylan. I work in Facilities. Nice to meet you." He smiled. Debbie was gorgeous. Long, blonde hair fell to her shoulders. Her smile was heavenly, displaying bright white teeth and sparkling blue eyes.

"I was just wondering," Debbie said. "Would you like to go for a drink on Friday?"

"Is there an office do, like? A work night out?"

Debbie laughed. "No, don't be silly! Just me and you. I'm asking you out on a date, Dylan. Don't make me feel silly and have to ask you again."

"Er. Yeah. Yeah of course. I'd love to."

6.

Dylan showered and dressed, spraying aftershave. His penis, now over twenty inches long, needed tucking into his jeans. He had been forced to buy baggier jeans to accommodate it. The growth had begun to worry him. *What if Debbie wanted to have sex?* He thought to himself. *Will my cock keep growing? When will it stop?* His confidence had grown in the past few weeks, at the same rate as the growth of his penis, but now for the first time he was beginning to feel fear. What would she say if she saw it? Would she be scared?

He met her at the pub. Debbie was fantastic, full of fun. She was Oxford-educated and had a keen interest in Art. Dylan liked her immediately. After a few drinks he began to feel a stirring in his groin. Fear filled him again, worry that he would hurt her, anxiety that she would be shocked by what she saw. But all the feelings of worry were swept away by a desperate, burning desire from his groin. A feeling of utter emptiness that could be filled and satisfied by taking Debbie to bed.

The stirring grew into an almost explosive excitement when Debbie looked at him with her bright blue eyes and said, "Shall we go back to yours?"

They went to Dylan's flat and immediately began removing each other's clothes. Dylan ripped open Debbie's blouse, exposing her large, firm breasts. Debbie went straight for Dylan's trousers. He gulped as she pulled them down. Debbie gasped.

"It's true. Oh, my God, it's true." She laughed and looked up at him.

"What's true?" he asked. A large grin on Dylan's face betrayed his combined feelings of relief and delight.

"They said they'd seen it . . . the bulge. Oh, my God, Dylan. It's absolutely *huge.* It's the biggest I've seen. How do you . . .?"

Suddenly, Dylan's penis moved. It twitched upwards.

"Oooh, it's a bit lively," she said, grinning as she took it in both of her hands. It moved again, snapping itself out of her hands like a whip.

"Dylan what are you—" Her words were cut off as the long, fleshy penis thrust itself at her. Debbie held her hand to her face and then brought it away. Her face was full of blood.

"What the fuck?" she yelled. But her words were soon cut off as Dylan's penis went forward again. It seemed to stretch into an even longer shape, elongating and bending. It wrapped around Debbie's neck. Dylan tried desperately to stop, pulling his hips away from Debbie's face and using his hands to pull it back. But it wouldn't move. It was thick, ropey and pulsating. Dylan had lost all feeling down there. It was as if his penis was completely independent from his body. He was powerless to stop it.

Debbie gurgled as it tightened its grip around her throat. Her bright white eyes began to fill with blood. Blood also ran out of her nose, spurting out with each struggling, suffocated breath. Dylan began to cry.

"Debbie, I'm sorry. I'm so sorry."

Debbie spluttered again and Dylan heard a popping sound. Her eyes were now bleeding and Debbie had defecated. The rancid smell filled the air. Debbie's lips turned blue, in contrast to her white, blotchy face. Dylan's penis loosened and Debbie's lifeless body fell to the floor.

Dylan put his hand over his mouth and cried. Surely this was a nightmare from which he would wake any minute? He slapped himself hard in the face. This couldn't have happened. *Surely it couldn't?* He looked down at his flaccid penis, the end of which was resting on the cold wooden floor. He put his hand around it and picked it up, staring at the shiny end.

"You bastard," he said. "You murdering bastard."

Suddenly the end of his penis glimmered. The urethra opening was large, around the size of a coin. Dylan looked at the blackness contained within and felt like he was looking into death, the blackest soul from hell. Suddenly there was a flash of white. *Were they teeth?* He thought so. They flashed again. Tiny white, jagged triangles in two circular rows were contained within the hole at the tip of his penis. He put his hands around it and squeezed. Maybe he could kill it. Maybe he could strangle it just like it had strangled Debbie in front of his eyes. Suddenly his penis darted forward and he felt a sharp pain in his right hand. *It had bitten him.* A fast trickle of blood fell from the wound. His own penis had bitten him on the hand. But this wasn't his own penis. Not anymore.

7.

Dylan put Debbie's body in a large holdall that usually held his Christmas Tree and dragged it to the woods. At two in the morning, it was unlikely that anyone would see him, but he had a cover story sorted all the same. He was carrying an old Christmas tree ready to make way for a new one. He worked nightshift and only had the middle of the night to do so. To make the story stand up against any possible police checks, he put branches of the tree around Debbie's body, which was covered in bin liners.

In the woods, he dug a shallow grave in the most remote area, right in the middle. It took him forty-five minutes to walk there and a further hour to dig. There was a creepy atmosphere in the dead of night, with the tree branches rustling in the breeze and several nocturnal animals scurrying, calling, crying, and squeaking. He pushed Debbie's body into the grave and re-covered it with loose dirt. He looked down to his dirty jeans and caught sight of the huge, long bulge down his right trouser leg. *Has it got even bigger since Debbie's death?* he thought to himself. *What is happening to me? When will this end?* He cursed his penis. He cursed his former self for making his penis the cause of all his problems. And he cursed the old witch for putting this terrible spell on him. Suddenly, Dylan had a thought. *The witch was in these woods!* He threw down his spade and ran farther into the dark woods.

He ran without direction for an hour, tripped over old stumps and caught sharp branches across his body, the trees over-looking him like eerie, dark pillars, judging him and tracking him. Suddenly he came across a small white caravan, partly hidden under a dead, fallen tree. The caravan was dirty and old, muddy handprints were stamped all over its battered façade. Dylan ran to the caravan and hammered his fists on the door.

"Come out! Come out, you old witch! What did you do, gypsy? What the fuck did you do to me?"

Suddenly the door swung open. A woman came out. She was young and beautiful. Long dark hair seemed to move and twirl of its own accord around her shoulders. Her skin was milky white and she was dressed in a bright red ballgown. The dress was strapless, ex-posing her perfect shoulders. Her lips were full and luscious and her eyes sang of beauty.

"You were looking for me?" she said.

"No. I was looking for . . . the witch."

"The witch! Ha! I take many forms, Dylan Turner."

"It was you."

She raised her delicate hand and moved her fingers lightly. Dylan looked down. He felt a stirring in his trousers. Suddenly his penis broke free and pushed its own way out of his jeans. He looked at the incredible sight in front of him. As the woman moved her hand, the penis was moving with it. She was *controlling it.* She snapped her fingers and the penis turned to Dylan, snapping at him with its awful ring of teeth. She clicked her fingers again and it fell back to his jeans limply. Still in terrible awe, Dylan tucked it back into his jeans. His mouth gaped open and he began to shake his head.

"But . . . why?"

"Why? No particular reason. I could see your pain, Dylan. Your stupid egotistical pain. It was running your entire life, heaping misery on you. I wanted to show you. To teach you a lesson. And it was fun. I enjoyed watching you. First the glee, then the ego, then the misery. Tell me, Dylan, what have you learned?"

"You're fucking evil! You're a psycho! I want to take it back! I want to go back."

The witch released a horrible cackle, the same one she had bellowed all those weeks ago. Suddenly her eyes brightened, the whites became larger and the pupils burned into a red fire. Her hair became grey and matted, with bald patches appearing all over her head. The gown fell from her body completely, revealing a bony, haggard torso, completely naked. Her breasts shrivelled and her skin sagged. The woman's nose grew into a hook and large warts appeared on her face. She raised a bony finger and pointed it towards Dylan.

"Go! You Go! The shame will return! The shame. The shame!" She cackled again, a sound that echoed across the desolate woods, rattling through Dylan's head and reverberating across his entire body.

Dylan fled.

8.

The following morning, Dylan was awakened by a knock at the door. It was the police.

"I'm Detective Inspector Dewsbury. I'd like to ask you a few questions about Debbie Field. A colleague of yours. I understand you went for a drink with her last night?"

"Yes," Dylan replied.

"Unfortunately, Miss Field's body was found in the woods in the early hours of this morning."

It didn't take Dylan long to confess. A witness had seen him dragging the bag across the woods. A dog walker had discovered the body when his German Shepherd had decided to dig the fresh earth, finding the large holdall buried below. Dylan had left the spade next to the grave. There was no escaping. He told the police everything. About the witch, the large penis, the growth. He even stood to undo his trousers to prove his story, which the Detective forcefully stopped him.

Dylan was arrested without bail and placed in a cell while a thorough investigation was carried out. Alone in the middle of the night, he sat in his cell and cried, with his head in his hands. How could everything have taken such a bad turn? He felt a sudden stirring in his groin and his penis burst out of his jeans, ripping the material around his button fly in the process. The penis hovered at his eyeline and its two rows of circular teeth glowed in the dim light of the prison cell. He looked at it with dismal resignation.

"You bastard. You've ruined my life." The penis looked back at him, the sharp teeth gleaming. *Was it smiling at him? Mocking him?* He put his hands up to grab it. He had nothing to lose. He was going to strangle the bastard, even if he took himself with it. The penis escaped his hands with ease, like a snake slithering out of its handler's grasp. It quickly wrapped itself around his neck. Dylan began to choke and splutter, his eyes filling up with blood. His bowels opened and his body slumped against the cell wall. He was dead.

9.

"Another one this morning," said Greg as he walked along the prison halls, talking to his colleague John. He swung his jailer keys around his fingers rhythmically. "Never get used to the suicides."

"Yep. Goes with the territory I suppose," John replied.

They stopped opposite Dylan's cell. His pale, lifeless body hung in front of them as other officers took photographs and surveyed the scene. Thin, tangled bedsheets were wrapped around Dylan's neck as he hung stiffly from the light fixture on the ceiling.

"Funny one this one, though. You've got to laugh."

"Really?' Greg asked. "What did he do?"

"Strangled his girlfriend. Not an uncommon one, gotta admit. But it was what he said to deny it which was bizarre. He said that his dick killed her. Jumped right out his pants and wrapped itself round her neck. He said a witch's curse made it grow to a massive length and then it killed her."

Greg laughed. "Aw that's a good one. I mean, I feel bad for laughing but that is a good one. First time I've heard that one. *It wasn't me governor, it was my tallywhacker that done it!*"

They both laughed loudly. Gregg laughed until his face went red and he had to bend down and regain his breath.

"But that wasn't even the funniest thing," John said. "Wait till you hear this. We gave him a medical when he came in. He stripped off, you know, the usual routine." Greg nodded.

"But when we checked him, his dick . . . it was the smallest one I'd ever seen. About the size of a baby prawn. That dick couldn't wrap itself round an ant's neck never mind a woman's!"

They roared with laughter.

NATURAL GROWTH
By M.B.Vujačić

"So, Mrs. Shane," Dr. Kramer said, leaning back in his chair, "I've been told you're interested in the Natural Growth Program."

Sarah straightened in her chair. "Umm, yeah," she said, and gave a tiny grin, her eyes sweeping across his office. It was all wood and leather and earth tones, the walls adorned with dozens of framed awards, diplomas, and certificates. Kramer watched her from behind an ornate desk. He was a small, clean-shaven, fifty-but-looking-forty type, clad in a business suit and a hundred-dollar haircut. She licked her lips. "Sorry, ah, I'm kinda excited."

The doctor smiled.

Greg chuckled and gently squeezed her hand. "It's okay, honey." He looked at the doctor. "We found an article about it on the internet. It sounded great, so we decided to give it a shot."

Kramer gave a slow nod. "A good choice. Natural Growth Program is not as swift as the traditional method, but I think you'll find the final result well worth the wait."

He opened a drawer and took out the largest, thickest brochure Sarah had ever seen. He leafed through it until he found a page showing the side view of a woman's breast, with five pink Xs marked around the areolas. "The hormones are introduced directly into the fatty tissue and the mammary glands. The procedure is performed wholly via infusions," he tapped the Xs with a pen, "with no more discomfort than what would be experienced during, for instance, a blood donation. The procedure consists of five major infusions spread over three months. The patient is closely monitored during this period to ensure everything goes well. The risk of scarring, rupturing, or infection is minimal, and there's no need for additional interventions."

Kramer turned the page. The next two pages displayed six photographs of a woman's naked torso. On the topmost photo, the one with *Before* written under it, the breasts were little more than nipples on a flat chest. The second picture showed the same nipples perched atop strong A cups. *Week One* was printed beneath it. The third, marked *Week Four*, displayed large Bs.

"And the best thing? They are *all yours.*" He spread his arms. "We implant no outside agents like silicone. We merely give your body a nudge and it takes care of the rest on its own."

Sarah barely heard him. She stared at the sixth photo, the one with *Week Twelve* written under it. It showed the kind of gravity-defying Ds that not only didn't sag, but also looked completely natural. The only time she'd seen their like outside of TV was in high school. They belonged to one Mona Jackson, an unassuming girl whom everyone liked but nobody invited to parties because she commanded the attention of every guy in the room.

"Honey? You with us?"

Sarah blinked, looked at Greg. "Oh. Yeah. I was just, umm . . ."

Kramer smiled, offering her the brochure. "Please, take a look. The available sizes are listed at the back."

Sarah leafed through it. There were more photos of successful procedures, not all of them ending with Mona Jackson-size Ds. Some women had stopped at Bs or small Cs, while one had had her already-strong Cs grown into Fs so bulky they bordered on vulgar.

Greg ran his hand over his mouth. "I gotta ask, doc, how is this so cheap? I mean, it costs less than implants at some clinics. I thought you guys would want to milk it while it's still new."

"Actually, that is precisely why it's so affordable," Kramer said. "The public tends to mistrust new medical procedures. Since we do not yet have the funding necessary to hire a famous actress or a model for promotion, we feel it's crucial to keep our prices as reasonable as possible."

"But it's all safe, right?"

"As with every procedure, some small complications may arise, but I assure you we're equipped to deal with them. We don't have a single unsatisfied customer and we intend to keep it that way." He looked at Sarah. "So, Mrs. Shane, do you prefer any size in particular? You do not have to decide right away, of cour—"

"*D cups,*" she said, grinning so hard the corners of her mouth itched. "I want *D cups.*"

"So what do you think?" Sarah said.

Greg smiled. "I still don't get why you wanted them so much. You were perfect just the way you were." He looked her up and down for the hundredth time in the last minute. "Not that I'm complaining."

"But they're lovely, aren't they?" Sarah said. She stood in front of the bathroom mirror, naked above the waist, holding one of her breasts. It felt warm and heavy, and it could barely fit in her hand. She couldn't have kept the grin from her face if she tried.

"They're awesome, baby."

Sarah's grin widened.

"How much longer is it going to take?"

"Eight weeks," she said. Round white patches, no bigger than shirt buttons, were glued to her breasts, three under each nipple, covering the spots where the syringes had punctured the skin. "Two more infusions."

"I read about those things they experimented on to make the hormones," Greg said, leaning against the washing machine. "Did you know they can lay, like, a million and a half eggs? Maybe you'll start laying eggs, too."

"If that's how it went, we'd all have tails by now from all those rats they use in labs."

Greg hugged her from behind and kissed her neck. "I just want you to know, I married you because I *love* you, and that's not gonna change. Not even if you grow a tail."

She giggled.

His hands slid up her belly and cupped her breasts. "They're so warm," he said. After a moment he made a puzzled face, then pressed his ear against her left breast. "Oh, weird."

"What?"

"It's like I can hear two heartbeats. One's faster than the other." He put his ear to the other breast. "Same here."

"What does that mean?"

"Nothing. There's probably a vein there and I'm hearing both its pulse and your heartbeat."

"You sure?"

Greg shrugged. "What else could it be?"

That night, Sarah had the first of what she'd come to think of as her baby dreams. In it, she walked on a seabed, lost in an aquatic landscape. Everywhere she looked she saw corals sticking to underwater reefs, jellies swimming in great swarms, and roe clusters hidden within forests of algae, but none of that fascinated her nearly as much as the two babies in her arms. She couldn't tell if they were boys or girls, and didn't care. They stared at her with bright blue eyes, same as her own, their lips mouthing a single word repetitively—*mama, mama, mama*. They asked her to promise she'd do something for them and, seeing no harm in it, Sarah gave her word.

By the time she finally woke up, her pillow was wet with perspiration and for a few moments afterward everything smelled of brine and rotten clams. Worst of all, her breasts itched. She tried scratching them, but the itch went too deep. It kept her up all night and didn't pass until noon.

Sarah mentioned the itch to doctor Kramer during the weekly examination. He told her not to worry, it was likely just a side effect of her skin stretching to accommodate her growing breasts. She left without telling him about the twin heartbeats, as that was something the babies had asked her not to do. Sarah didn't understand why she felt the need to keep a promise she'd made to a pair of imaginary infants, but there it was.

Oh well, she could always tell him next week.

"Oh, honey," Greg muttered, "oh, baby."

He lay on top of Sarah with his face buried between her breasts. His tie hung loose around his neck, his shirt unbuttoned, his lips purple from all the wine he'd drank. "I love you so much," he said into her flesh.

"Ow, you pinched me."

"I'm sorry, baby, I'm sorry," Greg said through a mouthful of nipple. "God, I love you."

Sarah giggled and ran her fingers through his hair. They'd just returned from a party at the factoring firm Greg worked at. It was an annual charity thing, held every year so his boss could show off to the investors. Although just a financial analyst, Greg had to attend and drop a little something into the charity box, and boy, oh boy did he hold a strong opinion about that. But not this year.

Sarah had read somewhere that the difference between a regular woman and a great one was that the great woman knew how to make her man feel powerful. She wore an unassuming black dress to the party, the kind you could wear to a funeral without being called disrespectful, but even so she made Greg feel very powerful indeed. He absolutely enjoyed how everyone—well, his boss, mainly—watched him with a mixture of envy and respect. He constantly smiled and laughed and cracked jokes, telling his bachelor colleagues a good wife was worth more than a thousand harems.

Sarah thought about her mother and sisters, and how they never noticed the way everyone—not just men—ogled them when they weren't looking. But she did. Skinny little Sarah, the one daughter in the family who never shared her bras with her sisters because they were too small for them. She'd always wondered what it felt like to draw such attention. Well, now she knew, and it gave her an unconscious smirk that stuck to her face like a tick.

"I love you, I love you, I love you," Greg said as he entered her. "God, how much I love you."

The sex was short and sweet, and ended with Greg falling asleep with half his body still on top of a satisfied Sarah, his hand laid over one breast. She let him sleep like that for a while, feeling way too mellowed to get up just yet. Eventually, the heaviness in her eyelids became too much and she went to the bathroom to remove the remnants of her makeup.

Sarah was standing in front of the mirror, wiping her face with a moist towel, when something *moved* inside her right breast. It was just a slight shift, but it produced a lance of pain so sharp it made her stagger and fall on the toilet seat with enough force to leave a bruise.

Second one this week, Sarah thought after the pain abated, *and it's only Friday.* Doctor Kramer had warned her rapid movements might cause a nerve to be pulled or skin to be stretched, but it had been six weeks since she'd finished the Natural Growth procedure, and these spasms still happened.

As for the babies, Sarah dreamed about them every night now. She'd fall asleep and find herself drifting in the murky depths, the twins side-by-side in her arms. She'd look at their blue eyes and hear them call her *mama*, and it'd disarm her so thoroughly she'd be unable to deny any of their requests.

One of the things they made her promise she'd keep to herself was the odd heaviness in her new breasts. Not only did they seem to weigh ten pounds each, if you squeezed them hard enough you'd come upon bone-hard matter. As if she carried rocks inside, hidden under all the soft flesh.

Also, something had begun to drip from her nipples. Sarah didn't notice it until five weeks after the therapy was over, when one morning she discovered brown smudges on the insides of her bras. At first she thought they were sweat stains. Then she washed them and realized they wouldn't come out no matter how hard she scrubbed. The babies begged her not to tell anyone about this and, though it worried her, Sarah just couldn't say no.

Not long after, she woke up to find brown stains on the inside of her nightgown. By the end of the week, her breasts were oozing brown liquid every night. Just a trickle, but it frustrated her to no end, doubly so once she realized how much it reeked. You couldn't smell it unless it was right under your nose, but it was there—a stale, salty odor reminiscent of filthy seawater and rocks slimy with algae. It embarrassed her so much she decided she'd tell doctor Kramer about it during the next examination, and to hell with the dream babies. In the meantime, she washed her breasts as many as five or six times a day. Greg never noticed anything wrong.

Sarah washed them again before returning to bed. She donned an old black t-shirt—that's what she slept in these days, to keep from ruining any more nightgowns—and snuggled next to Greg. He snored in big raspy wheezes, like he was coming down with the flu, so she gave him a nudge and he stopped. Sarah closed her eyes, yawning, and—

—and opened them to find the room flooded. The bed, the lamp, the night table, it all floated in what had to be at least two feet of water. Moonlight shone in through the window, but instead of blue it painted everything green. The babies sat at the edge of the bed, staring at her, muttering: *Mama, mama, mama.*

Sarah looked at them. "What is this? What are you—"

Something bumped the underside of the bed, right beneath where she was lying. She looked over the edge and saw long insect legs squirming just under the water's surface. They were covered in a jagged carapace, like that of a lobster.

"*Oh God! Greg!*" Sarah grabbed his shoulder and shook it, but there was no strength in her arms. "Jesus, Greg, *wake up!*"

The bed rocked, and then one of the insect-legs burst from the water and clamped its pincer on Greg's arm. Sarah shrieked and tried to push it away, but another one splashed out and bit into Sarah's thigh and she started screaming *screaming, SCREAMING* and—

—and then it was day and she was in her bed, facing the ceiling. Greg still lay there, asleep, his back turned to her. Her pillow was soaked, her hair sticking to her forehead, her breasts so sore the slightest touch made her wince. She shut her eyes and slowly pulled her shirt over her head.

"*No*," Sarah shrieked. "No, no, *no!*"

Black veins crisscrossed her breasts, branching out from her nipples and reaching all the way to her collarbone. They looked painfully swollen, as if the slightest bump might cause them to burst in a spray of black goo.

"Greg," Sarah said, crying. "*Greg!* Greg, wake up! Help me!"

He didn't move.

She dug her nails into his shoulder and shook it. "Greg, *please!*"

He still didn't move.

Screaming, "*Waaaake uuuupppp*," Sarah grabbed him with both hands and yanked, rolling him over. His eyes were already open. They stared straight ahead, glazed and empty like the eyes of a mounted animal. His mouth brimmed with brownish-red foam. It spilled over his lip, sticking to one pale cheek.

It reminded her of a dead slug.

Sarah saw the light.

It was a big white circle, with six little glowing circles inside it, like the wheel of a revolver. People, all of them dressed in surgical masks, medical caps, rubber gloves, and what appeared to be raincoats, all of it turquoise, stood around it, staring down at her. Machines, attached to her via a series of tubes, loomed within arm's reach of the bed, beeping and blinking. She was naked but for a turquoise medical cap and a pair of white panties the nurses had given her.

A nurse placed an oxygen mask on Sarah's mouth, and told her to count down from ten. Sarah tried, but her thoughts kept returning to the day she'd found Greg dead in their bed. The first thing she'd done was call 911. Driving to doctor Kramer's clinic was the second. When the woman at the reception asked her if she had an appointment, Sarah simply raised her shirt. Ten minutes later, while Kramer was holding an ultrasound stick against Sarah's left breast, the attending nurse gasped and said: "Oh my God, are those *legs*?"

Doctor Kramer gave the nurse a withering look, then gestured at Sarah with his free hand, waving it up and down as if to tell her to stay put.

"Legs?" Sarah said. "What legs?"

"Set Mrs. Shane up for an MRI," he told the nurse. He sounded as calm as ever, but his face had gone ashen and his Adam's apple kept twitching. "Full chest scan. The standard tests, as well."

"What legs is she talking about."

Kramer took a deep breath, exhaled slowly. "It, ah, it appears your mammary glands didn't react to the therapy as we intended. I . . . We need to do more tests to—"

"Jesus Christ, what *legs* is she talking about?!"

His mouth became a slit. He turned the ultrasound screen toward her and pointed at half a dozen segmented lines sprouting from and curving around a dark smudge.

"That doesn't look like a leg."

"I'm afraid it does."

"No, it doesn't. Where's the knee? Or the foot?"

"A moment." He took his cellphone, tapped its screen for a few seconds, then showed it to her. It displayed a photograph of an Asian man holding the largest bug Sarah had ever seen. Its armored body was bigger than the man's head, each of its six limbs five or six feet long. Its front limbs had pincers that looked vicious enough to shear an arm off. "This is a Japanese Spider Crab," Kramer said. "Look at its legs. Then look here." He indicated the ultrasound screen.

"What do you . . . Oh . . . Oh my God."

His forehead glistened with a thin film of perspiration. "I . . . I don't know how this could happen, but we will—"

"Are they *alive*?"

"No. Not truly. I can't tell for sure without additional tests, but I'd say they're equivalent to benign tumors."

"*Tumors*? You gave me *cancer*?"

"Uh, forgive me, poor choice of words. *Parasites* would be a better comparison. They live off your body's resources, but they're not a part of it. The excretions you experienced, the ones that poisoned your husband, they—"

"Poisoned? They fucking *killed* him," Sarah said. "No, *you* killed him. Your goddamn therapy did. And now you're telling me I have *fucking cancer*?"

Kramer swallowed. "I assure you, I understand your anger and I'm deeply shaken by all this. But we must act quickly if we're to prevent these parasites from doing more harm. Chances are, we'll have to operate."

"With . . . Am I gonna be fine?"

Even now, lying under the surgical lamps days after that ultrasound, Sarah still hated herself for asking that question. She couldn't shake the feeling Greg's death was her fault, that she had no right to worry about herself when he lay cold because of her. If she hadn't been so goddamn picky and just gotten silicone implants like everyone else, he'd still be alive.

His birthday was supposed to be in two weeks, Sarah thought as the six lights merged into a yellow blur. *I was going to buy him a gold tie clasp.*

For a while afterward, Sarah saw nothing but blackness. Then she heard a noise. It came and went, a soft *whoosh*, vaguely familiar. She eventually placed it. Waves breaking against a beach . . . Or against a ship.

Sarah could hear other sounds now: the hiss of sand drifting up then slowly settling back on the seabed, the click-clack of a rock bouncing down an underwater reef, the gurgle of air exhaled from a lung, and far above, the waves crashing. She was naked, her hair algae, her belly huge and swollen and covered in black veins. Everything glowed with a trembling green light.

The babies swam up to her. Their skin was brown and spiny, their blue eyes bigger than their mouths. They hugged her belly, showering it with kisses. One of them drifted away, crying and begging Sarah not to let it go. She heard screams in the darkness. They were close, but muffled, as if her ears were stuffed with cloth.

Her vision twisted at the corners. The babies' faces grew distant and vague, and so did the crash of the waves and even the sight of her own warped body. Soon all was blackness again, but now the screams grew louder. They stabbed at her skull, filling the space behind her eyes with ground glass.

She could see the lights now, all six of them. Only now there were scarlet stains on two of the lamps. The slow, rhythmical beeping of the machines had given way to what sounded almost like a klaxon. She tried to sit up and ask where all the doctors had gone, but her body ignored her commands. She could think, hear, even move her eyes, but aside from that she was paralyzed.

Oh, please God, no, Sarah thought, *don't let me die.*

God must've felt merciful that day. She sensed a coldness at her back and an uncomfortable tugging at her chest, but at least there was no pain.

Something clattered on her left. Sarah turned her eyes, trying to see. The doors stood wide open and people were shouting for help in the hallway beyond. A table lay overturned, the saws and scalpels scattered on the floor. Kramer lay next to it, his head bent at a grotesque angle, the lower half of his face a red ruin. Sarah felt more tugging at her midriff. She rolled her eyes down as far as they'd go . . . And realized God hadn't been merciful after all.

The thing on her belly was as big as a fist. Its pincers, caked with Kramer's blood, tore at her remaining breast, trying to free its sibling. Then, as if sensing her gaze, it backed up and turned to look at her, its chitinous legs dancing over her skin like skeletal fingers. It had a round face with a tiny pug nose and bright blue eyes, same as her own. It inclined its head, its mouth working, and uttered a single squeaky word: "*Maaa-maaa.*"

Despite the anesthesia, Sarah began to scream.

Millions, Mrs. Shane. Tens of millions.

That's what every lawyer who'd contacted Sarah during the nine months after the operation had told her. She could sue the clinic, hell, she could sue the entire medical system, for tens of millions of dollars, and that was just for the emotional damage. What she'd been through was awful, no question about it, but that was all the more reason to demand compensation.

Sarah supposed it was, but she still never called them back. She spent most of her time in front of the bathroom mirror, naked but for her slippers. She couldn't help comparing herself to a waterlogged corpse, with her pallid complexion and her damp skin, the two ragged scars that had replaced her breasts standing on her chest like botched skin-grafts.

Sarah returned to the living room and collapsed onto the couch. The apartment stank of brine and sweat, and the shadows seemed as deep as those in underwater caves. She didn't leave the house much anymore, nor did she talk to her family except on the phone. Not for some time now.

The crab-thing had almost managed to free its brother or sister or whatever it was from her remaining breast by the time the security guards had arrived. It charged them the moment they entered the room. They opened fire and—although inaccurate enough to graze Sarah's arm and destroy a fortune in medical equipment—

one of them managed to put a bullet in the thing's face. Its sibling lived only seconds longer.

Tens of millions of dollars, Mrs. Shane. We could ask for that in a settlement, and they'd count themselves lucky. That's enough to ensure an extravagant life for yourself and your family, not to mention whatever children you may one day have.

"Somehow, I doubt that," Sarah said to the empty room, and looked at her belly. It was so swollen she couldn't rest her arms on it without having them slide off. Its surface was rough and uneven and covered with thick black veins, the skin as craggy as if there were a thousand little knots just under its surface.

Knots? she thought. *Nah, not knots. Eggs.*

The doctors who had treated her after the surgery made her promise she'd notify them if something, *anything*, about her body felt or looked the slightest bit odd. Sarah wanted to be as good as her word. She really did.

But she couldn't, because she had other promises to keep, promises made to the new blue-eyed babies in her dreams. Sarah didn't know how they'd ended up in her belly or why she loved them so, and didn't care. What she did know, however, was that they numbered in the hundreds, and they relied on their *mama* to keep them safe until they were ready to hatch.

UTTER NO EVIL
By Joseph Watson

I keep asking myself why I was so stupid. Maybe I could have gotten help, real help. If I'd done something sooner, but I didn't.

It started at work. I snagged my arm on something when I was taking out the rubbish. They always leave loads of crap lying around the back of the shop. Most of it comes from the nearby factories, the guys there say it's not their fault, but shit, that's a big fat lie. The bosses' big pockets get them out of any serious trouble, so we have to make do with the back of our street looking like the world's just ended.

I'd caught my arm pretty bad. It was a bloody mess, to be honest. At first, I panicked and thought it'd gone deep, but once I'd cleared away the blood and gunk it didn't look nearly as bad. I got patched up in the back and didn't think any more of it; it'd be healed up in a few days.

When I got home it still itched like crazy. There wasn't any pain. In fact, I'd not noticed this until now, but there wasn't much pain when I'd caught my arm either. Just a strange itchy feeling, like nails were scratching under my skin.

I jumped in the shower. That should have sorted it out. I scrubbed it raw and for the first time got a good look at the wound. It was just an ordinary cut once you wiped away the blood. Well, an ordinary cut that didn't seem to hurt in any way, like I'd been anaesthetised. It was jagged and messy. There was a valley of torn skin surrounding the gash. Still, nothing to get all that worried about though. It looked worse than it was.

The itching, though, that was still there even after I'd put on some antiseptic. If it was still weird the next morning I'd made the decision; I'd go to the doctors. Maybe I'd have to get some antibiotics or something.

The next morning, the itching had gotten worse and when I rolled up my sleeve there wasn't any cut left. It'd healed already, within less than twelve hours. Let me just phrase that again; a cut running half the length of my arm had healed, *completely*, in less than a day.

The skin had healed funny too, it wasn't like a scab or scar was forming, instead the skin had sort of glued together over the cut. The texture looked like I'd kept my arm in water too long. It appeared to be healing, but in a strange way. The skin almost looked like it was pulling itself apart.

I went to the doctors.

The doctor who saw me was nice enough, young, just graduated maybe. She went through a lot of stuff, asked how I was eating, drinking, whether I was getting enough sleep. Eventually she prescribed me some new skin cream, said it's most likely an everyday infection. Trust those bastards that dumped all that shit out there to have made sure it was filthy too.

I didn't tell her that my arm had healed like I was Wolverine. Don't ask me why I didn't say anything, just figured, if they thought it was a normal injury then it'd be a normal injury. I was an idiot.

The cut still itched whilst I was at work. That feeling again, it was hard to describe, like fingers scratching. No, not fingers, that was the day before. Now it felt different. Like teeth, biting under my skin. When I got home the skin was still the same, perhaps even worse. It looked stretched, less like it was healing over and more like it had been pulled apart and was barely holding itself together.

I slapped on some more of the antiseptic, making sure to cover the entire wound. That was the other thing I noticed. The actual wound had gotten bigger. The cut had been fairly big but it'd been narrow at least. Now, the infection covered a good chunk of my forearm.

I bandaged it up and got ready for work. The first few hours were just about bearable, but then, I honestly thought I was going mad. I'd made an effort to simply not look at the bandage in an attempt to ignore it. Trying *not* to scratch an itch is almost impossible, and this was the worst I'd ever felt, it wasn't even as if I could get to the itch, it was like it was underneath the skin.

It wasn't until I had about an hour left before finishing that one of the other shop assistants came up to me. She gave me this slightly nervous, sympathetic look and told me my arm was bleeding.

Christ, I must have stood there for over half an hour at least, with blood flowing down my arm. I rushed into the back office and grabbed some paper towels from the bathroom. Unwrapping the bandages, I dabbed at the blood and wiped it out of the way. The wound had re-opened but was much messier than before. The skin had pulled back on both outer-edges of the wound, like it had been yanked open. Where the skin had given way, it looked as if it had dried up, peeling back to reveal a cavernous glistening hole buried in my arm.

The gash continued to bleed for several minutes as I wiped away at it, before eventually stopping. As I reached for the bandage, I glanced down at it once again. It was a horrible wound, and as I wrapped my arm up again I swore the opening quivered.

Why, for the love of god didn't I say anything?

My manager let me leave early and I made a trip straight to the hospital; I wasn't taking any more chances. They patched it up, stitching the wound and cleaning it, which burned something wicked. The guy told me it was the infection that was the problem and said to keep the wound as clean as possible, changing the dressing every few hours. I told him about the fast healing, but, if I'm completely honest, I don't think he believed me. I came in looking like a wreck, probably thought I was out of it.

That night I felt exhausted; by the time I got home I didn't have the energy to do anything. I collapsed in a heap on my bed and fell straight asleep.

It was a hot night; I felt hot. My arm thrummed with a dull, aching heat. Some horrible sickness was coursing through my body and it was starting to affect my mind. My dreams were horrid, sharp, painful things. Not actual dreams but more like flashes of nightmares, singular images that were lighting up at the back of my eyelids. Christ, I felt bad.

I awoke covered in sweat in the early morning. It was still dark outside and I glanced at my alarm clock. It was just past three in the morning, and I was due at work for eight. As I laid there staring up at the ceiling I heard a clicking sound from the side of my room. It was light and muffled, but I definitely wasn't hallucinating. It wasn't coming from the side of my room though, as I continued to look for the source of the noise, I realised it was coming from my arm, beneath the bandage.

I unwrapped the bandage and didn't know whether to laugh or cry. The wound in my arm was even bigger, running along the entirety of my forearm like a crooked smile. And it was moving. It quivered even more as I poked at the flesh, with soft clicking sounds whenever the two ends of the wound closed together. I probed at it for a bit, watching my own body seem to consciously react to my inspection before taking a deeper look. I still didn't know what was causing the clicking, but I found my answer.

I peeled back the edges of the cut, causing the wound to move more erratically, like some wild animal that was being pinned down. Beneath the edges I managed to get a glimpse at what was causing the noise. A row of small jagged teeth appeared to have erupted from my flesh; tiny crooked yellow daggers lined up in roughly symmetrical rows across the insides of my arm. I carefully pushed the flesh out of the way to look further in, only to see the bright red flesh and muscle, and, what looked curiously like a tongue. A sinuous slice of meat that seemed to move as I watched it. I let go in shock, and the teeth chattered once more.

I paced around the house for hours, watching the sun gradually creep in through the windows. I'd wrapped my mess of an arm in a clean bandage, and had not looked at it since. The steady gnashing of the teeth could still be heard, despite my best efforts.

I was losing my mind, this couldn't be real. Sleeping was impossible, not only did the wound constantly make noise; the steady chattering of teeth seemed to get louder. The pain had gotten worse too, covering the whole of my arm, not just the forearm where the cut had been, but all the way up to my shoulder.

By the morning I had that same itching sensation all the way up to the top of my back. I jabbed the side of my shoulder tentatively with a finger and it felt tight, yet oddly spongy. A dull heat had settled under the skin. Whatever I had was spreading.

Whatever I had wasn't in any medical book.

I unwrapped my arm to take a look again. The teeth were still chattering, the wound occasionally twisting itself into some kind of grin if I looked hard enough. I *was* looking hard enough, diseases don't grin for crying out loud. Bacteria isn't evil, it's just nature.

Yeah, try telling my arm that.

I was sick, really sick. What'd happen if I went to the hospital again? "Oh, come on in, sir, we're just going to send you to quarantine and turn you into a lab rat, can't have you infecting people now."

Work soon became impossible. The steady chattering too noisy to cover up. Returning to the hospital was also a no-go. I was a medical experiment now, some twisted miracle that'd be prodded and poked. No, I was alone.

Alone with a body that was no longer mine.

Soon, I had another mouth, similar to the first, which gibbered and clicked above my left shoulder. They continued with the same mumbling sounds. It'd be worse at night, locked in the silence of my room, trying to sleep, as the wounds would continue uttering nonsense.

Which brings me back to where I started. It's impossible to leave the house now. Last time I checked there's nine mouths spread all across my body. Wicked, ragged wounds with the same gnashing teeth and horrid supple tongues. They've gotten louder and louder, so much so that I've given up leaving the house, or even trying to sleep. They are wearing me down, attacking both my body and my mind. They're winning the fight and they know it.

They mutter things now. Maybe it's me going mad, but I swear that they talk in their own way. Murmuring in their own twisted language. And there's no way for me to escape it.

I could have done something sooner, gotten help, but I didn't. I was so stupid.

Last night, I tried to cut one out, the first one. I grabbed a knife out the kitchen draw and stuffed a towel in my mouth. It was agony, the thing began to croak and almost scream as I went at it with the knife. I couldn't keep it up though, I'm weak. It won out in the end, just leaving me in more pain than when I started.

And then they started chanting again.

I broke down. Snapped. I screamed until my throat gave out, anything to stop what is now a chorus of noise.

I yelled at it, the thing, this disease, whatever it is, that's slowly taken hold of my body.

"What do you want?" I screamed.

And it . . . *they*, answered.

"You."

I collapsed, and the mouths laughed in unison.

DOWN WHERE HER NIGHTMARES DWELL

By Sheldon Woodbury

They say the greatest heartache a parent can feel is to witness their child in pain and feel helpless to stop it. That misery is even more wrenching when it echoes the same pain they felt as a child, because then they know the soul crushing agony being inflicted on the flesh they created.

But what if that flesh *is* the cause of the pain?

The childhood of Molly Stark was brutal in a way that no child should ever have to endure. She'd been born with a face that was plump and sullen, with gloomy eyes, and a misshapen body. This woeful condition created other frailties as well, a halting stutter, a nervous twitch, a shuffling walk.

To make it even worse, she grew up in Los Angeles where beauty was worshipped above all else. The siren call of Hollywood lured striking faces from far and wide. Prom queens and heart-throbs strolled the streets in all their glory, as even more gorgeous faces shimmered on the giant billboards above.

Her teenaged years were nothing less than a daily crucible of terror and fear. She found out in the most painful way possible that the cruelty of kids had no boundaries. She felt like a prisoner of war and the collective duty of her classmates was to torment her with slashing insults and cutting taunts.

That's when something began to fester inside her, dark and secret. She didn't know what it was, only that it came from the place where her nightmares dwelled. It told her she had to change, no matter the extremes that needed to be taken.

Her course of action was obvious at first. She began to exercise with an obsessive compulsion, huffing and puffing in the tiny sanctuary of her room. She also bought beauty magazines and studied them by flashlight deep into the night. The glossy pictures and self-help articles became her sacred text, pointing the way to the promised land of beauty. Some modest gains were made, but that was all, a different hairdo, more pleasing make-up, some fat sweated off.

But even with that, the daily abuse didn't let up, because once the mean girls and bullies chose you as prey they couldn't be fooled by anything minor and modest.

In that secret place, the festering thing told her more radical measures were needed, because the problem was way too severe for small accomplishments. And the pain had gotten even worse, like a throbbing ache that had no limits either.

The next course of action presented itself when she was pushed down a flight of stairs at school by a football player and her plump face was horribly crushed by the tumbling fall. She was used to taunts and mocking sneers, but now it was obvious they wanted her dead. She was rushed to the hospital in an ambulance, and taken to surgery right away. And that's where her life was changed forever. Under the sizzling lights in the operating room, she met the gleaming metal god that had the power to change human flesh.

Her face had been smashed to a bloody pulp, so bones were rearranged, sinew attached, and the battered skin was sewn back together. The operation was deemed a success, but her face was even more revolting, a swollen atrocity mashed together with stitches.

The recovery process took months, another wrenching crucible of pain. When the healing was finally completed, the result was a surprise she didn't expect. It may have been the surgeon's miraculous skill, or just an unexpected accident, because her features weren't as dreary and dreadful as before. It wasn't a total transformation, but it was definitely better than what the exercise and make-up had been able to achieve.

All because of the gleaming god of surgical steel.

"This is your life . . ." she heard from that secret dark place.

The taunts and bullying continued through her teenaged years, then finally slacked off in college, only because the torment was now to make her invisible, as if she didn't exist at all. The beautiful people decided this was even more cunning and mean, to pretend they couldn't even see her. By this time though, she was so focused on becoming a doctor the new torture was something she could finally ignore.

But she didn't want to be just any doctor, she wanted to wield the metal god that could transform flesh.

She learned the mysteries of the human body in medical school, then studied the magic of plastic surgery after that. Late at night, in that secret place where her nightmares dwelled, the misery of her younger years still howled with an unforgettable agony and pain. But now she knew the slab of flesh that covered her body was not a physical prison, but merely a mushy facade that could be easily changed.

The years of study and building her practice were grueling, like climbing a mountain where her only desire was to get to the top. When money finally came, she quickly utilized the benefits of her chosen profession, sculpting her face and figure into a form that was unrecognizable from the pitiful creature she'd been before. She transformed her flesh into a captivating shape that wasn't that different from the glossy pictures in the beauty magazines from long ago.

With her new allure, suitors arrived and she picked the one that seemed the most pleasant. She'd never been overly attracted to men because of the psychic cruelty that still lingered inside, but she wanted a child so she accepted marriage as a necessary part of the process.

When her daughter was born, the flesh of her flesh, she felt a joy she'd never experienced before. Cradling the tiny bundle in her arms unleashed a part of her heart she never knew existed, the part where love was the most powerful feeling imaginable.

But then another emotion suddenly appeared one night when she realized her child was indeed the flesh of her flesh, but before her sculpted transformation. Her eyes were becoming dark and gloomy, and her wiggling body was twisting into a misshapen form.

They say the greatest heartache a parent can feel is to witness their child in pain and it echoes the same pain they felt as a child.

Down where her nightmares dwelled, and the memory of her tortured years still howled with pain, a plan formed that she accepted as the only right course of action. No loving mother would ever allow cruelty to the flesh of her flesh, so if ugliness was going to be her daughter's inheritance, then changes had to be made.

She divorced her husband, in case he didn't understand what needed to be done, then set up a make-shift operating room in the basement. She'd acquired skills that few people had, as a worshipper of surgical steel.

It was a slow process that wouldn't be detected by others, but it was extreme and radical in its own way.

She gradually transformed her daughter into a teenaged beauty, but it didn't stop at just that. She made her a bombshell beyond the limits of good taste, with a sexy figure, lusty lips, and cascading hair. She'd been attacked for being ugly, so she made the flesh of her flesh something totally new, seductive perfection in every way. And that's when it happened, the horror of horrors that no child should ever experience.

Her daughter came home in tears after a date with the captain of the football team, and the evidence was easy to see. Her clothes were ripped and her body was bruised, but the assault had gone much deeper than that.

Down where her nightmares dwelled, her rage erupted to monstrous proportions and she prayed to the metal god for an appropriate response. It came with a clarity that startled her with its stunning cruelty, but she accepted its depravity.

She needed her daughter's help, which she offered with the same need for payback and punishment.

With a soft and luscious voice, her daughter told the lumbering football player how much she wanted another date as soon as possible. This fed his brutish ego like a game winning touchdown run, so the trap was set.

"My Mom is away this weekend," she whispered in his ear at school. "Why don't you come over and we can have more fun . . ."

When he arrived lugging a bottle of cheap booze and flashing a horny grin, it was easy to knock him out with a super powerful tranquilizer slipped into his drink. It took both the mother and daughter to drag his bulky body down the thumping stairs to the make-shift operating room in the basement, then push him up on the table.

He was missing for a couple of days, because the operation was extreme and radical, not an easy fix.

He was one of the beautiful people, with sunny blonde hair, a square jaw, and blue-sky eyes.

It was close to midnight when his parents heard a scraping at the front door and stumbled downstairs. When they opened the door, it took a few seconds to see the whimpering thing on the stoop was their son, but now the flesh of their flesh was something brand new. He looked more like a pig than a human, with four stubby legs, a limp tail, pointed ears, and a snout that came from between his legs. The horror in his eyes was a pain no parent should ever have to see, but down where her nightmares dwelled, she knew the operation was a success.

PUBLICATION CREDITS:

ABOUT THE AUTHORS

Shaun Avery writes crime and horror fiction to the best of his abilities across a number of mediums. He has won prizes with his writing, and recently co-created a self-published horror comic. He sees "Slobber" as a laugh-out-loud comedy. But then, he always did have a pretty strange sense of humor.

Charlotte Baker is currently a PhD student studying cult horror, female identification and fandom. Her MA in Horror and Transgression and her research into the use of skin as a method of spectatorship won the 'Best Dissertation' award at the University of Derby. Charlotte is currently an associate lecturer in Film Production at the University of Derby and an author. She has published a series of novellas and over twenty short stories and articles.

Shadrick Beechem is a twenty-five-year-old aspiring horror writer from the Midwest.

David Beers writes thriller novels in Dallas, Texas. When not writing, he obsesses over stories in the news about unexplained deaths and paranormal happenings to the point that his friends and family wonder if he should see a psychiatrist.

Before publishing novels, David received awards for his short fiction seen in numerous publications, including the New York Times mentioned *Every Day Fiction*.

David scribbles weekly on topics from crime to horror movies at his website, http://www.davidbeersfiction.com. He loves interacting with fans through email, hand written letters, and smoke signals, so feel free to contact him!

Austin Biela currently lives in Forth Worth, TX. He has just finished attending Texas State University where he acquired a bachelor's degree in both English and Physical Anthropology. Though he is currently unemployed, he plans to work with law enforcement as a Medico-legal Death Investigator while also writing to his heart's content. He regularly runs 5Ks, has excavated a burial site in Poland, and volunteered with Texas State's Forensic Anthropology Center. Though humanity will always hold a special place in his heart, his mind is dominated by the thoughts of monsters, both surreal and all too realistic.

Chantal Boudreau is a speculative fiction writer with a focus in horror and fantasy. She is also an affiliate member of HWA and a current member of SF Canada. She has published in Canada with Exile Editions in their *Dead North* and *Clockwork Canada* anthologies and her other Canadian publications include stories in *Postscripts to Darkness Volume 5* and *Masked Mosaic: Canadian Super Stories*. Outside of Canada, to date, she has published more than fifty stories with a variety of American and British publishers.

Ed Burkley is a Social Psychologist living in Oklahoma. By day he works as a professor and researcher studying human behavior at Oklahoma State University. By night he writes about the darker side of the human condition. His short fiction appears in the forthcoming Smoking Pen Press anthology *Uncommon Pet Tales* and the new series *Night Shades* by Firth Books.

K.M. Campbell is a warmongering New Zealand librarian who writes when not sleeping. Breastfed on Stephen King, Karley now lives in some half-world where nothing terrifies her more than the monster that still lurks beneath her bed, whispering strange tales while she slumbers and insisting she scribe them lest he bite her foot off next time she leaves her bed. He is slowly draining her essence. His name is Brian, and he's an asshole!

A. Collingwood lives in a little town between forest and sea, and currently lives in a dank and dingy house on a hill, where a typewriter is the only thing that can drown out the scratching and slithering in the walls. If Collingwood must be contacted, do so on a full moon, at exactly midnight, on the blog "The Cabinet of A. Collingwood" at WordPress.com. Any misfortune that occurs afterwards cannot be held against the author. You'll have no proof. We promise.

Stuart Conover is a father, husband, rescue dog owner, horror author, blogger, journalist, horror enthusiast, comic book geek, science fiction junkie, and IT professional. With all of that to cram in on a daily basis, it is highly debatable that he ever is able to sleep and rumors have him attached to an IV drip of caffeine to get through most days.

A resident in the suburbs of Chicago (and once upon a time in the city) most of Stuart's fiction takes place in the Midwest if not the Windy City itself. From downtown to the suburbs to the cornfields—the area is ripe for urban horror of all facets.

Damien Donnelly was born in Dublin, Ireland. Damien juggles being a pattern maker by day for various fashion brands and a writer by night. He originally moved to Paris in 1998 before falling distracted by London and Amsterdam. Since returning to Paris in 2015, his focus has been heavily on writing and he was published in 2015's Irish short story anthology *Second Chance*, Eyewear Publishing's poetry anthology *Nous Sommes Paris* and various online journals including *Firefly Magazine* and *SickLit Magazine*. Aside from maintaining an online blog of poetry and photography, he is currently working on his first novel. For the rest of the time, he can be found in the kitchen baking high calorie cakes.

James Dorr's THE TEARS OF ISIS was a 2014 Bram Stoker Award® nominee for Superior Achievement in a Fiction Collection. Other books include *STRANGE MISTRESSES: TALES OF WONDER AND ROMANCE, DARKER LOVES: TALES OF MYSTERY AND REGRET*, and his all-poetry *VAMPS (A RETROSPECTIVE)*. Also be on the watch for *TOMBS: A CHRONICLE OF LATTER-DAY TIMES OF EARTH*, a novel-in-stories just released from Elder Signs Press in June 2017.

An Active Member of HWA and SFWA with more than 500 individual appearances from *ALFRED HITCHCOCK'S MYSTERY MAGAZINE* to *XENOPHILIA*, for the latest information Dorr invites readers to visit his blog at http://jamesdorrwriter.wordpress.com.

Spinster Eskie is a resident of California and has an M.Ed in creative arts education. With a background in women's studies, her focus as a writer is to expose the woman's experience through unsettling tales that highlight the dilemma of sexual repression and oppression. By combining the genres of feminist and horror/science-fiction she aims to not only disturb readers, but deliver a message that is informative and thought-provoking. In 2005, Eskie's play, *Tell Me About Love*, was featured in the Provincetown Playwright Festival. She has been featured in various online magazines such as *Deadman's Tome*, *Bad Moon Rising*, and *69 Flavors of Paranoia*. Eskie has a number of short stories published by Pill Hill Press, Post-Mortem Press, Scary Tales Publications, Cruentus Libri Press, and many others.

***

Santiago Eximeno is a Spanish genre writer who has published several novellas and collections, mainly horror literature and flash fiction. His work has been translated to English, Japanese, French, or Bulgarian. You can find him at www.eximeno.com or @santiagoeximeno on Twitter.

***

Balázs Farkas is a Hungarian writer of literary and weird fiction. So far, he's published two books and his works appeared in numerous anthologies and magazines. He also reviews books, movies and video games, and occasionally he also translates short stories from English to Hungarian. More recently, he started translating his own works to English.

He lives in Budapest and works at a video game development company as a community manager and contributing writer. Visit his website at www.balazsfarkas.com/english or follow him on Twitter: @fbdbh

***

Tarquin Ford *Tarquin Ford* is the pen name of an Atlanta-based writer of strange tales. He learned while working in the pennies-for-blogposts trade that his real name is so common that it renders him anonymous. His work has appeared in *thousandandonestories.com*, *Yellow Mama*, *J.J. Outre Review*, and *Infernal Ink*.

***

Ken Goldman, former Philadelphia teacher of English and Film Studies, is an affiliate member of the Horror Writers Association. He has homes on the Main Line in Pennsylvania and at the Jersey shore. His stories have appeared in over 855 independent press publications in the U.S., Canada, the UK, and Australia with over thirty due for publication in 2017. Since 1993, Ken's tales have received seven honorable mentions in T*he Year's Best Fantasy & Horror*. He has written five books: three anthologies of short stories, *YOU HAD ME AT ARRGH!!* (Sam's Dot Publishers), *DONNY DOESN'T LIVE HERE ANYMORE* (A/A Productions) and *STAR-CROSSED* (Vampires 2); and a novella, *DESIREE*, (Damnation Books). His first novel *OF A FEATHER* (Horrific Tales Publishing) was released in January 2014. *SINKHOLE*, his second novel, has been accepted by Bloodshot Books and will be published late summer 2017.

James Harper, a transplanted native in a city full of them, is a writer working in Washington DC. He has a short story, "Just for One Day," in the anthology *Stress City: A Big Book of Fiction by 51 DC Guys*, edited by Richard Peabody. In early 2015, the short story version of his novel, *Love Craft*, was collected in *Swallowed by the Beast*, an anthology edited by Samie Sands. Last year, a longer version was accepted for publication next year in *Dunhams Destroys Lovecraft*, a journal from Dunhams Manor Press. His novelette, "Return of the Caledonians," appears in *The Corpse Candle and Other Nightmares*, edited by Patrick Dotson. In addition, it appears in the Halloween anthology, *Tales of Horror on Halloween Night*, edited by Samie Sands. More recently, His short story, "Death Ray," can be found in *Busted Lip*, the inaugural anthology from Fat-Lip Press. Another short story, "Reptoid," appears in *Black Candy*, a Halloween anthology from Jaded Books Publications edited by Mitch Workman.

Kourtnea Hogan is a horror hound from southern Indiana. Raised on Stephen King novels and 80's horror movies, she fell in love with the genre at a young age and never looked back. She has recently finished her Master of Fine Arts and will be attending film school in the fall.

Carl R. Jennings is, by day, a thickly Russian accented bartender in Southwestern Virginia. By night, he is the rooster-themed superhero: the Molotov Cocktail, protecting the weak and beer-sodden. While heroically posing on a rooftop in the moonlight in case a roaming photographer happens by, he finds the time to write down a word or two in the lifelong dream that he can put aside the super-hero mantle and utility comb and become a real author.

━━━━━━━━━━━━

Christopher Vander Kaay has been published at *McSweeney's* and *Everyday Fiction*, has published three educational books about horror & sci-fi film history, and is a contributing writer at Bloody-Disgusting.com.

━━━━━━━━━━━━

Alexander Lloyd King is a proud resident of Sistersville, West Virginia. He appreciates his small town and finds inspiration there.

━━━━━━━━━━━━

Thomas C. Mavroudis is a Denver native, husband, and father. He possesses an MFA from the University of California, Riverside, where he studied under Stephan Graham Jones. He is the co-founder of the serial fiction blog *Saturday Morning Serial* (saturdaymorningserial.net) and his publishing credits include *Crosscurrents*, *Dreaming in R'lyeh*, and *Turn to Ash*, and forthcoming in anthologies from Frith Books and Muzzleland Press.

━━━━━━━━━━━━

Sean McCoy is a board game designer living in Dallas, Texas. He lives with his girlfriend and their two dogs. You can follow him on Twitter at http://twitter.com/seanmccoy.

━━━━━━━━━━━━

John S. McFarland's first novel, *The Black Garden* was published in 2010 to universal praise. His work has appeared in *The Twilight Zone Magazine*, *Eldritch Tales*, *National Lampoon*, *River Styx*, *Tornado Alley*, and in six anthologies, including *A Treasury of American Horror Stories*, along with work by Stephen King and H. P. Lovecraft. He has written extensively on historical and arts-related subjects and has been a guest lecturer in fiction at Washington University in St. Louis. He is a lifelong Bigfoot enthusiast, and *Annette: A Big, Hairy Mom* is his first novel for young readers. Its sequel will appear in 2017.

━━━━━━━━━━━━

Rick McQuiston is a forty-nine-year-old father of two who loves anything horror-related. He's had nearly 400 publications so far, and written five novels, ten anthologies, one book of novellas, and edited an anthology of Michigan authors. He is also a guest author each year at Memphis Junior High School. Currently, Rick keeps the wife happy while trying to conjure up new stories.

━━━━━━━━━━━

Jeremy Megargee was still a child when he picked up his very first *Goosebumps* book by R.L. Stine, and he knew he had fallen head over heels in love with all things horror. It's a love affair that has only grown stronger over the years, a borderline obsession with stories that explore the darkest recesses of the human imagination. He guesses you could say he's like a twisted explorer in that way . . . always stalking down those special stories that have the ability to invoke a creepy-crawly feeling right down to the marrow of his bones.

Jeremy weaves his tales of personal terror from Martinsburg, West Virginia with his cat Lazarus acting as his muse/familiar.

━━━━━━━━━━━

G.A. Miller discovered horror very early on, courtesy of Creature Features on television in the late-1950's/early-1960's. There, he first saw the Universal classic monster movies and many others. As he grew a little older, a friend's brother had a treasure trove of EC Comics from the mid-1950's and this only furthered his fascination.

In 1976, he browsed paperbacks at a newsstand, a cover catching his eye. Embossed black, with one spot of color on it: a red drop of blood. It was the first paperback printing of Stephen King's *Salem's Lot*, and it marked his induction as a Constant Reader, a position he still enjoys to this day.

━━━━━━━━━━━

Kurt Newton's dark fiction has appeared in *Weird Tales*, *Weird-book*, *Dark Discoveries*, and *Shroud*. He is the author of two novels, *The Wishnik* and *Powerlines*. He is a lifelong resident of the Connecticut woods.

━━━━━━━━━━━

Drew Nicks has always been fascinated by horror. Continued viewings of *Jaws* and *Aliens* as a youth skewed his young mind. His work has been featured in *Dark Corner Books*, *Road Maps and Life Rafts* and *The Lovecraft Lunatic Asylum*. He resides in Moose Jaw, Saskatchewan.

━━━━━━━━━━━

Sergio Palumbo is an Italian public servant who graduated from Law School working in the public real estate branch. He has published a Fantasy Roleplaying illustrated Manual, *WarBlades*, of more than 700 pages. Some of his works and short stories have been published on *American Aphelion Webzine*, *WeirdYear*, *Quantum Muse*, *Antipodean SF*, *Schlock! Webzine*, *SQ Mag*, etc., and in print inside 32 American Horror/Sci-fi/Fantasy/Steampunk Anthologies, 52 British Horror/Sci-Fi Anthologies, 2 Urban Fantasy/Horror Canadian Anthologies and 1 Sci-Fi Australian Anthology by various publishers, and 16 more to follow in 2017/2018.

Gary Power is the author of several short stories that have been published in respected anthologies such as *When Graveyards Yawn* (Crowswing Books), *Spinetinglers* (Spinetinglers publishing), The (BFS nominated) *Black Book of Horror—* (Mortbury Press) and most recently 'Hell's Bells' in *The Horror Zine* (USA) and 'The Road to Hell' with the Digital Publishing Corp of Canada.

Imminent publications are a radio/podcast play of 'Flitching's Revenge' with Manor House Audio and 'Deeper than Dark Water' with the 'Vault of Evil'.

He is a member of the British Fantasy Society and the prestigious Clockhouse London Writers group and was shortlisted for the Ian St James short story award.

Jenya Joy Preece found her love of horror when she was twelve years old while reading Poe's "The Tell-Tale Heart" and "The Raven" for a school assignment. From that day on, she couldn't get enough of the genre.

In 2009, she dedicated herself to writing only what she calls, "good honest horror." Her work is not for the weak of stomach or faint of heart, which she'd have no other way. Nothing brings her more joy in life than to spread fear and emotions through writing.

Frank Roger was born in 1957 in Ghent, Belgium.

His first story appeared in 1975. Since then his stories appear in an increasing number of languages in all sorts of magazines and anthologies, and since 2000, story collections are published, also in various languages. Apart from fiction, he also produces collages and graphic work in a surrealist and satirical tradition. They have appeared in various magazines and books. His work is a blend of genres and styles that can best be described as "frankrogerism", an approach of which he is the main representative.

By now he has a few hundred short stories to his credit, published in more than 40 languages. In 2012 a story collection in English *The Burning Woman and Other Stories* was published by *Evertype* (www.evertype.com). Find out more at http://www.frankroger.be.

Josh Shiben lives in the swamps of Fredericksburg, Virginia with his wife and two mongrels. An aerospace engineer by day and couch potato by night, Josh has from a young age been in love with storytelling. His work can be found in collections scattered across the various corners of the internet, covering everything from vampires to domesticated velociraptors.

Ian Steadman is a writer from the south of England. His fiction has most recently been published by *Black Static* and *Unsung Stories*. You can find out more at www.iansteadman.com, or he sometimes manifests on Twitter at @steadmanfiction.

Edmund Stone is a writer and poet of horror and fantasy living in a quaint river town in the Ohio Valley. It is a rural and backward area from which he derives a wealth of characters and strange ideas. He writes at night, spinning tales of strange worlds and horrifying encounters with the unknown. He lives with his wife, a son, three dogs and a mischievous cat.

Edmund is an active member of The Write Practice, a member only writer's forum, where he converses with other writers while perfecting his craft. Edmund's poetry is featured in the *Horror Zine*, Summer 2017 issue. He has a poem featured in issue #6 of *Jitter* by Jitter Press. He also has a short story to be featured in an upcoming anthology by Fantasia Divinity and another to appear in a February 2018 anthology by Schreyer Ink Publishing.

Aric Sundquist is a writer of speculative fiction. Born and raised in Michigan's Upper Peninsula, he graduated from Northern Michigan University with a Master's Degree in Creative Writing. His stories have appeared in numerous publications, including *The Best of Dark Moon Digest*, *Night Terrors III*, *Evil Jester Digest Vol. 1*, and *Division* by Zero 4: rEvolution. Being a writer and a musician at heart, he also enjoys tabletop board games, playing guitar, and traveling with his girlfriend.

David Turton has extensive training in Journalism, Marketing and Public Relations and has been writing as a career for over fourteen years. A huge horror fiction fan, particularly the works of Stephen King, David has written several short stories, all centred around dark tales of horror and dystopia. He is also in the final stages of his first novel, an apocalyptic horror set in the near future.

Mijat Vujačić is an economist by trade, storyteller at heart. He is a published author of three horror novels written in Serbian: *Krvavi Akvarel*, *NekRomansa*, and *Vampir*. His stories appeared in *SQ*, *Devolution Z*, *Crimson Streets*, *Encounters*, *Acidic Fiction*, *Creepy Campfire Quarterly*, *Under the Bed*, *9Tales*, and *Infernal Ink* magazines, as well as in professional anthologies *Toxic Tales*, *Silent Scream*, *The Nightmare Collective*, and *The Worlds of Science Fiction, Fantasy and Horror Vol1*. He believes a strong work ethic is the root of all success, and that it is best to err on the side of action. A fan of all things horror, he is also an avid gamer, hobby blogger, hookah enthusiast, and a staunch dog person. He lives in Belgrade, Serbia.

Joseph Watson hails from Chesterfield in the UK and graduated from Sheffield Hallam University with a B.A. in English Literature and Film Studies. When he's not writing stories, he blogs about video games at logicbutton.com.

Sheldon Woodbury is an award-winning writer (screenplays, plays, books, short stories, and poems). He also teaches screenwriting at New York University. His book *Cool Million* is considered the essential guide to writing high concept movies. His short stories

and poems have appeared in many horror anthologies and magazines. His novel *The World on Fire* was published September 2014
by JWK Fiction.

ABOUT THE EDITOR

C.P. Dunphey is an author, editor, Lovecraftian scholar, and the founder of Gehenna & Hinnom Books. He has edited thousands of stories for authors, novels, and collections, both mainstream and independent while also publishing work of his own. His science fiction/horror novel *Plane Walker* was published in 2016 and was met with critical and commercial success, going as far as being nominated for several awards. Dunphey is the editor-in-chief of Gehenna & Hinnom, helming both the anthologies released by the company and the bi-annual magazine *Hinnom Magazine*. When he isn't tirelessly steamrolling through editing, Dunphey can be found at his home in Hattiesburg, Mississippi with his beautiful pitbull Ripley Ellen, a book and movie shelf that holds all his secrets, and an insatiable thirst for everything horrific and imaginative.

If you enjoyed the *Year's Best Body Horror 2017 Anthology*, make sure to leave a review on Amazon and follow us on social media!

Facebook: www.facebook.com/gehennaandhinnombooks
Twitter: www.twitter.com/GehennaBooks
Website: www.gehennaandhinnom.wordpress.com

Look out for our new releases in 2017!

June 30th, 2017

Hinnom Magazine Issue 001

August 31st, 2017

Hinnom Magazine Issue 002

September 30th, 2017

Year's Best Body Horror 2017 Anthology

October 31st, 2017

Hinnom Magazine Issue 003

November 30th, 2017

Year's Best Transhuman SF 2017 Anthology

December 31st, 2017

Hinnom Magazine Issue 004